Loyalty's Haven

Book Three of the Victoria Chronicles

J. Robert Whittle

By J. Robert Whittle

The Lizzie Series
Lizzie: Lethal Innocence
Lizzie Lethal Innocence - *Audio Book*
Narrated by J. Robert Whittle
Lizzie's Secret Angels
Streets of Hope
Lizzie's Legacy

Victoria Chronicles
Bound by Loyalty
Loyalty's Reward
Loyalty's Haven
Paperback and Hardcover Editions

Laughing Through Life: Tales of a Yorkshireman (audio)

by J. Robert Whittle and
Joyce Sandilands

Whispers Across Time
Race for a Treasure
Yesterdays, A Collection of Short Stories

by Joyce Sandilands

Moonbeam Series
Leprechaun Magic
Leprechaun Magic - *Audio Book*
Narrated by Joyce Sandilands
3 On A Moonbeam
by Joyce Sandilands
3 On A Moonbeam - *Audio Book*
Narrated by Joyce Sandilands

Loyalty's Haven

Book Three of the Victoria Chronicles

J. Robert Whittle

Publisher's note: This book is a work of fiction set in the City of Victoria, Municipality of Saanich, and other areas of British Columbia, and Washington State. To enhance the story, real places and people's names have sometimes been used, although the characters are fictional and are in no way intended to represent any person living or dead.

Second Printing: 2010

Whitlands Publishing Ltd.
4444 Tremblay Drive, Victoria, BC
Canada V8N 4W5 250-477-0192
www.bestsellingbooks.ca

Original cover artwork by Barbara Porter Gorby
Cover design by Jim Bisakowski, Desktop Publishing
Back cover photo by Terry Seney

National Library of Canada Cataloguing in Publication Data

Whittle, J. Robert (John Robert), 1933-
Loyalty's haven / J. Robert Whittle.

(Victoria chronicles ; bk. 3)
ISBN 0-9734383-9-8 (bound)
ISBN 0-9734383-8-X (pbk.)

I. Title. II. Series: Whittle, J. Robert (John Robert), 1933- . Victoria

Chronicles ; bk. 3.

PS8595.H4985L68 2006 C813'.54 C2006-905318-9

Printed in Canada by Friesens, Altona, MB

To my fans
without whose friendship, loyalty,
confidence, and determination,
this book would not have been written.

Acknowledgements

My intention to turn the Victoria Chronicles into a series was never an issue—it was not a series! As many of you know, I had written the first two books as one, which we deemed too large for publication. I suppose when an author discovers he truly enjoys what he is writing, the results can sometimes be pleasantly disastrous! For in the two years following the release of *Loyalty's Reward*, I received so many hundreds of both verbal and emailed requests to continue Nancy and Dan's story, I just had to do so. Naming this volume became even less of a task when readers began referring to these books as the 'Loyalty' series. We thought this was a good suggestion and thus, *Loyalty's Haven*, it became.

I'd like to thank the local archives, readers, and members of the general public, for their support and assistance with my research. It's truly remarkable the amount of historical information available if one knows where to find it. I encourage those of you who have old documents sitting in your homes to please contact your local archives so that they may be preserved for others to enjoy and use. It's of little use getting mouldy in a box in the basement!

Once again, I must thank our hardworking team led by my wife, Joyce Sandilands, who wears the hats of editor, publisher, manager, and webmaster, besides looking after me (often a thankless task); Tara Poilievre, our effervescent and efficient office assistant who Joyce claims helps to keep her sane—brought a special honour to us in August by adding a new member to their family and naming him Danny; Barbara Porter Gorby, who has now produced five lovely covers for our books; Jim Bisakowski, who again lent us his graphic design skills, producing yet another of our well-loved covers; Deborah Wright, our faithful proofreader who keeps both Joyce and I on the straight and narrow; and Gerhard Aichelberger, our Friesens' printing rep, for his office's assistance and patience. Without the support and ever-willing assistance of these people, our books would never reach the required deadline.

If you're wondering what book is coming next, Joyce is working on a schedule to produce two more books over the next few years. If you continue to purchase these books, we will do our best to keep you supplied! Publishing is a very expensive endeavour when you are self-supporting. I am not as young as I used to be but sales and, your appreciation, helps to keep me going! Check our websites (listed below) as Joyce keeps them up to date, particularly our Events Page if you are looking for us at a particular venue. We will be doing different shows each year and moving around a bit more now that we've had our knee surgeries. We also send emails out when there is news to impart, if you would like to receive them let us know.

I *can* tell you that my next published novel will be *Whispers Across Time*, a book many of you already know about and for which you have been patiently waiting. *Whispers Across Time* is a time-travelling historical romance novel about a mortal ghost who lives in Seattle and visits Victoria, BC and Everett, WA between the 20th century and the present day. I think you'll discover it's a most pleasant and entertaining diversion from my norm and still with real history. Look for it in 2007.

Pre-sales are an excellent way to ensure you don't miss one of my new books and they are always gratefully accepted—you'll be one of the first to receive the book as well! Out-of-town readers especially appreciate being on our 'ship immediately list' but locals are also welcome. If you don't have access to the internet, please make arrangements by telephone with Joyce at the number below. Also, to clarify, only sales on the websites listed below (and by direct contact with us) give us 100% of the proceeds as they are run by Joyce and I. Watch for our shipping specials on these websites!

Last, but not least, on behalf of both Joyce and myself, thank you for purchasing and reading our books. There is nothing more pleasurable than to have a job you love—for us its writing and producing these books for you.

Addendum to Second Printing in 2010: All of our novels are now available as **ebooks**. Check our website for details.

J. Robert Whittle
October 2006
whitlands@shaw.ca
(250) 477-0192 PST (Victoria, BC)

www.jrobertwhittle.com
www.bestsellingbooks.ca

Main Characters (in order of appearance)

Mary Pickford – Canadian film star
Major General Greene – commander of Camp Lewis, WA
Nancy Wilson – Victoria businesswoman and Dan's fiancé
Nellie Cornish – Seattle music teacher and Nancy's pianist
Gus and Beth Jorgensen – Seattle businessman and wife
Meg MacDonald – Nancy and Dan's adopted aunt
Dan Brown – Nancy's fiancé and partner in Brown and Wilson
Bill and Christopher Jorgensen – Gus and Beth's sons
Jebediah Judd – Nancy and Dan's adopted uncle
George Cotterill – Mayor of Seattle
James Moore – owner of James Moore Theatre, Seattle
Tom Wills – Seattle newspaper reporter
Dr. Arthur Price – Victoria Health Officer
Dr. Tubble – Seattle Health Officer
Sam Smith and Flash – hermit and his dog
Kate Dumpford – Nancy's friend/business partner; wife of Jack
Dr. Henry Young, British Columbia health official
Jack "Dumpy" Dumpford – Brown and Wilson dock manager
Waldo Skillings – owner of Victoria Baggage Company
Mayor Albert Todd – Mayor of Victoria
Eva Todd – friend and Gordon Head neighbour
Captain John Gray – United States Coast Guard
Jane and Gilbert Mouat – mother and son; Mouat's store Salt Spring
Jack Duggan – friend and builder with Parfitt Bros.
Ezekiel Plunket – hermit friend of Jebediah
Admiral Johnson – United States Coast Guard
Don Melhope – director, RCA recording studio
Terry O'Reilly – Seattle gangster
Harry Maynard – friend and owner of Crystal Springs Brewery

(cont'd)

Main Characters (continued)

Chaplain Ralph Jordan – Canadian Army chaplain
Walter Bohannan – owner, *Island and Sidney Review*
Ruby Williamson – Gordon Head telephone operator
Fred Barrett – Senior Clerk, Harbour Master's Office
Algenon Pease – Gordon Head resident and harbour patrol
Dunnett Family – Gordon Head neighbours
Williamson Family – Gordon Head neighbours
Parfitt Brothers – local contractors
Bertha Landes – Seattle politician
Nellie Duggan – friend and wife of Jack
Eliza Marshall – owner of Gorge Hotel
Tom Irvine – Esquimalt farmer
Billy – Nancy's childhood friend
Millie Maynard – wife of Harry Maynard
Dick Radley – foreman at Roberts Pt., fish plant
Ormond Smythe – *Cowichan Leader*
Dora Alcock – Victoria widow with two children
May Coolridge – Red Cross Director
Teddy Lancaster – amputee living at Salvation Army
Jim Morrison – blacksmith
Maude Hunter – owner, Maude Hunter's corner store
John Sadlier – owner, *Gordon Head Store* on Tyndall
Premier John Oliver – Premier of British Columbia
Prof. Louis Turner – conductor of Empress Hotel Orchestra
Sergeant Morgan – Willows Army Base
Jim Goodwin – tugboat owner/operator
Eleanor Simpson – matron of Jubilee Hospital
Carlo Calza – manager of Empress Hotel
Tom Davis – retired Victoria fire chief
Simon Welsh – warehouse clerk, Bellingham, WA

Loyalty's Haven

Chapter 1

"Sorry darling," actress Mary Pickford giggled, "I can't possibly stay. I have a busy schedule to keep and must leave right away for Los Angeles."

"I'll come," actress-comedian Fanny Brice responded, followed quickly by tap dancer, Bill Robinson.

"You'll find my car at the side entrance when you're ready, don't leave without me!" General Greene quipped, his voice booming as he continued searching the backstage area for performers to invite to Mayor Cotterill's reception at city hall.

The successful Camp Lewis concert, held on the 16th of June, 1917, at the United States Army Base near Tacoma, was over and the not-so-surprising favourites of the evening proved to be the pretty and young Canadian vocalist, Nancy Wilson and her Seattle pianist, Nellie Cornish. It seemed their performance of familiar and favourite songs was even more popular than those of the famous Hollywood stars.

As Nancy and Nellie made their way back to their dressing room, both fellow artists and stagehands showered them with congratulations. Before reaching the door, they were surprised to find General Greene waiting for them, obviously pleased with the concert. He invited them to the reception, made sure they had a ride, and left.

"No need to change, girls, stay in your pretty dresses. We've already packed your clothes," Beth Jorgensen, Nancy's benefactor and the special friend she thought of as a mother, advised after the general had gone. "No doubt the mayor will ask you girls to perform again."

"Danny sent word he has gone ahead with Terry and the boys," Aunt Meg announced. "Here are your purses and shawls."

"Are any of the other performers joining us?" Nancy asked, her red hair bouncing about her shoulders as she turned excitedly.

Nancy's question and obvious concern brought a smile to Nellie's face and a soldier, given the task of seeing to their every need, called from outside the dressing room door, "They've already left with the general, ma'am."

Gus Jorgensen appeared with Peter, his chauffeur, quickly shepherding the women out to the car as soldiers loaded their bags.

"Ready girls?" Gus asked, waiting until they were seated before he shut the door and got in himself. "Hold onto your hats!"

Soldiers lined the route to the camp gates, all chanting Nancy's name. Peter drove slowly down the avenue and, upon reaching the gate, the guards sprang stiffly to attention and saluted the passing car.

"They don't know how lucky they are to have you for a friend Nancy Wilson," Nellie said emotionally.

"You were a sensation, you know," Gus babbled excitedly. "You knocked their socks off, girls. What a team! The world is yours!"

"I already have everything I want, Gus," the redhead said quietly, "and I'll never let him go again."

Whisked quickly back into Seattle, they were soon alighting in front of the city hall and saw the boys were waiting for them. Looking resplendent in evening dress, Dan winked at Nancy but held tightly to Bill Jorgensen's wheelchair and they all made their way toward the steps.

"Come on, sis, take my arm and we'll make a grand entrance," Christopher, the younger Jorgensen called excitedly to Nancy, offering his good arm.

Nancy hesitated, seeing the large crowd gathered outside. At that moment, the doors opened and some of the crowd began moving inside.

"Go on," Nellie urged, "lead us in. You've earned the honour!"

As the group entered the building, Peter collected the girls' shawls and quietly left them, while Christopher ran back to help his father and Dan lift Bill's wheelchair up the several stairs to the entrance.

"Follow us," announced the mayor.

"Not yet," the redhead replied looking around, "we need Uncle Jeb, he's part of this family, too. Where has he gone? He was here a minute ago."

The mayor turned to Gus Jorgensen who pointed through the crowd to where Jeb was standing looking at one of the wall displays. Sharp orders from the mayor sent one of the young female staff members scurrying away to get him.

"What's wrong?" Jeb growled as the woman informed him his party was waiting for him and pointed in their direction. His eyes searched the foyer suspiciously as he came toward them.

"Nothing's wrong, silly, we wondered where you had got to," Meg chuckled, reaching for his hand and pulling him in beside her.

"I'll slip in the side door," said Nellie, "and join you inside."

"Nellie!" Nancy turned to face the pianist. "You'll stay right where you are, like it or not you're part of our family, too!"

"Are you ready, Miss Wilson?" the mayor asked in frustration.

"Yes sir, please lead the way," Nan replied. "I'll push Bill's wheelchair and, Dan, you and Chris follow us, then Nellie and the others."

"But this is your night, sis," Bill pleaded over his shoulder as the group began to move forward.

"It's *our* night, Billy, and I want all Seattle to know how proud I am of all three of you," she whispered as they followed the mayor and his wife down a long hallway.

Stopping at a large set of double doors, they waited for the others to catch up. The doors opened and they moved into a large reception room full of waiting guests already sitting at tables. Upon seeing them, the room burst with applause, as the mayor, with his wife on his arm, strutted proudly through the gathering to the far end of the room where several empty tables waited.

"Ladies and Gentlemen," Mayor Cotterill proclaimed loudly when the guests had found their chairs, "may I present Miss Nancy Wilson and her family. I'm going to let her do the introductions for us."

"Thank you, Mr. Mayor," Nancy replied, taking the microphone he offered as the guests applauded enthusiastically. Smiling, she carefully pulled the long cable around behind her and went to stand behind Bill's wheelchair at the next table. Motioning for Dan and Chris to join them, she turned to the audience and smiled broadly. "Thank you so much, please take your seats, folks." She waited until everyone was seated before she spoke again.

"I would like to take a minute to introduce you to my special family. The lady wearing the tartan is my aunt, Meg MacDonald, and beside her is my uncle, Jebediah Judd." Some of the audience began to clap but she again held up her hand. "Then I'm sure you all know Gus and Beth Jorgensen, my American parents by mutual respect, and, of course, the young lady beside them is my talented accompanist and special friend, Nellie Cornish, one of your own talented musicians." At this point, the crowd once again burst into loud applause causing Nellie's cheeks to grow quite red as she mouthed the words 'thank you.'

"I also have the special honour to introduce three handsome young soldiers—war vets who are very important to me," she paused for a moment as a poignant stillness settled over the room. "This is my brother, Bill," she announced, affectionately resting her hand on his shoulder. "He's my favourite dancing partner and, on my right, is his brother, Christopher, who will talk your ear off if you give him half a chance! And this," she continued, taking Dan by the arm, "is Sergeant Dan Brown formerly of the Canadian Army, and my fiancé. I adore all three of them!"

"Thank you, Nancy," said the mayor when the applause had died down, "for introducing us to the special people in your life. Now, I believe a nice hot cup of tea will be welcomed by all and I'm told dinner is ready to be served."

As Nan went to take her seat, she realized General Greene and her aunt were seated beside her and they were talking to each other in hushed tones.

"That girl is truly a lady," he was whispering to Meg, sitting to his left beyond Nancy's empty chair.

"You don't know the half of it, sir," Meg retorted. "That girl is an angel!"

Whispered comments buzzed about the room as servers dressed in uniform quickly served up plates of food to each guest. Mayor Cotterill rose and held up his arms for silence.

"Make it short man, I'm starving!" Christopher commented loudly, causing a roar of laughter from those near enough to hear.

Gus dropped his head, shaking it in disbelief as he smiled at his son's audacity. Despite Christopher's obvious war injuries of a useless arm and an eye-patch, Gus was pleased his younger son still sported a sense of humour—his words now stirring the party into life.

As a testimonial to Gus' thoughts, the mayor threw up his hands in good-humoured resignation, telling everyone to enjoy their meal as he sat down again.

Later, as dishes were cleared away, members of a five-piece band entered and set up their instruments and music stands near a grand piano which had been quietly moved into place. Tables were shuffled around and a space was made for dancing.

When the band began to play, Bill and Nancy led off with their unique dancing routine, bringing sighs from many of the ladies and tears to Beth's eyes. Jebediah touched Meg's hand bringing her attention to the piano as Nellie slid onto the stool and picked up the song being played. As the song ended, the redhead rode back to the table on Bill's lap amid laughter and applause.

"Dance with Dan," Beth whispered across the table to Nancy.

Nancy nodded and, extracting herself from Bill with Dan's assistance, hand-in-hand they walked out onto the floor as the band began to play a waltz. Taking Nancy into his arms, he groaned quietly, not being much of a dancer. Nan began humming into his ear as she watched Nellie's fingers flash across the keyboard. At the end of the song, the pianist moved right into another, playing a gentle love song the redhead recognized as one she had often sung in practice. The band recognized it and managed to pick up the tune.

Someone gasped, telling everyone around them to be quiet as Nancy began singing softly to Dan. "I shall always love you," her beautiful soprano voice whispered. Nellie had to force herself to concentrate for she knew instinctively that Nancy meant every word and, although having heard her sing it many times, the song's tender simplicity still affected her.

This time there were no cheers or clapping as the last note hung in the air and Dan bent to kiss his bride-to-be on the cheek.

"Go sit down, honey," she told him softly. "These people have generously supported my war effort and now I need to show my gratitude."

Kissing her hand and winking, Dan returned to their table as Nancy went to join Nellie at the piano. His eyes met those of the Jorgensen boys as he passed their table and he shook his head emotionally.

"We know, brother. We love her, too," said Bill, a catch in his voice as Nancy began to speak.

"Dear friends," she began, "I'd like to thank each of you for your continuing support of my concerts and especially to Mr. James Moore for his generosity in allowing us the use of his theatre each month. You have all given so generously of your time, your hearts, and financial donations to Victoria's Widows' and Orphans' Fund and now I would like to thank you in the best way I know how … with a song from my heart."

"My word, that girl's a natural ambassador," General Greene muttered.

"Hush," Meg whispered as Nellie's fingers touched the ivory keyboard and their first notes floated through the silent room.

Singing for a full 30 minutes, the Canadian singer delighted the mayor and his guests with a selection of songs, for the most part, different from the earlier concert.

"That's enough, honey," Nellie whispered from the piano.

"Just one more," Nancy insisted. "I want to sing *My Island Home* for Aunt Meg."

The haunting melody caused Meg to reach for her hankie, dabbing at her eyes.

"She's singing this one for Aunt Meg," Dan quietly informed the Jorgensen boys.

There were speeches from Mayor Cotterill and a vote of special thanks to both the girls from General Greene before the party ended just after midnight. Long and protracted good nights were exchanged among the guests and Nancy hugged Nellie affectionately before they climbed into separate cars.

An hour later, laying contentedly between luxurious sheets in her room at the Jorgensen mansion, Nancy's still active mind began flashing back through the years beginning with the early pain of childhood and Dan's brotherly attention at the orphanage until their separation when he left seeking work. He promised to find her again, but she found him instead and, adopting each other as siblings, they built Cunningham Manor on the cliffs at Gordon Head naming it for the gold miner who had unexpectedly left her his fortune.

Her thoughts turned to the war years and Dan looking so handsome in his army uniform and the stress of separation which made them both realize their love had grown beyond their expectations. She remembered the terror waiting for news that did not come—news of Dan from the front, to turn into feelings of despair when he finally returned home desperately needing her help to recover his memory. A smile finally touched her lips as happy thoughts of her September wedding took over and sleep at last enveloped her weary body.

Sleeping in the next morning, Nancy awoke to the sounds of voices and laughter below her in the garden. Looking out through the gently blowing curtains, she saw Dan and the boys, along with Jebediah and Gus, waving newspapers in the air as they shouted to her.

"Hey you noisy devils," she called down to them, "can't a girl get her beauty sleep?"

"You're a star, sis," Bill yelled. "Every newspaper has your picture on the front page today!"

Despite her eagerness to see the newspapers, she refused to give up the luxury of her shower in the elegant Jorgensen bathroom. Afterwards, feeling more refreshed, she dressed quickly and hurried downstairs to the breakfast room where Meg, Beth, and Nellie were scanning a pile of newspapers on the table.

"Where did you get all the newspapers from?" she asked in surprise. "Hi Nellie, what are you doing here so early?"

"Nellie brought us some of these papers and Terry O'Reilly brought the rest," Beth giggled, as Nancy sat down. "It seems they're talking about you girls from coast to coast!"

"May we serve breakfast, madam?" the strained voice of the butler inquired.

"Yes, yes, of course, Joseph," Beth laughed. "Serve it in the dining-room and please call the men inside."

During the noisy, laughter-filled breakfast, Jebediah posed a sombre observation. "This may bring us too much attention, Gus," he growled. "We may have to curtail the liquor deliveries."

"Could also mean it's safer," the ship owner chuckled in mischievous amusement. "She'll be revered by the servicemen and we all know how the coast guard boys treat her!"

"Export laws and prohibition in BC could shut you down though," Chris offered quietly.

"Waldo said there's a way around that," Nancy interrupted. "There are still terrible hardships in many families and they need financial help. Maybe you should let Dan and I decide."

"Phone call, sir," the butler interrupted at the open door.

"Tell them nobody's home," Gus joked.

"It's okay, I'll get it, dad," said Bill with a grin, swinging his wheelchair away from the table.

Conversation stopped as he disappeared into the hall and Nancy glanced inquiringly at Gus.

"I have no idea who it could be," he murmured.

"Wow!" Bill's voice shattered the silence as he hung up the phone and wheeled into the room. "General Greene is going to visit you in Victoria, sis; he says the army wants you to sing at two more camps."

"When and where?" Nellie asked sharply.

"Philadelphia and New York."

"No, no, it would take weeks to get there," she laughed, "and we've lots to do in Victoria. When is he coming to see us?"

"He didn't say."

"Don't say no," Gus advised. "Wait until you hear what he has to say."

"It's the price of stardom, Nan," Nellie giggled, "there'll be many more offers coming in, don't worry!"

"Phone call, sir," the butler announced again, "and there's a newspaper reporter at the door."

"I'll get the phone," Bill said resignedly. "You get the door, Chris."

"I think we should move into the living room," Beth sighed. "I think everyone is finished and we don't need visitors in the dining-room."

Passing Bill in the hall, they heard him shout down the phone, "I'm her brother, so go get lost, pal!"

"Who was that, son?" his father asked.

"Some crook who wants to be Nancy's agent for 20 percent!"

Joining the others in the living room they were barely seated when Chris appeared at the door with a good-looking, blonde-haired young man of about 30 years.

"This fella says he's a newspaper reporter. I thought you might like to talk to him, sis!" said Chris, winking at Nancy as he took a seat next to his mother leaving the reporter looking quite uncomfortable as he stood alone in the centre of the room.

"Tom Wills, ma'am … er, folks!" the tall, slim figure muttered nervously, looking around the room as he adjusted his coffee-stained tie and deftly caught the pencil that slipped from behind his ear. "I'd like to interview Miss Wilson for the *Seattle Observer*," he announced uncertainly.

Nancy smiled, her eyes twinkling with mischief as she studied the young man.

Now what's she up to? Nellie wondered, noticing her friend's familiar playful expression.

"Well, of course, you can," Nan said quietly, "but I think you should start with the boys. They're heroes, you know. That's Bill in the wheelchair, Chris let you in and this one is Dan," she patted Dan's knee.

"No miss, it's you I want to interview," the reporter insisted.

"But you are interviewing me. That lady sitting over there is Nellie Cornish. Now don't tell me you don't know who she is—she's a legend in Seattle!"

"Yes ma'am I know about Miss Cornish."

Meg hid her smile behind her handkerchief, squeezing closer to Jebediah as the redhead teased the reporter.

"Mr. Wills," Beth took up the conversation, "Nancy Wilson is a Canadian from Victoria, a lovely young woman who sings at The James Moore Theatre once a month for charity."

"I know all that ma'am, but my readers want to know who she really is."

"Ach laddie," Meg sighed, "if we told all we know about our little angel, they'd noo believe it!"

Glancing around the room, Tom Wills grinned self-consciously and took a deep breath. "Thank you ma'am, but I know a lot more than you think. Miss Wilson owns a half interest in the *Wounded Soldier Restaurant* near the hospital in Victoria, and, with Mr. Brown, she owns a beautiful home in Gordon Head. They also own a shipping company on the docks in Victoria. She collects money for the Victoria Widows' and Orphans' Fund and comes here every Friday. But I figure there's still got to be more!"

Jebediah had suddenly sat up straight on his seat, his senses alert. This interview had the smell of danger. They had been investigated and he hadn't been aware of it. *What else does this reporter know*?

"Mr. Wills," the old detective asked, frowning heavily, "maybe we don't want you to tell the world about our Nancy."

"I'm sorry, sir, but Nancy Wilson is a star—a household name in Seattle. People want to know."

"And her privacy?" Gus intervened.

"All I want is a little background," the reporter pleaded. "Give me something to write about and I'll go away." He glanced over at Nancy. "You're a mystery woman, Miss Wilson, where do you come from?"

"I'm an orphan; in fact, we're all orphans, all four of us," Nancy replied, indicating Dan, Meg and Jeb.

"You mean none of you Canadians are related?"

"Not by blood, lad," Jeb growled, "we're all related by choice."

"Now there's a story I can write," Tom replied, looking quite pleased with himself. "How do the rest of you fit into this picture?"

"Well Nellie's my pianist," continued Nancy.

"And the rest of it is," Bill suddenly interrupted, "we Jorgensens adopted the whole lot of them!"

"Now that's what I want—a real human interest story, four orphans, three wounded soldiers, two cross-border families and a beautiful red-headed singer. My editor will love it!" replied the reporter eagerly spilling out his thoughts. "In fact, I'd like to know more about all of you."

"Don't push your luck, lad!" Jeb snapped. Coming to his feet, he put his hand on the reporter's arm and eased him toward the door.

Realizing he had all he was going to get this time, Tom extracted his arm from Jeb's grip, turned and thanked them, and left on his own. Driving away, his mind raced with the story he planned to write. "An orphan," he mused aloud. "I wonder how she met the Jorgensen family?" There were many more questions to which he would have liked the answers. He could feel the strong bond between those people and their fierce loyalty to the redheaded girl but he felt there was still more to be learned. *Does some dark secret draw them all together*? he wondered, his imagination running wild.

"He's going to be a nuisance," said Gus as they heard the car leave. "I could tell by his eyes he was fascinated and he'll be wanting more!"

The phone rang several more times and Bill and Chris took turns dealing with the calls. Later, they all went outside to admire the beautifully manicured gardens until Nellie announced it was time for her to leave.

"Walk me to the car, Nan," she said softly, taking her friend's arm and steering her toward the driveway. "I want you to know that last evening's concert was one of the most wonderful nights of my life," she said. "I never expected to reach such a dizzying height and I'd like to thank you for including me."

"It wouldn't be the same without you, Nellie," Nancy said warmly. "I know how you feel. I'm so happy I could scream!"

By early afternoon Nancy, Dan, Meg, and Jeb were travelling back across the choppy waters of the Strait of Juan de Fuca toward Victoria.

"You wouldn't think there was a war on, would you?" Meg commented as they watched several yachts running gracefully in the breeze alongside the San Juan Islands.

That week, even the local newspapers reported Nancy's singing at Camp Lewis, causing a short-lived burst of interest around Victoria which was soon forgotten as war news enveloped the city. Nancy got Dan involved helping out several of the war widows who needed odd jobs done, finding retired tradesmen who didn't mind getting paid very little or, nothing, for their services.

As the months passed, the city was pulling together even more to help the war-torn families of the area and, with Eva's help, they managed to keep the secret of where the funds were coming from intact.

Nancy changed her mind about having the wedding so soon, realizing she wanted more time to plan the most important day in her life. After talking with Dan and Meg, she decided to have it on the 4th of May, when spring flowers would be blooming. She knew the months would pass quickly as her thoughts became consumed with wedding preparations. Not having to worry about her wedding dress, as Beth made it clear that she was looking after that aspect. Nan and her friend, Kate Dumpford, her Matron of Honour, went shopping for Kate's dress and other necessary items.

Shipyards were once again busy with government contracts and skilled workers were at a premium as many tradesmen had long ago signed up and left for Europe. Hospital ships continued bringing their cargoes of wounded soldiers into Victoria harbour and, due to food rationing, many more families were discovered suffering desperate hardships. The breakwater at Ogden Point was completed, adding shelter to Rithet's outer wharf, and streetcars now ran out to the Dallas Hotel, not far from the breakwater. Victoria continued to grow despite the hard times.

During the summer and early autumn of 1917, reports began reaching the Pacific Northwest of an illness called Spanish Influenza that was ravaging the war-torn cities of Europe. In the following months, local newspapers carried reports of British hospitals full to overflowing and, with no sign of a cure, the number of deaths reported was terribly alarming, even from so far away.

"Do you think it will reach Victoria?" Nancy asked Dr. Arthur Price, the city's health officer, when he called for a meal at the *Wounded Soldier Restaurant* in early March of 1918.

"Oh I'm sure it will," he gruffly assured her, "there seems to be no stopping the epidemic."

"But by then you'll know how to treat it, won't you, doctor?"

"We're working on it, girl," Dr. Price replied sharply, "but cases have already been reported in Quebec, Boston, and Philadelphia."

"How is it spreading so fast?" she asked, a look of great concern wrinkling her brow.

“Soldiers are bringing it home with them,” Dr. Price replied shaking his head sadly. He paid his bill and, offering no further comment, left the restaurant.

Nancy watched through the window as the bowed figure slowly crossed the streetcar tracks and disappeared inside the hospital across the street. *He's more tired than usual*, she thought.

“What are you looking at?” Kate asked, coming up behind her with a cloth to wash the table. “What did Dr. Price have to say? Nothing good, by the look on your face.”

“He said the flu has arrived in Quebec and the United States already.”

“We live in troubled times, Nan. The war's not over yet and now this terrible influenza thing's killing thousands of people. At least we have the happy preparations of your wedding to keep us from going crazy with worry. I'm so glad you decided to have it in May rather than last September.”

“It certainly has given us more time to organize everything; I never imagined there would be so much to do!” Nancy exclaimed.

“Oh, we have lots of time now, we only have the influenza to worry about, it seems!”

“Don't even think of it, Kate, I've waited long enough to be Mrs. Dan Brown!” Nan retorted. “I'm not going to let a health emergency get in my way!”

Chapter 2

All through March and on into April, as wedding preparations continued reported cases of influenza drew closer to their area. Nancy was getting worried that it could impact the date of her wedding or worse—that friends or family would get sick, but she didn't say anything. She tried to dismiss the danger as wedding excitement accelerated, especially among the women in her circle.

General Greene, true to his word, promised the services of the Camp Lewis chaplain and then called again, enthusiastically offering their military ensemble band for the reception. Harry Maynard insisted he was providing the liquid refreshments and Waldo stated firmly he was arranging all the transport of guests and hauling of supplies such as tables and chairs.

Not having to worry about her wedding dress was also a great relief to Nancy but she talked to Beth by telephone insisting she keep it simple, worried that her small family wedding was quickly getting out of control.

By mid-April Victoria was alive with rumours of the dreaded influenza arriving in Vancouver and local health authorities found themselves stretched to the limit as they desperately made plans to combat the arrival of the deadly epidemic.

Fifteen minutes prior to her April 27th concert in Seattle, Christopher came to Nancy's dressing room accompanied by the city's health officer, Dr. Tubble, who made a startling request.

"Miss Wilson," he began very formally, "I must ask you to cancel your future concerts until further notice."

"Are you serious?" Nellie snapped, "she's an institution here in Seattle, people love her concerts."

"Steady Nellie," Chris intervened. "Let's hear the doctor's reasoning."

"The influenza has arrived in Seattle," the health officer announced with a grave expression. "We will be banning all gatherings of more than seven people in the interest of our citizens' health. I think your fans would take the news better if it came directly from you, Miss Wilson."

"You want me to tell them?" Nancy asked incredulously.

"Yes miss, they trust you. They'll believe you and it's imperative that they listen."

"No more concerts," the redhead whispered. "Have you talked to Mr. Moore?"

"Yes, I have. I'm sorry it's come to this but realize it is only a temporary measure," the doctor replied, turning on his heel and leaving.

Shocked into silence, Nancy felt Nellie's hand on her arm, gently reminding her of the ten-minute call to curtain time. Christopher gave her a solemn hug and also left.

Last-minute makeup touches were applied and they were getting ready to leave when a knock at the door revealed a sombre James Moore, his normal bubbling outlook replaced by an obvious sadness.

"Sorry girls," he said softly, "but we'll have one heck of a re-opening when this thing is over!"

The girls gave him a silent hug before following him to the backstage area. As he moved toward the curtain, he went over and took Nancy's hand and whispered something to her. The curtain began to rise and as they waited for James to introduce them, Nancy took Nellie's hand.

"This could be our last performance together," she whispered.

"Don't you dare even think that!" Nellie hissed back as they walked confidently toward the piano, putting on their best smiles. "We're going to give them a night they'll never forget."

Nellie seated herself and set up her music as the maestro entered to the usual round of applause. When ready, she nodded at him and Nancy took a deep breath, placing one hand on the smooth surface of the shiny black piano. Nellie winked at her and Nan turned to smile at her audience. The maestro tapped his baton, raised his arms and the concert began.

Nellie's fingers flashed across the keyboard and Nancy's clear joyous tones filled the theatre as they began with the lively favourite, *Oh How I Hate To Get Up In The Morning*. Dan, sitting on the edge of his seat in the owner's box, smiled as happy memories of his early days in the barracks flooded back to him. Then he frowned slightly when he detected a hint of tension in Nancy's voice.

"Something's wrong, Aunt Meg," he whispered over Meg MacDonald's shoulder.

"I know, son, I can hear it, too."

"The city health officer came to talk to Nan in her dressing room," Christopher whispered, hearing their comments.

"He did what?" Dan exclaimed.

"Quiet you two!" Gus hissed.

Dan now watched Nancy intently, his mind spinning as he wondered what was going on. He never took his eyes from the stage or off Nancy until she finished the last song and the curtain went down for the intermission. The audience erupted in wild applause and as Dan prepared to leave to go meet Nancy, the curtain rose and she stood silently alone at centre stage. She graciously acknowledged the applause then solemnly held up her hands for silence. The audience, sensing something unusual was happening, quieted almost instantly.

"Friends," Nancy's voice rang through the silent theatre. "I have been asked to make an announcement. Sadly, this will be my last concert for awhile."

"I knew something was wrong," Dan growled fiercely, standing up and turning toward the exit, as a ripple of surprise ran through the theatre.

"Stay where you are and listen," Chris hissed, sharply grasping Dan's arm.

"Apparently your beautiful city is being visited by the Spanish influenza," she continued, her voice amazingly calm, "and, for your safety, the city is temporarily banning all public gatherings. But be assured we will get together again soon when this sickness has passed. Now go have a drink on Mr. Moore and I'll see you back here in 15 minutes."

"Now you can go," Chris chuckled as the curtain closed and the theatre lights came on.

Shocked by Nancy's statement, much of the audience sat in stunned silence staring at the curtain before slowly moving toward the foyer, whispering among themselves.

"The drinks are on me, folks!" James Moore announced from the refreshment counter. "Enjoy the rest of the show and please look after yourselves."

Making his way down the stairs to the dressing-room area, Dan could barely hear the low murmur of voices coming from the foyer. What would normally have been a laughing crowd of happy theatregoers, was greatly subdued.

Knocking lightly on the girls' door, he waited for a call to enter before stepping inside.

"What was that all about?" he asked quietly. "You're not singing here anymore?"

"Didn't you listen to my announcement, Dan? Seattle health authorities are taking precautions, honey, they're trying to stop the flu from spreading. It's only temporary."

"Are they sure it's here?"

"Dr. Tubble seems to think so."

"They wouldn't dare issue orders like this, if they weren't sure," Nellie added.

They talked about it for a few minutes and then a knock sounded on the door with the ten-minute warning.

"We have to go, Danny," Nancy reminded him. "I'm sure Gus will find out all the details and tell us what's happening after the show. I'll see you after the concert, honey."

"Five minutes to curtain time," a shrill call rang through the back rooms of the theatre minutes later and the girls headed for the stage.

Back in James Moore's box, a discussion was raging as no one had left except Dan. A waiter was dispatched to acquire drinks as Chris defended the health officer's drastic measures.

"I'll get to the bottom of this," Gus promised determinedly.

Lights flashed in the theatre sending the audience hurrying back to their seats and the lively music of the second half soon drove all thoughts of the influenza from everyone's mind. All eyes were on the beautiful Canadian girl singing her heart out to leave them with a memorable evening. James stood in the wings, dabbing his handkerchief to his eyes as he hid in the folds of the curtain, knowing luck had dealt his theatre, and the city, an alarming blow.

There were many sad goodbyes to be said at the after-theatre party that evening. Tears were shed and Dr. Tubble became the target of much of their anger, quietly swallowing many insults in the line of duty as he struggled to keep his composure. Nancy said a sad farewell to Nellie and made her promise to look after herself and to keep in touch.

The ride to the Jorgensen mansion was a quiet one as everyone seemed to be keeping their thoughts to themselves. Stress had taken its toll and after quiet good nights and hugs, everyone made straight for their rooms.

The radio was announcing grey morning clouds and rain for Puget Sound as Dan and Nancy joined the family in the breakfast room. Thankfully, the mood had changed from the night before and the usual noisy exuberance was present. The boys, always eager with teasing comments, were greeted with kisses on the cheek from Nancy and a wagging finger as she took her place.

"Now, if you boys will keep quiet long enough for us to tell you the news," Beth warned them. Receiving nodded replies from Bill and Christopher, their mother continued, "Gus has already been on the phone to one of the city officials and he has confirmed the information Dr. Tubble gave us last night."

"I was told there had been an emergency meeting of council on the 22nd of April and at that meeting it was decided to enact emergency measures which would take effect immediately," Gus informed them.

"Maybe we should all stay here," Beth said softly. "We could seal off the estate."

"We can't do that, darling," Gus replied, patting her hand. "I have a business to run, but we certainly can take some sensible precautions."

"What about Nancy's wedding and her charity work?" Bill asked. "Can your fund manage without the theatre collection, Nan?"

"Oh, we could survive for awhile, but with the threat of this Spanish influenza things are going to get even worse for some of our destitute families," she replied candidly. "We have to think of some other way to find the money."

"You could always run more liquor deliveries," Bill suggested, looking at her out of the corner of his eye.

"It's probably the only way," she sighed. "I have no doubt Dr. Price will impose similar rules in Victoria very soon."

"I'm sure Terry O'Reilly would welcome that suggestion!" Gus muttered.

"Don't do it, lassie," Meg pleaded. "You've done all that you can already. You have to think of your own health, too."

"We can't just stop, Aunt Meg," Nancy replied, "those families are relying on us."

"Phone call, sir," quietly announced the butler standing in the doorway.

"Not just now, Joseph," said Gus waving him away.

"It's General Greene, sir," he insisted.

"I'll take it in the study, excuse me," he said, quickly leaving the room.

"It's time we got on our way," Dan announced, standing up. "It's going to be a rough ride home."

As they were putting on their coats, the door to the study opened and Gus came out.

"You're ready to be off?" he asked. "That was General Greene, he says the flu is already here and he'll be going to visit you in Victoria, Dan."

"When?"

"He didn't say, but he sounded mighty worried."

"We'll see you off," said Chris trying to be light-hearted as, with Joseph's assistance, he eased his good arm into his jacket. Then he threw a blanket over his brother's shoulders. "You can wheel the fat guy, Dan!"

"Cheeky brat," Bill flung back at his brother. "Run over him, Dan!"

"Stop that, you two," Beth snapped. "Can't you ever be serious?"

"Oh I'm serious, mum," Bill chuckled, "if Dan'll do it!"

"Okay if that's what you want, let's do it," Dan laughed, setting out to chase Chris down the garden path with the wheelchair right behind and the boys crowing with laughter.

"Blasted children, won't they ever grow up?" Beth laughed as they followed the boys down to the dock. She hugged Nancy and Meg then turned to Jebediah. "You look after these ladies for us, won't you Jeb?"

"I'll do my best, Beth, and you folks do the same," he replied, as they hugged each other and he shook hands with Gus.

As the *Stockholm* fought her way home through a gusting wind that often blew spray clear over the boat, the passengers were grateful for the protection afforded by the *Stockholm*'s cabin, remembering how uncomfortable their old boat had been. Nancy stood with Dan at the wheel watching for deadheads as they slowly moved northward through the Puget Sound toward Cunningham Manor, their home sitting atop the cliffs of Gordon Head.

Old Sam, the neighbourhood hermit, nudged his dog, Flash, with his foot when he heard the familiar sound of the *Stockholm*'s engine and, rising from his seat in the shadows of the manor's porch, shuffled toward the cliff stairs to watch.

"Looks like Sam's waiting for us," Jeb muttered, looking up and seeing them as he stepped onto the dock. He reached for Meg's hand. "He must have some news for us."

"I'll take Meg upstairs so she can get the fire on. I'll be right back," called Dan over the noise of the wind in the trees.

"Sam is probably hungry," Meg chuckled as they climbed the steep, stairs, still slippery after an overnight rain.

"You spoil him too much, Aunt Meg. He never had it so good until he met you!"

When they reached the top, puffing with exertion, Meg stood muttering to herself about growing old. Dan glanced around searching for Sam who was no longer at the spot where they had seen him. Finding the old man standing in his usual place at the edge of the trees watching them, he grinned.

"See, what did I tell you, Aunt Meg, he's waiting for your meal!" Turning back to the stairs, he started down.

"I'll have tea ready when you get back," she called after him, going in and shutting the door.

"Did you talk to Sam?" Nancy asked when he returned.

"No, Jeb can do that. The old fella seems to like our Mr. Judd!"

"I own him!" Jeb growled, offering no explanation for his statement as thoughts of the first time he and Sam met went through his head.

"Shut that door!" Meg called from the kitchen as they struggled into the house with their cases and parcels. "It's cold enough in here without bringing the wind in, too."

"I need a sandwich for Sam," Jeb called back, making no attempt to remove his hat or coat.

"Well make him one! You're not lame are you?" Meg snapped, "I'm busy trying to get this fire going."

"I'll do it, Uncle Jeb," Nancy chuckled, taking some bread out of the breadbox and going to the icebox to find some meat.

A few minutes later, armed with a thick sandwich wrapped in a sheet of newspaper, Jeb went back outside. Closing the door, he stood on the porch and looked out toward the tree line beyond the orchard. Finding Sam's outline in the shadows, he started out to meet him.

"Brown man come," the half-breed hermit grunted as he reached for the package of food.

"You mean a black-faced man?"

Biting hungrily into the sandwich, Sam shook his head. "No, all brown," he muttered through his chewing.

Watching him carefully, Jeb mulled Sam's words over in his head and suddenly realized what he meant. "A soldier's been here," he proffered, and saw Sam nod. "Today?" Jeb asked but a shake of the shaggy head told him no. "Yesterday?" Nodding, Sam turned and shuffled silently back toward the trees.

Now what the devil would the army want? Jeb wondered, stopping to light his pipe as he tried to make some sense of the information.

Dan, watching from the window, saw Jeb talk to Sam and could tell by Jeb's actions that something had happened.

"We had a visitor on Saturday," Jeb announced as he came inside and hung his coat on the hook behind the door. He met Dan's questioning gaze. "A soldier."

"A soldier, why?" asked Nancy.

"How the heck do I know?" Jeb retorted.

"Probably someone checking up on me," Dan mumbled.

It was after dinner, as they all gathered around a roaring fire, that the telephone rang and Nancy went to answer it.

"Hi Kate," she said loudly. "Oh, when? Thanks Kate, I'll tell him."

"Bad news, love?" the Scot inquired quietly, looking up from her knitting and seeing her solemn expression.

"The army was looking for Dan down at the dock on Saturday, too. Oh, and Danny, the Mouats want you to take their supplies over to Salt Spring on Tuesday morning."

"And so, why the worried look?" Dan inquired.

"It's the army," Nancy replied. "I don't trust them. They always want to make trouble for me."

"They can't, Nan," he said, grinning. "I'm retired now!"

"Did you say Dan's to go to Salt Spring tomorrow?" Meg asked.

"Yes, Waldo told Jack yesterday," Nancy replied.

"Well, you can bring me back some of their spun wool."

"Can't you get your wool here in Victoria, Aunt Meg?" Dan asked.

"Not the same quality, lad, and I like to give Jane Mouat the business. They try so hard with their little farm."

The next morning, the wind was calmer but a light rain was falling as Dan and Jeb left in the boat for Victoria. Nancy stood on the clifftop with her heavy coat wrapped tightly around her and skirts swirling about her legs as she waved goodbye. She knew they wouldn't be able to see her in the low light but she watched until the boat turned southward around the headland.

Before going into the house, Nancy cranked the little blue truck into life and then went inside to say goodbye to Meg. Picking up her hat and scarf, she loaded her packages into the automobile and waved to Meg on the porch. Stepping on the gas, her mind instantly thought of the restaurant wondering what sort of a day it would be.

Travelling Shelbourne at a fast clip of 20 miles an hour, there was hardly a soul in sight. It was pouring now and as daylight became more evident, she noticed the increased amount of water standing in puddles and small lakes in the paddocks. *It's been raining here all weekend*, she thought, turning east at Cedar Hill Cross Road and realizing the hollow was also deep with water. *It's a good job it's not winter time.*

When she turned onto Richmond, the road was swirling with blossoms blown from nearby trees. As she passed Mayfair Drive, water was gushing down Mount Tolmie. *No wonder there's so much water!*

At the corner of Richmond and Lansdowne, she waited for the Uplands streetcar to rumble by. Then, nearing the Jubilee Hospital, she noted the unusual number of cars and people in the area. She pulled into the back lane and was greeted by Kate as she entered.

"Good morning all," she called to staff and customers, throwing her weight against the door to close it against the wind. "What's happening over at the hospital?"

"All the provincial health officials are over there. A Dr. Price dropped in and ordered ten breakfasts. They should be here at eight-thirty."

"He's our Victoria health officer. Don't tell me the influenza has arrived already?" Nan said in an alarmed voice.

"I hope not but someone heard they have it in Vancouver," Kate replied, watching Nancy pull the top of her hair into a bun.

Quickly tying on her apron, Nancy swung into action, changing places with Linda so the waitress could go and help the cook.

Promptly at eight-thirty, a group of stern-faced men, most of them in suits, arrived and were shown to a corner table. When they sat down, there remained one empty chair.

"Shall we be waiting for the last member of your group, sir?" Kate asked the man they would later find out was Dr. Henry Young, the provincial health officer.

"No, my dear, he's coming from Seattle and may be a little late."

As the doctors' noisy breakfast discussion got under way, the other customers, hospital workers and bandaged men, eyed the argumentative group with suspicion. Fierce comments flew around the table and a heated argument raged back and forth until their meals arrived. Kate watched fascinated when the last member of their group finally arrived and sat down. Beckoning her over, he spoke quietly to her. She nodded before returning to the kitchen and making a bee-line for Nancy.

"An American officer with lots of fancy medals on his chest has joined the doctors and he's asking for you, Nan!" she said excitedly.

"For me?" Nancy cocked an eyebrow quizzically.

"Yes, he said to ask you to pop out there when you had a minute."

Straightening her apron, Nancy glanced in the mirror and brushed a stray hair from her brow.

"Go on," Kate urged, "you can't miss him."

As she entered the dining area, Nancy glanced over at the table where the doctors were sitting and let out a squeal. General Greene noticed her at the same time and was on his feet with his arms out when she got to him. Nancy noticed the frowns of disapproval from several of the medical men as they embraced.

"General, what a lovely surprise," she purred.

"Gentlemen," he said gruffly, keeping his arm around her waist, "I beg your indulgence for a moment, this lovely young woman is my Canadian sweetheart!"

"Oh, General Greene," Nancy giggled, blushing.

"Do you have time to join this meeting, sir?" Dr. Price snapped impatiently.

Ignoring the caustic comment, the general beamed at Nancy. "I'll talk to you after we finish here, my dear," he whispered, winking at her.

"Coffee and breakfast, sir?" Kate inquired from behind Nancy.

"Just coffee for now, please."

"Can I get a refill too, please miss?" a young man at a neighbouring table, sporting a heavily bandaged head, asked quietly.

"Are you a soldier, son?" The general turned to face the young man.

"Yes sir," he replied.

"Then serve him first, young lady."

He turned back to the table of sombre-looking men. "Now gentlemen," he growled, "I have some serious news for you."

"One moment, general," Dr. Young interrupted, "I should make some introductions first."

"Introductions are not important!" General Greene snapped. "I need to address a more serious issue and now—we have the European influenza in Seattle."

"Spanish influenza!" Dr. Price sharply corrected.

"Shut up man and listen!" the general hissed fiercely. "I came here to warn you and I advise you to act while you have time to do so."

"You're a medical man?" Dr. Price asked coldly.

"No, I'm army," he stated emphatically.

"And you presume to advise us?"

"No, sir, I presumed you'd heed a warning. Dr. Tubble of the Seattle Health Department directed me to give you a copy of the list of safety measures he has taken in our area. He thought it might be of some use to you." Reaching into his briefcase he produced a brown envelope which he pushed in front of Dr. Young.

Glancing at the envelope, the Provincial health officer slowly picked it up, frowning as he glanced over the papers. "Come gentlemen," he said firmly, "we have much work to do." Rising, he shook hands with General Greene, his face stern and brooding as he curtly thanked him for the information and made for the door. Each of the doctors, except Dr. Price, also shook hands with General Greene, quietly identifying themselves as they paid their bill and left.

"Breakfast now, general?" Nancy asked at his elbow.

"Just toast, please Nancy," he replied, his eyes twinkling mischievously, "and only if you'll sit with me."

"I'll do my best," she said with a smile, before heading to the kitchen. When she returned, she sat across the table from him and as they chatted she kept a wary eye on the tables as customers came and went. After talking with him for five minutes, she noticed a large group of men heading across the street toward the restaurant. "General Greene, I apologize, but I shall have to go and help Kate. Could I ask you to move to a smaller table?"

"By all means. Are all these men wounded soldiers?" he asked, looking up as they walked in.

"Most of them," she replied, pushing her chair in.

Taking his own cup and saucer, the general moved quickly to a table for two, watching with rapt attention as Nancy and Kate, in their white aprons, moved among the newcomers getting them seated and taking their orders. He heard the comments and giggles from the girls as each man vied for personal attention.

"I'm leaving tomorrow, Nancy. I'm going home to Vancouver," a young man on crutches called out, sending the restaurant into sudden silence. "Can I have a hug to remember you by?"

Some of the other men began to tease him, but Nancy went over to his table and put her hand on his shoulder.

"You certainly can, Jimmy. That's great news."

Now the men cheered and whistled as the redhead put her tray down and, as he rose, she slipped her arms around him, grinning when she heard his crutches clatter to the floor. His arms tightened around her as he leaned against the table.

"Sing for me, Nan," she heard him murmur into her hair.

The whistling and cheering subsided as the redhead stepped back and out of the soldier's arms. Holding him steady, one of the men picked up his crutches and handed them to him. As she began to sing, *You'll Always Be In My Dreams*, some of the soldiers hummed quietly along. When the song finished, Jimmy squared his shoulders and, even as tears ran down his face, he smiled and saluted Nancy, then quickly left the building.

Reaching for her hand as she passed his table, General Greene pulled Nancy around to face him. "Young lady," he whispered, "I know why your Aunt Meg calls you an angel. Because that's exactly what you are! I can see you are something special to these soldiers, just like you are to our's." Sighing loudly, the general kissed her hand and rose to his feet. He hugged her gently and left without another word.

Chapter 3

Later in the afternoon, the two health officials called back at the restaurant, marching up to Nancy who was behind the cash register. Their expressions were serious and she knew instantly that trouble was brewing.

"Ladies, this is Dr. Young, director of the provincial health department. We've decided to close your restaurant," Dr. Price informed her bluntly. "You're much too close to the hospital and we can't have patients running in and out of here as they do now."

"Oh no, you're not!" Nancy shot back angrily, trying to keep her voice down.

"But you can't," Kate begged, coming to stand beside Nancy.

"Come sit down and listen to us, girls," said Dr. Young, still frowning but relaxing slightly. He indicated an empty table and the four of them quickly went and sat down.

"We are going to recommend that the city close churches, schools, theatres, meetings and all places that people gather in numbers. Any gathering of more than seven people will be illegal." He paused, watching the effect his words were having on the young women. "We have to be prepared for the worst. The influenza will spread like wildfire if we don't take serious precautions now. It has happened already in Europe and back East. I know it sounds harsh but it's for everyone's good."

"I'm planning my wedding for next month, what will happen now?" Nancy asked solemnly. "People still have to mingle. What about workplaces, dockyard, sawmills, canneries and the railway?"

"Trains will be fumigated daily and great care will have to be taken by employers."

"Then we have some time before we have to close?" Nancy asked hopefully.

"We're afraid not, due to your proximity to the hospital, it's imperative that you close immediately."

"Oh my word, you are serious! I can't bear to hear another word. I'm going to call Jack," Kate retorted. Tears welled in her eyes as she went over to the phone, giving the operator the number for the Brown and Wilson dock.

Nancy sighed. *Was she going to be cheated out of her wedding by this sudden development*?

"Jack, could you come get me?" Katherine sniffled into the phone.

"What's the matter, honey?" Jack Dumpford, the dock manager at the *Brown and Wilson Speedy Deliveries by Sea* office, asked with startled concern.

"They've closed us down."

"Who has?" he snapped, but the phone had gone dead and he looked blankly at the receiver.

"What the hell are you talking about Dumpy?" Waldo Skillings, a neighbouring businessman, growled from the open doorway. "Are you talking to yourself again?"

"No, sir, it was my wife. She says they've closed them down."

"You mean the restaurant, lad?"

"I think that's what she meant. She was crying and asked me to go get her."

"Who's they?" the haulier asked fiercely, as he followed Jack out to his truck.

"That's what I'm going to find out," Jack mumbled, quickly cranking his vehicle, jumping in and accelerating up to Wharf Street leaving a cloud of dust behind him and Waldo shaking his head.

By the time he reached Fort Street, a knot of worry churned in his stomach knowing Kate rarely got so upset that she cried. His wife was as strong a woman as he had ever known, excepting Nancy whom he had known for some years longer. Her tears sent his mind into a panic.

Puffing hard on his pipe, Waldo watched Jack's truck swing into Fort Street and he went back to close the Brown and Wilson office door. Absentmindedly, he wandered out onto the dock pondering Jack's worried comments. He watched a freighter being moved into place at the Hudson Bay dock then, turning abruptly, headed back up the road.

Cursing a slow moving streetcar at Fort and Richmond, Jack brought his vehicle to a stop in front of the *Wounded Soldier Restaurant* and saw the CLOSED sign in the window. Leaping out, he dashed to the door and flung it open.

"KATE!" he shouted, hurrying past the empty tables.

"I'm in here," his wife answered from the kitchen.

Nancy grinned as they folded themselves into each other's arms.

"You tell him, Nan, I'm too upset," said Kate.

"They've closed us down, Dumpy. Simple as that." Nancy's voice came in a whisper as she answered Jack's questioning stare.

"Who has?" he asked.

"Dr. Price, the city health officer."

"Why?"

"He says it's a precautionary measure to stop the influenza spreading."

"Can he do that? I haven't even heard that it's arrived in Victoria yet," Jack noted.

"I'm not sure, but I'll talk to Waldo and Harry tonight, they'll know. Kate can have a few days off until I've sorted this thing out," Nancy replied. She hugged them both as they left, but even Jack's assurances that everything would be worked out did not dispel the foreboding feeling she had.

Standing in the middle of the restaurant, she looked around at the empty tables of the business she and Kate had worked so hard at and a tear slowly trickled down her cheek. Gathering up her belongings, she went to the door and switched the lights off. Brushing aside her tears she took another look back and the faces of the hundreds of wounded soldiers who had passed through these doors appeared. She had been happy to help by giving them a few minutes of pleasure and now it had all abruptly come to an end. She turned quickly away and locking the door she walked blindly to the truck.

It was almost four-thirty when she parked in front of their dockside office. The lights were on but Dumpy's truck was nowhere in sight.

"Hey girl," a familiar voice called from behind her as Waldo came up behind her. "What the devil's going on?" he demanded, noting her red face.

"Come inside, Waldo," Nancy muttered, getting out of the truck. "It's cold out here."

"Dumpy shot outa here over an hour ago," he grumbled. "I was waiting for him coming back when you turned up."

Opening the door, she yelped with surprise, for there sitting at the table was Dan, poring over his bookwork."

"Nan, what are you doing here? What's going on, honey?" he asked, also noticing her telltale colouring. He stood up as she came toward him.

"They've closed the restaurant down," she said softly, moving into his outstretched arms, "and we might have to put the wedding off."

"Like hell we will! Who has?" Dan reacted angrily and Nancy burst into tears burying her head in his chest. "Come on, Nan, sit down and tell me what's happened."

"Dr. Price says we have to close because of the flu."

"The Spanish flu's here?" Waldo growled, snatching his pipe out of his mouth. "No wedding, you say?"

"Easy, old friend," Dan tried to calm down the old haulier who owned Victoria Baggage Company. "Sit down and let her tell us the whole story."

"Well," she began, going to sit at the table and accepting the coffee Dan handed to her. "Dr. Price and eight other doctors had a meeting at the hospital this morning. They booked a table for ten at the restaurant and came for a late breakfast."

"Who was the 10th person?" Dan asked.

"It was General Greene, Dan. He'd come up from Seattle to meet with them."

"General Greene's here in town? Gus did say he was coming to see me but I haven't heard anything."

"Well, he was, I didn't ask how long he was staying."

"Did you hear why he came?"

"Oh yes, he came to warn them that the flu's already in Seattle but they wouldn't listen to him. He got really cross and shouted at them."

"It's the flu," Waldo growled. "I heard they had it in Vancouver, too."

"I know, Dr. Price came back this afternoon with the provincial health officer," Nancy sighed. "He said they were going to recommend closing schools, churches, restaurants and all meeting places. They want to ban any gathering of more than seven people; they hope it will stop the flu spreading. It's like we heard about in Seattle."

"Health emergency or not, they can't do that without a city ordinance," Waldo snapped, "and we'll soon hear when that happens. Why has he closed you down so quickly?"

"Dr. Price said we were too close to the hospital and he didn't want patients coming and going."

"It's after five," Dan pointed out. "I'll leave the boat here and go home with you in the truck. We'll sort this out tomorrow."

"Good idea, lad," Waldo agreed. "I'll be wanting a few answers myself in the morning."

Dan checked the *Stockholm*'s lines as Nancy turned out the lights and locked the office. Hooking arms, they watched Waldo barrel up to Wharf Street waving and yelling 'good night' as he went.

"Do you want me to drive, Nan?" he asked.

"No, but you can start it up for me," she said coyly, watching him go round to the front of the vehicle.

With the windscreen wipers brushing away the light rain, Nancy drove slowly behind a streetcar travelling up Government as they conversed about the boarded-up saloons and drinking establishments closed by the prohibition law.

"Between prohibition and the influenza, Victoria is being turned into a ghost town," Dan complained. "It's getting mighty hard for some business owners I'm afraid. We might be one of the lucky ones; a water service will always be in demand."

As they discussed how the influenza was going to affect the city, General Greene was entering the council chamber at Victoria City Hall only blocks away. Seated between Mayor Albert Todd and the Health Committee Chairman, Thomas Peden, General Greene was not at all surprised by the air of suspicious animosity which greeted him. He suspected it was not only the fact he was a uniformed general, but that these councillors and the health officials present were not happy with having an American at their meeting.

The emergency meeting was brought to order quickly and the mayor began by introducing Dr. Price. An instant buzz sounded throughout the room.

"Please gentlemen," begged the mayor, "we can get through this more quickly if you let me do the talking. As you know, we have been waiting for news on the scope of the influenza epidemic. Major General Greene, Commanding Officer of Camp Lewis in Washington State, is here to offer us some assistance with that information."

Dr. Price, seated nearby, kept a serious expression as he nodded a hint of recognition toward the general.

"I believe General Greene has already met with representatives from the hospital and local medical authorities," Mayor Todd continued, looking over at Thomas Peden and receiving a stone-faced nod of affirmation. "I invited him to meet with us to explain the measures the City of Seattle and Washington State are taking to protect their citizens against this epidemic. Perhaps he will be able to allay some of our fears by giving us a rundown on the effectiveness of these measures."

"He's a soldier, not a medical man!" one of the councillors snapped sarcastically.

"As commanding officer of Camp Lewis he is most concerned with the health of his soldiers—a contingent of ten thousand men. He is also the official representative of the Washington State Health Committee. I believe you will find he has some interesting observations to pass on to us," continued the mayor.

"Well, I think this is interference," Dr. Price interrupted, "and you're encouraging it, sir."

"Fool!" declared the general, unable to hold back his anger.

Banging his gavel in a vain attempt to gain control of the meeting, Mayor Todd watched in dismay as several of his councillors entered the argument resulting in strong words and abuse calling. Suddenly, the general rose to his feet.

"SHUT UP!" he bellowed, with the force of a drill sergeant major. When an uneasy silence prevailed, he continued, "This morning I detailed our recommendations to your doctors and Mayor Todd has a copy. I'm leaving now. I have no stomach for stupid bickering especially when there are lives at stake. You have a crisis looming here in Victoria—deal with it as you will!"

Turning on his heel, he left the room, his words having the desired effect. As he strode down the corridor he could hear renewed arguments being played out loudly behind him. He found himself out on Douglas Street and turned south toward the Empress Hotel. Walking along the deserted street, the sound of voices drew his attention to a store at the corner of Yates Street. Stopping to investigate, he noticed there were two drug stores on this corner and they were both bustling with people.

Easing closer to the window of Hall and Company Drugs, he watched with amused fascination as the druggist handed what appeared to be bottles of liquor over the counter to several customers.

I'll be damned, they're selling booze! Waiting until all the customers had gone, he entered and made his way to the counter.

"May I help you, sir?" the druggist asked.

"A pint of your best dark rum," said the general.

"Your prescription, sir?"

"My what?"

"Your prescription. You need a doctor's prescription to buy liquor."

“Then tell me, sir, what kind of malady would I be suffering from to need liquor as a medication?” General Greene asked with a twinkle in his eye.

Warming to the conversation, a smile tugged at the corner of the druggist’s mouth.

“A craving, sir, and a friendly doctor,” he said quietly.

“You could make an exception.”

“Certainly not, sir. Could I see your identification card?”

“Of course,” General Greene agreed, quickly flipping open his wallet to display his US Army identification card.

“One moment, sir.” Turning away from the counter, he reached for the phone on the wall and asked for a number, then he mumbled a short conversation into the mouth piece. “Right, sir, you said rum? You have a preference?”

“Yes, Jolly Roger, Dark Navy.”

“That will be two dollars fifty, sir,” the smiling druggist informed him, producing the required bottle of rum and wrapping it in brown paper.

Feeling pleased with his accomplishment, General Greene pocketed the bottle and thanked the druggist, noting several men now waiting behind him.

Out at Gordon Head, Nancy was once more relating the story of her day, telling Meg and Jebediah of Kate’s reaction to the unexpected news.

“Tell them about General Greene, Nan,” Dan reminded her.

“You should have heard him, Aunt Meg,” Nancy chuckled, “he sure told those stuffy doctors what he thought of them.”

“Is he staying in town?” Jeb asked.

“I don’t know, he didn’t say and he’d gone before I thought to ask.”

“I wonder what Eva knows about this influenza epidemic?” Meg asked. “Maybe we should give her a call.”

Just then, the phone rang.

“I’ll get it,” said Dan. “Cunningham Manor,” they heard him say, and then he burst into laughter. “It’s Eva, Nan, she must have heard you talking about her!” he joked, as Nan came to join him, taking the phone.

Jeb stirred the fire into life as Dan took his seat again. “You know, lad,” he said watching the rising sparks. “I once chased a bank robber clear down into Argentina. Caught him, too.” Pausing, he rubbed his bristly chin as if he were trying to recollect the event.

"This isn't the time for one of your tall tales, Jebediah Judd!" Meg chided.

"Hush yourself woman," the old detective countered, sending Meg a playful but withering look. "I followed that man right to his village."

Dan could hear Nancy chattering away to Eva and he tried to divide his attention between the two conversations. Dan knew the old man was trying to tell him something important, but he was also curious about Nancy's phone call.

"So you caught him?" Meg asked, trying to hurry the story along.

"If you'll just be quiet and let me think I'll tell you!" Jeb muttered. "The villagers were sick with fever. That bank robber offered to give himself up without a fight, but he wanted time to help his folks."

"I'll bet you helped him," Dan chuckled.

"Yes, I did. We went to see a medicine man in a village about 20 miles away and he told us to gather the bark of a certain tree, soak it in wine and give it to the sick folk."

"I should have known," Meg blurted out, "you're making it all up!"

"A few years later I found out that Kennedy's Tonic Port Wine is the same stuff."

"Hold up a minute," said Dan, "you didn't say if those villagers got well again."

"Every one of 'em recovered," the old man replied thoughtfully. "Me and that bank robber worked our tails off looking after them for almost a month."

"Then you brought the poor man back and collected your reward, I suppose?" Meg snapped.

"No I didn't!" Jeb hissed. "I just left him be and rode away."

"You let him escape?" asked Dan.

"No lad, I gave him a second chance at life. How could I arrest a man who gave himself up for a chance to help his family?"

No one noticed that Nancy had finished her phone call and was standing in the doorway.

"Did those villagers live or die, Uncle Jeb?"

"Every single one of 'em recovered, honey."

"And what was their ailment?"

"It was some kind of fever that caused wheezing and choking. I think we got there just in time."

"But what did the doctors say it was?"

"Doctors, lass? They had no doctors," Jeb replied with a chuckle. "There was just me and that bank robber."

"What did you say they called that mixture you gave them?" Dan asked. "I think we should try and find some."

"Kennedy's Tonic Port Wine."

"Uncle Jeb," Nancy smiled, walking across the room to sit on the arm of his chair and ruffling his hair affectionately. "I'm proud of you, you old softy."

"Soft? Me?" he snorted. "I'm as hard as nails, lass, and as tough as old boot leather!"

"Not with me, you're not," she laughed, putting her arms around him. "You're my wonderful Uncle Jeb."

He wrapped his arms around her and sighed, "Nancy, love, you're the only family I ever wanted. I inherited three of you instead and you three mean everything to me."

Meg stood up suddenly, quickly wiping a tear away with her apron. As she went toward the kitchen, she heard Dan ask Nancy what Eva Todd had wanted and she stopped.

"Money, of course," Nan replied, "but she told me some interesting news."

"What was that?"

"She said Victoria Council is having a special meeting tonight. They're discussing what precautions to take to prevent the epidemic spreading when it gets here."

"I hope it doesn't come to Victoria," Meg whispered, turning away.

"Eva says it's already here," Nancy replied, shaking her head sadly. "Maybe Dr. Price was right to close the restaurant down."

"What time does the drug store close?" Jeb growled, coming to his feet.

"You're not going into town tonight, are you?" Meg muttered. "Whatever you need can wait until morning."

"I'll go with you," Dan volunteered eagerly.

A startled look crossed Nancy's face as the men moved toward the door. "But why?" she asked helplessly.

"You tell her, Aunt Meg," Dan called from the door. "We'll be back in a couple of hours."

Standing like two statues, Meg and Nancy heard Jeb's car start and watched it roar away up the drive.

“They’ve gone to try to get that medicine Jeb was talking about,” Meg murmured. “That old man is doing his best to protect us, but he sure can get a mite cantankerous when he’s agitated.”

Nancy groaned softly and put her arm around the older woman. “Oh what a day this has been, Aunt Meg. I am so worried for the city.”

Meg silently kissed her on the cheek and patted her arm in an effort to console her fears and went to clear off the table.

Using Shelbourne Street, Jeb raced for the city. Impeded by the low light, the rain, and Dan’s constant grumbling about his speed, the old detective finally pulled up to the curb on Johnson Street at Shotbolt’s Drug Store. Banging through the door, Jeb marched up to the serious-faced, bespectacled, drug store clerk.

“I need a tonic, lad,” he demanded gruffly, “a bottle of Kennedy’s Tonic Port.”

“Yes, sir, that’s not a very popular brand; it comes from the United States,” the clerk sneered. “May I offer you one that I think is much more effective, sir?”

“No you may not, I said Kennedy’s.”

“As you wish, sir.”

Disappearing into a back room, he quickly returned wiping the dust from a medium-sized brown wine bottle which he placed on the counter.

“Is this liquor?” Jeb muttered, peering at the label.

“Medicinal tonic, sir, not covered by the prohibition laws.”

“How much?”

“One sixty three, sir.”

“How many of these bottles have you got back there, lad?”

“Approximately three dozen, sir.”

“Bring ’em out, I’ll take them all!”

Suddenly more enthusiastic, the clerk sprang quickly into action, bringing the three dusty cases to the counter. “There’s two full cases and seven others, that’s 31 bottles in all, sir,” he said, allowing a hint of a smile to touch the corners of his mouth.

“And the price for all of them?” Jeb growled.

“Fifty dollars and fifty-three pennies.”

“I’ll take them all, can you order me more?”

“Y-yes sir!”

“Then order me ten cases!”

Smiling, although offering no objection, Dan winked at the young clerk as he picked up the cases while Jeb paid the bill.

"Are you aiming to drown us all in that stuff?" he asked with a chuckle as they made their way out to the car.

"It might be a long shot, lad," Jeb snorted, after packing the boxes in the trunk. "Nancy's worried and I won't leave any stone unturned to keep her safe."

"I know," Dan muttered, realizing once again the deep protective feelings the old detective had for their Nancy.

They drove in silence for awhile with both of them deep in thought. Absentmindedly, Jeb swung the car onto Cedar Hill Road, sloshing through muddy pot holes made worse by the rain.

"Why'd you come this way?" Dan grumbled as they bounced and lurched through the deep ruts of the old road.

"Weren't thinking I guess, just eager to get home," he solemnly replied.

With her elbows propped on the kitchen counter, Nancy patiently watched the driveway. "They're coming, Aunt Meg," she called over her shoulder, as the dim glow of headlights came slowly down the drive.

"Come sit down, lassie," Meg sighed, her knitting needles clicking incessantly. "You've been at that window for the last half hour."

"Do you think they found that medicine?"

"Stop your fretting, we'll both know in a few minutes."

Laughing voices and the stomping of heavy feet on the porch caused her to jump to her feet but, before she reached the door, Dan stepped inside carrying two wooden crates and, to add to the confusion, the telephone rang.

"I'll get it," she called, easing around them as they went to hang up their wet coats. "Did you get that stuff, Uncle Jeb?"

"We sure did," he replied, grinning mischievously as the phone continued to ring. "Answer the phone, girl!"

"Cunningham Manor," she called into the receiver, squealing when she heard the voice of General Greene. "Are you still in Victoria?"

"Who's there, Nan?" Dan whispered, standing by her shoulder.

"You're coming over here in the morning—for breakfast—do you know how to find our place? All right. Goodbye."

Replacing the phone on its cradle, Nancy turned to Dan who took her in his arms. "He's coming for breakfast," she giggled.

"Who's coming for breakfast?" Dan asked impatiently.

"General Greene."

"What was that you said?" Meg queried. "He's funning, lass, he's noo coming out here."

"Well, that's what he said."

"I need you all in here," Jeb called from the kitchen. "Where's the corkscrew gone?"

"It's in the drawer where it always is," Meg replied, laying her knitting aside and going to Jeb's assistance. "Are you opening a bottle of liquor?"

"No, I'm opening a bottle of medicine—don't you know we have prohibition?" he chuckled, his eyes dancing with merriment.

Gathering around the kitchen table, they watched in interested amusement as the old detective eased the cork expertly out of the brown bottle then, filling a shot glass, poured one serving into each of four glasses, handing one to each of them. Meg sniffed the contents suspiciously, dipping her finger into the brown liquid and tasting it.

"Ach, it's noo too bad, laddie!" she stated with a sly grin, breaking into her native brogue. Raising it to her lips, she tasted a little more.

"I'd rather not Uncle Jeb," Nancy murmured. "You know I don't touch strong liquor."

"Drink it!" the old man ordered. "This is the medicine that'll keep that damned influenza away from us."

"Drink it, honey," Dan coaxed. "We can't afford to get sick."

Closing her eyes and grimacing, Nancy held her nose and sloshed the drink down her throat, coughing violently. Meg, meanwhile, held the liquid in her mouth and slowly let it trickle down her throat.

"A body could get used to a wee drop of that stuff," she said, smacking her lips.

"Right then," Jeb growled with a serious note in his voice. "We're going to take a shot of this stuff every day."

"Ugh, not every day!" Nancy complained.

"Yes, every day," replied the old man, his voice rising for effect. "Many times over the past year or two you've damn near killed us riding in that blasted boat of yours. I'll not be losing any of this family to an influenza bug from Spain!"

"She'll take it," Dan promised, "because I ain't about to lose her either, not now when I have her back and I'm supposed to be marrying her!"

Chapter 4

Many times during the evening, as they sat around the fire talking, Jeb's strange elixir was mentioned and Cunningham Manor rocked with the happy sounds of laughter. Later, as Nan lay in bed watching the moonlight from between the fast moving clouds, she quietly concluded the old American had their best interests at heart. She awoke early on the last day of April knowing that life must still go on despite the anticipated health problems.

"I'll deliver you to the docks and then I have some things to sort out for the wedding and the restaurant," Nancy told Dan as they came down the stairs together and heard Meg bustling around the kitchen finishing breakfast.

There was a heavy knock at the door, startling them.

"Who the heck could that be?" Dan muttered stopping at the bottom of the stairs to fasten the last button on his shirt.

"Answer it and find out!" Nancy laughed, from the kitchen. "It could be Eva."

"Good morning, folks!" General Greene's voice rang through the house as Dan opened the door. "Are you going to invite me in sergeant?"

"General Greene!" Nancy yelped, leaping up from her seat at the table.

"Well, I told you I was coming for breakfast," the general laughed stepping inside. "I guess you didn't believe me!"

"How in heaven's name did you get here so early?" Meg asked from the kitchen door, holding a frying pan full of fried eggs.

"I brought him so he didn't get lost!" said another voice from out on the porch and Capt. John Gray of the US Coast Guard stepped out of the darkness and into the doorway. "We thought we'd surprise you."

"You certainly accomplished that," the redhead laughed, greeting them both with a hug. "Better get Uncle Jeb up, Dan, he won't want to miss this."

"I'm right here," the old detective growled from behind the men. "I've been watching these two arriving for the last hour or so."

Meg shook her head in bewilderment. "You were outside in the dark?" she muttered going back into the kitchen.

“I couldn’t sleep,” he grumbled, stepping into the light. Now clearly visible, Jeb presented an ominous picture as he stood on the doorstep wearing his heavy belted coat, hat pulled down over his eyes, and his Winchester held across his chest. “It took me awhile to figure out what that ship was out in the strait but when I saw who it was I remembered the general’s phone call,” he chuckled.

“Shut the door, you old fool, and put that gun away!” Meg ordered. “Och, it looks like we’ve got two extra for breakfast.”

“No, no, not me,” Capt. Gray objected backing toward the door. “I’m not staying. We’ll come back for the general in an hour.”

“Sit down,” Jeb hissed, picking up his rifle. “The lady just invited you to stay.”

“Better sit down, captain,” General Greene chuckled, “or I think he just might shoot you!”

Meg dished up what she had cooked and then put more on the stove surpassing herself as everyone wolfed down a delicious breakfast of bacon, eggs, fried potatoes and wonderful salt-cured ham, finishing off with home-baked scones, marmalade, tea and coffee. Blushing, she accepted the accolades liberally heaped on her by the visitors. Self-consciously she shooed the men away while Nancy helped her clean up.

“Where’s the *Stockholm*, Dan?” asked John Gray.

“Left her in town. I came home with Nancy last night.”

“I was at a meeting at the restaurant yesterday,” General Greene announced as they went out onto the porch.

“Yes, Nancy told us just before you called.”

“She didn’t believe me when I said I was coming for breakfast?”

“We never thought you’d come in a coast guard cutter, sir.”

“I figured it out when I saw the cutter with my binoculars,” Jeb admitted with a grin. “I had you in my sights before you even stepped on the dock.”

“Now, why doesn’t that surprise me?” Capt. Gray commented with a frown. “You must have been a hell of a man to tangle with when you were younger, Mr. Judd.”

“He is now,” Dan said sharply. “He’s more than a match for anyone I know.”

Jeb turned away to hide his grin, satisfied with Dan’s words of confidence.

“I stayed last night to meet your city council,” said the general, smiling wryly. “I wanted to tell Nancy her wedding’s still on, that lot won’t have made a decision by the end of June!”

“We have to go, sir,” Capt. Gray announced, watching his men row toward the dock.

“Right, son,” General Greene murmured, “but not before I say goodbye to two lovely ladies.” He turned and went back inside calling loudly to Meg and Nancy.

“Och, sounds like the general is leaving, lassie,” Meg announced.

“Come on, we’ll see them off,” said Nancy, going to get their coats.

They joined him on the porch and walked over to the clifftop together. After one last hug, they watched the visitors bound down the steps and wave as the small boat pulled away from the dock.

“He says the wedding’s on,” Dan commented as they drove into town.

“I heard him, too,” she admitted, snuggling in closer to him on the truck’s bench seat. “I hope nothing else goes wrong.”

“Has your wedding dress arrived yet?” he asked.

“Beth called Aunt Meg yesterday to say her seamstress had sent it off to us. It should arrive around noon today.”

“Hmm, are you going to model it for me?”

“Just you stop that Danny Brown. You’re teasing me and I don’t need anything extra to worry about, thank you.”

“Aw heck, Nan, let’s just go to Seattle and quietly get married there. I don’t care about all this ceremony.”

“No, Dan,” Nancy whispered, “I’ve waited too long for this day to come and I intend it to be a special one.”

Not daring to look at her as he recognized that sound in her voice, Dan kept his eyes on the traffic avoiding pedestrians as he turned the truck onto the Brown and Wilson dock.

“Waldo’s on his way over,” he commented as he brought the truck to a stop and got out.

Nancy hadn’t moved when the haulier came storming down to the dock.

“Where’s Nancy?” he called after Dan who had stopped partway to the office. “I had a word with that damned council. Is she with you?” Then, he stopped and noticed Dan was solemnly watching the truck. He snatched his pipe from his mouth and looked more closely. Seeing Nancy, he went over to the passenger side intending to open the door. “Young lady,” he began, as the door opened and Nancy stepped out. She looked up at him with a tear-stained face and he did the same thing he had done many times to a much younger girl, he held out his arms and she stepped into them.

"I'm sorry, Nan," Dan sighed, realizing there was something wrong and feeling he had no doubt caused it. "I was only being silly."

"Not your fault, Danny," she sniffled, "it's just ... everything."

"Hey," Waldo snapped, easing the redhead away from him and looking at her with squinted eyes. "I think I lost somebody today."

"Who?" she asked.

"Oh, she was once a friend of mine."

Nancy frowned at the haulier, wiped her eyes and straightened her hat. "What are you taking about Waldo?" she asked.

"A girl I once knew. By golly, she could fight a dozen cougars single handed."

"You're being silly aren't you?"

"No, lass, this girl I knew fought like hell for three years and never gave in. She bent every rule until she won the biggest prize on earth."

"Are you talking about me?" she mumbled, her cheeks growing pink.

"No, I'm talking about Nancy Wilson. She used to live here, but she's left us."

"I didn't leave," she sniffed.

"Then, damn it, stop your blubbering and fight, girl!"

A smile tugged at the redhead's lips. Breathing deeply, she squared her shoulders, adjusted her hat again, and looked the haulier in the eyes. "All right, old friend. You're right, of course."

"That's my girl," Waldo beamed. "I talked to the mayor this morning. Dr. Price tried to introduce new regulations at last night's meeting but the council wouldn't agree to them. He overstepped his authority by closing your restaurant down. You're free to continue if you want."

"Thank you Waldo. I'll talk to Kate," she replied, not sure whether to believe it was true or not.

"Better now, love?" Dan asked quietly, resting his arm over her shoulder and kissing her lightly on the cheek. He steered her toward the office door. "Let's see if Dumpy's got some coffee on."

"Hi Nan!" said a voice from inside as Dan opened the door.

Nancy was surprised when Kate looked up from her book as they went inside.

"What are you doing here, Kate?"

"I was just going to ask you the same question," her friend replied. "I needed to do something, just to take my mind off what's happening."

"Where's Jack?" Dan asked, flipping through the order book.

"He said to tell you he's taken three men out to Renfrew and loaded the *Stockholm* for Salt Spring. There were two extra boxes, but Jack said Mrs. Mouat or Gilbert would take care of them for you. He also said to remember the hay barge for Mr. Skillings."

"Are you coming with me to Salt Spring, Nan?" asked Dan.

"No, I've got too much to get done seeing as the wedding is on again!" she replied, looking over at Kate and grinning.

"What!" exclaimed her friend excitedly. "Tell me what's happened, don't you dare keep me guessing."

"Right girls, I think you'll find enough to fill your day somehow! I'll gas up at Turpel's then be off," Dan announced.

"No need, Jack gassed both boats before he left, Dan," Kate told him as she came round the counter to stand beside Nancy, obviously bursting to ask more questions.

"Efficient little devil, isn't he?" said Nan.

"Yes, he is," Kate said fondly, making a face at her friend as they followed Dan outside. They watched him check his cargo and then start the engine.

The telephone rang and Kate dashed back inside.

Loosening his mooring rope, Nancy waved to Dan, blowing him a kiss as he expertly wheeled the *Stockholm* away from the dock.

"Phone, Nan," Kate called through the open door and Nan came hurrying back inside.

"Hello, Nancy here," she said, picking up the receiver.

"Miss Wilson, this is the Hudson's Bay Company delivery service. We have a rather large package for you. Would you like it delivered to the Brown and Wilson office?" a feminine voice asked.

"How soon can you deliver it?"

"Right away."

"Yes please, that would be fine."

Kate cocked an eyebrow inquisitively as Nancy replaced the receiver and sighed. "I think my wedding dress has just arrived."

"Oh, that's wonderful!" Kate replied, a note of excitement in her voice. "Now are you going to tell me what's going on before I burst?"

"Well, how do you feel about re-opening the restaurant?" she asked, pouring herself a cup of coffee and sitting down at the table. "Waldo says the council refused to implement Dr. Price's recommendations last night at an emergency meeting. It seems he didn't have the authority to close us down after all!"

"Yes! Let's do it. Those boys need us, Nan," Kate exclaimed. "But what about the wedding? I thought all gatherings were cancelled."

Nancy then had to tell Kate the whole story of General Greene's visit. She was almost through when the phone rang again followed quickly by a knock at the door.

"Your parcel, Miss Wilson," the delivery man announced handing her the large parcel. "It's marked 'fragile' so please be careful."

Laying the parcel down on the table, she thanked the delivery man and he left. She noticed Kate was cheerfully telling someone on the phone that the restaurant would be open tomorrow as normal. Her eyes glazed over as her hands moved slowly over the brown paper-covered box.

"It's really happening, Kate, it's really happening," she murmured, as Kate put the phone down.

"Well, aren't you going to open it?"

"No, I had better wait until I get home."

"Then let's go over to the Wounded Soldier, we have some cleaning up to do and I can't wait to open those doors."

"Jack's going to be surprised when he gets back," said Nancy.

"So is Dan."

"I wouldn't blame him if he were cross with me," Nancy replied. "I was awfully touchy this morning."

"He won't be cross with you, but I'd better leave my man a note or I might not be so lucky!"

Across the road, in the stable doorway of Victoria Baggage, Waldo puffed on his pipe as he watched the two young women climb into the little blue truck and slowly drive up the hill to Wharf Street. Hiding behind his bushy eyebrows, a mischievous glint sparkled in his eyes when they turned onto Fort Street and Nancy waved to him. He knew then that his pep talk had worked.

Meanwhile, Dan had left the harbour feeling like a heel; he wasn't sure what had caused Nancy's tears but felt somehow he must have been responsible. Quietly cursing himself for being insensitive, he opened the throttle of the *Stockholm* and was streaking across the water behind James Island when a glint of light caught his attention. Easing off on the throttle, he picked up his binoculars and soon realized what he had seen was the Victoria harbour patrol boat. Moving slowly toward it, he pulled the *Stockholm* alongside.

"WHAT DO YA SEE, ALGY?" he shouted, easing off on the throttle.

"That boat out yonder," Algenon Pease called back to him, pointing. "I've seen them around here a few times of late."

"Probably fishermen dumping a catch at the cannery in Sidney."

"No, I checked that out," said the patrolman frowning with concern. "Where you heading?"

"Salt Spring."

"Say hello to Jane Mouat if you see her."

"That I will," Dan called, waving goodbye.

Carefully avoiding a CP Rail barge heading to Deep Cove as he rounded Coal Island, he grinned to himself and speculated on the hundreds of tiny, secluded places a boat could use to load an illicit cargo. Roaring on through the open waters it was a couple of hours later when he caught sight of Ganges Harbour and Mouat's dock. Raising his glasses, he spotted Gilbert in his wheelchair watching him arrive. As he tied up to the jetty, two men were quickly on hand to help him unload.

"There's two extra boxes for somebody else on there," Dan shouted at the men. "Just put them aside, Mrs. Mouat knows about them."

"We'll take care of them, lad," Gilbert grinned. "Come sit with me and chin wag for a minute or two."

"I need some spun wool for Aunt Meg and I'd better get some white paint for our new fence," Dan told him as he climbed up to join the store-keeper.

"We can tend to that in a minute. How are the wedding arrangements coming along?"

"I thought fine, but Nancy's getting very sensitive. She was crying again this morning."

"I don't blame her," Gilbert said with a grin. "I'd be bawling if you were marrying me!"

"Chump!" Dan flung back good-naturedly.

Having known Gilbert for many years, it came as no surprise to hear his humorous remark. Struck by polio in the prime of life and doomed to a wheelchair, he had long ago shown his metal. Never whining or grumbling, he'd accepted his new situation causing Dan to have great admiration for his courage.

"Look out, Mum's here," he muttered.

Balancing a steaming cup of hot coffee and a piece of pie on a plate, Jane Mouat beamed as she strode down the jetty toward them.

"You're needed in the store, boy," she informed her son sharply, handing the plate to Dan. "I'll take care of this rascal."

"Bully!" Gilbert laughed as he sent the wheelchair rolling along the jetty, well used to his mother's bossy ways.

"How's Nancy and Meg? Are you ready for the wedding? Do you need anything to take back with you?" asked Mrs. Mouat, her words spilling out as she got more excited.

"Easy, easy, Gran, give me a chance to answer!"

"Oh it's so exciting. The whole island's buzzing about your wedding. Ben Wall was down here yesterday talking about it. He said his wife is embroidering a tablecloth for you."

"I hope you're not all disappointed," Dan began, a frown creasing his forehead. "There could be a hitch in the works."

"Oh, and what would that be?" Jane asked, raising an eyebrow.

"Dr. Price and that blasted Spanish influenza."

"Glory be, who's got it in these parts? Newspapers say it's a killer."

"Nobody's got it yet that I know of," Dan replied with an audible sigh. "It's the precautions the health officer's taking that are becoming a problem. He closed the girls' restaurant down yesterday and says they're going to ban all gatherings of people."

"He can't do that, can he?"

"He can't it seems, but council can when they're ready to."

"You won't let them do that, will you, son?" Mrs. Mouat's voice trembled with concern. "Nancy's had enough trouble to contend with, what with the war, you going missing, and then your sickness. She must be terribly concerned."

"She is."

"How much wool did your aunt want, Dan?" Gilbert called from the back door of the store, "and how much paint—two gallons be enough?"

"Same as she got last time and yes, two gallons should be plenty."

A wave of his hand told Dan that Gilbert had heard. "Sorry about that, Gran, what were you saying?"

"Darn it, son, I don't know what to say but you take care of that girl, she's a treasure."

A smile bent his lips as he handed the cup and plate back to the well-loved Salt Spring Islander and she headed off toward the store.

"Did she tell you about the strange boat that's been nosing around here?' Gilbert asked, rolling up alongside and handing Dan a wrapped parcel.

"No, but Algy was out off James Island when I came by and he mentioned a strange boat had been in the area. How much do I owe you for the wool?"

"Dollar fifty. You be careful out there, Dan. That's probably a rum runner nosing around, could get dangerous."

His mind on Sidney and the hay barge for Waldo, Dan made his way leisurely down the inlet, taking note of the fishing boats and vessels he passed, but today there were no unfamiliar boats in the vicinity.

As the girls drove up Fort Street, Nancy was having second thoughts about opening the restaurant and conveyed her concerns to Kate.

"Maybe we should wait and see what the council does," she said to her partner.

"Waldo said we could reopen," Kate argued.

"We'll look terribly stupid if the council closes us again though."

"Why don't we talk to the hospital staff before we make a decision?"

"That sounds like a good idea, let's do it," agreed Nancy.

Kate stared blankly out of the window for the next two blocks, her disappointment obvious. Then, she suddenly turned to face Nancy.

"If we don't open, we could use the time to redecorate the place!"

"Now that's a good idea," Nancy chuckled. "We could paint and add a little wallpaper—give it a touch of class."

"It's a diner, not the Empress, Nan. Just a fresh coat of paint and a picture or two would be fine."

Tossing ideas around as they pulled into the alley, they noticed a soldier trying to open the back door.

"Hello, are you from the hospital?" Nancy called getting out of the truck.

"No ma'am, I'm looking for Dan Brown."

"Dan, why?"

"To deliver an order from my commanding officer, ma'am."

"But he's not in the army anymore."

"I'm just following orders, ma'am."

"Well, you can stop looking now, soldier, he left on a ship this morning."

"He's gone abroad, ma'am?"

"Yes."

"Thank you, ma'am. I shall inform my commanding officer."

Saluting the girls, he quickly marched away.

Standing silently watching the soldier leave, Nancy took a deep breath and put her key in the door.

"Are you keeping something else from me?" asked Kate, looking puzzled while she watched her friend. "I thought Dan had gone to Salt Spring."

"He has."

"But you just told that soldier he'd gone abroad."

"Salt Spring's over the sea, isn't it?"

"Nan, you deliberately lied to that soldier."

"Yes," Nancy replied, sighing as if the weight of the world was on her shoulders, "and if that keeps them away from us, I'll be glad."

Kate shook her head but realized that Nan was still so afraid of Dan being taken away from her she would do almost anything to prevent it. Trying to forget the soldier, they wandered around the restaurant swapping ideas on the décor. They laughed at each other's silly suggestions and Kate was relieved that Nancy seemed more relaxed. Finally they came to a mutual conclusion. The walls would be painted cream coloured and in each panel around the room they'd have the insignia of a Victoria regiment, in memory of the wounded men who had spent time in this very room.

"It sounds good, Kate, but how on earth are we going to paint these insignias?"

"You just leave that to me, Nan. I have an idea."

"We should also go see the hospital staff and see what they think about us re-opening," Nancy suggested, "but I've a feeling they're going to agree with Dr. Price."

"Tell you what," Kate grinned, "let me organize the decorating and we'll re-open after your wedding."

"Yes, I think you're right, that would be the best way to go. You're not too disappointed, are you?"

"No, I'll be all right now that I can keep busy. Let's make a cup of tea and a sandwich and then you can help me get the curtains down. They might as well go to the Chinese laundry."

By the middle of the afternoon, Kate had luckily found a painter who could start early the next morning, and they had moved all the furniture into the middle of the room and washed window frames and doors. Exhausted and relaxing over a cup of tea, the phone rang.

"Hello," Nancy purred. "No."

Kate frowned as she waited for her partner's next words.

"Yes, sir, we're leaving immediately." Turning to Kate, she grinned, "That was Dan. He wanted to know if we'd opened the restaurant and if we weren't busy would we go down to the office."

"Did Dan say if Jack was back?" Kate asked as they drove back to the city.

"He didn't say. Why, are you afraid of what he will say?"

"Aren't you?"

"No I'm not. Dan and I have always supported each other and I know Jack is always there for you, too. We'll drop the curtains off at the laundry on the way."

Chapter 5

Driving down onto the dock, Nancy parked beside a familiar car and murmured to Kate, "Harry's here."

"We're out here, Nan!" Dan shouted from behind the office building.

Walking around the back of the office, she found Dan, Harry, and Waldo looking down toward the end of the jetty at a loaded hay barge.

"I thought you'd gone to open the restaurant," Waldo grunted.

"We decided to redecorate, brighten up the place, and open again after the wedding," she announced.

"Good idea, lass, it's time you had a break."

"It won't be much of a break," Harry chuckled, "the wedding's only four days away."

"Oh, by the way, Mr. Brown," Nancy interrupted with a grin, "my wedding dress arrived this morning."

The sound of the *Highliner*'s engine coming up the harbour stopped the conversation as they watched Dumpy arrive.

"What's happening?" he asked. "Where's Kate?"

"Good news," Dan replied as he tied up the *Highliner*. "Council has refused to shut things down yet so the wedding is on. Kate's in the office, she'll fill you in on the rest."

"Are you loaded for Seattle, Dan?" Nancy inquired.

"Yes, and we'll be leaving early. I think Jeb wants to call at Apple Cove and check up on old Ezekiel."

"I'm going with you," said Nancy.

"Don't you have enough to do with the wedding and all?"

"If you're trying to get rid of me it won't work. I want to come," she retorted, pretending to pout.

Dan just laughed at her, patting her behind before climbing aboard. Waldo and Harry went over to Harry's car and Kate noticed they seemed to be arguing about something. These men were astute businessmen, both having weathered the changing times in Victoria. She knew that over the years each in his own way had taken a deep interest in Dan and Nancy.

"Are you going home now?" Nancy asked Dan after the others had left and the four of them were sitting around the table drinking coffee.

"Yes, I want to be out of here before Waldo's men move that hay. The dock will look like a barnyard by the time they're finished."

"I won't be far behind you," she added. "I'm going to call into city hall before I go home."

"Why?"

"Just to check things out and put my mind at ease."

Shrugging his shoulders, Dan drained his coffee cup and rose to go. Reaching across the table, he took Nan's hand and pulled her to her feet, giving her a quick kiss.

"Come throw my lines off for me, honey."

"I'll do it," Dumpy volunteered, coming to his feet.

"No, you won't you're staying here with me," Kate murmured and, with eyes sparkling with intuition, she grabbed his jacket.

Nancy looked back at her and smiled as she followed Dan outside. Before Dan climbed aboard the *Stockholm*, he came up behind her and wrapped his arms around her. She turned to face him enjoying the closeness they didn't often experience. Wrapped in each other's arms, Dan tenderly kissed her.

"Only four more days, honey, then you're mine," he whispered.

"I've always been yours, silly, ever since we were in the orphanage," she replied, touching his cheek then bending to release the rope.

He kissed her quickly, untied the other mooring line and jumped across the widening gap onto the *Stockholm*'s deck. "See you at home," he called starting the engine and moving the boat away from the dock.

Going back to the office, she stopped in the doorway to look back at the disappearing boat. "Only God knows how much I love that man," she murmured. The Dumpfords were deep in conversation and didn't hear.

Victoria City Hall was buzzing when Nan found a parking spot across the street from the main door. A group of people standing nearby were arguing loudly as she pushed her way inside. Locating the mayor was easy by following the sound of shouting voices farther down the hall.

"THERE IS NO EMERGENCY!" Mayor Albert Todd was screaming at a crowd of people. "WE ARE IN CONTROL OF THE SITUATION."

"What's all the fuss about?" Nancy asked a bonneted older woman.

"Damned idiots are talking about regulations again."

"Regulations for what?"

"Who knows girl, this is Victoria!"

Wincing, Nancy squeezed past and carried on down the short corridor, turning abruptly when she heard the sound of Dr. Price's voice coming from a nearby office. Tapping lightly on the door, she pushed it open and the doctor looked up from the papers he was reading.

"Who are you?" he asked vaguely.

"Nancy Wilson, you were in my restaurant yesterday morning."

"Yes, yes, I remember. I closed you down."

"It appears, sir, you acted without authority."

"I gave you my reasons, what more do you need? Go away, I'm busy."

Calmly, Nancy moved farther into the room and pushed the door shut with her heel. It was then she realized there were two other gentlemen in the room.

"I said go!" Dr. Price demanded, rising from his chair.

"No, sir, you will hear me out before I go!" Nancy objected.

"Calm down, Arthur," said one of the men as he also stood up. "Would you like a seat, young lady?"

"No thank you, sir." She smiled at the familiar-looking man who she remembered as being Dr. Price's provincial counterpart. Before turning her attention back to Dr. Price, she quickly looked at the other man and realized she recognized him also from the restaurant. "Dr. Price, I believed you yesterday and we closed down the restaurant. Have you any idea what that place means to all the wounded soldiers who feel trapped at Jubilee Hospital? It's like home for them, sir. It's a place that's warm and friendly. It relieves their loneliness and gives them a measure of comfort for a short time. And yesterday, without a moment's thought, you took that all away and, I might add, without the proper authority. I hope you feel proud of yourself, doctor."

As Nancy spoke, the city health officer slowly sank back down into his chair and, elbows resting on his desk, now cradled his head in his hands. Nancy's words were obviously having some effect.

"Aren't you the girl who sings in Seattle?" asked the other doctor.

"Yes, sir, I was until last week."

"I was at that concert last week. The Seattle City Health Committee cancelled your future concerts, didn't they?"

"Yes, sir, but with good reason, they have confirmed cases of the flu in Washington State."

"Let me introduce myself, Miss Wilson. I'm Dr. Henry Young, the Provincial health officer."

"Yes, I know who you are, sir, you were also at our restaurant yesterday," she said slowly.

"Arthur, I think you owe this young lady an apology," he continued, turning abruptly to the man behind the desk.

"I do not!" Dr. Price retorted fiercely, raising his head and giving the appearance of a harried man losing his self-control. "We need to take precautions, Henry. I can't allow council to interfere with my job."

"Arthur, you must operate within the rules," Dr. Young said sternly, "or would you rather be terminated and leave Victoria to take its chances with someone less qualified?"

"Certainly not!" retorted Dr. Price, going red in the face as he realized the severity of his superior's statement.

"Then dang it, use a velvet glove, Arthur. Now, this young lady is waiting for your apology!"

Breathing deeply, Dr. Price rose to his feet. "Miss Wilson," he began hesitantly, "I offer my apology for causing you such distress. I assure you my action was out of concern for the health of our citizens."

"I understand, sir, thank you," the redhead replied softly. "Now may I suggest you use a little caution and try to earn some respect from those citizens. Victorians don't appreciate being bullied, you need to educate us. We're really just simple folk."

Reaching out, she offered her hand to the doctor. Surprised at the gesture, he took it and held it briefly.

Nancy whispered impishly, "You, sir, almost ruined my wedding day!" Nodding to the others, she turned and walked out of the door. Dr. Young caught up to her in the hallway.

"I'll let you out by the side door, Miss Wilson," he offered. "The crowd at the front is getting rather rambunctious tonight."

Thanking him, she found herself on Pandora Street and was easily able to reach the truck by skirting the crowd near the main entrance.

"Who was that girl?" asked Dr. Fred Underhill from Vancouver.

"That's Nancy Wilson," he replied coldly. "She and Kate Dumpford run the *Wounded Soldier Restaurant* opposite the Jubilee Hospital."

"They own the place?" Underhill asked showing his surprise as Dr. Price nodded in the affirmative. "She's certainly an eloquent speaker and seems wise beyond her years." Dr. Young returned just in time to hear his comment.

"Yes, she is," he chuckled, "and there's a lot more to that young woman than you realize. I think you'd do well, Arthur, to make an ally of the future Mrs. Brown. She was determined to have a go at you and perhaps the threat of her wedding being postponed had something to do with it!"

With her wedding worries overcome, Nancy drove along Douglas to Bay Street, singing quietly to herself until she turned up Cedar Hill Road. Sniffing the air, she smiled as she noticed the gardens with their beautiful displays of daffodils and tulips in a myriad of colour. She soon picked up the smells of the countryside and watched as several farmers industriously tilled their land in the late afternoon sun. *Dan's right*, she thought, *this is God's country. We're so lucky to live here.*

A wonderful feeling of home settled over Nancy as the truck chugged its way up Ash Road and turned into Cunningham Manor. Looking over at the orchard she sighed as she became aware of how many of the little trees were filling out with spindly young branches. She saw the Parfitt Brothers' truck parked at the side of the house and whispered, "Oh good, Jack's here."

Jack Duggan, Dan, and Jebediah smiled as she came around the corner stopping when she saw the new fence stretching out along the clifftop in front of the house. Going to park, she walked toward them.

"Come here, you little beauty," Jack flung his hat in the air and held out his arms. "There aren't many more days we can do this, you know!"

"Do what?" Nancy giggled, wriggling free.

"Hug you like this."

"Why not?"

"Because, my little colleen, you'll be a married woman!"

"Oops, I almost forgot," she squealed. Throwing her purse to Dan, she raced back to the truck and quickly reappeared carrying a large parcel. "My wedding dress came today! Do you want to see?" she asked excitedly, not speaking to anyone in particular.

"We'd better go take a look, Jeb," Jack winked at the old detective. "Dan can finish nailing that last rail in place."

"I'm going with you," Dan retorted.

"Oh no, lad, you're not," Jack frowned, "it's unlucky for the groom to see the bride's dress until your wedding day."

"That's just a silly superstition," Dan retorted.

"Well, let's say we're not going to tempt fate. You're staying right here!" the builder insisted.

"Where's Danny?" Nancy asked as the men followed her inside.

"He can't see your dress, child," Meg declared, watching Nancy carefully lay the parcel on the table and begin to fumble with the string. "That would be bad luck. I think they left him outside."

"Oh, that's right," she giggled, paying more attention to the parcel. With trembling fingers, she folded back the paper revealing the beautiful white satin dress. Touching it almost reverently, her fingers daintily explored the silk and lace frills and delicate embroidery work. "Isn't it beautiful? I can hardly believe this is really happening," she whispered, turning to her aunt as tears threatened.

Meg put her arm around the girl's waist and kissed her cheek, unable to speak herself.

"It's almost too nice to wear," Jack commented gruffly. "You know that Nellie's bringing your bouquet of flowers, don't you?"

"Yes, we know," Meg murmured, "we women have it all arranged."

Jeb caught Jack's attention and nodded toward the door. He hadn't spoken a word and they silently went out and joined Dan. Cocking an eyebrow, Jack Duggan glanced over at his friend.

"Well Jeb, what the devil have you got on your mind?" he asked. "Your silence is deafening."

Grinning, Dan also looked over at Jeb.

"Well, I'll tell you, lads," Jeb began, scratching his chin. "It seems to be an awful lot of trouble to go through just to get attached to a woman. Why I saw two folks get coupled in a saloon once, it must have took all of two minutes!"

"Aye," Jack laughed, "and some gal's daddy was nearby with a preacher and a shotgun, I'll wager!"

The men were picking up the tools when Meg appeared at the door and shouted, "I HOPE YOU'RE PLANNING TO PAINT THAT FENCE!"

"Are you sure you don't want a row of trees planted as well?" Jeb called back sarcastically.

"I want it painted, you heathen!" Meg shot back. "It's taken you four years to get the fence up. I'm not waiting another four years to get it painted with a wedding here on Saturday. I assume you have some paint, dinner will be served when you're finished!"

"What did she call me?" Jeb chuckled, turning to Dan.

"I think she means we had better paint her fence," Dan snickered. "Good thing I got the paint while I was at Mouats!"

After seeing the builder off, Dan went down to the boat and got the paint and brushes and he and Jeb got to work. Grumbling incessantly, Jeb kept Dan laughing until the job was finished and Nancy called them in for a late dinner.

While they ate, she told them of her interesting visit to city hall.

"The council should have supported him," Jeb growled.

"I agree," Nancy retorted, "but he should have waited until council were more prepared to agree."

"How's Kate feeling about it now?" Meg asked, having heard about Kate's reaction the day before.

"Oh Kate's all right, she's tough. It just took us completely by surprise when Dr. Price told us to close."

"Will she be opening the restaurant tomorrow?" Meg continued.

"No, we've decided to redecorate and open next week, after the wedding."

"You're not going in to work on Monday, are you?" Meg asked, sounding surprised.

"Yes, why shouldn't I?"

"I thought you'd want to take some time off."

"What for?"

"For a honeymoon—to get used to being a married woman!"

"Aunt Meg," the redhead giggled, "that man has been on my mind for as long as I can remember. We've taken care of each other for the last ten years, built a house, and lived together, there can't be much more to get used to!"

"There's more to marriage than being concerned for each other, lass," Meg blushed, glancing over at Jebediah, who averted his eyes and puffed heavily on his pipe.

Reaching for Dan's hand, Nan's eyes sparkled with devilment. "I wonder what it'll be like around here when we've a bunch of children running around?" she whispered.

"Heaven!" Meg gasped, reaching for the hem of her apron to wipe her eye. "It'll be heaven, lassie."

"That's enough of that," Jeb growled, "are we going to Seattle tomorrow, Dan?"

"Yes, I've already loaded."

"We calling to see Ezekiel?"

"Yes, that's what you wanted."

"Right then, off you go, you two," Jeb commanded. "I'll help Meg with the dishes and, don't go touching that fence, the paint'll still be wet."

"Put a coat on, Nan," Meg warned, "that wind's still chilly in the evening."

Hand-in-hand the young couple walked over to the orchard, following Sam's well-worn path. "You can almost feel them growing," Nancy exclaimed happily. "I can already smell the blossoms."

"That's manure you're smelling, honey!" Dan laughed, ducking as she swung at him.

Laughing, she began to tease him, running away between the saplings. Dan took chase and they playfully ran toward the darkness of the tree line. Nancy slowed down, allowing Dan to catch up to her.

Suddenly, he took her into his arms and kissed her, "NANCY WILSON," he shouted into the evening sky, "I LOVE YOU!"

"Oh shh, Danny, someone might hear," she objected.

"I don't care, I want the whole world to know," he retorted.

"I can't believe our wedding day is almost here. I am so happy and I love you, too."

He pulled her closer and they looked silently into each other's eyes, then their lips met and for a brief moment they forgot about everything except each other.

When they returned to the house, Dan helped Nan with her coat and with faces pink from the cold, they went into the warm kitchen where Meg and Jeb were just finishing up the dishes.

"We had a phone call while you were out," Jeb informed them.

"Eva?" Nancy asked.

"No, Tom Wills."

"The reporter from Seattle," said Dan, frowning. "What did he want?"

"He asked for an invitation to the wedding."

"What did you tell him, Uncle Jeb?" asked Nancy.

"I said 'no' and, if I caught him around here, I would break his neck!"

"You should have given him that invitation, Uncle Jeb," Nancy scolded. "He could have found plenty to write about and maybe would have left us alone for awhile."

Jeb slipped his pipe out of his mouth and nodded, "Never thought of it like that, lass."

Chapter 6

Waking, as the first rays of sunshine streaked across the gently rippling waters of Cordova Bay, Nancy stood at the open bedroom window listening to the excited squawking of seagulls. Taking a deep breath of the fresh sea air, her gaze moved across the skyline taking in the beautiful vista of Mount Baker and the islands.

"Oh how lucky we are to have found this special haven … heaven at our doorstep," she whispered.

A call from Meg caused her to grab her housecoat and she scurried down the stairs tying it snugly around her small waist. She hugged her aunt who was holding two plates of steaming eggs and bacon, placing them on the table just as Dan and Jeb arrived.

"Don't forget the parcel for Ezekiel," the Scot gently reminded Dan as breakfast finished.

"And a bottle of tonic," Jeb muttered, going to the cupboard and taking down the bottle. "Oh, and by the way, girl, you haven't drunk yours yet."

"I'll drink it later," Nancy replied, averting her eyes.

"You'll drink it now!" he demanded.

"I don't like it."

"Drink it, honey," Meg coaxed, "humour the old fella."

Nancy picked up the glass, eyeing it suspiciously. Pinching her nose, she put the glass to her lips, closed her eyes and swallowed the contents in one gulp, grimacing as she finished.

Dan chuckled.

"It's not funny, Danny," she gasped, "that stuff is awful!"

"I know, Nan," Dan retorted, "but it just goes to prove that sometimes you can do as you're told!"

"Oh does it now?" she retorted, punching his arm. "We'll see about that, my lad."

"Hey you two," Meg interrupted, "behave yourselves, you can argue all you want after Saturday."

It was two hours later when Dan eased the *Stockholm* through the overhanging trees into Apple Cove and Nancy got out the whistles, blowing one sharp note on the regular whistle followed by the duck call.

Continuing slowly into Ezekiel Plunket's hidden lair, Dan cocked his head and listened until he heard the whistled reply.

"IDENTIFY YERSELF!" yelled a wild-looking figure, just visible in the trees at the edge of the shoreline.

"GO TO HELL YA CRAZY OLD COOT!" Jebediah yelled back.

BOOM! Ezekiel's old long-barreled rifle spit out fire and noise and Nancy blinked in surprise as the old detective's hat flew off his head.

"He's gone too far this time," Jeb snarled, grabbing his Winchester and jumping into the shallow water.

"STOP IT YOU TWO," she screamed, "OR I'LL SHOOT THE BOTH OF YOU!"

Jeb stopped, glancing back at Nancy as he hurled his rifle onto the sandy foreshore. He waved his arms wildly at the casually approaching recluse who spit a long stream of tobacco juice right at his boot.

Walking right past him and into the water without saying a word, Ezekiel arrived at the boat and held his arms out. Scooping Nancy into them, he carried her onto the shore.

"I got him mad this time!" the hairy old man chuckled with satisfaction, setting her down on a log.

"I'm sure glad you two are friends," giggled Nancy, kissing him lightly on a dirty cheek.

Dan moved the *Stockholm* over to Zeke's rickety jetty, picked up Jeb's hat, and went to join them. "One of these days," he said, handing Jeb his hat, "that old coot is going to kill you."

"Look at my hat," Jeb fumed. "You lame-brain, it's ruined!"

"Go get that parcel of Algy's jam Aunt Meg sent," Nancy whispered to Dan.

"Just listen to him squawking," Ezekiel continued, winking at her. "I'm really glad to see ya girl, but I won't be coming to yer wedding."

"That's all right, Ezekiel, you wouldn't enjoy yourself anyway with all the fancy stuff these women are planning," Dan assured him.

Jeb finally settled down and a grin appeared as he poked his finger through the bullet hole in his hat. When Dan returned with the jam, he glanced over at Jeb's hat and laughed aloud.

"That was one heck of a shot, old hoss."

"No it weren't," retorted Ezekiel. "I missed him!"

"That's enough from you two," giggled Nancy. "You've had your fun now behave yourselves. We can't stay long."

Turning his back on his guests, Zeke reached behind a tree stump and produced one of his own bottles. Going over to Jeb, he held it out to him.

"Have a drink while you can, lawman," he chuckled, "'cos next time I won't miss!"

Jeb rolled his eyes but ignored the remark as he took the bottle of homemade moonshine from his old friend. He turned to Dan and asked, "Did you bring the bottle of tonic, son?"

"No."

"Then go get it, lad, we don't want the old devil getting sick."

"But he just tried to kill you."

"If I'd tried to kill him, lad," Ezekiel growled, "he'd be dead! That were just a practice shot!"

Shaking his head, Dan started back across the sand toward the wharf but hearing the throb of an idling engine just beyond the entrance to the cove, he hurried back to the others.

"There's a boat out there," he hissed.

"Coast guard," Ezekiel muttered, his keen senses already aware of it. "Get yer rifle, Jeb, I'll go check."

Dan took Nancy by the arm. "Hurry," he commanded, "get behind the house, just in case." Then he took cover in the shadows a few feet away.

Nancy tried to watch the entrance from her vantage point and saw that Jeb had taken cover behind the logs they used for a seat.

"Surely, we're not going to fight the coast guard boys!" she hissed nervously to Dan.

"No, but we need to make sure that's who it is first."

Impatiently waiting for something to happen, she felt Dan's arm on her shoulder as he pointed out Zeke moving through the trees coming back toward them.

"It's the coast guard and they have a fishing boat in tow. Looks like it had engine trouble," Ezekiel growled.

"Do you know the fisherman?" Jeb questioned.

"Yes, one of them."

"Who?"

"Harris Copley from Bay View."

"The boat builder from Useless Bay?" Dan asked. "Copleys aren't fishermen."

"We should wait until they've gone," Jeb countered.

"No," Dan replied, already heading for the boat, "we'll go out and see what's happening."

"There they are, sir," a crewman aboard the coast guard vessel informed Capt. Gray as the *Stockholm* came toward the cove's entrance. "They're coming out now, sir."

"Hail them, sailor, and order them alongside," the captain said sharply and the crewman immediately waved his arms to attract the *Stockholm*'s attention.

Pulling up alongside, Dan handed the controls to Nancy and joined Jeb on deck, catching the coast guard rope and tying the boats together.

"What's the problem?" asked Dan.

"Capt. Gray would like you to come aboard, sir."

"Careful lad, watch what you say," the old detective muttered.

Quickly shown onto the bridge, Dan noted the presence of a senior officer and saluted.

"Sgt. Dan Brown, retired sir."

"Admiral Johnson, United States Coast Guard," the senior officer returned gruffly. "You're army, sergeant?"

"Artillery, sir, invalided out."

"Wounded at the front?" the admiral asked, his eyes fastening on the still vivid scar on Dan's forehead.

"Yes admiral."

"We're stopping all vessels heading for Seattle and Tacoma, but I'm told you're from Victoria."

"Yes, sir."

"Capt. Gray informs me you're on your way to the Jorgensen dock."

"Yes sir, that's as far as we're going."

"And your business?"

"Taking my fiancé to visit her folks, sir."

"You mean Nancy Wilson is with you?" the admiral asked, suddenly relaxing. Seeing Dan's smile, he eagerly continued, "Call her aboard."

"Nan!" Dan called over the rail. "Come aboard, honey, someone wants to meet you."

As Nancy came aboard the cutter, she whispered anxiously, "Who is it?"

"You'll see," he replied secretively, leading her to the bridge.

"Hello Nancy," John Gray greeted her pleasantly. "This is Admiral Johnson, my superior officer."

"Pleased to meet you, sir," she said, blushing slightly as he took her hand. She noticed how large it was but his touch was remarkably gentle.

"Major General Greene has told me all about you, young lady," the admiral chatted. "He thinks you're wonderful, says you're their mascot at Camp Lewis."

"He's a dear, sir."

"Well, Miss Wilson, I've heard him called a lot of things, but never a dear! Now tell me, how are you related to the Jorgensens?"

"By love, sir. It was the Jorgensens who first coaxed me to sing in Seattle."

"And now you're a star. I believe they call you 'Seattle's Sweetheart'."

"Yes, I know," she replied, blushing again.

"Did you know we have our first suspected case of Spanish influenza at Camp Lewis?"

"Oh no, we didn't, that's terrible," Nancy replied, showing her surprise.

"Any sign of it in Victoria yet?"

"Not to my knowledge, sir, but they're talking about new regulations to deal with it when it does arrive."

"Sgt. Brown!" Admiral Johnson called to Dan who was talking with Capt. Gray, "if you give me your assurance that you will take this vessel no farther than the Jorgensen dock, I will give you a pass."

"You have my word, sir."

Turning to the chart table, he quickly signed a lengthy form and handed it to Dan, then reached into his briefcase and withdrew a diary.

"Now, Miss Wilson," he asked, grinning broadly as he opened the book and offered her a pen. "Would you do me the honour of signing my diary?"

"But of course," Nancy giggled with surprise, taking the pen and signing her name under the date May 1, 1918.

As they were shaking hands, Capt. Gray interrupted indicating that Dan was waiting on board the *Stockholm.* Escorting her back down to the lower deck, he offered his arm for support as she climbed over to the other boat.

Looking back as the coast guard vessel moved away, they breathed a sigh of relief but felt the deep seriousness of the new situation and understood Washington State's efforts to keep its residents free of the dreaded disease.

“I would have thought they could have found a cure by now,” Dan muttered, “maybe I was lucky to get wounded so I got out before the influenza started.”

“We won’t get it now,” Jeb growled as they moved back to Ezekiel’s wharf and handed his friend a bottle of their tonic. “We’ve got our cure.”

“What was happening with Copley’s boat?” asked Zeke.

“Just like you thought,” said Dan, “he had engine trouble.”

“How did you know that?” asked Nancy.

“Capt. Gray told me while you were busy signing autographs!” retorted Dan, winking at the others.

Giving Zeke instructions to take a swig of the tonic daily, they left him and headed off down Puget Sound. At the Jorgensen dock, Terry O’Reilly and Bill Jorgensen were using binoculars to search the waters of the sound for the expected arrival of the *Stockholm.*

“Here they come,” Bill announced, his wheelchair moving precariously close to the edge of the dock. “Just look at that boat fly!”

Sweeping into the little harbour, Dan’s experienced hands quickly had the red-and-gold craft backed into the boathouse out of sight.

“I brought as much as we could carry,” he informed the gangster. “Better keep a check on the extras.”

“I’m surprised you didn’t get stopped by the coast guard,” Terry snorted. “They’ve been stopping every ship coming into Seattle all week. Seems we have our first case of the influenza at Camp Lewis.”

“They stopped us, too, told us the news, and gave us a pass to come only as far as this dock.”

“They turned a freighter away on Monday, Roy told me. Wouldn’t let it near a dock until doctors had checked the crew over.”

“Yes, they’re talking about restrictions in Victoria. There’s quite a ruckus going on between the health department and city council. They shut Nancy’s restaurant down illegally.”

Nancy jumped down onto the dock allowing Bill to pull her onto his knee, giggling as he hugged her. Meanwhile, Jeb stood silently watching at the outer door of the boathouse, his eyes constantly probing the area for hidden danger.

“Will you marry me, Nancy?” Bill asked as Dan pushed him up the garden path toward the house.

“Sorry pal,” Dan laughed, “she’s marrying some other fella on Saturday. You’re too late!”

Beth and Gus, waiting at the back door, could hear them laughing even before they came into sight. They ushered them into the living room where tea and sandwiches were waiting.

"We have good news and bad news for you," Gus announced thoughtfully.

"Give us the good news first, please," Nancy requested. "Good news would be quite a change these days."

"James Moore has arranged for you to sing for a record company," Gus announced.

"But I can't, they've closed the theatre down."

"No, honey, you'll sing in a studio, there won't be an audience."

"What good will that do if nobody's listening? I need a theatre and a collection," Nancy complained.

"Don't worry, James will explain it to you. He's coming over to pick you up in 15 minutes. They're eager to get on with it."

"Today?" Dan asked, frowning.

"It's all right, Danny," Beth assured him. "James said it wouldn't take long and I'll go with her."

"And the bad news?" Jeb asked bluntly.

"General Greene won't be coming to the wedding," Gus responded, lowering his voice, "he's got the flu."

"He's at Camp Lewis?" asked Jeb.

"Yes, he is. He was the first patient they had."

"My gosh, he had breakfast with us only a few days ago!" Nancy exclaimed, a chill running up her spine.

You'd better find yourself a new minister, Nan, because he won't be coming either," Jeb declared, ignoring her worried comment.

"Oh the minister's all right," Beth whispered, "it's only General Greene who is sick."

"Well, the minister will not be officiating at this wedding!" Jeb ranted. "I'll not have him bringing sickness to my family."

"Jeb's right," Dan agreed, "it's foolish to take a chance. We'll find a minister in Victoria, if you would contact him at the base for us please Gus."

A tap on the door drew their attention as the butler appeared. "Mr. Moore has arrived, sir. I've shown him into your study."

"Bring him in here, Joseph," Gus gestured impatiently.

"Do we need to get changed?" Nancy asked with a puzzled expression.

"No dear, but you might want to change and freshen up a bit," Beth said, smiling. "I'll brush your hair and you can use a bit of my makeup, we'll only be a few minutes."

Passing the theatre owner in the hallway, Nancy greeted him with a hug as Gus called out inviting him to join them. Going up the stairs with Beth, she changed out of her heavy sweater into a light blouse and cardigan, then sat down and stared into the mirror, watching the reflection of her adopted mother as she gently brushed her long hair.

"I never knew what it was like to have a mother or father," she mused. "I'm so lucky to have found so many special people to fill that void in my life."

"It works both ways you know, dear," Beth replied softly, kissing the top of her head.

They were both lost in their own thoughts until Nancy suddenly changed the subject saying, "I'll need Nellie to play for me, Beth."

"James has it all arranged, dear," Beth replied. "Don't worry."

Downstairs, the men were listening to the theatre owner as he explained the financial arrangement he had made for Nancy.

"She gets a lump sum for the initial recording and a royalty for every record sold," he announced. "This way she'll be able to keep her charity fund going."

"You're acting like an agent!" Bill interrupted.

"Not quite, son," James sighed. "I won't be taking a fee, I'm just happy to help."

"Where is this recording studio?" the wheelchair-bound young man asked.

"Here in Magnolia, just off McGraw. We'll be back in an hour."

Frowning, Jebediah's mind swung back to his lawman days and he knew what Bill was getting at—they were about to let Nancy out of their sight with a man they hardly knew and into an unusual situation.

When Beth and Nancy appeared, he winked at Bill. "I think I'll go with you."

There were no objections from the theatre owner as he led them out to his car, chattering incessantly with excited enthusiasm for the project he had arranged. Soon they were weaving their way through the lunchtime traffic of Magnolia and pulling into the yard of the RCA Recording Studio.

Met at the door by Nellie Cornish and a stranger wearing a cowboy hat, Nellie grabbed the redhead's hand and pulled her inside the building. Not wanting to spoil the girls' fun, Beth followed at a distance.

"Glad you got her to come, Jimmy," said the stranger, "and who's this old fella, her Pappy?"

"Don't call me Jimmy, it's James, if you please," James retorted, sounding aggravated, "and this gentleman ..."

"Leave it, James," Jeb hissed, his eyes flashing annoyance as he stopped in front of the cowboy before entering the building. "I'll introduce myself if he doesn't mind his manners!"

Don Melhope paled a little under his tan, his position as recording director for the newly amalgamated companies of Victor and Columbia was delicate at best. Orders had come down from the executive office to sign and record the Canadian singer, nation-wide coverage of the Camp Lewis concert assuring them of Nancy's popularity.

Glancing around the studio, Nancy shook her head in dismay at the bare-looking interior. Glass walls separated technicians from the performers and an upright piano and an odd-looking, cone-shaped mechanism standing in the centre of the room, completed the picture. This was not what she had expected at all.

"What is that, Nellie?" she asked, staring at the large, cone-shaped object.

"It's an acoustical horn, I'm told," Nellie replied. "It records the sound waves of our performance into that machine attached to it which cuts a wax-coated master disc. Amazing don't you think? I've never seen one before but that's what they have to use to record voices."

"Why can't we just use a microphone?"

"Voices don't record clearly through a microphone," said a male voice as Don Melhope entered the studio. "Hello ladies, I'm Don Melhope and I'll be producing this record for you today."

"Oh!" exclaimed Nancy, looking rather perturbed. "This isn't at all as I expected, Mr. Melhope."

"We're going to make it as painless as possible, Miss Wilson. All you have to do is sing and we'll do the rest!" he said, his cocky attitude very obvious. He left the room abruptly.

His attitude unnerved Nancy a bit but Nellie, having already tried the piano, was eager to discuss the repertoire of songs and run through a warm-up. She quickly got Nancy's attention back to the job at hand and they went to work. Meanwhile, in the outer room, the manager found seats for Beth and the men.

"James, have you discussed specifics of her payment with Nancy yet?" Jeb asked the theatre owner.

"Later, later," James Moore whispered excitedly, "wait until he hears her sing."

"Quiet please," Melhope ordered sharply, "we'll start recording in three minutes."

"I can't sing to an empty space," Nancy moaned, following their short warm-up.

"Of course you can," Nellie whispered, "just think of singing to Dan or at the theatre in Seattle."

"Nancy doesn't look a bit comfortable in there," Beth commented. "I hope she'll be all right."

"She can't see us," Jeb growled, picking up his chair and moving toward the separating door. "I know what she needs."

"No, no, no!" Melhope rushed to stop him entering the room. "You can't go in there."

Ignoring the frantic, arm-waving director, Jeb put his chair down against the wall and went to get Beth's, indicating for her to follow. James followed suit, placing his chair against the wall and sitting down.

"We'll be very quiet," Beth assured the director.

"No, madam, no! This just will not do," Melhope spluttered.

Nellie giggled, putting her head down and continuing to play to get Nancy's attention, but the commotion unnerved the singer and she stopped and glared at the director.

"Leave them, Mr. Melhope, or would you rather we all went home?"

The unmistakable threat and determination in Nancy's voice caused Melhope to grudgingly throw up his hands and concede defeat. Smiling coldly at the girls, he turned and nodded to the control room then, turning back to face the girls, he raised his arms.

"We will begin when I drop my arms," he commanded loudly.

When the signal was given, Nellie's poised fingers flew like magic across the keyboard and Nancy's beautiful voice instantaneously filled the studio. Beth closed her eyes and gripped Jebediah's arm. When the director gave the signal to stop at the end of their time, 20 minutes had seemed to pass in the blink of an eye. Once again the redhead's singing had mesmerized her audience.

"My God, what a talent," Melhope gasped almost inaudibly, continuing out loud, "take a break, girls, we'll finish up in 15 minutes."

"You were both wonderful," Beth said excitedly giving them hugs. "I can't wait to hear the record."

Linking arms with Nancy, Nellie requested three glasses of water and once they arrived she beckoned to Beth. "Let's step outside for a breath of fresh air." Leaving the men to deal with any business matters, she led the women outside. "Think of it, Nan," Nellie said excitedly, spreading her arms and breathing deeply of the pleasantly scented air from a next door garden. "Your voice will be heard right around the world."

"She's right," Beth sighed, "I'm afraid we're going to have to share you after this record comes out!"

Jeb came out to join them and they were talking as a car came around the corner, pulling up beside James Moore's large black Ford. Becoming instantly alert, he moved to put himself between the driver and the ladies.

"Back inside, girls," he hissed. "It's that nuisance reporter again."

Pulling his gangly frame out of the car but stopping when he saw Jeb's reaction, Tom Wills leaned against his car and grinned at his adversary. "I'm here by invitation, Mr. Judd."

"Who the hell invited you?" Jeb demanded.

"I did!" Don Melhope called from the door. "Come inside Wills."

Holding his temper in check, Jeb returned to the studio quietly seething at the newspaper reporter's unwanted intrusions into their lives. Taking his seat, he winked reassuringly at the redhead, then tried to relax as they waited for the second recording session to begin.

"Marvellous, absolutely marvellous!" the recording director shouted when they had finished.

"The contract?" James Moore reminded him.

"Later Jimmy, wait until I hear the recording," replied Melhope, brushing him flippantly aside.

"Now!" the theatre owner insisted.

"Well, if you insist. Would you all step outside, while I discuss it with Miss Wilson in private."

James cursed under his breath and turned to Jebediah for support. Smiling coldly, the former Pinkerton detective moved closer, menacingly flexing his shoulders, when suddenly a voice was heard from the direction of the control room.

"You're not planning to cheat these talented ladies, are you, Mr. Melhope?"

Following everyone's gaze as they looked toward the voice in the control room, Jeb frowned when he saw Wills in the doorway--his dishevelled appearance making him appear anything but threatening.

Well I'll be damned, Jeb thought, *he's actually trying to help*!

"Just a minute here," Nancy interrupted. "I thought Mr. Moore had all this arranged."

"Only verbally," James admitted, looking confused. "It was a gentleman's agreement."

"I only need the singer," Melhope exclaimed. "We have our own pianists."

"What did he originally offer in this gentleman's agreement, Mr. Moore?" asked Tom Wills, his back to Melhope as he grinned slyly and scribbled more notes on his pad.

"Five thousand for Nancy and one thousand for Miss Cornish."

"What, no royalties?" asked the reporter.

"Yes, but we haven't discussed any figures yet."

"I think you'd better do that now," the reporter suggested. "May I suggest five percent."

They could all see the anger building on the recording studio director's face and he suddenly cut loose in a tirade of abuse at Tom Wills, ordering him out of the building.

"If he goes, we all go," Nancy responded angrily. "We don't really want to work for this man anyway, do we Nellie?"

"But this is what you need, Nancy," Nellie whispered behind her hand. "This would keep your fund going."

"We don't need all this arguing so let's just go home and forget about the recording," Nancy said stubbornly.

Jeb chuckled to himself. He heard the determined tone in Nancy's voice and recognized that expression. He knew her mind was made up. Blocking the path of Don Melhope who was trying to follow the retreating girls, Jeb noticed that the reporter was still scribbling notes feverishly on his pad as he went and stood near the door.

"Well lad, are you coming?" he asked Wills.

"Yes sir," the reporter agreed readily, "but first I want to thank Mr. Melhope for the wonderful story he has given Seattle readers!"

"Don't you dare print what you've heard here today," Melhope threatened, "or we'll sue!"

"I would be very careful making such a statement, sir," Wills declared. "I think Miss Wilson could very well be the one suing!"

Chapter 7

"What a mess," exclaimed Nancy, getting into the car and falling back against the soft leather upholstery. "Everything's gone wrong this week and I'll be glad when it's over."

James' hands were shaking as he grasped the steering wheel on the quiet trip back to the Jorgensen mansion. He had made a mistake trusting Don Melhope, a blunder he would have to take responsibility for. Beads of sweat formed on his brow as he pondered how he was going to explain this to Gus.

Unnoticed, Tom Wills followed them in his battered old car, having difficulty keeping up with the sleek modern Ford but suspecting they were going to the Jorgensen estate. Nevertheless, he was chuckling to himself at the way things had turned out at the recording studio.

Meanwhile, staring out of the window, Jebediah was re-evaluating this same reporter. Had he really tried to help or was he just stirring the mire and hoping to cause some revealing reaction from the Canadians. Truly his persistence was a nuisance but the old detective recognized a strange kind of courage in the skinny young man. *Maybe we can make him into an ally*, he thought.

Still silent and with red eyes, Nellie fought back her deep disappointment as James brought the car to a halt in the shadow of the Jorgensen's porté cochére.

"I'm awfully sorry, girls," he said sadly, resting his head on the steering wheel.

"Don't be silly, James," Beth murmured as they got out of the car. The front door of the house opened and Joseph stood waiting to let them in. "You tried your best and Gus will deal with it now."

Leading the way past the butler, Beth followed the sounds of laughter into the living room. Bill swung his wheelchair to face them, his smile disappearing when he saw the serious looks on their faces.

"What's wrong, Nan?" Dan leapt to his feet.

"They tried to cheat us," Nancy replied sadly. "Uncle Jeb'll tell you, Nellie and I need to go upstairs for a few minutes." Taking her friend's hand she tugged her gently toward the stairs. "Let's go repair the damage, Nellie."

"What damage?" Bill snapped. "Is she hurt?"

"Her make-up, son," Beth whispered, "she's been crying. This has been quite an experience."

Striding across the room, Gus took his wife's hand and led her to a chair, his smile hiding his anger.

"Sit down dear, Jeb and James will do the explaining," he quietly advised.

"It's all my fault," James began, as the door bell rang.

"Mr. Wills for you, sir," the butler addressed Gus.

"Bring him in," Jeb ordered, "we need him, Gus."

Gus frowned sternly as Joseph returned followed by the young reporter who appeared somewhat ill at ease.

"Jebediah," Gus announced, "the floor is yours."

"Just a minute, let's wait for the girls," Jeb replied indicating a chair for the reporter.

Hands behind his back and head bowed Jeb slowly paced back and forth in the hall, staring fiercely at the floor. A pencil appeared in Tom Wills' hand and he hurriedly scratched some notes on his notepad balanced on the arm of his chair. Finally, Nancy and Nellie returned.

"Right," said the old detective standing in front of them all, "here's the way I see it. James was duped into thinking he had a contract for Nancy and Nellie and all they had to do was turn up at the recording studio and perform."

"Yes you're right, Jebediah, I trusted him," agreed James.

"Well it didn't quite turn out that way Gus, because that Melhope fella tried to pull a slick manoeuvre," he explained pausing to glance around the room at their faces. Then he continued more slowly and deliberately. "He had no contract ready, but he got his recording then tried to cut Nellie out."

"He also wanted to negotiate with Nancy directly and alone," Tom Wills reminded them. "I believe it was his plan to get the Northwest's biggest star for peanuts!"

"Tell me, lad," Jeb faced the reporter, "why did you interfere at the studio when you were invited by the recording company?"

"Because," Tom blushed, "the more I found out about you people, the more I respected you all … and the less I respected them!"

"Have you written anything about us yet, Tom?" Gus asked.

"Yes sir, I told you I would. My editor was ecstatic, he wants more."

"You're a persistent little devil, aren't you?" exclaimed Jeb.

“I write the truth, sir, and I won’t stand aside and let someone get cheated. I will expose those crooks in my newspaper column, you’ll see. There will be lots of other record offers coming Nancy’s way in the near future. Remember, Miss Wilson, I heard you sing and I know you’re a star. By the way, my editor is also one of your fans.”

“Seems to me you’re a one-man army, son,” Gus sighed. “I think we should leave the whole dang mess in your lap.”

“Thank you, sir,” Tom said gratefully, raising his eyes from his pad. “My newspaper will really enjoy tearing them to pieces!”

“We should be going, Nan,” Dan interrupted. “Aunt Meg soon takes to worrying if we’re late.”

“Not yet,” Beth exclaimed, rising quickly to her feet, “we have some wedding presents for you to take back. I’ll get the servants to carry them down to the boathouse. Billy, go tell cook to make some sandwiches, Nancy must be starving,” she called over her shoulder, as she hurried out of the room.

Following her upstairs, Nan quickly changed back into her boating clothes then hurried outside to catch up to the others as they went down the path to the boathouse.

“You’re coming down to the boat, too, are you Mr. Wills?” she asked, finding him at the back of the group.

“Well, I’d sure like to look it over,” he replied eagerly.

“Look all you like, lad,” Jeb growled over his shoulder, “as long as you keep your feet on the dock.”

Some shouting from back up the path drew Nancy’s attention as a servant raced toward them with a basket of food and a large thermos.

“I’ll get it for you,” called Wills, turning back to meet the servant. With the basket in hand he caught up to them again, handing it to Nancy once she was aboard.

“Don’t leave yet, Tom, I would like to talk to you,” Gus informed the reporter as they waved to the departing Canadians.

“How long have you known Miss Wilson, sir?” Tom asked without taking his eyes off the *Stockholm*.

“Oh, quite a few years.”

“Where did you learn so much about recording contracts, Tom?” Nellie asked, joining the conversation.

Wills grinned as he pushed Bill’s wheelchair back to the house. “Same way I learned about you, Miss Cornish. I ask questions and somebody tells me.”

“Why were you at the recording studio?” Bill asked over his shoulder.

“Don Melhope, the studio director, told the newspaper Miss Wilson was going to make a recording today.” He stopped and chuckled. “I suspected both Miss Cornish and Mr. Moore would be there, also.”

“Free advertising,” Gus growled.

“Exactly, sir.”

“And what will you write now?” the shipping magnate prodded.

“The truth. I shall tell our readers how the recording company tried to cheat their sweetheart, Nancy Wilson. My editor will love it and you can imagine the reaction of the readers who know of her and there are many! By Friday, word will have spread outside the area and she’ll be inundated with offers for a new recording contract!”

“I think you’d better teach me a thing or two about this recording business, Tom; you sound to be quite knowledgeable about it,” said Gus.

“What I would really like,” Tom continued as they arrived at the house, “is an invitation to the wedding!”

Chuckling to himself, Gus rubbed his chin leaving the request unanswered. *The audacity of this young man*, he thought, *he’s actually trying to bargain for a chance to be at the wedding*. He glanced over at James. “You’ve been very quiet, James. What do you make of all this?”

“I’m sick to my stomach about the whole mess. It’s entirely my fault, Gus. I can’t believe I was taken in so easily. Nancy will never forgive me for this fiasco.”

“Nancy doesn’t blame you, James,” Nellie assured him. “She was grateful you were trying to help her cause.”

“Maybe I can be of some further assistance,” Tom interrupted. “My editor wants to sell more newspapers. If the newspaper sponsors Nancy’s first recording, they could make it obtainable solely with the purchase of a newspaper.”

Beth giggled at the innovative idea and seeing her husband’s eyebrows shoot up, she knew Tom had set Gus thinking.

“That’s a great idea!” Bill cried enthusiastically, banging his hand on the arm of his chair.

“It’s too restrictive,” replied his father. “We need nation-wide sales, not just here in Seattle.”

Unaware of their American friends’ scheming, the *Stockholm* sped up Puget Sound toward the Canadian border. Crossing the line, Dan pointed to a barge making its way through Haro Strait on tow behind a tug. It was loaded high with snow-white shells from the fish plant in Sidney. They were almost home.

Looking out the window at Cunningham Manor, Meg cocked her head and turned to her visitor. "They're coming."

"I can't hear them yet," Eva Todd replied, "you must have awfully good hearing, Meg."

"No, lass," replied the old Scot. "Sam was out on the cliff and he just went back into the trees, no doubt toward his home, wherever that is."

"Doesn't he bother you?"

"Ach noo! He's always close by when Jebediah's away. I like it that way."

Eva reached for her coat and went out onto the porch. Listening, she heard the *Stockholm*'s engines and her eyes glanced over at the tree line searching for the old hermit but he was nowhere in sight. Going over to the fence, she watched the red-and-gold boat docking below and felt a twinge of envy as Nancy stepped onto the dock and waved.

Loaded down with parcels, Nancy screamed when her hat blew off halfway up the cliff stairs, allowing her red hair to stream out behind her. Still giggling when she reached the top, she quickly accepted a peck on the cheek from Eva, then transferred the parcels to her friend and went scrambling over the rocks to recover her hat. Nimbly she jumped from rock to rock until she was back at the dock.

"Use the stairs, girl," Jeb growled as they passed, "you're not a goat!"

Picking up another load of parcels, she met Eva and Meg at the top of the stairs.

"What on earth have you brought home this time?" Meg asked.

"They're wedding presents!" Nancy exclaimed.

"How wonderful!" said Eva.

"From who?" asked Meg.

"I don't know," the redhead giggled, "they were left at the Jorgensen's. They must be from their friends who go to my concerts."

"We'll put them in the front room," ordered the Scot, then smiled when Dan and Jeb arrived with more parcels. "Glory be, we won't have room to move!"

After hanging up their coats, Nancy and the men gladly sat down at the table and accepted steaming bowls of soup from Meg.

"Sit down, Eva, you don't have to rush off yet. You might as well have a bowl, too," coaxed Meg.

Eva's eyes sparkled mischievously as she sat down and whispered across the table.

"Are you all ready for Saturday, Nan?"

"Ready and willing, I need a change in my luck."

"Why, what's happened?" asked her friend.

"Oh you wouldn't believe what's happened to me this last week or two, Eva. It's been an absolute mess."

"I saw Kate at the restaurant today. I was surprised when I saw the closed sign in the window but the tables were outside and full of soldiers from the hospital. They were eating as normal but she had the painters in and said she was redecorating the place.

"Good for her, was she on her own?" asked Nan, looking surprised.

"No, it was a madhouse, all the girls were working," she replied, pausing when she saw the redhead smiling. "You didn't know?"

"They closed it down on Monday!" Meg muttered clearing off the dirty dishes. "Anyone like a piece of lemon cake?"

"I do!" Jeb and Dan chorused.

"Let me tell you what's been happening to us Eva, and some of it Meg doesn't even know yet. It's enough to give a body sleepless nights," said Nan, pausing to take sip of tea. "It all started last week when the Seattle health officer shut my concerts down without notice."

"Why?" Eva gasped. "My goodness, what are we going to do for money?"

"It's because of the flu. They're taking precautions, but that's not all. My wedding dress was late coming and I got a bit weepy and Dr. Price ordered our restaurant closed on Monday. He said it was too close to the hospital."

Eva stared at Nancy, her eyes wide with shock. "Can he do that?"

"Apparently not, as the council wouldn't back him, so we were allowed to open again, but by that time Kate and I were so frustrated we decided to redecorate to cheer ourselves up."

"So you're open again?" Eva asked, shaking her head.

"Yes, we had permission to open but right now Kate was only supposed to be organizing the painting and we were going to wait to re-open after the wedding."

"Well, she's open now and doing a roaring business!" Eva declared.

"Do you want to hear the rest? There's more yet," Nan added with a grin. "Today we made a recording in Seattle."

"Did you really?" Eva's eyes sparkled with excitement. "Oh, Nan, what a triumph for you."

Meg came to sit back down at the table, paying close attention to the conversation. She knew by their expressions there was something amiss and she waited patiently for the redhead to tell it all.

"Don't get too excited yet, there's more," Nancy continued. "They didn't have a contract ready and they tried to cut Nellie out. It finally ended when we all walked out."

"You wouldn't cut Nellie out, would you?" asked Eva.

"Certainly not, I need her!"

"So there's no recording?" demanded Meg.

"Yes there is, but they can't use it without my permission and we won't agree to their terms."

"It's a wonder you're sane after a week like that," Eva sympathized. "Now I feel guilty bringing you more problems."

"Nan? Sane? Oh, I won't vouch for that," Dan chuckled. "Hasn't she told you she's marrying some layabout lazy bum on Saturday?"

"Oh Danny! You two have found the end of the rainbow—the pot of gold you've dreamed of and worked so hard to achieve," Eva said softly, feeling very envious.

"And only two more days to go," Nancy replied, smiling at her friend. *Poor Eva, it must be terribly hard to see me so happy these days as she waits for news from Tom.* Then, suddenly remembering that Eva had come with a problem, she said, "Now you'd better get your problem off your chest."

"Mine's money, of course," Eva said making a face.

Meg got up and going into the other room, returned with the money box and her book. "How much do you need, lass?" she asked, her hand hovering over the open box.

"Sixty should do it," Eva murmured.

"It's month end," Meg reminded her, "what about rents?"

"Oh yes, better make it a hundred then, that should be enough."

"I've got the booze money," Dan reminded them, pushing a thick envelope across to Meg. "We just need the cost of the liquor out of it."

"My goodness, I wonder if Victoria will ever know you're their guardian angels," Eva commented, tears coming to her eyes.

"Hush woman," the redhead warned her. "Victoria has given us everything and this is simply a little we can give in return."

It was after dinner when Meg finally broached the subject of the recording again not being able to stop thinking about the sketchy details Nancy had given. Jebediah took up the story first, telling in graphic detail Nancy's reaction and how Tom Wills had jumped into the fray.

"He looks a bit simple," Jeb chuckled, "but the lad's not without courage."

"Gus and Bill were quite impressed with him," Dan added.

"Ach, I don't understand these new-fangled things." Meg's knitting needles clicked fiercely. "How do they make your voice come out of a box, when you're not there?"

"They make a recording, then play it back on one of those phonograph machines we saw last week in Fletchers' window," Nancy explained, looking over at her adopted aunt. "Remember Fletcher's Music Shop in the Spencer Building in Government Street, Aunt Meg?"

"Can't say I do, lassie," the old Scot shook her head.

"She knows what you're talking about, lass," said Jeb. "She's just being stubborn."

"I am not!" Meg's fingers stopped knitting and she glared at Jeb. "And anyway, how do you know?"

"Because you do it to me all the time woman, but I'm onto your tricks!" he declared, winking at Nancy.

"You don't know nothing," she replied as a smile tugged gently at the corners of her mouth. "You just know about men things and rubbish!"

"Hold it, you two," Dan laughed, climbing to his feet and pulling Nancy up with him. "If you're going to start arguing, we're going for a walk."

"Put your coats on!" the old lady snapped.

"Yes, Aunt Meg," they both chorused from the door.

"What the hell's bitten you, old girl?" Jeb asked, going over to the hearth and knocking the ash from his pipe into the fire.

"Nothing, you silly old fool! I've bought them one of those phonograph players for their wedding gift and I don't want them to know."

"Well you've sure been sneaky."

"Oh shut your blather man, and come with me."

Easing out of her rocker, she reached for the old man's hand, tugging him gently toward the door.

"Put your coat on," she whispered, pulling a heavy woollen shawl around her shoulders, quietly opening the door, and peeking outside.

"Why are you whispering? Where are we going?" he asked.

"Shush, listen."

Stepping out onto the porch, they could see the silhouette of the young people sitting close together at the top of the cliff stairs in the moonlight. The sound of Nancy's voice softly singing to the man she adored wafted toward them on the light breeze.

Instinctively Jeb put his arm around Meg's shoulder and she responded by snuggling in closer.

"They're our children, Jeb," she whispered. "We are so blessed."

"Come on woman, let's get to where we're going before they see us and ask questions," he insisted, allowing her to take his arm and lead him down the stairs. They turned the corner of the house and disappeared from view.

The house was in darkness when Dan and Nancy crept quietly upstairs, taking a last lingering kiss before moving off to their bedrooms. Sleep came easily to the redhead and soon her mind was tumbling through a recurring dream of wedded bliss, children, and their quiet haven at Cunningham Manor.

Dan and Jeb left the house early Thursday morning as bookings were heavy for the freight service and, with Kate back at the restaurant, Jeb had his regular duties at the office. Nancy left an hour later. Rain had fallen in the night causing puddles and muddy holes everywhere as Nancy drove along Richmond. Lights were on at the Wounded Soldier when she pulled into the back lane. She smiled as she heard the clatter of pans and good-natured laughter emanating from the open back door—things were back to normal it seemed. Inside, the bright new paint welcomed her and the names and insignia of local regiments painted on the walls brought a triumphant smile to her lips. Kate had worked wonders with the place.

"You don't need to work today, Nan," Kate called to her.

"Oh yes she does!" called a young soldier with his head wrapped in bandages. "If you try to close this place again, the boys are going to demote you both."

"They wouldn't let me close," Kate giggled. "The painters took the tables outside and the customers quickly filled them and yelled for service, even the streetcar men wouldn't take 'no' for an answer!"

"But didn't it rain?"

"Yes a little, but they still sat there. I just had to serve them, Nan."

"No one tried to stop you, from the health department, I mean?"

"Dr. Price came in," Kate chuckled recalling the incident, "but the soldier's booed him away!"

"I'll bet he was mad."

"No, he actually left here laughing, but shaking his head," Kate giggled, rolling her eyes at the memory.

"You love this place, don't you Kate?" Nancy whispered reaching for her partner's hand.

"I never really knew how much until I thought we'd lost it. I'm so glad to get it back."

"Well now, young lady, you just remember no matter how hopeless it looks, no matter how impossible the task, we'll always get there if we never stop trying."

"You live by that motto, don't you?"

"Oh, I've had my moments of despair, too, my friend. Now tell me Kate, how on earth did you get those insignia pictures painted on the wall? They're wonderful!"

"Well, it's amazing how it all fell into place. The painters knew an old guy who used to be in the army. He'd taken up painting for a hobby and had studied all these different regiments and their insignia. Need I say more?" she laughed.

"Boy, you never know who you'll meet these days. He must have worked all day and night, but he's done a superb job and I hope he'll come in one day so I can meet him."

A sudden call from the kitchen interrupted further discussion as Kate rushed off to investigate, leaving Nancy to deal with the customers.

All through the morning, well-wishers called in to offer their congratulations and a group of nurses brought a very special gift from the hospital—a painting of the restaurant done by one of the soldiers who had recently succumbed to his injuries. The inscription on the back drew tears to the redhead's eyes when she read, *The Home of a Red-haired Angel*. It was signed *Randy*.

"He thought the world of you, Nancy," a nurse whispered emotionally, fighting back tears. "The funeral's today."

"Where?" asked Nan.

"Ross Bay, at 2 o'clock."

Kate quietly understood when Nancy showed her the picture and informed her she would be attending the funeral. Promptly at one-thirty, Nancy nosed the truck into Richmond Road traffic, following a slow-moving Hudson Bay truck that mercifully turned back toward Oak Bay

Avenue leaving the way clear for her to speed along to Fairfield Road and reach the gates of the cemetery.

Parking behind two other vehicles, she steeled herself against the sadness she felt knowing that funerals always made her feel this way. She quickly spotted a small group of people standing around an open grave some distance away. As she joined them, she recognized the nurse who brought her the painting and four of the soldiers from the hospital.

Squeaking along on a gurney, the coffin arrived a few minutes later and was lowered to its resting place. A simple ceremony followed, conducted by an army chaplain as two old grave diggers in dirty overalls waited in the background to complete their task.

"Thank you for coming," the chaplain murmured to the small gathering going around and shaking their hands.

"Would it be in keeping with your service, sir," Nancy murmured, "if I sang one last time for Randy?"

"By all means, please do," replied the chaplain, his eyebrows raised in surprise.

Nancy's voice softly rang through Ross Bay Cemetery as she sang the words to the tender lullaby, *Tonight, little man, you'll sleep with the angels, you'll be at peace with the world forever*." The soldiers stood stoically with squared shoulders, the nurse stood at attention with tears running down her face, and the chaplain clutched his prayer book tightly to his chest. It was a touching tribute to a brave young soldier and friend.

Turning, as the song ended, Nan hurried away hardly hearing the chaplain's thanks. Driving toward the city, her thoughts turned to Harry Lauder, the popular Scottish singer who had taught her that song at Camp Lewis. Pulling onto the dock in Wharf Street, she dried her eyes and caught a glimpse in the mirror of Waldo dashing across the street behind her.

"Hey there, girl," he puffed reaching the side of the truck. "Who's the minister for Saturday's shindig?"

"Minister?" Nancy repeated. "Oh my gosh, I forgot! We were going to use the chaplain from Camp Lewis."

"Well," Waldo bellowed, "Dan says he can't come now."

"They've got at least one case of influenza at the camp. Uncle Jeb says he won't allow him on the property."

"He's right, but you'll have to find a replacement or there'll be no wedding."

"I know where to find one, don't worry!" Nancy thumped the steering wheel in frustration.

Starting the truck again she turned around, gears grinding into reverse, and drove quickly out onto Wharf Street. Waldo winced at the blaring horns and screams of irate drivers that the redhead ignored as she sent her truck bounding toward the Empress Hotel.

"Where's she going in such a hurry?" Dan inquired as he came around from behind the office.

"Damned if I know, something about a minister," Waldo grunted. "I'm just glad I didn't have to ride with her!"

Driving as fast as she could, the truck hurtled along Dallas Road to Ross Bay Cemetery. Could she catch the army chaplain? Would he still be there? Her heart sank when the gates came in sight and she realized only one car remained.

"Oh please let him be here," she whispered, hurriedly parking and getting out of the truck.

She peered past the monuments to where the service had been held and breathed a sigh of relief. The chaplain was still there talking to the grave diggers. Waving her hat, she caught his attention. He raised his Bible as a signal and started walking toward her. Frowning, Nancy watched him limp over the rough ground to the pathway and hurried forward to offer her assistance.

"Are you hurt?" she asked, taking his arm.

"No my dear, I was wounded in that hell we call a war."

"But you're a minister."

"We go where we are needed my child, and sometimes suffer the consequences," he replied, smiling despite the pain. "Now, how might I be of assistance to you?"

"Can you marry me?" Nancy blurted out.

"Well no, my dear, I'm already married, but thank you for the offer," he said his eyes twinkling.

Blushing and stammering for words, Nancy smiled as she realized what she had said and quickly regained her composure.

"What I really meant to say was, I need a minister to officiate at my wedding on Saturday and I wondered if you would be so kind."

"You're getting married this Saturday? Congratulations, my dear."

"Thank you. The chaplain from Camp Lewis was going to officiate but he can't come because there is influenza at the base."

"Which church do you belong to?"

"None really, we're getting married in the garden at Cunningham Manor … our home."

The chaplain's eyebrows raised and he murmured solemnly, "I will if you'll answer me one question."

"I'll try."

"Why did you sing that beautiful song at the graveside?"

Nancy's head dropped and she took a deep breath, her teeth biting into her lip as sadness again welled up inside her.

"I hardly knew him," she whispered, "but he painted me a picture which I received earlier today. I just wanted to say thank you … and goodbye."

"What is your name?" the chaplain asked.

"Nancy Wilson."

"Well, young lady, my name is Ralph Jordan. I'm chaplain at the Willows Camp and I would be honoured to conduct your wedding. This world would be a much better place with a few more Nancy Wilsons in it. Now, I have a form in my car we must complete and you can give me the pertinent details."

Completing the form on the hood of his car, Chaplain Jordan pencilled in all the pertinent information and assured her he would be there.

It was almost four-thirty when she passed the Dallas Hotel at Ogden Point and waited for the Outer Wharf Street car to clang noisily into its terminus at Rithet's Wharf. Farther along, she saw the fishboats returning to Fisherman's Wharf and the paint factory at Laurel Point that blocked her view across the harbour. Moving a little faster past the Parliament Buildings, she breathed a sigh of relief that the CP dock was free of hospital ships.

Standing at the end of their dock, Dan saw the blue truck cross the harbour bridge in front of the Empress and went to the driveway to watch her arrive.

"Where the devil have you been?" he asked, as she stepped from her vehicle. "You were here one minute and gone the next!"

"Making sure you don't escape," she grinned impishly.

"Me?" Dan asked with a puzzled expression, reaching out to hug her.

Ducking under his outstretched arms, Nancy dashed into the office, scurrying behind Jebediah's chair. The old detective's eyes narrowed, watching the door as his hand quietly opened a drawer and reached for his unloaded revolver.

“Is this fella bothering you, honey?” he growled, levelling the gun as Dan appeared. “Do you want me to plug him?”

“Not today, Uncle Jeb. Just make sure he marries me on Saturday, please,” she giggled.

“If he don’t,” the old man grinned, “I’ll plug him for sure!”

Skipping around the table, Nancy flung herself into Dan’s arms.

“Tell me, where did you go in such a hurry?” he murmured into her hair. “You had everybody worried.”

“When I talked to Waldo, I remembered we didn’t have a minister.”

“You went looking for a minister?”

“Yes.”

“I bet she found one, too,” Jeb chuckled confidently watching as Nancy nodded her head. “It’s time we loaded for tomorrow, lad. That liquor has been stood on the dock since noon.”

“It’s loaded,” Dan replied, “we loaded it before Dumpy left for Sooke.”

“Then it’s high time we went home!” Jeb countered.

Leaving the boys to come home in the boat, Nancy locked up the office with a feeling of contentment that things were finally going right. The newspaper had forecast a sun-filled weekend and they had only one more trip to Seattle before the big day. Taking the old way home along Cedar Hill, she found time to slow down and enjoy the view over the valley’s farmland. Smelling the orchard blossoms, she couldn’t help but smile. This was the Gordon Head they loved and Cunningham Manor was the end of their rainbow, just as Eva had said.

Chapter 8

Hanging her coat up in the hall, Nancy went into the kitchen and greeted her aunt.

"Don't come in here," commanded Meg, "you better go have a look at the living room table."

"My goodness, where has all this stuff come from?" Nancy called from the other room, sounding puzzled.

"Read the labels, honey, folks have been dropping by all day with those parcels!"

"They're wedding presents!" the redhead squealed. "I think everyone in Gordon Head must have sent something!"

"And everyone in Washington State, too!" Meg declared. "Leave them until later, lass, I need you to set the table for dinner. The men will be here before we know it."

With the table set and Meg refusing her help in the kitchen, Nancy wandered out to the clifftop searching the water for a sign of the *Stockholm*. Suddenly she heard the faint sound of an engine and, looking out toward Cormorant Point, she saw a flash of light and knew Dan was almost home. She ran back to the house and burst through the door.

"They're coming, Aunt Meg!" she cried.

"Calm down, lass, they'll be 15 minutes yet."

Later, they had just finished eating when the telephone rang and Dan went to answer it, frowning as he listened to the caller.

"You're who, sir?" he asked. "You met her where? Yes, I'm Nancy's bridegroom. Full uniform please, sir. Thank you."

"The chaplain," Nancy whispered. "I'd better tell you how I met him."

"I know how you met him, he just told me, but how come you were at a funeral?"

Meg looked mystified while Jeb grimaced trying to make sense of the conversation. So Nancy related the story of how the nurse had brought the picture over to the restaurant and how the artist was a young soldier who had died causing her to decide to attend his funeral.

"I just thought I should go and say goodbye. He was a nice young man. So sad."

"Why did you ask the chaplain to marry us?"

"Because General Greene has the influenza and Uncle Jeb said he wouldn't let the base chaplain come."

"That's why you raced off this afternoon," Jeb stated, grinning. "You had just remembered that you needed a minister?"

"Yes, but I had to act fast to get back to Ross Bay. There was no time to explain or I might have missed him and I had no idea how to find him again in a hurry."

"You did right, Nan," said Dan. "I should have known it was something important."

Later, Meg insisted they retire early as they wanted an early start to Seattle in the morning. Nancy, suddenly feeling very tired, got up and went over to hug her aunt.

"Thanks for working so hard on our wedding, Aunt Meg. I'm so glad you're here," she murmured.

Meg smiled and silently gave the girl a kiss.

Once in bed, although so tired she couldn't keep her eyes open, Nan wasn't able to get to sleep, tossing and turning as her mind kept jolting back to thoughts of the wedding.

Somehow morning arrived, coming much too early as she heard Meg's call echo up the stairway. Groaning, she blinked her eyes open, reluctantly pushed back the covers, and went over to the window. Opening the curtains she couldn't help but smile at the beautiful sight. Dawn was breaking and orange and yellow streaks spread across the sky.

Thank goodness, no rain today! *Please make it nice for tomorrow*, she pleaded silently, stretching her arms above her head, and then she hurried to get dressed.

"Where's Uncle Jeb?" she asked, entering the kitchen and easing a chair out from under the table.

"Outside looking for Sam. Nobody's seen the old fella for a couple of days and he was worried," explained Dan, coming in from outside.

"Oh, he'll be all right," Meg muttered, "he wanders all over the place especially when he thinks no one is watching!"

Footsteps noisily stamped on the porch outside, the door opened, and Jeb stepped in. Slipping his still-smoking pipe into his vest pocket, he went to hang up his coat.

"It's cool out there," he grumbled.

"Yes, lad, and it'll be cool in here if you burn anymore holes in that pocket!" Meg snapped.

Winking at Dan and Nancy, he extracted the still-smoking pipe from his pocket and placed it carefully on the kitchen hearth.

"Satisfied honey?" Jeb whispered when Meg brought his breakfast plate.

"I don't need any of your Texas blather this morning, m'lad," the Scot replied, but gently rested her hand on his shoulder. With a mouthful of egg, Jeb glanced up and winked at her. Meg giggled girlishly, fondling the hair on the back of his head. "I think you've still a lot of the devil left in you, old lad."

"Aunt Meg," Dan chuckled, "are you telling us a secret?"

"There's no secrets here, son," his aunt murmured. "I just wish we could stay this way forever."

"I don't," Nancy chirped through a mouthful of toast. "I need to get tomorrow over first!"

Glowing fiery red, the sun was just rising above the mountains as the *Stockholm* slipped out of the cove and roared off down the coast. Meg stood for a moment enjoying the view and listening to the fading sound then, turning away, caught sight of Sam standing at the tree line.

Leaving the redhead at the helm, Dan joined Jebediah on deck and they watched the shoreline carefully for danger. By nine they were passing Whidbey Island and the Edmond's Light. Jeb used his binoculars and checked Apple Cove. The weather was clear and several freighters were clearly visible chugging in an orderly line toward Seattle's docks.

Sweeping up to the Jorgensen jetty, Nancy quickly backed the *Stockholm* out of sight in the boathouse. Slickly efficient, Terry's men went to work unloading while the young gangster chatted with the Canadians. Bill arrived with two servants carrying a thermos of coffee, a package of sandwiches, and more wedding presents. They were all quickly stowed away.

"Dad talked to the recording company," Bill informed them. "He also talked to Tom Wills' editor at the newspaper. Seems Dad knows the owner, they're horse racing pals."

"You're having trouble with somebody here in Seattle?" Terry growled ominously.

"No," Bill replied quickly. "Dad seems to be handling it."

"Did you hear anything from General Greene?" Nancy interrupted.

"Yes, Dad talked on the phone to him briefly, he does have the flu but so far it doesn't seem to be life threatening."

"Oh my, that is good, and poor Mr. Moore?"

"Oh, he's over his embarrassment and now talking of starting his own record company."

"How are you getting to our house tomorrow, Bill?" Dan inquired.

"Company launch. Mum said Dad had to take her in style. Don't worry, brother, we'll be there!"

"Right, let's go," Jeb grunted, draining his coffee cup. "That's enough jawing, it's time we went home. We have a wedding to organize!"

"Not without this!" said Terry handing the redhead a bulky envelope.

"And not without this," Bill laughed, grabbing Nancy and pulling her onto his knee and hugging her. "If that big lump doesn't turn up tomorrow, you call me. I'll marry you in an instant!"

"Oh he'll turn up," Nancy chuckled. "Uncle Jeb's got a loaded shotgun ready!"

Laughing, Terry pushed the wheelchair out onto the dock as the *Stockholm*'s engines burst into life and Dan brought the boat outside, thundering away as Nancy and Jeb waved from the stern.

Only one small incident marred their run home. A lone yacht with its sail ripped from the mast, wallowed in distress just before they reached Marrowstone Island. Dan quickly changed direction taking her in tow over to Port Townsend. A quick shake of the captain's hand conveyed his thanks and they were speeding toward home again.

Standing on the porch, Meg heard them coming and smiled, wiping her hands on her apron as she moved toward the steps. The ringing of the phone made her hurry back inside.

"Nancy?" a gruff, unfamiliar, yet educated voice stated.

"I'm her Aunt Meg, and who might you be?"

"*Island and Sidney Review*, Walter Bohannan, ma'am."

"And your business, sir?"

"I would like to announce Nancy and Dan's wedding in our newspaper. I wonder if you could answer a few questions for me?"

Meg was thrilled, she was actually talking to the man who wrote the little newspaper Dan often brought to her. Its bits of Island information and gossip had kept her amused through many dark winter evenings.

"What is it you want to know?" she asked hesitantly.

"Nancy is twenty-one, how old is Dan?"

"He's twenty-nine."

"And they both live with you over there at Gordon Head?"

"No, sir. Me and their Uncle Jebediah live with them. They own this place."

"You mean they have been living together?" the voice snapped pompously.

"Of course we all live together."

"That's sinful, madam!"

Instant anger raced through Meg's mind.

"Do you know them, sir?" she snapped.

"Slightly, I met Nancy at the Resthaven Hospital and Dan calls here occasionally."

Totally engrossed in the phone call, Meg had forgotten the *Stockholm* and, unnoticed, the threesome in the doorway listened to the one-sided conversation.

"Then you're a stupid man, sir, and I hope your beard catches on fire!" the Scot hissed fiercely, slamming the phone down onto the hook.

Startled by their laughter, Meg turned around and they noticed she was red in the face.

"That's my girl," Jeb spluttered, "you set their damned beards on fire—that'll smarten 'em up!"

"Who in heaven's name were you talking to, Aunt Meg?" asked Nancy.

"It was that stupid newspaperman at Sidney!"

"Bohannan?" Dan frowned. "What did he want?"

"I don't want to talk about it," Meg exclaimed continuing to chunter away as she went out to the kitchen. "He's a stupid man."

Nancy followed her into the kitchen to calm her down and Jeb glanced over at Dan and raised his eyebrows.

"Well lad," he growled, nodding at the phone, "you or me?"

"I'll do it," Dan replied, reaching for the phone. He jiggled the hook a couple times to call the operator, then put the phone to his ear.

"That call we just had from Sidney," he said into the receiver, "can you reconnect us, Ruby?"

"Of course, Danny," Ruby Williamson, the local telephone operator, whispered, "just hold the line."

"*Island and Sidney Review*, Bohannan here," said the voice.

"It's Dan Brown, Mr. Bohannan, you were just talking to my Aunt Meg and I'd like to know what you said to her."

"I was going to report your wedding until I found out you and your fiancé are already living in sin!"

"What are you talking about? Is that what you said to my aunt?"

"Well, yes, I'm a God-fearing man you know."

"From now on you'd better be a Dan Brown fearing man too, Mr. Bohannan, because the next time I'm in Sidney, I shall stuff you into your printing machine!"

"Threats won't change the facts, boy."

"No, sir, they won't and you had better get yours right before you print a word about us."

"Then you explain it to me."

"Go to hell," Dan replied, grinning at Jeb who was listening from the doorway, as he also hung the phone up on the man.

Ruby Williamson clenched her teeth in annoyance. She had heard the conversations at her Tyndall Avenue station and felt a desperate need to put Mr. Bohannan straight. Nervously she made the connection, answering quickly when a voice came on the line.

"Mr. Bohannan, Nancy and Dan are good people and they're neighbours of ours. My mother says theirs is a love story that might have come out of a book. Please don't write bad things about them."

Unplugging the connection, Ruby breathed a sigh of relief and smiled, wiping a trickle of sweat from her forehead.

Meanwhile at Cunningham Manor, Nancy finally got Meg calmed down and they were all sitting around the table when she remembered something she wanted to ask her about.

"Are those tents over by the orchard, Aunt Meg?" she asked as her aunt handed her one of the dishes of food.

"Yes, I had the orchard men put them up when Harry came with the truckload of tables and chairs for the wedding," Meg explained. "Harry got them organized before he left. We thought it would be a good idea to put the tables and chairs inside the tents so they didn't get wet from the dew."

"I didn't realize we were having tents but I guess it's a good idea," Nancy murmured, the thought of rain making her cringe.

"It was Waldo suggested them, love," Jeb piped up, reading her mind. "He thought it would be a good idea to have them, so I told him to look after it. I think he was more concerned about the sun melting the wedding cake than rain!"

Nancy smiled gratefully. Her one fear was that they were going to forget something important and Waldo was always a step ahead of her or so it seemed. It had been like that since she first met him when she was a youngster.

After dinner the phone kept ringing as friends called offering their help and Nancy and Meg went over their lists checking on last-minute details.

"The wedding cake hasn't come has it, Aunt Meg?" Nancy asked in a worried tone as the time pushed on close to midnight.

"Kate's bringing it in the morning," replied her aunt. "Come on, lass, stop worrying, I want you to get to bed or you'll have dark circles under your eyes and that will never do!"

Moonlight bathed the clifftop as Nancy got ready for bed and finally slid between the sheets. Yawning, yet still wide awake, her mind raced toward her wedding day and the realization came to her that this time tomorrow night she would have Dan lying beside her. Hugging herself, she smiled in the darkness and lay quite still. She listened to the sound of the rustling trees and the faint calling of night-time creatures in the forest until sleep finally overtook her weary body.

Waking to Meg's gentle touch the next morning, her aunt sat down on the side of her bed and lovingly stroked the girl's soft hair. Voices in the garden were noisy with laughter as neighbours and friends, under Dan's direction, organized tables and set up chairs. The Williamson and Dunnett girls were talking and laughing with excitement in their voices as they helped Eva organize the table settings.

"It's really happening isn't it, Aunt Meg?" Nancy whispered sleepily, turning over and opening her eyes. "I can hardly believe it."

"Yes, dear, it is," Meg replied, kissing her forehead. "You'd better come down and have your breakfast, we have a bride to get ready, and 2 o'clock will come too fast."

"What time is it?" Nan asked, sitting up and stretching.

"It's eight-thirty. People started arriving soon after dawn! They seem to all want to be a part of your special day, lass."

"Oh my, you let me sleep so late and I have to wash my hair. I can't believe I didn't hear them," she exclaimed, suddenly panic-stricken. She jumped out of bed and went to the window. "Oh gracious, look at all the people! Aren't they wonderful."

"Calm down, lass, this is your day and they want to help make it special. Just come down when you're ready and no rushing is necessary," Meg assured her, quietly leaving and closing the door behind her.

Nancy dressed quickly and went to sit at her dresser looking at herself in the mirror. "It's my wedding day at last! I still can't believe that little girl at the orphanage is marrying that sweet boy who looked after her all those years at that horrible place," she whispered, hugging herself as tears came to her eyes. *Stop that*! she silently scolded herself, *no red eyes today*!

Leaning back, she ran her fingers through her long hair and smiled giddily. Picking up her brush she slowly brushed her hair, deep in thought then remembering she had to wash it she quickly stood up and went over to the washstand. Realizing Aunt Meg had brought her a pitcher of hot water, she poured some into the washbowl and added some cold from the other pitcher. Dropping her head into the water she carefully wet her hair and added the soap, being careful not to make a mess. When she finished she wrapped it in a towel and prepared to go downstairs. Realizing that wouldn't be a good idea with all the people about, she towelled it dry and ran a comb through it, yelping softly as the comb encountered a knot.

Eating breakfast proved to be quite a chore as the house was full of women and girls all eager to help. Men tramped in and out getting last-minute direction from Dan or Meg. The beer arrived in a Crystal Springs truck and Jack Duggan and two of the Parfitt boys were setting up the lectern they had borrowed from their church.

"I haven't seen Waldo, is he here?" Nancy asked Dan on one of his trips into the kitchen.

"You were still in bed when he arrived so he supervised getting the chairs set up for the ceremony and has gone home to change," Dan explained, giving her a hug and a quick kiss on the cheek. "Now, how's my beautiful bride-to-be feeling this morning?" he teased not waiting for a reply before going outside again.

Suddenly at 11 o'clock, things began to quiet down as people left for home. Everything that could be ready had been done, even the breeze dropped and a warm stillness enveloped the cliffside property.

Eva stayed for lunch, chattering like a school girl, teasing Jebediah when he asked Meg for a pack of sandwiches.

"Are you leaving home?" she called after him as he went outside with his package.

"Come watch him, Eva," Meg invited mischievously. "You'll be surprised."

Following the Scottish woman onto the porch, Eva stood and watched as Jeb wove his way through the tables and out past the orchard. He stopped just inside the tree line and sent a shrill whistle out to the forest.

"He's got a pet bear," Eva giggled. "I hope it's not dangerous."

"Hush child and watch," Meg whispered.

A movement in the trees caused Eva to take a step closer to Meg as Sam and his dog appeared.

"It's Sam," she said with surprise in her voice, "and they're talking! He hardly ever says a word to anyone, how does Jeb do it?"

"Jeb's feeding him, lass, he's been watching out for him ever since we moved here."

"Well I'll be darned and I never knew."

"My goodness, it's time Jeb and I got dressed for this 'do'," Meg exclaimed. "Jeb!" she called to him. "Come and get dressed, guests will be arriving soon and we need to be ready."

"When Jeb reached the porch, he glowered at her. "I thought I was dressed!"

"You get yourself upstairs and into that new suit we got you. You won't be giving away the bride looking like a hermit!" Meg declared.

He winked at Eva and they disappeared into the house.

"The Jorgensens are here!" Dan called from the porch half an hour later.

"Wonderful!" Nancy exclaimed, giving her almost-dry locks a shake.

They all watched as the big red-and-gold Jorgensen Company launch entered the cove. Behind it came the familiar US Coast Guard cutter. Dan went down to the dock to greet them and, with help from two of the ensigns, Bill and his wheelchair quickly arrived at the top of the stairs. Nan went over to hug him but they were interrupted by Beth's joyful shout from below.

"Nancy, we brought everyone!" she exclaimed, reaching the top of the stairs. Stopping to get her breath, she greeted Meg and Eva with hugs and turned to Nancy who noticed there were tears in her eyes. "Well, honey, how does it feel?"

Suddenly overcome with emotion, Nan could only hug her.

"Oh sweetie, I'm sorry, let's not have any red eyes," Beth exclaimed, putting her arm around the girl. Leading her away from the group they walked toward the house. "Look at this place, what a perfect setting. It looks marvellous! You've all been busy this morning."

"Not me! Aunt Meg let me sleep in while an army of people arrived, close to dawn, I was told. I slept right through it!"

"We have such wonderful friends and neighbours," Dan mused, coming up behind them. "Look at all these people, Nan, it's unbelievable!"

At that moment, Nellie Cornish, Bertha Landes and her husband, James Moore, and Capt. Gray arrived at the top of the stairs waving and shouting their greetings. Bringing up the rear was Terry O'Reilly, helping Seattle Mayor, George Cotterill, and his wife, and Tom Wills, looking surprisingly splendid in a new suit.

"Time to get dressed you two," Meg suggested, finding Nancy and Dan standing together. "Jeb, come over here and introduce everybody to Eva; I have a bride to get ready. Dan won't take long and he'll be back to help you."

"And I'm going to help, too," added Beth, taking Nan's arm and easing her gently away from the well-wishers as another car drove in and tooted its horn.

It was Jack and Nellie Duggan with the Parfitt boys and their wives, but Nancy, Dan, Beth and Meg had already disappeared into the house. More cars began arriving and Jeb was so busy with his introductions he hadn't noticed Chaplain Jordan, in full military uniform, limp across the lawn until he was standing on the edge of the group.

Moving quickly to intercept the unfamiliar military man, Jeb's eyes flashed with suspicion.

"They're not going to spoil Nancy's day," he muttered to himself.

"Hello," Chaplain Jordan smiled disarmingly at the fierce-looking old man approaching him. "I'm the chaplain. I believe I have a wedding to perform."

"Chaplain Jordan!" Eva exclaimed, rushing over to welcome him, saving Jebediah from his embarrassment. "Are you officiating?"

"Take care of it, Eva," Jeb muttered, backing quickly away.

Above the chatter of many voices, the sounds of a piano suddenly floated across the lawn. The Parfitts had brought the piano out onto the porch and coaxed Nellie into playing a medley of popular songs. To the pianist's amazement, the Parfitt boys' delightful voices led the singing and soon everyone was joining in.

"Oh listen to them, Aunt Meg," Nancy sighed, sitting at her dressing table in her new lace-trimmed undergarments and applying Nivea cold cream to her face. "Doesn't that sound wonderful?"

"A perfect beginning for the wedding of a perfect couple," Beth whispered emotionally, brushing Nancy's hair.

After about half an hour, the music suddenly stopped and Nancy, just having stepped into her dress, went to look out the window. Dan, looking terribly handsome in his army uniform was talking with the chaplain near the lectern.

"They're ready, I have to go!" Nan declared, feeling her first touch of panic.

"There's no rush, honey, they'll wait. Now keep still while I get these buttons done up," Beth chided. "The bride is always allowed to be fashionably late, another few minutes isn't going to matter in the least!" Beth twisted the last tiny button through the buttonhole and hugged her affectionately. "There, now put your hat on, dear."

With trembling hands Nancy sat down in front of the mirror and picked up her little white hat with its multi-layers of fabric forming a shoulder-length veil. Meg, holding two large hatpins, attempted to stabilize it.

"Keep still, lass, I don't want to stick you!" her aunt exclaimed.

"There, you're ready, Nancy!" Beth declared. "Take a deep breath and let's look at you, dear."

Chapter 9

Jebediah, waiting in the hall, went over to the stairs when he heard the sound of a door open and listened as excited women's voices drifted down the stairway. Nancy appeared on the upstairs landing and he caught his breath. As she moved slowly down the stairway, her red hair sparkled against the whiteness of her calf-length satin-and-lace wedding dress. Unashamedly, Jebediah wiped a tear away and held out his hand to her.

"You're a beauty, little lady! I'm so danged proud of you," he exclaimed, shaking his head and smiling broadly.

"Ooh, don't you look handsome in your new suit, Uncle Jeb!" Nancy said softly, as a nervous excitement enveloped her.

"Give us time to get to our places," Meg murmured as she and Beth squeezed by them. "I want to see you walk every step of the way, lassie."

Beth stopped, remembering something, and went back up the stairs to stand over Nan gently taking her veil and lifting several layers to cover her face. She gave Nan a quick kiss on the cheek as she passed her on the way outside. The chattering of guests settled to a low murmur as Meg and Beth walked down the centre aisle to their seats near the lectern. Through the partially open doorway, Nancy could see Dan and Jack, his best man, waiting with their backs toward the house.

Whispers rippled through the gathering as the house door opened and Jebediah stepped outside winking to Nellie, at the piano. This was her signal and, through a sudden rush of emotion, she began to play the wedding march. A loud sigh rose from the waiting guests as Jeb extended his hand and Nancy appeared framed in the doorway. Taking Jebediah's arm, she noticed Nellie wink as she took her first step toward the stairs.

As Nancy and Jebediah walked slowly down the stairs and onto the lawn, Eliza Marshall, owner of the Gorge Hotel, reached out and tucked a silk handkerchief into her hand.

"Something borrowed, my dear. God bless you both," she whispered.

Holding tightly to Jebediah's arm, Nancy forced her feet to keep walking as uncontrollable tears began to fall under cover of her veil. Her dream was only ten strides away from reality. When they reached the front, Jeb left her standing beside Dan and went to sit next to Meg.

Nancy looked up at Dan and tried to smile knowing he wouldn't be able to see her clearly, but the events were slowly taking their toll. As the ceremony proceeded, she hardly heard the chaplain's words, whispering '*I do*' when he prompted her. She was only aware of Dan's gentle touch as he slipped the wedding ring onto her finger. Hearing Chaplain Jordan's voice loudly boom out, '*I pronounce you man and wife*,' finally brought her back to reality before hearing his next comment.

"You may kiss the bride!" gave Dan the permission he needed. Oblivious to the loud cheers and the sound of foghorns rattling through the still afternoon air from the Jorgensen launch and the coast guard cutter, he smiled and lifted her veil, taking his bride lovingly into his arms. Finally, the dream had come true.

Noisy congratulations were shouted from every corner of the garden. A second cheer erupted when Kate appeared on the porch with the tall wedding cake, carrying it over to one of the tents. Harry Maynard and Eliza Marshall organized the illegal bar tent and soon the ladies were sipping on wine and men's beer glasses clinked noisily.

Now totally composed, Nancy made sure they personally thanked all the guests and it wasn't long before Dan cheerfully admitted that his body ached as a result of the shaking of hands and back-slapping.

"It's all right, honey," she assured him with a giggle, "I think we've been around to say hello to everyone. Let's escape for a bit."

Arm-in-arm they started out the driveway and over near the cars, quietly sitting on a tree stump, they found old Tom Irvine sipping on a beer, dutifully watched over by Nancy's Indian friend, Billy. Billy and his sister had often visited her through the orphanage fence sharing food with her. They were her first friends, other than Danny, and she always remembered their kindness. Bending over, she kissed the old farmer on the cheek.

"Holy bedoodle Billy, lad," he chuckled, "that's the first kiss I've had in 50 years!"

Laughing, they moved on toward the orchard but a shout interrupted them from the porch and they saw Waldo standing with his arms raised trying to get everyone's attention.

"We need to cut the cake before it melts!" he chuckled. "So fill your glasses and get your cameras ready folks; I'm going to propose a toast to the bride and groom, if I can find them!"

"I guess he means us, my wife," teased Dan, putting his arm around her waist and kissing her. "We'd best be getting back."

Moving off toward the house, they made their way over to the cake tent where a crowd was gathering—many with Kodak Brownie cameras in hand. Kate got the newlyweds placed behind the cake, knife in hand, and explained how she wanted them to perform the ritual cutting.

"Are we all ready?" Waldo asked and, receiving a nod from Kate, he turned toward the guests. "Friends, let's raise our glasses to the finest young couple ...," he paused, bowing his head as emotion suddenly gripped him. Taking a deep breath, he raised his head and continued, "… to the finest young couple on Vancouver Island. To a long and happy life together."

Everyone raised their glasses, some clinking them with their neighbours before taking a sip. A loud cheer rose as they waited for Nancy and Dan to cut the cake.

"You can cut it now," Katherine urged from the sideline, noticing a number of cameras being focused on the couple, "both your hands on the knife, please."

Cameras clicked as the couple solemnly cut the first piece of cake then, obeying the taunts from the crowd, kissed each other playfully with Nancy blushing as usual.

All afternoon the garden at Cunningham Manor rang with laughter and the hungry guests devoured plate after plate of food. Finally at 5 o'clock, the air began cooling down as a breeze came off the water and some of the guests said their goodbyes walking away down the drive or leaving in their cars.

Eliza came over to say goodbye, telling them her ride home was ready to leave.

"How did you get here?" Dan asked, "I can take you home."

"Oh, Dan, you can't leave," she laughed. "I'm with Tom and Billy."

"You risked your life with Billy driving?" Nancy giggled.

"Oh, it wasn't too bad, I took Tom's advice and kept my eyes shut most of the time!" she laughed, giving them each a hug as the men came over to collect her and say their own 'good-byes.'

"I haven't seen Jeb or the Jorgensen boys for quite awhile," Dan muttered, glancing around when they were alone again.

"They were talking to some of the men over by the orchard. I suspect they're waiting for Tom and Billy to leave," Nancy replied, giggling as she turned to face that direction.

"Who's that stranger with them? I don't recognize him from here."

"I don't know, let's go see," she replied, taking his arm.

As they walked toward the group, Meg came up beside them. As they got closer, Dan whispered, "That's Bohannan from the *Sidney Review*."

"Oh, is it?" Meg hissed loudly. "Well, I'll soon give him a piece of my mind!"

As she spoke, Bohannan turned around and saw them.

"Please accept my apologies, Mrs. MacDonald," the Sidney newspaper man boomed, going toward her with hand outstretched. "I didn't quite understand the situation, but your husband has put me right."

"Well, Mr. Whoever-you-are, for your information, Jebediah Judd is not my husband and I'm a Miss not a Mrs.!" The Scot glowered at the man while collecting her thoughts, then continued her roasting. "I think you make too many stupid assumptions, Mr. Newspaperman. I'd be surprised if your paper has any truth in it at all!"

"Easy, old girl," Jeb whispered, coming up beside her, "the man tried to apologize."

"Don't you 'easy' me, Jebediah Judd—you were ready to shoot him last night!"

Unnoticed, Tom Wills heard the commotion and came over to see what was happening. "Would it help," he asked, "if I gave him a copy of my write-up about the wedding?"

"And who are you?" Bohannan snapped.

"Tom Wills, *Seattle Observer*."

"I write my own columns!" Bohannan exclaimed.

"Suit yourself, I just thought your readers might enjoy reading a pro for a change," Tom continued sarcastically.

"You cheeky ...," the Sidney editor began, cringing when Jebediah stepped between them.

"Stop right there, Mr. Bohannan! You will accept this man's offer or I'll be calling at your office with my shotgun!"

With the blood draining from his face, W. H. Bohannan backed away mumbling incoherently and stumbling in his sudden eagerness to leave.

"Thank you, Mr. Judd," Meg purred, winking at him as she went to join the remaining guests.

"Wow!" laughed Bill Jorgensen, "I'll bet in your younger days you would have done it, Jebediah!"

"Don't you ever chance it, son," the old detective growled over his shoulder, going after Meg.

"He means it," Bill commented to the others. "I'd hate to get that old codger mad at me!"

"Have you boys seen our orchard?" Dan asked, changing the subject.

"Yes, we've seen everything," Chris replied with a broad smile. "We even walked down Ash Road to the bridge. This is such a lovely area and so many farms. No wonder you like it so much."

As they made their way back toward the house, the newlyweds watched the Parfitt brothers move the piano back inside. Out on the lawn, amazingly everything had already been dismantled and Eva was giving directions. Jack Duggan and Waldo were stacking and loading the borrowed tables and chairs into one of the trucks and the Parfitts now joined them. The rest of the men were keeping out of the way gathered by the stairs on the clifftop but the women had disappeared.

"Why don't you go join them, honey," Nancy suggested squeezing Dan's hand. "I'll go find the ladies."

"We're even now," Kate giggled when Nancy came into the house.

"Even?" asked Nan, frowning.

"We're both married women now!"

"It only seems like yesterday when we first met you, Nancy," commented Millie Maynard. "Jack and Nellie brought you over to our house. Do you remember?"

"The Joyce brothers introduced us," added Nellie Duggan. "We knew then you were meant for each other. In fact, Danny even said so that night—he just didn't realize it was in a marrying way!" she giggled.

"I heard all about you from Waldo," Margaret Skillings chuckled. "He could never stop talking about his red haired waitress. Of course, she was just a youngster then, working for George Dunn at the Occidental."

"Oh my, you all have such good memories," laughed Nancy, blushing at their comments.

"Do you remember how we met you and Dan on a streetcar after visiting the Gorge Park?" asked Beth. "We were enchanted by your devotion to each other. Danny was so protective of his little sister."

This brought a whoop of laughter from the ladies and Nancy blushed again.

"More tea, anybody?" Eva chuckled, bringing the teapot to the table. "I'm just a neighbour from up the hill on Ash Road, but seeing as you're reminiscing I can tell you it was this awful war that brought us together. Our men were in the forces overseas," she paused for a moment and added sadly, "mine still is."

"Yes, I'll take a little more tea, please Eva," said Kate holding out her cup and saucer. "Nan was my boss when I started working in Victoria. I came from Seattle to look after my grandparents and got a job at the Balmoral Hotel. She introduced me to my husband, Jack." She paused to giggle at a memory.

"Tell us what the joke is, Kate," Eva prodded filling her teacup.

"Don't you go telling tales on me, Kate Dumpford," Nancy warned her. "You're all embarrassing me!"

"Oh, now we really want to know," Eva teased, causing Nancy to sit down and cover her face with her hands. "Come on, out with it, girl!"

"Oh, she used to bully Harry Tabour, our boss who was the hotel manager," continued Kate. "It was so funny how sheepish-looking he got when she attacked him but she was very protective of him too, and kept him from getting fired several times."

"Nancy wouldn't attack anybody, would you love?" Millie interrupted glancing over at the bride.

"She ran that place like clockwork," Kate elaborated. "She kept everybody in their place and was the best friend I ever had … and still is," she paused to look up at Nan and make a face. "Jack and I owe everything to Dan and Nancy."

Nancy got up and went over to Kate and hugged her. "Dear Kate, you've always been there for me, too."

The others could see that the girls were getting emotional about their special friendship and Meg quickly jumped into the conversation.

"Girls, girls, no tears, this is a happy day," she gently rebuked them.

"Well, if we're reminiscing about happy times," Mrs. Cotterill murmured, "we met Nancy at the James Moore Theatre the first time she sang there. Just like Hattie Rhodes, we fell in love with her instantly and we love that red hair!"

"That's right," Hattie laughed, "and that voice of yours is such a special gift, Nancy. I hope you will never stop using it to entertain us."

"Seems like I'm last," Nellie Cornish sighed as she watched Nancy blush. "I met our Nancy at the Jorgensen's before any of the concerts. As a music teacher and singing coach, I was struggling to keep my school open, existing on charity and handouts. She changed my life from the moment I heard her sing and, just like Kate, she's a very special friend."

Meg took Nancy's hand and pulled her gently onto her knee, straightening her wedding dress before folding her arms around her lovingly.

"The truth of it is, ladies, this is my little girl," she whispered looking around at the serious-looking group.

"Whatever's wrong?" came a voice from the doorway as Dan entered and found everyone wiping their eyes.

"Oh, go away, Danny. You wouldn't understand. You're a man," Eva snivelled.

Retreating back outside, Jeb watched him approach. "They didn't want you in there, did they, lad?" he chuckled.

"They're all sitting around crying," Dan exclaimed, shaking his head.

"They're happy tears, lad," Waldo growled, "but I don't suppose you'd know the difference yet."

Loud laughter followed the haulier's observation as Chris pushed his brother's wheelchair closer to Dan.

"Don't pay no heed to these old coots, Dan," Chris chuckled. "Me and Billy will keep you straight."

"The blind leading the blind!" their father added, glancing down at the dock below. "Here comes John Gray, it's probably time he was leaving."

Followed by two crew members, Capt. Gray came bounding up the steep cliff stairs, two at a time. "Sorry Dan, but it's time we were leaving. I'll just go say goodbye to Nancy, then we're off. If you need a hand with the wheelchair, Mr. Jorgensen, my men will help you down to the dock."

"Tell the girls we're leaving, too, will you Danny?" Gus called, watching Dan head toward the house again.

As the Americans prepared for their departure, Dan and Nancy were overwhelmed by their displays of affection and best wishes until finally the Jorgensen party were all down at the launch and ready for leaving. Off to one side, Meg and Jeb quietly held hands, congratulating each other that the day had been such a success. Horns blared below, signalling the ships' exit as they backed out of the cove and turned for home with everyone on deck waving frantically.

As the newlyweds stood arm-in-arm alone on the clifftop watching their friends get smaller and smaller they, in turn, looked like tiny dolls to the several pair of binoculars watching from the Jorgensen launch.

The breeze suddenly changed direction blowing Nancy's long hair and swirling it about her shoulders. Dan looked at her with a sly smile, took her in his arms and, brushing the hair away from her face, kissed her tenderly.

"My goodness, I almost forgot, we still have presents to open," she exclaimed as they walked back to the house, "and everyone has gone!"

She took his arm and tugged him toward the house. When they reached the porch, Dan suddenly bent down and picked her up in his arms. She screamed and Meg and Jeb came up behind them, laughing when they saw what was happening. Dan stopped in the doorway and kissed his bride before carrying her over the threshold.

"Another of those old traditions, I assume!" laughed Nancy, as he set her back down on the floor.

"We have presents to unwrap," Nancy declared.

"You can unwrap the presents after we've tended to the cleaning up—I don't want it waiting for me tomorrow. You should change your clothes first," Meg suggested.

"Thank goodness!" Dan exclaimed, taking the stairs two at a time. Reaching his room, he stopped suddenly. The wardrobe and some of his dresser drawers were partly open and he could see they were empty.

"Hey, who's been in here?" he called.

"You don't live there anymore, Mr. Brown!" he heard Nancy giggle.

Smiling wryly, he turned around and saw her standing behind him. At that moment, with the light from the hall illuminating her, he thought he had never seen her more beautiful. Taking three quick strides toward her, he swept her into his arms again and carried his giggling bride into their bedroom kicking the door shut with his boot.

"I love you, Nan," he whispered, dropping her onto the bed and laying down beside her. He stroked her cheek and kissed her gently.

She returned his kiss and hugged him quickly. "Then help me out of this dress, husband!" she murmured into his ear. "We've one heck of a job to finish downstairs!"

Dan turned over laying on his back and watched Nancy struggle to her feet and turn her back to him.

"Well!" she teased. "I can't undo these buttons by myself."

Realizing she was serious, he sat up on the edge of the bed and looked at the row of tiny white buttons running down the back of her dress.

"You've got to be kidding, Nan!" he declared as his fingers fumbled with the top button. "These tiny things certainly weren't designed with a man's fingers in mind!" Before long, he figured out a system and finally succeeded with his task.

Nancy dropped her dress to the floor, stepping out of it and standing in her petticoat. Bending over to pick up the dress, they bumped into each other; laughing and blushing, they searched for where Meg had put their clothes. Dan finally found his shirt and Nancy giggled again as she complained of having to share her closet.

Dishes rattled in the kitchen as they came down the stairs. With everyone helping, they finished the cleanup and were surprised when they found it was almost 10 o'clock. Mutually they decided to leave the present unwrapping until the next day. Finally collapsing on comfortable chairs in the living room, Jebediah produced a bottle of high-quality wine.

"I think we should drink a private toast," he announced, somberly filling four glasses. "This has been the best day of my life and I just want to thank you all for allowing me to be part of this family. May you two youngsters always be as happy as you are today."

"Ach, you silly man," Meg whispered, "diya not know we love you!"

"Drink!"

"Now, you two get off to bed," she chuckled, "and I'll try to talk some sense into this old man."

The next morning as sun streamed through the curtains, Nancy awoke and thinking it was still early, lay in bed with her eyes closed. Thoughts were going through her head about the wedding and how wonderful it was to be Mrs. Dan Brown when she sensed something and opened her eyes—Dan was leaning over her about to kiss her. She giggled and kissed him back reaching up to hug him but instead pulled him down on top of her.

"You're dressed!" she exclaimed between his kisses. "What time is it, Danny?"

"It's 9 o'clock, you sleepy head. I just had to get up. I'm not used to sleeping in late," he said defensively, kissing her on the nose and pushing himself onto his feet.

"I think I'll like being Mrs. Brown if you let me sleep in like this. I feel like a lady of leisure. I didn't realize I was so tired."

"Don't forget we still have presents to unwrap. Aunt Meg is wondering where we are going to put them all. You'd better come down or she's sure to be on the warpath, Nan. She wants to finish up with breakfast."

"Tell her I'll just be a few minutes," Nancy replied, throwing back the covers. Swinging her legs over the side of the bed, she modestly pulled her nightie down to cover her legs.

Dan leaned against the closed door, his arms crossed over his chest as he watched her, a smile curling his lips.

"And what do you think you're doing, Dan Brown? I'm not going to dress with you standing there gawking!" she retorted, standing up and obstinately placing her hands on her hips looking like a dishevelled child with her mussed hair hanging about in all directions.

Dan smiled even more and began to laugh causing her to blush. Frowning fiercely at him she went over and tried to reach behind him for the doorknob but he wrapped his arms around her and held her tightly.

"Nan, is it as hard for you as it is for me, to believe this is really happening? We've known each other for so long, I just ...," he said softly, his voice trailing off as he nestled his head in her hair.

She reached up and touched his face looking into his eyes.

"Want to pinch myself?" she asked softly, finishing his sentence.

"Something like that," he replied, pressing his body against hers and kissing her in a way he had not done before.

Is this what happens when you're married? thought Nancy. *I just don't want to let him go.*

Suddenly, Dan broke away from her, kissing her once more on the forehead and opening the door.

"You'd better get dressed, honey, I'll wait for you downstairs."

She stood watching him go, then closed the door, and sat down quickly on the edge of the bed. Her heart was beating so fast she thought she was going to faint. In a minute she sighed and stood up. *Come on Nan, you have things to do. Just because you're a married lady doesn't mean you can laze about all day*!

Later that morning, Jeb lit a small fire in the living room and they all gathered for the present unwrapping. One by one, Meg chose a parcel from the piles on the floor and table and handed it to Nancy and Dan, but it soon became evident that this would take too long.

"I think you'd better give them both a parcel, Meg, or we're going to be here all day!" Jeb suggested.

"Good idea," Dan agreed, selecting a parcel for himself. "We'll just have to speed it up if we want to have lunch sometime today!"

With Meg writing a list of the presents in her book, so they knew who had given them each gift, they soon had a heaping pile of empty boxes and torn paper all over the floor. Jeb soon realized this would be his job and began throwing it into the fire. Towels, feather pillows, sheets and all manner of kitchen utensils were oohed and aahed over until Meg, smiling coyly, finally handed them the last parcel—a large, heavy box.

"To our special children," Nan read from the small attached card, a lump forming in her throat as she looked tearfully up at Dan.

"Well, open it, girl!" Jeb encouraged.

"You do it, Dan, it's so heavy, I can't imagine what it is," she exclaimed.

"No, we'll do this together, honey," he said solemnly, getting the feeling this box contained something very special.

As they slowly tore the paper off and opened the box, Nancy let out a squeal.

"A phonograph!" she screamed, "Oh my gosh, Danny, we'll be able to listen to my records. Thank you! Thank you!" Jumping up she went over to Meg and almost bowled her over with a hug.

"Och, that was the general idea, lassie!" Meg announced, very pleased with Nan's reaction.

Nancy next went and gave Jeb a hug. "What a perfect gift from two perfect parents. Thank you both," she said through her tears.

"You're very welcome, lassie, we want to have lots of music and laughter in this house," said Meg.

"Don't thank me, it was all Meg's doing, honey. She got it before I even knew about it. I never did find out how she did it."

"All I had to do was phone Waldo and he looked after it for me!" Meg laughed. "We did a good job of keeping it a secret, didn't we?"

"You sure did," Dan agreed, standing up and stretching. "Now, I don't know about you all, but I'm famished. Opening all these wonderful presents has exhausted me. I find it a bit overwhelming so many people that we barely know took the time and effort …."

"And spent all this money in such hard times … on us!" Nancy said softly, tears welling in her eyes again.

"It just shows you what these people think of you, Nan," said Dan, taking her in his arms.

"People want you to be happy, lassie. You've done so much to bring happiness into so many people's lives and they love you too, Danny. Your love story has touched far more people than you realize," Meg added.

"Well, I don't know much about love stories, except we should be hearing the sound of little feet one day and that would really make your aunt and I happy!" said Jeb, looking a bit sheepish.

Nancy blushed and Dan began to laugh, not saying a word but holding her tightly as he looked into her eyes.

Chapter 10

Married life suited Dan and Nancy, quickly settling back into their grinding workload. Money for the widows and orphans was scarce since the cancellation of her Seattle concerts and hospital ships were still regularly depositing their cargo of human suffering on Victoria's docks. War news continued to fill the newspapers reporting that although the enemy was in full retreat, the heartache and suffering remained.

By the middle of May, General Greene thankfully recovered from his bout of influenza and he managed to keep Gus informed of the epidemic's relentless progress through Washington State and other areas. By the end of June, as several of his soldiers came down with the disease, he grew very frustrated with the slow speed in finding a cure.

It was early in July when Gus announced he acquired shares in a recording company and Nancy went back to Seattle to make her first recording under a real contract with Nellie at the piano. Tom Wills continued his interest in Nancy's singing, finding them national coverage through his newspaper column, which created an instant demand sparking remarkable interest and healthy sales despite the health crisis.

Later in the month, Nancy was at the restaurant when Kate made a startling announcement.

"I want to help you with your charity work, Nan. I really need to feel that I am doing something useful other than running the restaurant and I know the workload has been getting too much for both you and Eva. You're working so hard but you are doing a remarkable amount of good for these poor people. Please let me help," she pleaded.

"Oh Kate, how thoughtful of you. Of course you can help us, we'd be grateful for any time you can fit in and it does give us a feeling of doing something in these troubled times. The restaurant is running so well now and Linda is quite capable of looking after things in our absence," Nancy assured her.

So it was agreed Kate would start as soon as they could set up a new schedule both for the charity work and the restaurant. No further contact was made with Tom Wills throughout August and they heard he had gone to Chicago on assignment. Then, in early September, the sad news arrived through the Jorgensens that disaster had struck and Tom had sadly succumbed to the flu without returning to Seattle. The speed at which this disease took the life of the young reporter who had become such a friend hit Nancy hard and a new feeling of intrepidation began to consume her. Jeb decided to keep a more careful watch on his family making sure they and, Nancy in particular, took their daily dose of tonic.

By mid-September, Seattle newspapers ran a story announcing they were in the midst of a nightmare as the 13th case of influenza was confirmed from the outer suburbs. General Greene locked down Camp Lewis in an all-embracing quarantine and union trouble erupted on the Seattle waterfront. The city was shut down and they prepared to face the rampaging epidemic alone.

In Victoria, Dr. Price fought long and hard with city council making frenzied preparations for the inevitable. As a regular customer at the *Wounded Soldier Restaurant*, he constantly complained about the lax mentality of the city councillors.

Bill Jorgensen, meanwhile, had taken over the task of watching out for Nancy and Nellie's interests, becoming their agent and assuring them that the recording company lived up to its contract. Nancy's records were now producing a nice income from royalties, easing the ever-growing financial burden of her charity work. The numbers of families requiring assistance had grown substantially as the war continued, often over-extending both she and Eva to the point of exhaustion.

On the 9th of October, it came as no surprise to Nancy and Kate and, of course, many throughout the city, when Dr. Price convinced city council to take drastic precautions, shutting the Canadian city down. Businessmen and church ministers were very upset when these far-reaching restrictions were finally announced, also closing theatres, churches, and schools. Gatherings were limited to nine people causing the girls to close the restaurant once again, this time officially and, sadly, for an unknown period of time.

Vancouver reported rising death figures reeling under the shock of the first published casualties from the dreaded epidemic. Fear raced through Victoria's streets as masked citizens scrambled to buy herbal cures. Jeb found the situation taking care of itself as worry caused their friends, for the most part, to take his special tonic, swearing it was keeping them safe.

The waterfront buzzed with rumours and wild stories of hundreds of deaths in prairie towns. Miners from Northern Canada travelled southward hoping city doctors had found a cure. When Jack returned from Sooke, reporting the little town up the coast had discovered their first case of influenza, renewed fear spread quickly. It was here,and the fight for survival now began in earnest.

Hearing the news, Jebediah jumped into his car and hurried off to Shotbolt's. Sick with worry, he took delivery of ten more cases of his tonic, startling the clerk when he ordered still more. Over the next few days he handed out bottles to the Dumpfords, Eva Todd, and several neighbours.

Dan's deliveries took him to Maple Bay, Ladysmith and Nanaimo, where he found ample evidence of a rampaging disease. Death and sickness were everywhere and no one appeared safe from the deadly malady. Although he wore a mask when meeting people, he was becoming fearful to travel. Not wanting to worry Nancy anymore than necessary he decided not to say anything for the time being.

Adding to the city's despair, on Friday the 25th of October, Fred Barrett, the senior clerk at the harbour master's office, informed the waterfront workers that the Canadian Pacific Steamer *Princess Sophia* had gone down in a storm after striking a reef in Lyn Canal near Juneau, Alaska, losing all 343 of its passengers and crew.

"Damn!" Dan barked emotionally, kicking angrily at a mooring ring after hearing the sad news. "I knew Capt. Locke and his crew, they were good men."

"We all knew them, lad," Fred added with a sigh. "You be careful out there; the weather forecast is warning of another storm."

Newspapers quoted Victoria health officials calling desperately for volunteers to help—hospitals were full and volunteers needed. Eva now worked night and day at her Red Cross duties and having no transportation often slept in town leaving Nancy and Kate to take care of the charity.

Worry was also a daily occurrence for Meg watching Nancy's blue truck go up the drive each morning, fearful of what the day would bring. Many evenings, Nancy broke down and cried while relating heartbreaking stories from the families she was visiting. More often now, she didn't dare enter their houses so she would slip their envelope under the door or put it in the mailbox. The situation was definitely getting worse.

On Monday the 28th of October, a new panic set in when Kate collapsed after visiting one of her widow ladies. Jeb took the call at the office and immediately got on the phone to Waldo.

"I just got word that Kate has collapsed over on Duchess Street and been taken to the hospital. Both the lads are out on deliveries and I need somebody to find Nancy," the old detective's voice pleaded.

"Leave it to me," the haulier growled, putting the phone down and hurrying away to alert his drivers. "We'll find her," he muttered hopefully.

In no time, all the waterfront companies were involved—their delivery trucks searching the streets for Nancy's truck. A Hudson Bay driver spotted the vehicle on Cook Street and delivered Jeb's message.

"Oh no," she whispered on hearing the news, her knees suddenly feeling weak and her mouth going dry. "Have they taken her to the hospital?"

"Don't know, miss," the driver admitted. "The message came from Waldo Skillings."

Quickly completing her business with a grieving young widow and her youngster, she left money for food and rent and left quickly for the office. Tearing down Fort Street, she panicked a streetcar driver by cutting in front of him and almost ran a pedestrian over as she pushed her way into the Wharf Street traffic. Turning off at the narrow entrance to the dock, she bounced the truck down the washboard hill and onto the Brown and Wilson dock.

"She's at the fire hall in Kingston Street," Jeb called, rushing out to meet her.

"The fire hall's empty!" Nancy gasped. "Are you sure Uncle Jeb?"

"Yes, just go!"

Turning around, she drove back up to Wharf Street, breathing a sigh of relief when Waldo calmly walked into the street and stopped the traffic, holding it up until she was safely onto the road.

"She can't be at the fire hall," she muttered to herself crossing the causeway in front of the Empress Hotel and taking a sharp right onto Belleville. "That place has been empty for months."

As she approached, she was surprised to see a number of city trucks lining the street in front of the old fire hall. Two city workmen came running toward her trying to wave her away.

"YOU CAN'T LEAVE IT THERE, MISS," one of the men shouted officiously.

"YES SHE CAN!" Dr. Price yelled from the doorway. "We have Kate in here, Nancy," he told her when she got out of the truck.

Pulse racing as she imagined the worst, Nancy raced into the fire hall to find beds being set up in long rows. Then she noticed several men standing near a bed in the corner.

"Hold it, young lady," said Dr. Price hurrying to block her way. 'I need a word with you first."

"How bad is she?" Nancy asked, trying to step around him.

"Stand still, Nancy!" Dr. Price snapped.

"Get out of my way!" she cried, giving him a push that set him off balance, her panic-stricken eyes darting around the room totally oblivious to his plight.

Finding himself suddenly sitting on the floor, he scowled angrily as she marched off to see her friend. Brushing away a workman's helping hand, he quickly struggled to his feet and charged after her.

"Has she got the flu?" Nancy demanded of one of the white-coated men standing at Kate's bed, pushing her way through and taking her friend into her arms.

"If she had, you'd both have it by now, foolish woman!" Dr. Price retorted angrily, coming up behind her.

"I'm sorry, Nan," Kate whispered. "I don't know what happened."

"Hush now, we'll soon have you better," Nancy gently consoled her, noting how pale and helpless she appeared.

"Mrs. Brown!" Dr. Price snapped, roughly grasping Nancy's arm and angrily pulling her to her feet. "Will you please listen to me?"

"Take your hands off that girl!" a gruff voice ordered from behind them. "What is going on here?"

Swinging around to face his aggressor, Arthur Price could barely control his temper as he shouted at the well-known haulier, Waldo Skillings.

"All I'm trying to do, sir, is tell her Mrs. Dumpford is fatigued, worn out, and needing bed rest. This is a very dangerous situation and Mrs. Brown appears not to be aware of that."

"You mean she really doesn't have the flu?" Nancy whispered suddenly feeling very tired and a bit embarrassed.

"No, she doesn't! Now would you please take her with you and leave me to get on with my work. I am turning this place into a hospital as the situation is getting out of control in the city and we're running out of space in other facilities."

"I have my car, Nan," Waldo said quietly as the doctor left them. "We figured you'd get yourself into some sort of trouble!"

"Who's we?" she demanded, trying to keep her mind focused.

"Fred, your Uncle Jeb and me."

With assistance, they got Kate up and slowly walked her out to Waldo's car, settling her on the back seat of the big Ford and wrapping her in a blanket. She whispered something to Nancy and handed her friend her purse.

"Where do you want me to take her, Nan?" the haulier asked.

Nancy closed the car door and leaned against the vehicle, catching her breath and shielding her eyes from the sun.

"Take her out to Cunningham Manor, would you please Waldo. Aunt Meg'll take care of her for a day or two."

"Are you all right?" he asked with a worried frown, watching her nod. "Are you going to come with us?"

"No, I'll phone Aunt Meg from the office and tell her you're coming. I need to make Kate's last call."

"Next news, you'll be going down," Waldo grumbled as he opened his car door and began to climb in.

"Mr. Skillings," Nancy retorted, smiling impishly despite her weariness, "how long have you been watching out for me?"

"I'm not watching out for you!" he muttered defensively, puffing hard on his pipe. "You've been a blasted thorn in my side since you were barely 13 and worked at the Occidental."

Feigning hurt, she replied, "I had no idea I was so much trouble."

From the back seat she heard a weak giggle.

"Trouble, girl?" Waldo declared, his voice rising as he watched her walk back to the truck. "Why, if I'd been a younger man, and free, I would have given Dan Brown a run for his money!" He climbed into the car, turned the key, and drove away without looking back.

Waving after them, Nancy stood with her door open and watched them leave thinking about Waldo's comment. She knew the haulier would be chuckling to himself after making a confession like that. Noticing another truck pull up and stop, obviously waiting for her spot, she jumped in and moved out of the way. She couldn't help but wonder how much worse this situation would get for Victoria.

There was one call she needed to make in James Bay to complete Kate's visits. Working out the route in her mind, she quickly arrived at Dock Street. As she got out of the truck she heard the sound of waves crashing onto the nearby breakwater and stood listening for a minute, again realizing how tired she was.

She knocked on the door of the small cottage and waited. Through the window, she saw two very young children playing near a pot-bellied stove, and then a very thin young woman opened the door.

"I'm the stand-in for Kate Dumpford, Mrs. Hall," she quickly explained going inside but staying near the door and looking around the sparsely furnished room. "Are you managing all right?"

"I get terribly worried and it eats away at me, especially at night. I can't sleep wondering what's to become of us."

"Do you have family close by?"

"No, only the lady in Gordon Head."

"What lady in Gordon Head?" Nancy questioned her, curiously.

"The lady that helps us every month, but I hate asking for charity."

"Is there a fire in that stove, it's quite cool in here?"

"We're out of wood. I collect it on the beach after a storm, if I get there quick enough."

Opening Kate's notebook at the appropriate page, she read the notation, *firewood needed.*

"Oh yes," she said. "I see Kate has made a note of that. I'll make sure you get firewood tomorrow, Mrs. Hall. Did your army pension come?"

"Not yet, I think the influenza scare has messed up the mails."

"Well, here's your rent money," Nancy said kindly, sliding a pre-marked envelope out of her purse and adding a ten-dollar bill, "and an extra ten dollars to tide you over for food. I'll check around again in a week and try not to worry."

Ella Hall dropped her eyes to hide the tears. Life was hard for a war widow with two children to feed. Desperation had driven her to the Red Cross for help and Eva Todd had stepped into her life bringing regular help from the lady at Gordon Head. Unable to speak, she gently lay her hand on Nancy's arm.

Nancy left quickly before her emotions got the better of her, but broke into tears upon starting the car. Seeing storm-driven debris and logs on the road ahead of her, she avoided Dallas Road and turned down Niagara Street heading back to town.

On Government, she stopped abruptly when confronted by a number of cows herded along by the wild, dishevelled figure of Emily Carr waving two walking sticks to keep the animals moving. This was enough to dry up her tears, affording a smile and a wave at the comical figure of the well-known rebel. Skirts and hair blowing in the wind, Emily waved at the familiar blue truck.

The streets were almost bare of people—storm and city ordinance rules probably keeping folks at home, she thought to herself, as the streetcar she was following failed to stop in front of the Empress. Remembering she had promised to pick up some tea for Meg, she parked on Fort Street having no trouble finding a spot.

Dan and Jack were back when she walked into the office, struggling to close the door against the wind as Jack began a barrage of questions.

"Where's Kate, Nan?" he pleaded dejectedly. "Jeb said she's ill."

"Give her a chance to put her bag down!" Jeb snapped.

"Tea, honey?" Dan asked. "Come on, take your coat off and tell us what's happened before Jack goes crazy."

"Yes I'll have tea and a sandwich if you've got one," Nancy sighed. "Kate's all right, Jack, so stop worrying. Dr. Price says she's just overtired, needs a couple of days to rest up. Waldo's taken her out to Cunningham Manor so Meg can look after her. You should come out and stay with us for a day or two."

"It's not the flu then?" he asked, beginning to relax. "Thank God for that."

"No, it's not the flu. Dr. Price checked her out at the fire hall."

"What fire hall?" Dan muttered, handing her the tea and a sandwich. "I didn't know they took sick folks to the fire hall."

"If you'd just hold on a minute, I'll tell you all about it," she interrupted.

Suddenly, the door banged open and Waldo stepped in, crashing it shut behind him. "There's a tree down on Cedar Hill Road, better use Shelbourne to get home tonight," he said breathlessly, easing a chair out from the table and sitting down. "Pour me a coffee will ya, Dan?"

"Slow down, Waldo, did you get her home all right?" Nancy asked.

"Of course I did!" he snapped, his voice softening when he continued, "Meg's taking care of her."

Jack's eyes rolled in frustration as he looked from Nancy to Waldo. "Please, will somebody tell me what happened to Kate?"

"Yes, Jack, I will. I'm sorry," Nancy said softly. "Kate collapsed with fatigue this morning while making her rounds to the widows. City workmen saw her and took her to the old fire hall in James Bay."

"Why?" Jack interrupted.

"Will you listen?" she snapped. "Dr. Price and a city crew were turning it into a holding place for influenza victims as all the hospitals are full. They were just installing beds and setting up equipment when

Kate arrived. A doctor checked her out and then called here. Uncle Jeb took the call and got a message to me."

"How did he find you?" Dan asked.

"I found her," Waldo growled. "Every truck driver in the city was looking for that damn blue truck!"

The conversation stopped abruptly as the telephone rang and Dan went to get it.

"Danny!" a familiar voice shouted, loud enough for everyone to recognize the caller as Fred Barrett. "Algenon's in trouble. He's trying to tow a boat in but they're getting battered off Harling Point."

"Right, we're on our way," he replied, hanging up the phone and grabbing his heavy coat. He snapped an order to Jack as he opened the door. "Get your coat, Dumpy, Algy's in trouble!"

Neither Jeb nor Waldo made a comment as Nancy's lips bent into a smile. "Algy will be fine with Dan on the job—he's the best darned seaman on this coast," she said proudly.

"LONG DRAGLINE AND TWO BUOYS, DUMPY," the ex-whaler commanded above the noise as the *Stockholm* powered out of the harbour and into the crashing waves. "KEEP YOUR EYES PEELED, LOOKS LIKE A LOG BOOM GOT AWAY."

Running straight out, the *Stockholm* proved her worth slicing through giant waves. The deck was instantly awash with salty foam. Dan swung hard on the helm as a 30-foot log almost speared the wheelhouse, bouncing down the side and tearing the deck rail loose.

"CLOSE ONE, DAN!" Jack shouted. "JUST LIKE OLD TIMES ON THE *BELFAST*!"

"GET READY, DUMPY!" Dan yelled. "TURN THOSE BUOYS LOOSE, WE'RE GOING IN."

Algenon Pease, the harbour patrolman, saw the flash of red-and-gold through the thundering spray as it enveloped his small speedboat. Pulling hard on full power, his boat *Legal Limit* was barely able to keep its tow from smashing onto the rocks.

Dan's timing was perfect, though dangerous, as he swung the *Stockholm* in close. Using the crest of a wave, he hurled the buoys watching as the water moved them quickly toward the struggling patrol boat.

Algy wasn't prepared for what happened next as the rope and buoys crashed into him, knocking him off his feet. He struggled to grab hold of the line, finally succeeding and, tossed about by the waves and spray, at last managed to tie the rope fast to the bow. Holding on for dear life, he felt the jerk as the *Stockholm* took up the slack, and he sighed with relief.

"WE GOT 'EM, DANNY," Jack screamed. "WE GOT 'EM!"

Workers at the Gonzales Weather Station crowded to the windows and cheered as they watched with binoculars, having a perfect observation point to witness the rescue—an emergency they had reported to the harbour master.

"That's Dan Brown down there," someone announced. "He's the whaler who harpooned that freighter off Albert Head a few years back."

"Are you suggesting he used that wave on purpose to toss his buoys over to the other boat?" the radio operator asked skeptically.

"No, I'm not suggesting anything; I'm telling you he did just that! This man has a reputation as long as your arm. He's a legend on this coast. You better call Fred and tell him Algy's all right."

A few minutes later, the phone rang in the Brown and Wilson office. "Now what?" Jeb grumbled as he walked across the room and picked up the receiver.

"Jeb!" Fred Barrett's voice was chuckling now. "Danny's got 'em. He's on his way back in."

"They got him," Jeb stated matter-of-factly, looking over at Nancy as he hung up the phone.

Back out on the water with the tow rope straining almost to breaking point, the *Stockholm* slowly pulled all three vessels away from the rocks, across Gonzales and Ross Bays, turning them loose in the safety of the harbour.

"They're here," Nancy murmured awhile later, picking up the familiar engine sounds. "What time is it, Uncle Jeb?"

"Almost 5 o'clock. It's time we were heading for home when the boys get here. Remember there's a tree down on Cedar Hill Road—you'll have to go Shelbourne way."

"I know," she replied, sighing.

Although cold and wet, Dan and Dumpy were laughing when they walked into the office. "We got 'em, Nan!" Jack chuckled. "I bet Algy got a shock when that rope landed in his boat."

"It was just a matter of timing," Dan admitted modestly with a grin, giving Nancy a kiss on the cheek.

"You're wet!" she sputtered, pushing him away. She could tell the two former whalers were enjoying working together again, something that didn't happen very often anymore. The strong bond as shipmates on a whaler still held them fast. Flirting with danger had little meaning to these two young men.

"You need dry clothes," she said, "both of you. You'd better go home and pack a case for you and Kate, Jack. Aunt Meg will love the company and by the weekend she should be almost back to her old self. Now let's all get out of here!"

Changing into dry clothes he kept on hand, Dan slipped into his sea coat. There was one more call he had to make before heading home.

"Where's he going?" she asked Jeb as the *Stockholm* pulled away from the dock and turned toward the railway bridge.

"Turpel's for gas. He's going to Cowichan Bay in the morning."

The long drive home in the rain did little to settle Nancy's thoughts and she was grateful when she turned into the familiar drive.

"Nancy's home," Meg called to Katherine in the living room.

"Is Kate in bed?" Nancy asked as soon as she opened the door.

"No, listen!" Meg replied, putting a finger to her lips and nodding to the other room.

"That's me!" the redhead giggled hanging her coat up then going to hug the Scot. "She's playing my record on the phonograph."

"Leave her, lassie. She's wrapped up like a kitten, sipping rabbit stew and listening to you singing. Just what the doctor ordered. Where's Jebediah?"

"Right behind me, his lights were coming down the drive when I came in."

"Danny's bringing the *Stockholm* home?"

"Yes, can you hold dinner for a little while, Dumpy's coming too."

Sneaking quietly into the front room, Nancy grinned at the scene in front of her. Just as Aunt Meg had described, Kate was wrapped in blankets curled up in the big stuffed chair close to a roaring fire. Her eyes were closed and she was smiling.

Chapter 11

Outside, under the sheltering eaves of the workshop, Jeb puffed on his pipe as he watched the *Stockholm* arrive through the pounding rain and white-capped waves. Turning away, now that he knew Dan was safe, he heard a vehicle coming down the drive and went to the corner of the house to look. Seeing their dock manager climb out of his truck and come toward him, struggling with an oversized case, he shook his head.

"How long have you come for, lad?" he chuckled. "I've not had that many clothes in my entire life!"

"Where's Kate?" Jack whined, standing in the pouring rain, but ignoring the old man's comment.

"In the wood shed, you chump, where else would she be?"

Jack turned and walked toward the house. Even after so many years he still had difficulty dealing with Jeb's sense of humour. Knocking on the door, he stood and waited until the old detective shouted, "Go on in, they're expecting you!"

Timidly opening the door, Jack stepped inside and put the suitcase down on the mat, starting to remove his boots.

"Ach laddie, aren't you a sight to behold," Meg chuckled, calling from the kitchen. "Take him upstairs, Nan, and get him out of them wet clothes."

"But Kate ...?" Jack began to ask then, seeing the old Scot point a stern finger toward the stairs, he blushed and quickly capitulated, hanging up his dripping coat and starting up the stairs.

"She's asleep in front of the fire and not going anywhere, Jack," Nancy said gently, handing him a dry towel. "Wipe your bag off, and anything that's dripping, and I'll take you to your room."

Halfway up the stairs, Jack suddenly whispered, "Where's that music coming from Nan?"

"It's Kate, she's playing one of my recordings on the phonograph."

"On the what?"

"Oh Jack, it was a wedding present. We'll show you later," she replied. "Get changed, we're waiting dinner for you and Dan and he's just arrived."

Taking him to the door of Dan's old room, she pushed him gently inside closing the door. When she got back to the bottom of the stairs blocking her way was Dan, still in his wet sea suit. He quickly grabbed her and slid his arms around her waist.

"Get away from me!" she whispered as he pressed her against his wet body. "Shh, we'll wake Kate up." Wriggling wildly, she escaped and ran into the kitchen hearing her husband's laughter behind her.

Ten minutes later, Jack appeared at the kitchen door. Nancy took his hand leading him into the living room. He groaned with relief when he saw his wife, pushing past Nan to drop onto his knees beside her. Sighing wistfully, the redhead closed the door.

A few minutes later, hanging onto Jack's arm, Kate came out to the kitchen, her presence the centre of attention as the family ate dinner and related the events of the day. She broke into laughter when Nancy told them how she had given Dr. Price a push, in her anxiety, and he had fallen on his behind.

"Waldo said they're making a house in Fort Street into a hospital," Jeb informed them. "I think he said it was 1124 Fort."

"Oh golly, I just remembered, I need firewood for one of our families tomorrow," Nancy groaned. "Has anybody got any ideas?"

"Try asking Eva," suggested Meg.

"She's not home yet, I already called her."

"Tom Irvine and Billy had a load on their truck when I saw them today," Jack eagerly informed them. "I bet they're clearing land again, you should call them."

"Do you have Tom's number, Aunt Meg?"

"Yes dear, it's in my little black book on top of the phone stand."

Kate's eyes followed Nancy as she picked up the book and searched though Meg's numbers, then dialed Tom Irvine. She smiled weakly as they listened to the one-sided conversation.

"Billy, are you selling firewood? No, no, it's not for us. Can you deliver me four loads tomorrow? No, call at the office, Jack will give you a list and pay you. Thank you Billy, I'll tell her what you said."

"Let me guess," said Dan, when she hung up the phone, "he's going to do it, and he's told you to say hello to Aunt Meg."

"Absolutely right, now all I need are those four addresses for Jack and a 20 dollar bill, then that's another problem solved."

"Leave your book out," Meg advised. "I'll make sure you get your list for the morning."

"It's time you took that girl to bed, Jack," Jeb suggested showing his concern as he noticed Kate's eyes beginning to droop. "She's falling asleep."

"Give me a minute," Meg chuckled, hurrying toward the stairs. "I'd better get those warming rocks out of the bed!"

Frowning as they watched her go, Kate's expression told Nancy she was looking for an explanation.

"Aunt Meg warms rocks in the oven all day," she explained with a serious expression, "then, just before dinner, she puts them in our beds. It takes the chill off the sheets. I thought everybody did it."

"You're pulling my leg," said Kate.

"Wait and see then."

"Your bed is ready," Meg called from the head of the stairs.

Grinning, Nancy hugged Kate and watched the guests climb the stairs. Sighing, she pulled her book back toward her, scanning the pages as she worked out her visiting list for Tuesday. It was coming to the end of the month, rents would have to be paid, and her workload was doubled now that Kate was sick. *However did Eva manage it all on her own*? she wondered.

It was almost 10 o'clock when Nancy and Dan gave in to their own weariness and, wishing the old folks goodnight, they quietly crept off to bed. Laying in each other's arms in the darkness, they watched the moon flit from cloud to stormy cloud as it moved across the sky.

"What are you thinking, Nan?" Dan whispered.

"Oh, just how lucky we are," she yawned, nestling closer to him and sighing contentedly.

Long before dawn, Cunningham Manor was buzzing with activity. Leaving Kate asleep, Jack crept downstairs to join the family for breakfast.

"Did you sleep well, son?" the Scot asked slipping a plate heaped with eggs, potatoes, and sausages in front of him.

"Sure did," he grinned. "Kate loved that warm bed!"

"Eat your breakfast," Jeb growled, "you've a load for Port Renfrew this morning."

"Yes, and I've got to go to Cowichan Bay," Dan informed them through a mouthful.

"Were you loaded when you went out after Algy yesterday?" Nancy asked.

"No, it's a pickup at the cannery in Sidney."

Grey streaks of dawn were creeping across the sky as Jeb and Dumpy left for the city and Dan grabbed his oilskin coat before hugging Meg and kissing Nan goodbye. Striding across the lawn to the cliff stairs, he glanced back, catching sight of Kate in the upstairs bedroom window and waved.

Now they were alone, Nancy and Meg began sorting out her work for the day. Envelopes were carefully filled for each widow—rent, food and allowances for the children. Nancy suddenly remembered the money for Jack Irvine and Billy.

"Did Jack take that money and the firewood list for Billy?"

"Jebediah took it, honey; he'll look after that for you."

Unnoticed, Kate quietly came down the stairs and stood watching at the doorway.

"I'm sorry, Nan," she whispered.

Meg reacted immediately, gently shepherding her over to the table and pulling out a chair. "Don't stand there in that draft girl—come sit down. I'll get you a blanket," she scolded.

Smiling across the table, Nancy reached for Kate's hand, a lump forming in her throat as she saw the sad look on her friend and business partner's face.

"What you need, young lady," she said, "is some of this wonderful Gordon Head air, if it would only stop raining! You'll be doing me a favour by keeping Aunt Meg company for a day or two."

Up the coast, Dan had reached Sidney by the time Nancy left home. He docked at the fish plant at Robert's Point and stared at the huge machine he was supposed to transport. Dick Radley, the foreman, told him there was also a load of asphalt shingles to go to the Cowichan Bay Cannery.

"I can't get that blasted thing aboard the *Stockholm*," Dan grumbled. "We'll have to put it on floats and tow it."

Finding a log float proved easy, but loading the canning machine was nerve racking. Fingers were trapped and tempers exploded as workmen lowered it from the government dock onto the floating platform, got it balanced and lashed it securely.

"It'll be a miracle if that gets to Cowichan," the foreman growled at John White, the owner.

Life never seems to be without its challenges, Dan thought as he started the engine and slowly pulled the strange-looking barge away from the Sidney dock. There were wild scrambling moments as he rounded

Piers Island and the fast-running tide of Satellite Channel seemed intent on causing disaster pushing the cargo toward the seal-infested rocks.

It was almost 2 o'clock when, with a sigh of relief, he arrived at Cowichan Bay and help in the docking was at hand. Workmen were full of praise as they quickly unloaded the roofing material from the deck and laughed at Dan's ingenious method of transporting the machine.

Ormond Smythe, the owner of the local *Cowichan Leader* newspaper, was there to meet him, always ready to glean tidbits of information from visiting ships. A dour-faced man, Ormond was well known to Dan and it came as no surprise when he offered Dan lunch at the dockside café.

"I want to know about the influenza," he asked as they waited for their lunch. "How many deaths have there been in Victoria?"

"I'm not sure, the newspapers aren't telling us much, but there are a lot of people sick."

"Dr. Young was up here," Ormond muttered, "had me print a whole host of rules and regulations. We've had three deaths already and Duncan's had more."

"Seattle has it bad," Dan added. "Soldiers are dying after they get home. They thought they were safe and then this hits them."

"It's going to be rough, lad, and you mark my words; we haven't seen the worst of it yet."

"I have to go," said Dan after hurriedly finishing his sandwich, having no stomach for the depressing conversation. "Did you bring me a newspaper for Aunt Meg?"

"Yes lad, I put it on your seat in the *Stockholm*, I didn't want you to forget it."

Walking back to the dock, Ormond told him of a railway derailment in the lumber yard at Chemainus and how a native Indian was found drowned in the bay.

"Don't you have any good news?" Dan asked in frustration, before jumping into the boat. "I'm sick of listening to doom and gloom."

Ormond watched him leave and shook his head. *That boy's mighty worked up about something*, he thought.

Back in Victoria, Nancy's well-laid-out plan for the day was quickly going amiss as her first stop in Fernwood brought an unexpected problem. Dora Alcock's two young children were sick and, with no money for doctors adding to her worries, she was becoming a nervous wreck. She tried so hard to maintain the two-acre property at the corner of Fernwood and Denman, but since the news of her husband's death early in the war, it had all become too much for the poor woman.

Nancy's reaction was predictable. With no thought to her own safety or even considering the children might have the deadly flu, she bundled them all into the truck and raced up Denman to the Jubilee. Luckily Dr. Price was just leaving when she pulled up to the door. Scowling fiercely, he recognized her and strode over quickly to investigate.

Things happened fast when he saw the children. Shouting orders to staff, he quickly had the family bundled away inside.

"Park your vehicle away from the door and I want you in there, too," he snapped with a wry smile.

"I'm fine," Nancy objected.

"That's not a request, it's an order!" his voice rang with authority, causing heads to turn.

Reluctantly going to park the truck, she began to realize the seriousness of her actions. If the Alcock family had influenza, she might also have contracted it. The thought sent a shudder of cold down her spine.

Crowds of people milled about in the hospital hallway as she pushed through the door. Looking around to find the Alcocks, she felt a nurse gently take her arm and lead her down the corridor into a room where the family were sitting. Dr. Price came in nodding to the nurse and pointing to the empty seat as he went to examine one of the children.

Frowning, he prodded each of the Alcocks with his stethoscope. At last he came to Nancy. Blushing when he tapped at her chest, she brushed his hand away when he reached for the top button of her cardigan, glaring at him.

"You're as strong as a horse, wonderful lungs," he growled with a hint of a smile at her embarrassment. "The children have a chill and Mrs. Alcock is quite run down—overwork, no doubt. Take them home, Nancy and make sure they take care of themselves. Next time they might not be so lucky."

"Dora, I think it's time we found you some help on that place of yours." Nancy spoke her thoughts aloud as she and Dora carried the sleepy children back to the truck and bundled them inside.

"I can't afford help, Nancy," Dora said softly. "With Jim gone, I don't …."

"Would you accept help if I could find you someone?"

"But I couldn't pay them," she said dejectedly.

"Maybe you wouldn't have to if he could share in the profits."

By the time she got the family settled comfortably back at home, she realized it had taken all morning to deal with her first call.

I'll just make these three quick calls by Quadra and Hillside, she told herself, *and then I'll need some lunch.*

She was able to make the calls without meeting anymore emergencies and by 1 o'clock she was travelling down Bay Street heading for the dock. She was almost there when she remembered that Eva had sent her Kent Macleod, the amputee gardener. *Perhaps a call at the Red Cross office would be beneficial.*

She turned onto Government and then down Fisgard, pulling up to the curb in front of the Red Cross office where she was quickly directed next door to the Salvation Army.

"Ask for the director, May Coolridge," the clerk suggested.

"Hello Nancy," May greeted her warmly. "I haven't seen you in ages. They tell me you're married."

"Yes, we've been married six months now."

"And what brings you here?"

"Eva once brought us a war amputee to do some work for us at Gordon Head."

"Yes, I remember, that was a couple of years ago."

"Well, a friend of mine is in need of some help around her little farm. I thought I could contact the organization on her behalf. Could you tell me how to do that?"

"Oh, that's easy, Nancy, the Red Cross finds wounded soldiers employment if we are able."

"I want a man who's used to farm work and can take care of a little market garden. Someone who's quiet, reliable and likes children."

"How soon is he needed?"

"Yesterday!" Nancy laughed.

"And the pay?"

"She isn't able to pay him, but she'll share the profits."

"Accommodation?"

"Oh, I'm sure something can be worked out."

Sliding out a desk drawer, May flipped through her files pulling one out and placing it on her desk.

"Yes, I remember now, you've got Kent Macleod out at Gordon Head."

"Kent's a good man," Nancy replied, thinking of the brave soldier who had lost a leg but refused to feel sorry for himself. He had been tending to the trees in their orchard ever since they'd been planted.

"You need someone else in Gordon Head?"

"No, only Dora Alcock. She's in Fernwood and in desperate need."

Pulling another file, May flipped through the papers, stopping as a look of sadness came across her face. "Thomas Alcock, killed in action, June 1914, wife Dora Alice, two children ages one and two. My heavens, that poor woman!"

"Yes that's her, the children are a few years older now, of course."

Turning back to her files, May's fingers began to shake and her eyes clouded over as she extracted a form and handed it to the redhead. Tears began to roll down her cheeks and she dabbed quickly at them with a handkerchief.

"A relative?" Nancy whispered.

"No, my own two sons were killed in that battle. Would you excuse me for a moment?" Leaving her desk, the director was heard sobbing quietly behind the partition.

Nancy bit her lip as her own emotions welled up. She could feel May's pain and her heart went out to her.

"Darn," she whispered under her breath, "I hate this war."

Struggling with her composure, May returned to her desk. "I'm sorry Nancy sometimes it's the little things that start the memories. Now, let's sort your problem out. I have an Edward Lancaster, both his legs are missing below the knee. He's living right here in town at the Salvation Army hostel. Would you like to meet him?"

"Yes, I would," Nan replied, her mind conjuring up a picture of Mr. Lancaster.

"Then come with me, we'll try to find him."

Leading Nancy through the building and into the hostel area, May called to the desk clerk.

"We're looking for Teddy Lancaster."

"He's usually sitting by the window in the upstairs living room," came back the instant reply.

"Teddy!" May called as Nancy followed her up the stairs. A young man with strawberry-blond hair and sparkling blue eyes turned to smile at them. "Hello Teddy, you have a visitor."

Hopping off his seat, a handsome young man came toward them. Once a big man of six-foot-five, he had towered over the other recruits when he enlisted at the Bay Street Armory in 1914. His injuries were now obvious as he came toward them with a jerking motion and stopped at the head of the stairs. His legs were missing below the knees and in place of feet he wore wooden rockers.

"Well howdy ladies," his voice tinkled with amusement. "I sure hope this lovely visitor is a relative of mine, Mrs. Coolridge!"

"Stop it, Teddy, be serious for once," May chuckled. "This lady is Nancy Wilson … sorry Nan, I mean Mrs. Nancy Brown, and she might have a job for you."

"Tell me a little about yourself, Teddy," Nancy invited.

"There ain't much to tell," he replied, his eyes sparkling as he remembered his youth. "I'm just a simple Alberta farm boy."

"How are you with children?"

"All right I guess, Dad said I never really grew up. It's the adults I have trouble with!"

"Well I've a job for you," Nancy replied, smiling at him. "How would you like to help a widow woman with two young children on a smallholding in Fernwood?"

May carefully watched Ted's reaction.

"I hope the mud ain't too deep," he laughed, "my backside's awfully close to the ground!"

"You might have to stay here at the hostel for awhile until we can sort out accommodation," Nancy giggled, warming to the young man.

"Who cares, I'd be useful again, anything's better than watching these trains all day."

"He can stay here as long as he likes," May interposed.

"There wouldn't be any wages for awhile, but I can promise you'd get 50 percent of the profits," explained Nancy, "and I would appreciate a quick answer."

"YES!" Ted yelled. "If that's quick enough, how soon can I start?"

"I'll go and talk to the lady after lunch."

"Take me with you," Ted pleaded. "She would need to see me. Sometimes people get scared when they see I'm only half a man."

"Half a man," Nancy grinned. "I'll wager you're twice the man you used to be and far exceed many others! My husband was badly wounded in France and also my two brothers, one of them in a wheelchair. They are wonderful people and my guess is they've grown up a lot since they went to war."

Listening closely, May was surprised at the way Nancy's forthright and honest manner had a good chance of solving two problems. Disabled soldiers had a devil of a time finding employment and no one seemed prepared to accept responsibility for the growing number of widows and orphans needing help. Her thoughts were suddenly disturbed when a call came echoing up the stairs. The familiar voice of Dr. Price sounded a little annoyed at having to search for the Red Cross director.

"Yes, I'm here," May called, hurrying away.

"Get your coat, Ted, we'll go for lunch, then I'll take you to meet Dora," Nancy announced.

Hopping from step to step, Ted made a tremendous noise with his wooden feet banging on the stairs, but Nancy smiled at the ingenious way the wounded soldier was overcoming his disability. She was curious how he would manage going up a flight of stairs.

"Now what are you up to?" the city health officer exclaimed in surprise, when Nancy and Ted appeared in the hall. "Where are you taking this young man?"

"It's all right, sir, they have my permission," May whispered, embarrassed at his questions.

"I'm taking him for lunch," Nancy replied, offering no further explanation but turning to wink at May.

Ted eagerly left the building and climbed into the truck without assistance appearing very excited about his new adventure. Nancy felt the doctor's eyes boring holes in her back as they walked away and he sardonically reminded her that restaurants were closed.

Chapter 12

Steam-belching trains blocking Store Street caused the redhead to detour along Government slipping into Yates as a streetcar rumbled around the corner. She pulled up to the sidewalk in front of the boarded-up Palace Saloon and the Olympus Café.

"They're open?" Ted muttered in surprise.

"Only for take-out. You stay here, I'll get us a sandwich. Would you like beef or ham?"

"Beef with pickles, please."

Coming up the street, Jim Morrison, the old blacksmith, waved a blackened hand at the girl and followed her into the restaurant.

"Who's that with you, Nancy?" he asked.

"Ted Lancaster, he's a war amputee living at the hostel."

"What's he got missing?"

"Legs, both of them below the knee."

"Is he going to help you at Gordon Head?"

"Oh no, I think I've found him a job helping a widow lady on her small farm over on Denman. We're on our way over there now."

Frowning, Jim puffed on his pipe for awhile before replying. "Stop at the smithy when you leave, Nan, I want a word with that lad."

"Do you know him, Jim?" Nancy asked, turning to give her order to the girl.

"No, it's just an idea. You bring him over after you've eaten," he said firmly.

"That old man's a friend of yours, isn't he?" Ted asked, when she returned to the truck.

"You'll know in a minute," she chuckled, handing him his sandwich. "He's the blacksmith and he wants to meet you. So we're stopping before going out to Fernwood. I hope that's all right with you."

"I guess so, but why would he want to meet me?" Ted asked.

"I guess that's what we're both going to find out," she replied, pulling the truck up to the curb in front of a sign that said 'BLACKSMITH'.

She got out but stepped quickly aside as a man leading two carriage horses went into the dark shop.

"Have you seen Jim, Nancy?" the man called out to her.

"He's coming down the street," she called back, then turned to Ted. "You might as well get out."

As Jim Morrison walked toward them, Nancy noticed she was taller than Ted. Jim's brow furrowed into deep lines as his eyes took in the young man's legs and strange wooden feet.

"Stay there, I'll get you a seat," he muttered as he passed, having a quick conversation with the man inside.

Rolling an empty ten-gallon barrel out of his workshop, Jim pointed his pipe stem at the barrel and Ted jumped up and sat down, a puzzled frown on his face. Next, Jim brought out a flat board and propped it under Ted's knee. Without looking up at the young man, he pushed Ted's trouser leg up revealing the ugly, scarred stump. Jim was silent as he studied the leg and how the strange wooden foot was attached, all the while grunting and muttering to himself. Finally, groaning softly, he straightened his back and eased the pipe out of his mouth.

"Want me to make ya a new pair of legs, lad?" he inquired.

"Can it be done, Jim?" Nancy asked excitedly.

"How tall do you want to be, son?" the blacksmith grunted, ignoring Nancy's question.

"About six feet, I used to be six-five but that's too big, you've no idea how it feels when everybody stares at you."

Nodding, the old blacksmith glanced quickly over at Nancy and clamped his pipe between his teeth. Frowning in thought, he began making chalk marks on the board under Ted's knee. Stopping to scratch his chin, he carefully examined the straps that held the wooden foot in place and again muttering to himself, he turned away.

"Nothing to it son, just like walking on stilts. Have him back here on Saturday morning, Nan."

"Right, Mr. Morrison."

"This ain't really happening," Ted said softly as they walked back to the truck. "I have to be dreaming."

"Do you want to wait for the new legs before you meet the Alcock family?"

"No ma'am, I want them to see me as I am."

"Hop in, I want to call at the dock first," Nancy called putting her hand on the door handle, then suddenly blushing when she realized what she'd said. "I'm sorry, Ted, I didn't mean it like it sounded!"

"Oh stop your blathering, woman," Ted laughed. "This is the best day I've had in the last three years. It feels like my life is starting all over again and it's good."

Traffic was unusually light and the street was noticeably empty of shoppers as she pulled into Wharf Street. The influenza scare and restrictive city ordinances were certainly keeping people at home. Ted's face showed his interest when the redhead bounced the truck down to the Brown and Wilson dock.

"You can get out if you like," Nancy carefully picked her words this time. "We'll be here for a little while."

"Your husband works here?" Ted inquired.

"Nancy," Eva called from the office doorway, her eyes straying to the passenger. "Teddy?" she murmured. "What are you doing here?"

"Hello Eva, I'm in the hands of a red haired angel," the amputee replied with a grin. "She's rebuilding my life for me!"

"She's doing what?" the Red Cross worker laughed.

"She's found me a job and arranged with Mr. Morrison …."

"Hold it," Nancy interrupted. "Let's keep that our secret for now, Ted. There's nothing for certain yet."

Ted looked a bit disappointed but smiled resignedly and Eva asked no more questions. Leaving them talking, Nancy went in to see Jeb. He looked up from his order book as she entered.

"Who's talking to Eva?"

"A wounded soldier from the Salvation Army hostel. Anything new happening around here?"

"Orders are coming in and Waldo says there are more cases of flu breaking out all over the city."

"Oh goodness!" Nancy muttered, going to look at some papers.

Outside, Eva gave Ted a tour of the dock explaining that Dan and Nancy owned the business and two boats which ran a delivery service to coastal towns and businesses.

"You came here from Vancouver didn't you, Ted?" she asked. "Were you ever in the Jubilee Hospital?"

"Yes, I was there for six months."

"Have you heard of the *Wounded Soldier Restaurant*?" Eva asked.

"The boys told me about it," Ted replied, "and I heard the lady who owns it singing one day, but I never saw her because I couldn't get out of bed. That was just after my surgery."

"Oh yes you have seen her," Eva giggled. "You've been with her all morning!"

"Mrs. Brown?" Ted gasped.

"Yes, Nancy Wilson, now Mrs. Dan Brown. Do you remember what you said about her when you got out of the truck?"

Frowning, Ted looked a little embarrassed. "Oh gosh, I wasn't meaning it disrespectful," he groaned.

"I know you weren't, but what did you say?"

"I said she was a red haired angel. I hope she wasn't offended."

"Well you hold onto that thought, my lad, because it's true and some day all the world will know just how much of an angel Nancy Brown really is."

"Sounds like she's touched your life, too, Eva."

"You'll see, but don't tell her what I told you."

"Ted!" Nancy called from the doorway. "Come meet my Uncle Jeb."

Moving as quickly as he could, Ted's wooden feet rattled on the deck boards announcing he had heard. Entering the office, he saw the older man sitting at the table. He looked to be a pleasant old fellow and he was smiling broadly. Pre-warned of the soldier's disability, Jeb showed no surprise and stood when Nancy introduced them, bending to shake Ted's hand.

"Looks like you've had a little trouble, lad," he proffered. "How big were you before your accident, son?"

"Six-five and it wasn't no accident, sir."

Jumping up onto a chair and landing on his behind, Ted appeared normal as he sipped a cup of tea allowing Jebediah's questions to extract details of his past. Chuckling as he told of his childhood on their family farm and the humorous antics he got up to, he hesitated when he mentioned enlisting.

Not wanting to hear of the war, Nancy quickly drew the visit to a close. "I think you'll have to save that story for next time, Ted. We really need to get going."

Driving to the corner of Fernwood and Denman, Nancy soon became aware that Ted's mood had changed. He was no longer talkative and she surmised that he was worried about receiving rejection at the Alcock home.

She pulled into the yard but before she had a chance to open the door, some movement caught her eye and she lay her hand on Ted's arm. He followed her glance. Dora and the children were coming out of the back door of the house. The children were looking much better as they ran ahead of her, shouting as they went into the nearby barn, and Dora, carrying a large basket, followed.

Climbing out of the truck, Nancy and Ted stood and waited. Suddenly excited children's squeals and some clucking was heard causing Ted to laugh aloud.

"They found some eggs," he confidently predicted.

Reappearing, Dora immediately noticed the truck and tried to send the children into the house but when they clung shyly to her dress she quickly gave in. Setting her basket of eggs on a tree stump, she moved slowly toward the truck, seemingly oblivious of the children.

"Hi Dora, children!" Nancy greeted them, peeking around behind Dora. "This is Ted Lancaster—he wants to help you out. He's a farm boy from Alberta and well used to working on the land."

"Did you warn him I can't pay?" Dora asked softly, looking at him doubtfully.

"He knows and you can see he's been hurt. All he wants is a chance to be useful."

"I'm not sure he could handle the work," Dora muttered.

"Well whatever he is able to do will mean less for you. Why don't you give him a chance, Dora," the redhead continued, lowering her voice.

"I'm sorry Nancy, but I think he will frighten the children," she whispered.

Unnoticed, the children moved from behind their mother and although still holding onto her skirt, were studying Ted with obvious interest.

"Don't you have any legs, mister?" the boy asked.

"I keep them at home," Ted replied, grinning at them. "I don't want to wear them out!"

Giggling, both children let go of their mother and moved closer, watching intently when Ted picked up a tiny stone from the ground. Rubbing it in his hands, he opened them and showed it to them, then he clapped his hands and opened them again. The stone had disappeared.

"What do you think of that?" he chuckled. "I'm a magic man!"

Dora smiled; her son and daughter had made her mind up for her. Anyone who could instantly make friends with her children deserved a chance.

"We can try it for a month," she suggested, "but I don't have a spare room."

"That's all right, Mrs. Alcock, I have a bed at the Salvation Army hostel," Ted replied, watching the children out of the corner of his eye as they went around behind him.

Nancy took Dora's arm and they walked toward the house keeping an eye on the interplay between Ted and the children. Reservations were gone and the youngsters began to chat happily to their new friend.

"When would you like him to start?" Nan asked.

"Tomorrow morning if he can," Dora replied, sounding more enthusiastic now.

On the drive back to the city, Nancy glanced over at her passenger. Deep in thought, he stared out the window. Totally oblivious to his surroundings, Ted's thoughts were in the future.

"You'll be able to get over there in the morning?" she asked, standing with him outside the hostel. "The Spring Hill streetcar will take you up to the quarry."

"I'll get there," Ted assured her with a boyish grin starting toward the building. "Thanks Mrs. Brown."

"Please call me Nancy. I'll pick you up at the Alcock's on Saturday morning, Ted, about nine-thirty." She watched him wave as he got to the door, reached to open it and with difficulty held it open to get through.

He won't have trouble with doors much longer, thought Nancy with a little giggle.

Leaving the hostel, Nancy made her way into Store Street, avoiding a number of rail cars left along the track. She smiled with satisfaction and a feeling of elation buzzed through her brain as she thought of the day's accomplishments. Up ahead she could see Waldo standing in the middle of the road, puffing on his pipe as he watched her approach.

"Are you trying to commit suicide?" she asked her old friend.

"Business has slowed to nothing," the haulier growled. "It's like the city has died!"

"It's the influenza."

"All I've seen for the last hour are ambulances and mortuary wagons," he continued.

"Look on the bright side," she advised. "The war sounds to be nearly over and Dr. Price thinks they have the influenza contained."

"Like hell they have," Waldo snapped. "Blasted officials wouldn't tell the truth if it jumped up and bit 'em."

"You're too hard on them, Waldo."

"No lass, I've known them longer than you have," the old man barked, snatching his pipe out of his mouth. "I wouldn't trust them as far as I could throw them!"

Continuing down to the dock, she parked the truck. As she turned off the engine, she could hear Dan and Dumpy laughing and she looked around to see where they were. She found them loading the *Stockholm* for the next day's run to Seattle and waved to them before going inside.

"Fred Barrett says Seattle's been closed up tight," Jeb informed her.

"You mean it's closed to shipping?"

"Almost, they're checking every boat that goes down the straits. Fred seemed worried about us."

"Have you told Dan?"

"Yes, he didn't seem particularly bothered."

"I'll go and see Fred."

"He's on the dock with the boys."

"Is he? I didn't see him. Why don't you go home, Uncle Jeb? I'll answer the telephone," she offered, noticing how tired he looked.

Looking relieved, Jeb reached for his coat, the sound of heavy footsteps alerted them that the men were finished loading. He called to them as he headed for his car and they went into the office and sat at the table. Nancy went over to the stove and picked up the old metal coffee pot.

"Did you ask Fred to contact John Gray, Dan?" she asked pouring her husband the first cup.

"I already did it, Nan," the harbour master chuckled. "He'll be waiting at the border to escort you to the Jorgensen's."

"Have you talked to Kate since this morning, Jack?" she continued, changing the subject.

"Yes, she's feeling a lot better."

"I got the deck rail fixed on the *Stockholm*, Nan," Dan advised her, watching her smile. "She's as good as new again."

"Dan says they have the influenza in Cowichan, too," said Fred, a frown furrowing his brow, "and a few deaths."

"It's all around us, Fred," Nancy whispered. "Victoria is going to suffer just like the other towns."

Dan and Jack left for home in the *Stockholm*, while Fred stayed on for awhile talking to Nancy. They found themselves reminiscing about how things had changed in Victoria over the years. They laughed at their memories of streets lined with saloons and taverns before prohibition and then of the years before the war when the harbour was filled with the whaling fleet. They agreed that times were hard back then but there had also been much happier days.

"I was like the others," Fred murmured, reaching back in his mind. "I thought the war was a big adventure. I was really disappointed when the army wouldn't take me but now I figure I was one of the lucky ones."

Listening intently, Nancy realized she'd not heard Fred talk this way before and wondered why his mind had suddenly taken this train of thought.

"Just think of the heartache this damn war has brought to Victoria, Nan," he continued. "All those young men we knew who will never come home again—the broken families they've left behind, and now we have the influenza. I'll be glad when we can get back to normal."

"We all will, Fred. I've never heard you talk like this before," she stated with a questioning expression. "Has something happened I don't know about?"

"Yeah, I got word last night that my aunt in Vancouver just died of the flu."

"Oh, I'm so sorry, Fred."

"I hardly knew her, but it makes a man think. Thanks for listening, Nan," he said sadly, slowly pulling himself to his feet. "Thanks for the coffee, I better get going."

Stocking the stove with wood, she followed him out into the chilly evening air. Locking the office door, she watched him walk slowly back up to Wharf Street.

Almost empty streetcars rattled back and forth on Government Street, not often stopping, and she was glad to leave the unusually quiet city. *It's like a city under siege*, she thought, noting the lack of both automobiles and pedestrians.

Dusk was folding its dim light over the land when she turned onto Cedar Hill Road, the tall trees making it even darker as she wound her way home. Farmhouse lamps twinkled in cottage windows across the fields as she cut down the crossroad to Shelbourne. This was Gordon Head and home.

Humming a tune as she crossed the little bridge at Ash, she suddenly burst into song. Approaching the house, her headlights caught a glimpse of Dan, standing waiting by a Parfitt Brothers' truck under the trees. *Jack and Nellie are here*, she thought, parking the car quickly and running into her husband's waiting arms.

"Will you marry me, young lady?" he whispered in her ear.

"No, sir," she giggled. "I've already caught my man!"

"Jack and Nellie are here."

"I know, silly, we're stood next to Jack's truck, aren't we?"

"Well, who could this be?" Dan murmured, releasing her and watching the headlights of a car coming down the drive.

Stopping, the mystery car blinked its lights, and then slowly started to go backwards.

"Who is it?" Nancy asked suspiciously, moving closer to Dan.

Suddenly the car stopped and roaring into life sped down the drive toward them.

"DAN!" Nancy squealed as the car skidded to a stop and the lights went out.

"YOU MUTTON HEAD, HARRY MAYNARD!" Millie yelled at her husband as she jumped out and slammed the car door. "Won't you ever grow up?"

"You tell him, Millie," Dan chuckled.

"What's going on?" Nancy asked as the two women hugged.

"It's party time!" Millie giggled. "Meg and Kate rang us this afternoon. I think it's a great idea."

Moving quickly inside, the Duggans jumped up to greet Nancy as she entered. Glancing at the table laden with food, she quickly cornered Kate in the kitchen.

"What's the party for?" she asked.

"Meg's birthday."

"Is it Aunt Meg's birthday?" Nancy asked, looking confused.

"Actually, I don't know," Kate giggled, "she said something this morning about turning 60 but when I questioned her she became very secretive."

"She's never told me when her birthday was but then I don't think I've ever asked her either. She's 60, is she?" Nan said thoughtfully.

"We needed an excuse for a party, so I'm calling it Meg's birthday!" Kate exclaimed. "The last party was your wedding and that was almost six months ago!"

As the evening went on, no one seemed to be concerned about the reason for the party as they swapped yarns and news. They were simply a group of friends suffering the pains of oppressive government regulations, municipal restrictions, and a fear of the unknown which they didn't want to mention. Cunningham Manor was soon ringing joyfully with conversation and laughter.

The men cheered when Harry produced several cases of real beer, brewed in secret, and illegally, at his brewery. A bit later, they all went into the living room and listened to Nancy's recording on the new-fangled phonograph player.

"It's good," Jack Duggan hesitantly agreed, "but it isn't like the real thing."

"You want me to sing for you, don't you Jack?" the redhead asked giving him a coy smile.

"Aye lass, I do," Jack admitted, hopefully batting his eyes at her. "It seems like it's been years since you sang for us."

"She was singing when she came down the drive tonight, Jack," Dan chuckled, pulling his wife closer. "Go on, honey, make the old fella happy."

"Millie, I need your help." Nancy beckoned to the brewer's wife as she slipped from under Dan's arm. "Let's do it. I feel like singing tonight."

Clearing the embroidered runner and ornaments from atop the piano, Millie felt a tingle of excitement as she sat down on the stool, letting her fingers caress the smooth keyboard. She loved to play and didn't often do it these days. Nancy joined her, turning to face the eagerly waiting faces.

"Let me tell you what happened today first," she bubbled. "I met a nice young lad, an amputee soldier who's getting some new legs on Saturday. I'm thrilled for him knowing his life will soon be so much better."

"New legs?" Harry asked softly, but his comment was ignored as his wife began to play.

The room went absolutely quiet as if everyone was suddenly holding their breath in expectation. When she began to sing the sound of her glorious voice filled every corner and she motioned to them to join in with the old favourites.

"That's enough, Nan," Millie whispered after five or six songs.

"All right, but I have just one more," Nancy replied, speaking to everyone. "I learned a lovely little song from the young daughter of one of my widows this week and I want to share it with you."

Realizing she didn't need to play, Millie sat back and listened as Nancy softly began singing without accompaniment and, the childlike yet poignant, words were soon tugging at their hearts. Kate buried her head on Jack's chest, unable to control her emotions while Meg dabbed at her eyes. They all realized Nancy was singing for the women suffering through the horrible period of waiting for their men to come home.

There's a hope in every rainbow, a wish in every star, until you come home again, the song concluded.

"What a gift you have, dear," Millie said quietly, closing the piano lid and not daring to look around as her own eyes filled with tears.

"That's enough for tonight," Nancy whispered. "I hope all those men still away from their loved ones heard me."

"You do get to a body, girl," Jack Duggan growled. "I don't know anyone else who can sing like you do."

Jebediah lit his pipe and walked slowly to the door, stepping out into the darkness.

"Where's he going?" Harry asked, frowning as the door closed.

"Oh, he isn't one for showing his feelings, is our Jeb," Meg informed him. "He just needs to be on his own for awhile."

It was almost ten when the visitors left and Jeb emerged from the trees, watching the tail lights of the cars disappear up the drive. Hardened by years on the trail as a Pinkerton detective and lawman, he considered himself almost immune from feelings. Tonight, however, Nancy had touched his heart, as she often did, and he found himself again worrying for the safety of these special people … his family.

Chapter 13

Dawn was breaking as Jeb and Dumpy left for work the next morning, although it was very difficult to tell due to the thick blanket of winter fog which tightly wrapped the area. They made their way cautiously down the drive and out onto Ash Road. Almost at Cedar Hill, the car ran off the road on the bend and Jeb cursed the weather in a blunt stream of expletives.

"I hope the others have enough sense to stay home!" he muttered, hanging over the steering wheel and peering out at the swirling grey darkness.

"You've got to be kidding!" Jack muttered back. "Dan's a sailor, a little pea soup won't keep him landbound!"

True to his prediction, with fog lanterns hung fore and aft, at that moment Dan was casting off the *Stockholm*'s lines as Nancy applied light pressure to the throttle.

"East by south, Nan," he ordered, poking his head into the cabin. "Watch for my signals, I'm going up front."

Moving painfully slowly, it was almost an hour later when Dan waved for her to stop. Knowing there had to be a reason, she did as he ordered and listened intently. She could hear the dull throb of a freighter's engine nearby. Dan slipped in beside her and gave her a quick kiss on the cheek.

"Go out on deck, Nan," he ordered. "Hold on tightly to the rail and hang your hand in the water."

"Whatever for?"

"You'll be able to feel the vibrations. Try to tell if it's coming this way or away from us, but hang on tight, honey, we might have to bounce out of its way!"

Again following his orders, she worked her way onto the deck and knelt by the deck rail. Holding on tightly, she dangled her hand in the water, giggling when she felt the strange vibrations running through her fingers. Concentrating, she tried to ascertain if they were getting stronger or weaker.

"It's going away I think," she called to him, suddenly hearing two distant foghorns.

"I think you're right," Dan replied with a grin. "I reckon we're coming into Admiralty Inlet and we've just passed Keystone. Did you hear the horns?"

"John won't find us in this fog!" she exclaimed, coming back into the cabin.

"No, but we'll find him!"

"How?"

"Think, Nan. I'll bet you he's in Useless Bay."

"That's just a guess."

"No, it isn't. He's out of the shipping lane, but close enough to hear what's passing and ready to pounce if he feels the need. He's a good sailor, but we're going to surprise him!"

Following the noise of the freighter, Dan suddenly turned toward the coastline. Easing slowly closer and closer, he pulled the lever down until they almost stopped, backing away when a jagged rock appeared.

"No talking now," he whispered, going to the door, "keep the engine low and follow my directions." Shutting the door, he jumped onto the deck and went back to his position on the bow.

Funny, she thought, *how at home he looks, sitting out there.*

Suddenly, he jumped up and scuttled back into the cabin.

"I think they're just ahead of us, I heard somebody talking."

"It could be anybody," she argued.

"Not when they call someone 'sir'! It's them all right. Cut the engine, we'll float right up to them."

Ten more agonizing minutes passed before the hazy shape of the US Coast Guard cutter appeared out of the fog. Dan was right and they had floated silently right up behind it. He scrambled out onto the bow and hand-over-hand worked them alongside, preventing them from colliding before securing his lines.

"Are you ready?" he hissed, poking his head in the doorway. "Let's go surprise them."

"A'hoy on board!" he called across the cutter's deck.

"What the …?" a startled sailor hissed, running to look over the rail. "Capt. Gray, sir, over here!"

"Dan, Nancy!" John Gray laughed. "How in Sam Hill did you find us in this pea soup? Come aboard."

Escorting them to the wheelhouse, he shut the door behind them and spoke to one of the sailors.

"Bring three teas, my bottle of Jack Daniels, and make sure …."

"I know, sir, a cup and saucer for the lady!"

"Good man," Gray hissed. "Is the *Stockholm* secure, Dan?"

"Yes, sir," he saluted mischievously.

"Then let's get under way this blasted fog is a menace."

Visibility was at a minimum as the cutter slowly moved off. With crewmen lining the rail, alert for any sign of danger, they made their way south into the shipping lane. Even above the engines they could hear the strange musical sounds of the warning foghorns which were stretched out along Puget Sound.

"We're standing off the Jorgensen dock, sir," a voice shouted from above them sometime later.

"Right you two, off you go and say hello to our mutual friends."

Still surrounded by thick fog, Dan moved eastward through the haze and the cutter disappeared from view. Suddenly, the shoreline loomed ahead. Quickly making the necessary adjustments, Dan smoothly pulled into the Jorgensen boathouse.

"I thought you weren't coming," O'Reilly called as his men closed the doors. "How on earth did you find your way in this fog?"

"We had company," Nancy replied, "the coast guard escorted us in!"

"Next you're going to tell me elephants can fly," quipped the gangster.

"How are things in Seattle, Terry?" the redhead inquired, ignoring his sarcastic comment as she took his hand and jumped down onto the dock.

"Locked up tight, but nonetheless, we're selling lots of booze!"

Making their way up the garden path to the house, Dan suddenly stopped and looked skyward.

"This fog will be gone in an hour," he stated solemnly.

"How do you know?" asked Nancy as the house door opened and Joseph stood waiting for them.

"Rain's coming!" replied Dan. "Hello Joseph."

Doubting his forecast, she put her thoughts aside concentrating on what Joseph was telling them as he ushered them inside.

"Good morning, Mr. and Mrs. Brown, you're a welcome sight on this foggy day. The family are in their apartment. I'm to tell you to go straight up," he instructed, trying to sound chipper although Nan got a hint that there was something bothering him.

Dumping her coat in Dan's arms, Nancy raced up the stairs to the family's private apartment. Barely tapping on the door, she burst into the room but stopped immediately staring in disbelief. Beth was lying in her favourite chair with her feet up on a stool. Still dressed in her housecoat with a blanket wrapped around her, she looked shockingly pale.

"What's wrong?" Nan whispered, her heart beating heavily as she moved quickly across the room.

"A mild case of the flu," Gus murmured heading her off. "Maybe you shouldn't go too close, honey."

Nancy's heart sank, tears welling in her eyes as she hugged the shipping magnate and gently pushed past him to gaze down on the lady she had come to love like a mother. Pale, drawn and looking somewhat older, Beth bravely put on a smile and hoarsely croaked her name.

"She could be highly contagious," another voice, one of authority, sharply informed her.

Startled, but realizing the voice was slightly familiar, Nancy quickly turned around and saw Dr. Tubble standing in the doorway.

"Gus, did you give her Uncle Jeb's medicine?" Nancy asked.

"No, Nan," he mumbled. "Dr. Tubble said it's only a cheap port wine and wouldn't do any good."

Dan entered the room just in time to see Nan's determined look as she turned to face the doctor—he knew trouble was brewing. Striding quickly over to her side he tried to hold her back but she fiercely brushed him aside.

"What harm would it do to at least try it, doctor?" she demanded, her voice rising to a hysterical pitch.

"N-none, I don't suppose," the medical man replied, unfamiliar with having his word questioned, especially by a woman.

"Do we have a bottle on board, Dan?"

"It's all right, I'll look after it, Dan," Gus murmured hesitantly, taken aback by Nan's fierce insistence.

Issuing quick directions to a hovering maid, Gus turned back to Nancy, "I hope it does some good."

"It will!" the redhead assured him, gently taking his arm and leading him over to his chair. "Uncle Jeb said he'd seen it work many times."

"Foolishness," Dr. Tubble rasped. "There are hundreds of those stupid remedies circulating the city."

"Stupid remedy?" Nancy repeated, her voice rising angrily again. "Then I presume you have a cure that will work better, sir!"

"We're doing all we can."

"And that's what I'm doing! I'm trying to help my mother!"

"You've no training and no medical skills. You're working at a disadvantage, young lady," the doctor continued, going red in the face.

"Sir, I was born with a disadvantage!" Nancy spluttered in frustration.

"Your bottle and a glass, sir," the halting voice of the maid interrupted their bitter exchange. Taking the tray and pouring a liberal amount into the glass, Nancy moved toward Beth.

"Stop!" Dr. Tubble demanded, moving to intercede. "I forbid this ridiculous experiment."

Dan sprang forward, blocking the doctor's approach as she knelt beside Beth's chair.

"Don't you dare touch her," Dan hissed menacingly. "You're lucky I'm here and not Uncle Jeb—he'd have shot you by now!"

Smiling weakly, Beth opened her mouth to accept the spoonful of tonic Nancy offered, slowly tasting, then swallowing it, and nodding to signify she wanted more. Gus watched in amazement as a hint of colour returned to Beth's face seconds later, and a more relaxed expression showed in her eyes.

"Sleep now, Beth," Nancy whispered gently. Going to sit in a chair near the door, she took a deep breath and closed her eyes. *Uncle Jeb, your medicine has just got to work*!

Gus came over and took her arm, ushering everyone quietly out of the room. He ordered the maid to keep an eye on his wife and followed them out. Even as they descended the stairs, the doctor again began to grumble, loudly proclaiming that perhaps Beth did not have influenza. As Gus tiredly thanked him for coming and showed him to the door, he continued ranting that his time was being wasted and he wouldn't take the Canadian girl's interference lightly.

"I think this is all getting too much for the poor man," said Gus, entering the kitchen to join Dan and Nancy at the table, spread with refreshments.

"I suppose I shouldn't have been so hard on him," Nancy said shaking her head sadly as she nibbled on a sandwich. "I just felt so helpless seeing Beth lying there."

Throughout the early afternoon, Nancy looked in on Beth several times, noticing a slow but marked improvement in her colour and breathing. Each time she awoke, Nancy dosed her with tonic. By two-thirty Beth was asking for some hot broth, her first food in two days. Nancy breathed a sigh of relief and her confidence in Uncle Jeb's elixir soared.

By the time they left the Jorgensen's, they knew they would be racing against the darkness and seeing Dan was right with his weather prediction. Dan opened the boathouse doors and Nancy quickly climbed aboard, stowing the thermos and food given to her by the maid. She started the *Stockholm*'s engine and was surprised to find a newspaper lying on her seat. Opening it, the large, bold headline glared out at her, *PEACE WITH CONDITIONS TURNED DOWN BY ALLIES.* Shaking her head, she noticed both the doors were open and Dan was waving to her. She quickly put the newspaper aside and began to ease the *Stockholm* slowly out of the boathouse. She was pleased when Dan came up behind her and she allowed him to take over.

"Look who's closing the doors!" he exclaimed, pointing back to the boathouse.

Looking back she was surprised to see Peter, the chauffeur, waving to them through the rainy mist. Waving back, she moved to her own seat and picked up the newspaper again, silently mulling over the news until she could safely talk to him.

"I don't understand why they wouldn't want the war to end," she commented as they picked up speed.

"What the devil are you talking about?" he asked, glancing over at her.

"Look at this newspaper headline," she replied, holding up the paper so he could see it.

"Where did this come from?" he asked, obviously surprised and taking it out of her hand.

"Someone left it on my seat, probably Terry. Here, trade places with me so you can read it."

When he finished reading, he grinned ruefully. "Gus was right, Gerry is trying to talk peace."

"Well, why don't they call a truce and get this horrible war over with?"

"They will, when the enemy surrenders unconditionally."

"I don't understand why they'd want more killing when it could be over."

"We don't, but these things take time, honey. You'll see, it will be over within the week, they're beaten and just have to realize it."

"I just hate to think of all the men who could be getting killed or injured while these powerful men decide what to do," she said sadly.

"It's as dark as the inside of a whale's belly," Dan quipped, coining a phrase his old boss, Ned Joyce, used to say on many a whaling trip.

"Oh golly, we should have called Aunt Meg!" Nancy said with a worried note in her voice. "We're much later than usual and she's going to be worried."

"She already knows, honey," Dan assured her, taking her hand. "Gus said he would call and tell them we'd be late."

Slowing a little as they came to the Edmond's light, they checked Ezekiel's signal beacon at Apple Cove. Satisfying themselves that he was not needing their help, they picked up speed, roaring off toward Kingston and the open waters of the Strait of Juan de Fuca.

"There's the coast guard," she warned, pointing to the shore just south of Kingston. "Looks like they want us to stop," she added as they got closer and saw their signal. "I wonder what the problem is."

As they drew alongside, Capt. Gray hailed them with the bullhorn.

"PERMISSION TO COME ABOARD, CAPTAIN BROWN?" he shouted formally. He handed the bullhorn to his lieutenant and casually saluted Dan.

"PERMISSION GRANTED!" Dan shouted back, returning the salute.

Jumping over the side, they were relieved to see that the captain was looking unusually happy.

"We just received a radio message," he informed them, "the Turks have surrendered!"

"That's a good start," Dan replied, showing his relief. "It's the first positive sign that this war is finally coming to an end. Thanks for telling us, John."

"Won't be long now," Gray added. "I thought you'd want to know, Dan, being a veteran and all." He returned to his own boat and several of his crew lined up and saluted as the *Stockholm* pulled away.

"You're quiet tonight, honey," the redhead murmured over her shoulder half an hour later. "Did John stir up some bad memories?"

"I don't have any good memories of the war, Nan," he replied, continuing to look straight ahead. "It was hell, plain and simple."

As they passed Oak Bay, the rain finally abated and the clouds were breaking up playing hide-and-seek with the moon and stars. She realized they had travelled the last hour in silence, Dan's eager chatter had disappeared.

At Cunningham Manor, worry disturbed the minds of Jeb and Meg and their guests, Jack and Kate. Jeb went outside as it was getting dark waiting for half an hour and lighting the two cliff beacons before returning to the house. He tried not to act concerned although he was sure something was amiss, the youngsters would have called if they had known they'd be late.

By six-thirty Jack was taking his second turn outside, pacing the clifftop and watching the strait for any sign of a light. Suddenly, he heard the faint sound of a powerful engine and knew instantly it was the *Stockholm*.

Racing across the lawn, he leaped onto the porch and threw open the front door. "They're coming!" Going back to the clifftop, he picked up one of the lanterns and went down the dark stairs to wait for them. It wasn't long before the *Stockholm*'s bow light turned into the cove.

"WHERE THE DEVIL HAVE YOU BEEN?" he yelled over the engine noise as the boat bumped the dock and Dan threw him one of the lines.

Ignoring his old shipmate's question, he helped Nancy onto the dock as Jack continued his barrage of questions.

"Dumpy, will you stop! We'll tell you all about it when we get something warm in us," snapped Dan.

Hearing the exchange between the men, Nancy urged Jack to go back to the house. Knowing Dan even better than Nancy, from their many years together on the whaler, he knew when his friend was in a bad mood it was best to leave him alone. He also knew there was probably something wrong to put him into this mood and he would just have to wait until he was ready to give an explanation. Starting up the stairs, he left the lantern near the top and went into the house.

When Jack left, Nancy also started up the stairs but stopped when she realized Dan wasn't following her. Lighting the lantern hanging outside the cave entrance, he seemed to be puttering around although not doing anything in particular. He looked up and realized she was watching him.

"You go up, Nan, I've a few things to do here yet," he called.

"All right, but don't be too long, Aunt Meg will have dinner waiting."

When she looked back from the clifftop, he was still standing in the same spot and she wondered what thoughts were going through his head. He had never talked much about his war experiences because so many of them had been erased by his loss of memory. *Was it something John*

Gray said today, she wondered, *or will he always be tormented by this terrible war*?

Meg noticed Jack's worried expression when he returned to the house but, seeing a light move outside shortly after, she knew someone was coming and didn't question him. When she realized it was Nancy, she looked behind her for Dan.

"Where did you leave Danny?"

"He's finishing up on the dock," the redhead slowly replied, then stopping suddenly, she set her bag down on a chair and turned on her heel. Going back outside, she ran over to the stairs. Picking up one of the lamps she carefully descended the wet stairs looking for Dan. When she was almost at the bottom, he came out of the cave and, seeing her, smiled boyishly catching her as she sprang into his arms.

"I was worried, let me share it with you, Danny," she whispered, hugging him fiercely.

"Don't worry, Nan, it was only a few ghosts visiting me momentarily." He reached up and, with that faraway look in his eyes again, touched her face. "I am so lucky to have you."

She looked into his eyes and kissed him tenderly. "You'll always have me, Danny. We belong to each other forever."

Puzzled at Nan's disappearance and still feeling something wasn't right, Meg put her coat on and went to stand at the clifftop. Joined by Kate, they watched Dan and Nancy embracing in the shadows below.

"Is everything all right, Meg?" Kate murmured apprehensively.

"Ach lassie, I hope so. I just have a feeling gnawing at my old bones," Meg took her arm and led her back toward the house. "I do know that they're doing what they've always done."

"But they weren't doing anything except hugging!"

"Ah yes they were, lass," Meg replied softly. "They were loving each other and sharing each other's problems."

As Dan and Nancy slowly started up the stairs together, Dan talked of the war and several of the men he had known—men who would never come home—comrades he'd fought with who died in the mud of Vimy and Flanders.

"We're the lucky ones, Nan," he whispered as they reached the top.

"Don't look back, Danny," Nancy consoled him, squeezing his hand. "We've so much to look forward to. I want you to be happy."

"I am happy, Nan, happier than I've ever been. You're right of course. Sorry for being a misery." He put his arm around her and kissed her forehead.

Now watching from the kitchen window, Meg patted Kate's hand reassuringly.

"Whatever the problem was it's gone now," she muttered, hoping she was right.

"We're home … again!" the redhead cried, entering the warm kitchen and hugging her aunt. "A nice cup of hot tea would sure go down well right now. It was a miserable day out on the water first with the fog and then the rain."

Soon they were all sitting around the table drinking a hot cup of tea.

Kate's inquisitiveness got the better of her and she suddenly broke the silence. "Why did you go back down to the dock, Nan?"

Meg's tea cup rattled on her saucer, but Nancy smiled and reached for Dan's hand.

"I realized I'd left him to face his pain alone."

"Dan's in pain?" Kate asked, frowning.

"Not physically, but we'd been talking to the coast guard about the war and the conversation shook his memory. Do you remember when I caught you crying in the kitchen at the Balmoral? You were so distraught over looking after your grandmother it just got too much for you one day, didn't it?"

"Yes, it was a tough time," Kate replied, "but you helped me get through it."

"She helped me too, Kate," Dan whispered, "and not for the first time."

"I'm sorry Nan, I shouldn't have asked," Kate replied, dropping her head. "It's really none of my business."

"No you shouldn't have, lass, but the damage is done now," Meg retorted softly. "It's time I got dinner on the table, come help me."

"You two gave us quite a turn tonight you know. We were expecting you before dark," Meg commented putting the plates on the table. "I'd die if anything happened to either of you!"

"We're sorry, Aunt Meg, but Gus was going to telephone and tell you we'd be late. He must have had too much on his mind," reasoned Nancy.

"I wonder if there's something wrong with the phone. Now that you mention it, the darn thing has been unusually quiet today," Meg mused. "Has anyone used the phone today?"

"I'll go check it, Aunt Meg," offered Dan, getting up and going out to the hall. Returning a minute later he was able to solve the mystery. "Ruby says there have been some phone problems today due to the weather, they think. That could explain not hearing from Gus. I'd better give him a quick call."

They heard him talking on the phone and when he came back Meg ordered everyone to the table. She began dishing up her staple meal of rabbit stew with big fluffy dumplings. As they ate, everyone listened intently as Nancy and Dan described their eventful trip. Nancy told them about finding the coast guard vessel in the thick fog and everyone laughed when they heard how they were able to sneak up on them and gain safe passage to the Jorgensen's. Dan, with interruptions from Nancy, told them of Beth's illness, the wild argument with Dr. Tubble, and giving her a dose of Jeb's tonic.

"Dan told him," Nancy giggled, "if you'd been there Uncle Jeb, you'd have shot him!"

"Damned right I would have!" the old detective muttered.

"Did it make a difference?" Meg asked hopefully.

"Not straight away, but she certainly looked a lot better and ate some broth before we left."

"Gus said she's sleeping more peacefully than she has in days."

"That's good news," said Nan.

"You were in the same room with her?" Meg asked in concern.

"Well, only briefly. I wanted to stay but Gus wouldn't let me, so I looked in on her several times."

"On the way back, the coast guard stopped us, John gave us the latest news of the war. It seems the Turks have surrendered," Dan announced.

"Thank heavens," Meg declared, "maybe peace is close at hand at last. Now you tell them your news, Jeb."

"Heywood's man called at the office," Jeb growled. "This flu's really hitting hard and the funeral home is running out of boxes."

"Boxes?" Nancy asked, raising her eyebrows and frowning.

"Coffins, lass," Meg whispered solemnly.

"They want Dan to bring a load in from the Grahams' sawmill on Denman Island," Jeb growled.

"Why me?" Dan grimaced. "They could send them on the *Beaver*."

"They're in a hurry, lad."

"How many do they need?"

"Fifty."

“Fifty? We’ll need a barge to transport that many!” Dan exclaimed.

“They said it was urgent so I told him you’d do it tomorrow.”

They finished their dinner and continued discussing the influenza epidemic, now obviously taking hold in the Victoria area. Jeb pointed out that newspaper reports were still giving only sketchy details but it appeared hundreds of cases had been reported in both Victoria and Vancouver and up-island deaths were even higher than Victoria.

“They’re trying to play down the severity, so people don’t panic,” said Nancy.

“But reports coming from Seattle and Vancouver can’t be disguised so easily,” Jeb said bluntly. “Fred tells me that freighter crews are bringing almost daily news of the rising death toll and sickness from the Mainland. And I don’t like all this travel you two are doing to Seattle, it’s too dangerous.”

“But we’re taking your tonic, Uncle Jeb, and we’re being careful,” Nancy assured him but he looked at her doubtfully, knowing she still didn’t understand the severity of the disease.

Settling into bed that night, despite Dan’s attention and soothing words, Nancy couldn’t stop the thoughts that filled her head with worry for their American friends and, especially, the Jorgensens.

Chapter 14

As dawn broke on the last day of October, 1918, Dan and Jack checked the weather from the clifftop noting the red streaks on the horizon.

"Looks like it'll be a cool one but no rain in sight, Danny," murmured Jack.

"This is one job I'm not looking forward to old friend."

"Hopefully, they won't need you to make anymore of these trips."

Dan merely sighed and turned back to the house. As the boys entered the kitchen, Nancy and Meg were arguing with Kate who was already dressed and insisting she felt well enough to return to work.

"The exercise will do me good, Jack, please tell them," she begged feebly.

"Honey, you know they're right," he said softly, putting his arm around her.

"Stay with us for at least two more days, Kate, you've gotta admit that it's nice being waited on and not having to make meals!" Nancy reminded her as Meg nodded her head in agreement.

Feeling outnumbered Kate gave in and dropped the subject. Ten minutes later, Nancy and Meg, bundled up in their warm winter coats, stood watching as Dan took the boat out of the cove. He waved one last time and turning north toward Denman Island, soon disappeared behind his own wake.

"He'll be late home tonight," Meg commented as they went back inside to get warm. "It's a long way to Buckley Bay."

"He'll be trying to get back while he has light," said Nan, silently talking to herself as she went upstairs. *I don't like him travelling these waters alone after dark, it's too hard to spot deadheads.*" When she returned, she sorted through her notes gathering what papers she needed.

"I'll be going out to Sidney today and to a lady down West Saanich Road," she informed anyone listening, donning her coat, scarf, and hat.

"Drive carefully, lass," Meg reminded her as they hugged at the door.

Preparing her mind and contemplating her mission as she drove through the forest below Mount Douglas, Nancy tried to dodge the deep, water-filled potholes in the rough track. Sitting for a moment at the

Royal Oak rail crossing, she watched the Cordwood Express as it puffed across the valley's marshlands belching black smoke as it climbed the Royal Oak hill on its way to Sidney. Crossing to West Saanich Road, she made her way toward Brentwood, stopping at the Morris farm at the corner of Prospect Lake Road.

Clara Morris was a strong, independent lady, who worked hard on the family farm. Her husband had been listed as missing in action for more than three years. But there was no time for tears for Clara. With seven youngsters to feed, out of necessity, she quickly became mother and father to her brood, never grumbling at her 16-hour work day. She had come to Eva's attention through the Red Cross when she confided she was having a struggle with her mortgage payment. Nevertheless, she impressed all who knew her with her determination to provide for and keep her family together.

The worry of her mortgage payment was dealt with by the Widows' and Orphans' Fund, although she knew little about it or of its founders. Visitors were always a welcome addition at Clara's table. Seeing no newspaper, her thirst for gossip and news was almost insatiable. She knew nothing of the deadly influenza epidemic or of the present state of the war—her efforts and thoughts totally directed on survival.

Driving away, Nancy realized how much she admired Clara Morris. *That dear lady has such determination and her outlook on life is undaunted despite her hardship and worry*, Nancy mused silently. *There must be lessons to be learned from women like her.*

She took the bumpy West Saanich Road through the village of Brentwood and past the rolling farmlands to the Deep Cove Railway Station. Turning sharply at the corner of Mills Road where the little Holy Trinity Church stood proudly looking out to sea, she followed a rough dirt road through the heavily wooded hillside to Sidney.

Groaning when she saw the ankle-deep mud in front of her along Beacon Avenue, she eased the truck forward as slowly as she dared, knowing that no matter how she drove, the splashing thick spray of mud would require her to wash the truck later. Shooting a quick glance at the ramshackle buildings fronting the main street of the little town, she remembered that they housed the Asian mill workers so important to this area. She turned up Fifth Street and found the house she was looking for.

As she opened her door and saw the mud at the side of the truck, she grimaced and leaped to the safety of a small patch of grass. She could hear Mrs. Wright's chuckle of amusement as she watched from the doorway.

"I was hoping you'd come," the old lady said simply, inviting her in with a wave of her hand. Silently producing a letter still in its government envelope, she placed it slowly and deliberately in front of the redhead.

Nancy's blood raced through her shaking fingers as she saw the official army endorsement.

"When did this come, Mrs. Wright?" she asked with a quivering voice.

"Monday, I been waiting for you to read it to me, dearie."

Biting her lip and trying to appear calm, Nancy hesitated, hating the inevitable task. Too many times through the last few years, she'd seen the hopes and dreams of wives and mothers shattered by the contents of such a letter. Steeling herself, she ran her finger across the flap, extracted the letter, and slowly began to read.

"To Mrs. Ida Wright," she read, "we must inform you that your son, Sergeant James Arthur Wright," she stopped to poke at a tear, hardly daring to continue reading the last short sentence, "will be coming home on the fourth of November. Oh my goodness, isn't that wonderful, Mrs. Wright?"

"Jamie's coming home?" the old lady whispered as if she didn't yet believe it was true. She had both hands around her teacup now as it sat on the saucer and rattled with her nervous excitement. "My boy is coming home."

"Thank God for that," Nancy added under her breath, barely able to contain her own emotions.

After two cups of tea, she handed Mrs. Wright an envelope containing the rent and food money, adding a five-dollar bill from her own purse to help Ida get something special for her son's homecoming.

"Will you go meet Jamie at the docks, Ida?" she inquired.

"No dear, I could never travel that far—he knows his way home."

Hugging the dear old lady, Nancy could feel her spirits rising as she walked back to the truck. This time she cared little about the mud squishing under her feet and cheerfully returned Ida's wave.

In Sidney, she found two of her families suffering with the flu so she slid her envelope under the door and talked to them briefly with the door closed. Feeling a great sadness envelope her body, she was glad to be on her way home up East Saanich Road before dark.

As the late afternoon sun perched low over the Sooke hills, a cold breeze blew in off the sea and Nancy felt a desperate need to raise her spirits so she began to sing. Her voice rising majestically, she startled a teamster leading his logging horse team home for the night and he waved.

Reaching the end of Elk Lake and turning onto hilly Cordova Bay Road, soon she was able to look over the trees at one of her favourite views of Mt. Baker. Although getting dark, it was still a majestic sight similar to theirs at Gordon Head, but she never tired of it. Here, the land was a good deal higher and, on a clear day like today, each nook and cranny of every island in the strait was visible and she slowed to take it all in.

"Marvellous!" she exclaimed aloud, then began to sing once again as she descended the hill. Now much of the road hugged the coast and her spirits lifted even more as she drew closer to home. Once again, driving through the forest and heavy underbrush below Mt. Douglas, she thought of the beach where the native Indians used to park their canoes and walk into town, wisely not chancing the treacherous currents.

Between the trees she looked out at the sea and her heart took a leap when she spotted the *Stockholm* towing a barge across Cordova Bay not far from home. The race was on. She giggled, adjusting the throttle a bit, only to bounce heavily into several large potholes. Slowing, she began to sing as she turned onto Ash Road. Reaching their gate she turned down the drive bouncing through more potholes as she descended the little hill. Parking quickly, she raced for the cliff stairs and watched the boat arrive.

"I beat you home!" she called to Dan as he tied up.

"Only just, you little devil!" he shouted back, laughing as he came up the stairs to sweep her off her feet. "I saw you through the trees, driving like the devil was after you. I knew what you were up to, girl!"

"Put her down," Jeb grunted as Dan carried her into the house. "She ain't lame, is she?"

Dan laughed lowering her onto her feet and giving her a peck on the cheek.

Kate giggled at the unusual show of affection between her friends and watched as Nancy walked over to Jeb sitting at the table. She removed the pipe from his mouth then tossed the newspaper onto the table. Sitting down on his lap, she slipped her arms around his neck and kissed his forehead.

"Get away with ya!" he growled, though Kate noticed he had wrapped his arms around her waist. "What are ya doing, woman?"

"Only loving one of the special men in my life," Nancy purred.

Sighing, the old detective's head slowly came to rest on the redhead's shoulder, his arms tightening around her.

"Sweetheart, you're the only girl I'd ever kill for," he whispered emotionally before pushing her away.

"I feel rejected," Nancy pouted, grabbing the pipe from his hand.

"You'll never be rejected as long as I breathe," he continued, "now give me that pipe back, and go help your Aunt Meg."

"I wonder where Jack is?" Kate asked with concern.

"You'd better get used to it, lassie," said Meg, "a seaman will always keep you worried."

As they waited on dinner for Jack, Dan told them of his trip to Denman Island and how much he enjoyed the unusual humour of the Graham brothers.

"Any sickness on Denman?" Nancy inquired.

"None at all. I went and said hello to Pat and Bessie at the store. They said folks are on edge but thankfully nobody's got the sickness yet."

"Did you tell them what you'd gone there for?"

"Didn't have to, everybody knew. They've been busy filling orders for many places on Vancouver Island. Seems Nanaimo's been harder hit than us with over a hundred deaths so far."

"That's awful!" Kate declared.

"We want to hear about your day, Nan," Meg interrupted. "Hopefully you can tell us something more pleasant."

"I had a pretty good day, but that drive to Sidney's a pain in the neck. They badly need a new road and the mud was ankle-deep even on main street."

"Not that, silly, I want to know about Clara Morris and old Mrs. Wright," Meg declared.

"Oh, Clara's Clara! She's a mountain of strength that poor woman; we should all take a leaf out of her book. I've nothing but admiration for her, and Mrs. Wright was the happiest woman in Sidney when I left her."

"Why," Dan frowned, "what's happened?"

"I read her a letter saying her son Jamie is coming home. He lands in Victoria on the fourth of November."

"Wounded?"

"I don't think so, I hope not—at least the letter didn't say so."

“Now that’s what I call good news,” agreed Dan.

The sound of a truck in the drive caused Meg to turn back to the stove as Kate ran to the door to meet her husband. Within minutes everyone was sitting down and Nan helped Meg put the plates on the table. They were partway through the meal and the men were just having seconds of venison roast, when a knock came at the door and it opened slowly. Eva poked her head inside.

“Anybody home?” she asked enthusiastically, grinning when she saw them.

“Hello Eva,” they all chorused.

“Get another chair, Danny,” Meg ordered, “you’re staying for dinner, aren’t you?”

“No thanks, I’ve already eaten, I was actually home early today, finding an unexpected ride,” Eva bubbled, “but I will have a cup of tea. I wanted to talk to you about Dr. Price’s restrictions. They’ve now been passed by council!” Taking her coat off and sitting down, she realized everyone was waiting for her to continue.

“The provincial government has given Dr. Young the authority to override council if he feels it’s necessary. They’re clamping down on everything and business owners are screaming blue murder. Churches have been closed—schools, too. Theatres are locked and even the Union Club has orders to shut its doors. I brought you a list of the new regulations.” She opened her bag and extracted a sheet of paper and handed it to Dan.

Their conversation continued as Nancy and Kate helped Meg clean up the kitchen getting the dinner dishes washed and put away in quick order.

“We can only hope Victoria isn’t hit as hard as some of the eastern cities which are reporting thousands of dead already,” Eva reported. “And I know you won’t like to hear this, but figures are coming from Europe now with millions dead over there. It’s hard for a soul to imagine. I just hope the Lord and Jeb’s port wine will keep me safe so I can carry on as normally as possible!”

“Amen!” Nan agreed solemnly as the others nodded in agreement. “There are too many people who depend on us these days.”

On Friday, Dan went off to Seattle on his regular run vowing to be even more cautious and, up at the house, rejecting Meg and Nan’s arguments, Kate insisted she accompany Jebediah into the office. She promised she would take it easy by working on the shop’s books and going window shopping in town, something she rarely had time to do, assuring them she would stay away from people and not go into any shops.

"I was going home tomorrow anyway, so I'll just go home with Jack tonight and save everyone the trouble of having us overnight again," she argued.

"Ach, you know you are no trouble at all, lassie. I have enjoyed the company and we just wanted to make sure you were all right," Meg assured her.

"I know you did and I appreciate it so much," she said gratefully, hugging the older lady. "You're like family, Meg. Thanks for your concern."

"Kate, I haven't heard you mention your grandparents for awhile, how are they doing?" asked Meg.

"Oh they're remarkably well, thanks. I drop in to see them quite often. I hope they're all right with this flu around; grandpa is quite frail."

"Wait a minute, I have an idea, Kate," Nancy called from the hall, as she put on her coat. "Awhile back I heard you say you've been wanting to have a ride in the *Stockholm*."

"Yes, I did, but what does that …?" Kate asked with a puzzled expression.

"Well, first of all, I'll be coming home by mid-afternoon today and I can pick you up so it's not such a long day for you. This means you'll stay another night and can go into town with Dan in the morning!"

Kate's face lit up. "Oh all right, you've got me hooked! We'll come back tonight then. Thanks … both of you, you're dears!" Then hearing Jeb calling, she opened the door. "I'M COMING!" she called, hurrying to grab her coat and give each of them a hug.

It wasn't long before Jeb's big car was disappearing up the driveway with Nancy following. Meg realized she was again back to her usual routine. It was so nice having Kate around to talk to for a few days and, as she finished cleaning up the kitchen, a feeling of stark quietness seem to descend over the big house.

Must be my old age creeping up on me! she thought. *It's hard enough turning 60, maybe I should have admitted it last week when they pretended it was my birthday.* She let out a deep sigh and went to do her ironing.

At 3 o'clock, Nancy finished up her visits and went to pick up Kate as planned. Upon arriving home, Kate admitted she was tired and Meg shooed her away to have a nap before dinner. Nan changed her clothes and when she returned downstairs found Dan in the hall.

"I didn't hear you come in, Dan. Did you see Gus or Beth? How is she?"

"Gus came down to the dock to tell me Beth was sleeping but feeling much better and still taking Jeb's tonic. He'd been able to get some in town, seems no one else knows about its benefits except us!" he laughed. "Thankfully, he now has everyone taking it!"

"Why don't you two go into the living room and enjoy the fire I lit for you," Meg suggested. "Everyone is home early except Jeb and Dumpy. Kate's asleep and I have to get dinner, so shoo!"

Left on their own, Dan stoked up the fire and they snuggled up together on the chesterfield. In conversation Dan mentioned the shortage of hospital beds being a big problem in the city.

"I wonder why they don't requisition the empty Hudson Bay building on Douglas Street for a hospital?" the redhead mused. "It's been empty for years."

"That's right, it was built before I went away." Dan replied. "Tom Ben says it's been wrecked and he thinks it'll never open."

"Thousands of soldiers will be coming home very soon. After risking their lives for four years, do you think there'll be jobs for them, Dan?"

"Premier Oliver's a good man; he'll make sure there's work."

"I hope you're right, honey," she replied, not sounding convinced.

"Terry said Seattle's having a terrible time with the influenza bug and I told him about my trip to get coffins," Dan sighed. "Would you ever imagine Heywood's Funeral Home running out?"

"Don't say that word!" Nancy shuddered, nestling in closer to him. "It gives me the willies."

They were quiet for awhile and soon both drifted off to sleep. Later, the sound of plates rattling in the kitchen and Kate and Meg's voices woke them. Dan got up and put another log on the fire.

"The boys are home, come on you two, dinner's ready!" Kate called from the doorway as the sound of heavy boots were heard on the steps outside.

Soon they were all gathered in the kitchen and Jack went over to greet his wife, getting in Meg's way.

"Blacky said not to forget you're going to see him tomorrow, Nan," Jeb growled as he took his place at the table.

"Get out of my kitchen, Jack Dumpford," Meg scolded, causing him to sheepishly release his wife, then go and sit down.

Setting the last of the food out, Kate avoided Nancy's eyes, blushing as she took her place next to Jack.

"Grace please, Mr. Judd," the Scot ordered, settling into her seat.

Jeb lowered his fork and winked mischievously at Meg.

"Whoever you are who causes all this trouble, I wish you'd quit!" said the old detective staring up at the ceiling. "Stop the war, get rid of the flu, and maybe help me and the old gal get some grandchildren! Amen. Now get on with it!"

Kate giggled and Meg rolled her eyes and whispered, "Amen!"

All through the meal Jeb and the young people filled Meg's need for news. Dan began by describing Gus' tales of empty streetcars, shops operating on limited hours, and the fishing fleet which had moved out of Seattle Harbor, all in an effort to avoid contact with the flu.

Jeb and Jack told them what they had heard of the war from downtown mentioning that a rumour was circulating that it was over. Fred Barrett corrected the misinformation explaining that it was the Turks who had capitulated.

"Why didn't you bring me a newspaper?" Meg asked sullenly.

"We did," Jack muttered. "Jeb had it in his pocket."

Jeb just sat and grinned while Meg shook her head in frustration, marching out to the coat rack to search his pockets. Meanwhile, Jeb picked up the paper from Meg's seat and held it up to show the others, causing a ripple of laughter.

"What's so funny? There's no newspaper here!" she grumbled, coming back to the table. "Where is it, you old goat?"

"It was on your chair, Aunt Meg," Nancy giggled.

"You've been keeping it warm, lass!" quipped Jeb, winking at the others.

"You'll be the death of me someday!" Meg snapped, trying not to smile.

"Please don't use that word, Aunt Meg," begged Nancy.

Later, Kate raised the issue of her travelling in the boat with Dan to see if Nancy had mentioned it to him.

"I know it's Saturday, but are you going into the city tomorrow morning, Dan?" she asked coyly, looking over at Nancy.

"Yes, as far as I know Jack and I have some work to do at the dock." He looked over at Jack who nodded his head, knowing what Kate was on about.

"Can I go with you, Dan? I've never been on the *Stockholm*."

"Of course you can," he laughed. "I'll give you a ride in a real boat!"

"You'll love it, Kate," the redhead predicted, "the *Stockholm* is perfection on the water."

So, the next morning, Nancy and Jack were on the clifftop waving as the *Stockholm* left the cove with their spouses aboard. A cold rain was now falling, lashing the coast as they headed out into the swells of a typical West Coast storm.

"I hope she's a good sailor, Dumpy," Nancy commented. "They're going to get tossed around today!"

"Farthest Kate's been is across the harbour in a row boat!' Jack grunted.

"Oh my gosh, I thought she would have been out with you on the *Highliner* by now."

"Nope, never showed much interest!" he declared.

"Too late now, she asked for it!" Nancy chuckled. "You better go catch your ride with Jeb so you can be there when they arrive. I'll drop by later."

Chapter 15

Waiting until Jeb's car was up at the gate, Nan giggled knowing he had gone first to avoid getting his precious car covered with mud, flung from her rear wheels. By the time she reached Ash Road, he was out of sight.

Taking it slowly, she grumbled aloud about the never-ending rain. As she bounced through mud-filled holes, hard to miss on old Cedar Hill Road, she wondered if taking the shortcut may not have been the best idea. She grumbled even louder when she descended the hill and saw the amount of water running in the stream by North Dairy Farm, flooding the nearby marshland and the little farm's lane.

Driving slowly until she was clear of the water, she continued up the rise. Here, the road was much better as the potholes at the end of the street by Susan White's cottage had been carefully levelled. She slowed, peering through the rain-splattered windscreen when she saw the early morning streetcar crossing Cedar Hill at Lansdowne. *I'm almost there*, she thought.

Pulling into the muddy drive at the Alcock farm, she saw Ted watching her from the barn and waved. Parking the truck, she quickly picked her way across the yard to join him.

"Well Ted," she said, breaking into a smile as she wiped rain from her face with the end of her scarf. "I see you're on the job despite the weather!"

"Already milked two cows, fed the hogs and chickens," he replied, grinning back at her. "Would you mind taking this bucket of milk inside, Nancy, then I can bring some logs for the stove. It'll save me a trip."

"Certainly, is Dora up?"

"Oh yes, she's in the house with the children."

Nancy heard Ted laugh as she struggled across the muddy yard with the heavy milk bucket, kicking the door with her foot until Dora came to open it.

"Oh, hello Nancy. Take it into the kitchen, would you please," Dora instructed. "Ted enlisted you, did he?"

"Yes, he said he was going to bring in some wood."

Followed by three cats, Nancy set the bucket down where Dora indicated and soon realized she would have to guard the precious white liquid from the eager meowing felines.

Noisily Ted arrived, clumping in on his strange rocker feet. He dumped his armful of logs into the box and turned to answer the eager calls of the children who were playing at the table.

"Who's calling for Mr. Teddy Bear?" he asked, jovially.

"You're not going away are you, Ted?" five-year-old Laura whispered.

"Only for an hour or two; I'm off to find some magic legs," he said mischievously.

"Can we see them?" her older brother, George, asked eagerly.

"Yes, I promise I'll show you as soon as I get back."

"He's marvellous with the children," Dora whispered to Nancy. "I hope he'll stay when he gets his new legs."

"Are you ready, Ted?" Nancy asked, smiling to Dora. "We'd better be going."

As they drove away from the farm, Nancy turned to the young man.

"You seem to have made quite an impression on the Alcock family."

Nodding, Ted continued looking out of the window but made no reply. Driving into the city in silence, Nancy understood his quietness considering he might be experiencing some doubts about the legs Jim was making for him. She knew this could be a life-changing day for him.

Ted *was* experiencing some tormenting thoughts. His expectations were high but would Jim Morrison have accomplished the impossible? Was it feasible to think he could ever appear to be normal again and how would it change his life?

Stopping at the curb in Wharf Street, she noticed beads of sweat standing out on Ted's brow as he sat rigidly in his seat.

"We're here, Ted. I'm coming with you if that's all right?" she commented, watching his face.

"That's all right, but Nancy, what if they don't work?" he asked suddenly, as tension gripped his stomach.

"You won't ever know if you don't go and see," she said softly.

"I'm actually scared to death. Strange isn't it, I had the courage to go to war but this is even harder," he confided.

"Cheer up, the Magic Man can't be scared. What would the children think, Ted?" she reminded him with a smile.

This must have hit the right nerve because he opened the door and was just climbing out when Jim came around the corner.

"Hello Nancy, Ted," he called as he backed a horse out of the smithy. "Bring that lad in, I'll be with you in a minute."

Spurred into action by the blacksmith's appearance, Ted followed Nancy into the building.

"Sit!" the blacksmith ordered roughly as he came through the door, pointing to a barrel. "Get them feet off him, lass, we're going to put him back to normal right now!"

Nancy cringed watching as Ted pulled his pants up to reveal the strapping. There was no escape and she had to face the sight of the badly scared stumps of his legs or embarrass herself. With shaking fingers she fumbled with the straps trying not to look. She turned away quickly as the wooden feet came loose and fell onto the dirt floor.

"Out of the way, girl," Jim ordered, coming up beside her and forcing her to move. With heat-blackened hands, he attached some new metal contraptions, first one, and then the other, as Ted and Nancy watched with fascinated curiosity.

"Right lad," the blacksmith announced, groaning as he straightened his back. "Let's see if you can use 'em."

Nancy moved to offer Ted her arm for support but he raised his hand to stop her.

"I-I can do it," he said, slowly bringing himself up to his new six-foot height. "Wow, this is great. I feel normal again!"

"Well, you look a hell of a sight with your short pants and steel legs," chortled Jim, but he was grinning with satisfaction. "I'd suggest you find some new pants before anybody sees you!"

"Can you walk on them—don't they hurt?" Nancy asked.

"Yes, no, and just you watch me!" Ted laughed.

As Jim cleared up some pieces of metal from the floor to make room for Ted to walk, he didn't take his eyes off the new legs.

"Now that ain't right," he grunted, spitting a stream of tobacco juice into the dust, "and I know just how to fix it."

"Fix what? They're great, Mr. Morrison, can't I keep them like this?" Ted pleaded taking two confident steps toward the blacksmith.

"Sit down, lad. I just have to make a bit of an adjustment. They'll be ready in an hour, go have a chat with old Jebediah."

Disappointment showed on the young soldier's face, as he unbuckled the new legs and strapped his wooden rockers back on.

"Do you have any of your old trousers?" Nancy inquired as they went back to the truck.

"Hell no!" Ted's smile returned. "They were all chopped off at the knee when I got my feet!"

"Well you're going to need some now. Do you think the Sally Ann will have some?"

"Sure, can we go there now?"

In less than ten minutes, they were standing in front of May Coolridge and the smile on her face told them she was glad to see them.

"Hi Nan, Ted, how's the new job going?"

"It's going good," Ted admitted.

"We need some men's trousers, May. Can you help us?" asked Nan.

She immediately rang a bell for a volunteer.

"How many pair do you need?" she asked.

"Two pair of heavy work pants and three pair of decent ones," Ted quickly decided.

"What size? Who are they for?" May frowned, giving her order to the volunteer.

"Me, I'm going to grow new legs in an hour!" he chortled, enjoying the surprised look on both May and the volunteer's faces.

"Don't be silly, who are they for?" May insisted.

"He's telling the truth, May," Nancy advised, "we'll come back and show you."

"Now that would be a miracle," May chuckled as the volunteer hurried off.

While they awaited her return, May made some notes in a file and talked to Ted about his work at the Alcock farm.

"Five pairs of pants, three pair of suspenders and three belts, ma'am," the girl announced on her return, leaving quickly but not without checking Ted out rather thoroughly.

"Would you like a bag, Nan?"

"No thanks, May. We'll take one pair of work pants with us—could you have the others put in Ted's room, please?"

"Certainly and don't forget to come back and show me," she added, her expression telling them she still had some doubts about the situation.

They went over to have a quick visit with Jeb and, before they knew it, the hour was up. When they arrived back at the blacksmith's shop, they couldn't see Jim anywhere so Nancy peeked inside. He was standing in front of his fire, his back to her, chuckling loudly to himself.

"Right on time," he growled, hearing Nancy call to him. "Come right in and sit down, lad. Let's see what you think of these."

Eagerly, Ted sat back down on the barrel and unstrapped his wooden feet, winking at Nancy. Jim handed him the new metal legs and they gasped in unison.

"You've put boots on them," Nancy giggled nervously, "how did you do that?"

Ted was speechless as he examined the metal leg complete with foot and boot. Slipping the leather cup over his stump, his fingers were noticeably shaking as he fastened the straps.

"I bolted a shoe tree and boot onto the end, I'm sure it'll work. When you get your new pants on, nobody will know they ain't for real!"

"Wow," Ted squealed, "even the knee bends!"

"'Course it does," the blacksmith said proudly. "I welded a gate hinge onto it with some slight modifications!"

"Put your new pants on, Ted," Nancy ordered. "Let's see how you look. They'll fit over your boots."

"I'm not taking my pants off in here!" he pleaded with Jim, looking over at Nancy.

"Nancy, go outside and guard the door," Jim ordered with a wink, "now get on with it, lad!"

Going out onto the sidewalk, Nancy listened to the conversation taking place behind her back. She smiled when she heard Jim cursing, then laughter and more harsh words, suddenly everything went quiet.

"Can I come back?" she called as a hand touched her shoulder and Ted stood towering over her.

Standing back, she checked him over from his boots to the top of his head. He looked perfectly normal and so handsome it took her breath away. The transformation was a miracle.

"You're a handsome devil, Teddy," she chortled, causing him to blush. "Let's go show Uncle Jeb."

"First things first, Nancy," said Ted, turning back to Jim. "How much do I owe you, sir?"

"Not a cent, son," the old blacksmith growled, "just promise you'll come see me now and then."

"That's a deal, Mr. Morrison, you're partly my father now. You gave me my legs!"

"Take him away, lass," Jim sighed, turning his back and moving inside before they could see him wipe his eyes with a work-blackened hand.

"Jump in the truck and we'll go down to the dock," Nancy suggested.

"You drive and I'll walk. I need the practice," he replied, grinning with anticipation.

Striding off along Wharf Street, Ted made slow but steady progress, wobbling a little as he adjusted his balance.

"I've got the hang of it now," he boasted loudly when she pulled up beside him. She slowly drove down onto the dock and, with his long legs, he was almost able to keep up although she was a bit apprehensive about the speed he was taking on the rough hill. But he manoeuvred himself just fine, arriving beside her truck glowing with excitement.

Smiling through wet eyes, Nancy felt the glow of Ted's achievement. Jim Morrison had performed the impossible; he had given a young man his life back.

Coming out of the office to meet them, Jebediah stared at Ted in disbelief. Removing his pipe, he stood dumbfounded, shaking his head.

"What the hell has she done to you, lad?"

Ted pulled up his pant legs slightly and Jeb whistled.

"Now ain't that something, did Blackie do that for you?"

"Blackie?" asked Ted.

"That's what Jeb calls Jim because he's a blacksmith," Nancy explained. "Is Kate inside, Jeb? How did she like the ride in with Dan this morning?"

"She was here then she went over to James Bay to see some lady. Dan says she ain't no sailor!"

"Where is Dan?"

"Gone to Renfrew, they've got the sickness and he took Dr. Young to check things out. It doesn't look good."

"And Jack?"

"Delivering supplies to a logging camp."

"I've got to take Ted back to Fernwood right away, do you want me to come back?"

"Yes."

Nancy's eyebrows raised in surprise at Jeb's quick answer. Was there more he wanted her to know that was not for the ears of strangers? Anxious thoughts rattled through her brain as she shepherded Ted into the truck and they waited for traffic at Wharf Street.

"Do we have time to call at the Sally Ann, Nancy?" Ted asked.

"Of course we do. Oh dear, I had my mind on something else. We promised May, didn't we? We'll have to hurry and get you back to the farm though."

Driving past the hissing steam engines on Store Street, Nancy wrinkled her nose at the smell and noise of the cars on the E&N siding. She pulled in tightly to the sidewalk in front of the Salvation Army and honked her horn at May who was standing just inside the door talking to someone.

"Nancy," she called, coming closer, "did you accomplish that miracle yet?"

"Miracle?" the redhead asked coyly. "Oh, you mean Ted's legs?"

"Yes! He said he was growing some new ones."

Grinning mischievously, Ted opened his door and, lifting out his metal legs, brought himself to his new height.

May's reaction was just as they expected. Gasping, she watched him walk toward her.

"I don't believe it!" she exclaimed, her eyes racing over the new six-foot frame. "You weren't kidding. How the devil have you done it?"

"A red haired angel helped me," Ted murmured, assisting the Red Cross supervisor back to the shelter of the door. "Look Mrs. Coolridge," he pulled up one of his trouser legs. "I'm walking on steel legs!"

Regaining her composure, May bent over and examined his leg, her fingers delicately touching the steel and the boot.

"Who made this, Nan?" she asked excitedly. "How is it fastened to his leg?"

"He'll tell you all about it later, May; right now I have to get him back to work. He just wanted to show you his miracle."

Laughing together at May's reaction as they drove out of town, by the time they turned up Bay Street, Ted was humming happily. Then, suddenly, in the most wonderful mellow voice, he began to croon a cowboy song from his childhood.

"I can play a mean guitar, too," he added with a grin, seeing her delighted smile. Arriving at the Alcock farm, Dora was out on the porch as they drove in.

"Teddy's back!" she called inside to the children.

Running past her to the steps, George and Laura's eyes goggled as their new friend walked toward them.

"You growed new legs!" George whispered.

"Mummy, Teddy grew bigger!" Laura giggled.

Gingerly tromping through the mud, Ted reached the porch and gathered both children in his arms. He hugged them affectionately and they all waved goodbye to Nancy.

As she drove up Fernwood Avenue, she noticed several ambulances coming and going to Sir James Douglas School. The playing field was deserted of children and all the activity seemed to be centered on the open front doors. *They're using the school for a hospital*, she quickly assumed, watching as several white-coated men and women moved about near the entrance.

Turning down Fort Street, next she became aware of several homes belonging to the Victoria elite with their blinds still drawn. At 1124 Fort, a city truck with its crew of workmen were unloading materials which looked like parts of beds—evidence that Waldo's information had been correct. The seriousness of the influenza epidemic was now growing in the provincial capital.

Clocks were striking 3 o'clock as she bounced the truck onto the Brown and Wilson dock. Despondently, she got out and slowly walked across the boards to the end of the dock. For the first time, she noticed a hospital troopship standing at anchor in the harbour instead of being tied up at the wharf. Many people were moving about on deck and small boats were coming and going between ship and shore. She soon realized they were carrying injured soldiers as ambulances and trucks were lining up along Belleville Street waiting to transport them.

"What the devil's going on?" she said aloud.

Heavy-booted footsteps sounded behind her and Waldo and Fred joined her.

"They've got influenza on board," said the harbour master as if he had heard her.

"Yes, and the bloody hospitals are full of influenza victims already," Waldo added gruffly. "What the hell are they going to do with them all?"

"I just came past the school at Fernwood," she sighed, "they've taken that over and, Waldo, you were right about 1124 Fort Street, too."

"And don't forget the old James Bay Fire Hall," Waldo added, "what a tragedy."

"Seattle has it worse," Fred continued, "people are dying by the dozens every day."

"Newspaper says Vancouver ain't doing too good either," the haulier added.

"Hold it!" Nancy said solemnly. "That's enough doom and gloom for today. I don't want to hear another word about it. Is Kate back yet?"

"Yes, ten minutes ago," Fred replied, smiling at Nancy's outburst. "Jack and Dan are both on their way in. Jack's towing the Muir barge, Waldo."

Leaving the two men to finish their conversation, she headed for the office to find Kate.

"Tea's just fresh made, Nan," her friend murmured, glancing up from the books. "Pour me one, too, please. I just have to find this wrong entry."

"Uncle Jeb is cooking the books, is he?"

"'Course not silly, it's probably an entry in the wrong column."

"It's not my fault," Jeb grumbled, closing the door behind him. "I wrote everything down like you told me."

"Don't you worry," Kate replied cheerily, "you're doing a wonderful job, but you put a sale in the expenses column, see." She pointed to an entry on the page.

"How did you like your ride in the *Stockholm* this morning, Kate?" Nancy asked with a coy smile in her direction.

Adjusting the mistake, Kate slammed the book shut and reached for her cup.

"I had a wonderful view of the coastline. Dan's a marvellous sailor and full of interesting information. He showed me the explosives factory at Ten Mile Point, Oak Bay harbour and the Gonzales Weather Station. I never realized how high up it was, then he let me see Ross Bay Cemetery through his binoculars. When we passed the breakwater at Ogden Point, he told me it was only finished last year!"

"Sounds like you really enjoyed your trip," Nancy continued, fishing for information.

"You knew it was going to be rough, I had a heck of a job keeping my breakfast down and when we got here I couldn't walk straight without Dan's help!" she laughed. "I think next time I'll ride with you in the truck!"

"I love that boat!" Nancy added, laughing with her. "I didn't realize you weren't much of a sailor until Dumpy told me after you'd gone. You sure picked a stormy day to want to try out your sea legs!"

"I suppose you have no trouble with your sea legs, Nan. Dan taught you everything he knows," Kate retorted.

“Not quite, he still has a few tricks he never showed me. Did you hear the story of what he did with Algenon Pease?” asked Nan, pouring a cup of coffee and sitting down at the table.

“No I don’t think so,” Kate replied. “Tell me.”

“He used a wave to fling a buoy line over his boat so he could be towed in a storm. I’ve never tried it but I’ve heard some of the men say it takes a special skill.”

“Jack says Dan is the best seaman on this coast.”

“Oh, I don’t know about that, but he’s certainly one of them,” Nan agreed.

Jeb, who had left the office unnoticed during the girl’s conversation, now stuck his head back in the door.

“Dan’s back and Jack’s just behind him.”

Going outside, they joined Jeb, Waldo, and Fred on the dock watching the *Stockholm* sweep around the hospital ship and stop. It held steady in the water as the *Highliner*, pulling a barge, passed him and turned into the dock.

“Isn’t that something!” Fred muttered in admiration, coming up to join them. “Dan can stop on a button!”

Their attention taken by the two boats, no one answered as Jack brought the *Highliner* into the dock, coaxing the barge to swing in an arc before miraculously bringing it in tight against the boards.

“DON’T TIE UP, DANNY!” Jeb yelled hurrying toward him. “You’ve a pickup at the rice mill and another at the Hudson Bay Wharf, both for Salt Spring tomorrow.”

“For the Mouats?” Dan called back. Watching Jeb nod his head, he restarted the engine, waved to Nancy, and eased the *Stockholm* away from the jetty.

Chapter 16

The following Wednesday, with rain and wind buffeting the *Stockholm* as soon as they crossed the imaginary line of the US border, standing off Keystone, the coast guard cutter watched but made no effort to contact them. With little conversation, the redhead's thoughts projected ahead to Beth, hoping she was on the road to recovery and that the news from Seattle was not as grim as the week before. Glancing over at Dan, checking the coastline with his binoculars, she knew from the hard set of his jaw, he was also concerned about something.

Watching them dock, Terry scowled as he quickly set his men to work unloading. Cursing, he gave them the bad news that the influenza was still tearing through Seattle, creating a deadly impact on the city.

"There ain't no sense to it," he complained, "nobody's safe these days. You two don't want to stop here for long."

Impatient to check on Beth, Nancy hurried up to the house leaving Dan to deal with Terry and business. Tension bit at her stomach as Joseph solemnly took her coat, giving her no indication of anything, and she went up the stairs. Damp beads of perspiration formed on her brow as she lightly tapped on the door. Hearing Beth quietly say 'come in,' she took a deep breath and pushed it open.

She was surprised to see her sitting up in a chair sipping on a cup of fluid. Nancy sighed with relief and went quickly to her side.

"You're better!" she gasped ecstatically, dropping onto her knees.

"Not quite, honey, but certainly better than last week."

Nancy reached for Beth's hand and whispered emotionally, "Mother Jorgensen, you sure gave us a scare."

"Well, you can thank Jebediah and that awful tonic of his!" Beth chuckled. "I started feeling better from the moment you gave it to me. We should have believed in it from the start."

"Where are Gus and the boys?"

"Gus is on the phone and the boys are at the ranch. Their father told them they had to stay there until this thing is over. He got them some bottles of the tonic and insisted they take it."

Voices and footsteps on the stairs told them Dan had found Gus. When the door opened, a beaming Gus strode quickly across the room, helped the redhead onto her feet, and hugged her. Dan greeted Beth, although keeping his distance, expressing his delight at her recovery.

"Sit down, Nan," said Gus, a note of excitement in his voice. "I've got some news for you."

"Order some food first, please Gus," Beth said softly, "these two must be starving."

"I already did, darling," Gus replied, "now listen to this you two. After that debacle with your first recording Nan, James and I bought the controlling interest in the recording company."

"I thought you said they wouldn't sell?" Beth interrupted. "See, he doesn't tell me everything. I don't know about this."

"They wouldn't," Gus chuckled, "that is until Bill called them as Nancy's agent and told them you would be suing. They were selling copies of your recording which they had no authority to do as you hadn't signed a contract or given permission."

"You mean you own that same recording company now?" Nancy asked incredulously.

"Yes, James Moore and I own it," the shipping magnate reiterated with a twinkle in his eye. "The recording studio just called to say they would accept our offer, if you drop the lawsuit."

"But that means, I will need a contract with you now!"

"Yes Nan, it does and it's on my desk," Gus winked mischievously. "It also includes Nellie."

"Don't worry, sweetheart," laughed Dan. "Bill is the official agent for both of you now."

"But, but," Nan gasped.

"Hold it, Nan," Gus laughed. "I know you don't fully understand, but believe me, you'll get everything you want and more. You'll also get a copy of the contract and Bill will keep you well informed. He said to tell you he won't make any decisions without consulting with you."

The maid arrived with a tray of food, passing it around and then serving tea and coffee as Gus kept on talking.

"We are already arranging a Christmas concert for November and next week we'll have another recording session when you're here."

Nancy's head was spinning—her money troubles were over. *Thank goodness, our Widows' and Orphans' Fund will be able to survive now*, she thought, *but with all the health restrictions, how can there be a concert or more recordings*? Out loud she interrupted him. "You're boggling my mind, Gus. With the influenza all around us, how can we be sure what the future will bring—how can we hold concerts?"

"Leave it to me, Nancy dear," Gus smiled. "The war will soon be over, the influenza will be gone, and we'll be back in business before you know it."

They visited for only half an hour more, noticing that Beth was looking strained with the excitement. Gus appeared to have the business matters well in hand so Nancy and Dan said reluctant goodbyes and made a dash through the pouring rain to the boathouse. Again, Peter followed them down to the boathouse ready to close the doors when they left. Climbing aboard, while Dan and Peter opened the doors, Nancy started the engine and they headed for home.

Over the next few weeks, life became hectic on the West Coast as Seattle, Nanaimo, Victoria, and Vancouver suffered terrible losses from the influenza epidemic. November was remembered for the dark days it brought as few communities in the Pacific Northwest escaped the dreaded disease and death became commonplace.

Victoria counted themselves lucky compared to many BC and Canadian communities and Nancy worked herself almost to a standstill. Having taken care of her widows and orphans for so long, her heart almost broke when the influenza claimed victims in several of her already war-ravaged families. Neither young nor old, rich nor poor escaped, and soldiers happy to be returning home, also found themselves succumbing to the fateful illness after surviving the unspeakable horrors of war.

Newspaper reports finally told the seriousness of the situation bringing to light the disturbing statistics from October. Jeb showed Dan the reports but agreed to give the women only selective information. One report claimed there were 525 cases of sick and dead in Victoria in mid-October, increasing from 230 cases in just two days. In Vancouver, they had nearly 800 cases in the same period but this increased disturbingly to nearly 2,000 cases by the end of the month. One day alone, 1,304 cases were reported in the mainland city.

Nancy forced herself to carry on, driving the streets each day. Near to exhaustion, she tried her best to help the families she had supported for so long. Each time Dr. Price saw her, he warned of the danger of spreading the infection. Through luck, Jebediah's strange port wine elixir, or divine intervention as Meg called it, the inhabitants of Cunningham Manor thankfully remained in good health.

On Friday the 8th of December, 1918, Dan finally brought news that the epidemic was waning in Seattle. His visit with the Jorgensens and Terry O'Reilly's gossip left him with the feeling that the worst was finally over. They had suffered hundreds of fatalities in the Seattle area and newspaper reports feared the number would reach 2,000. With cases thankfully now declining, the city was even considering opening up again.

In Victoria, it was announced they had treated 2,439 cases with 127 deaths. Up-island communities had suffered heavier losses with deaths numbering 143 in Nanaimo and 188 in Alberni, accounting for the majority of over 500 deaths on the Island.

The war, Gus assured him, was also in its last stages and negotiations were ongoing—not made any easier by the enormity of the influenza spreading among soldiers of all nations. His world-shipping contacts reported that the war was virtually over and only the extent of humiliation the British and American generals could heap on the Germans was being discussed.

Rumours circulated in Victoria that the war was over, yet still no official announcement was forthcoming. By Sunday, the 10th of December, citizens by the thousands filled the streets, many wearing face masks as they disregarded city regulations. They milled about on the lawns of the legislative buildings where loudspeakers broadcast warnings by Dr. Price, but even the threat of renewed disaster didn't stop the crowds from booing him.

The Browns watched from their dock, joined by Harry and Millie Maynard who had come into town to see what all the noise was about. Patriotic singing broke out and quickly spread through the crowd until it sounded like the whole city was singing.

When the wind increased blowing in colder air for a time, it helped to quell and dissipate the noisy crowds and Dan and Nancy left for home in the truck. Yet still no announcement came from the legislature and only the rasping voice of the health officer continued.

Darkness blanketed the Shelbourne Valley and tonight no moon or stars shone through the overhanging storm clouds as Nancy and Dan travelled home through familiar farmlands. Windblown leaves swirled across the road in front of them, picked up by dim-headlight beams.

"Peaceful isn't it?" Dan muttered.

"Uh ha," the redhead agreed, "but blasted cold!"

A light flickered in the kitchen window as they came down the drive, causing Nancy to quietly chuckle to herself, knowing the old folks had waited up for them.

Inside, Jeb cocked an eyebrow, folded his newspaper neatly, and got up to stir the fire into life while Meg poured four mugs of hot tea.

"Much happening downtown?" the old man inquired innocently, as they came inside.

"You know there is,'' Meg snapped, "that phone's been ringing all night!"

"Gus called from Seattle," Jeb admitted. "According to him, the fighting will stop tonight and the announcement will come in the morning."

"He said it was over on Friday," Dan replied.

"I don't care which day they pick," Nancy intervened, "just let it be over."

"Eva rang, too," Meg murmured, taking her seat by the fire. "She said the mayor and council want the restrictions removed but Dr. Price won't hear of it yet."

"He was using that awful loudspeaker system to yell at the crowd in front of the legislature tonight," Nancy yawned. "One of these days that man's going to have a heart attack!"

"Is he completely in charge, Nan?" Jeb asked.

"No, Dr. Young's the provincial health officer. He's really the boss."

"What's he like?" Jeb continued.

"Dr. Young is a real gentleman and more inclined to be reasonable I'd say. I guess Dr. Price does his best and it is a thankless job right now."

"Has Vancouver lifted their restrictions?"

"I don't think so; they've had a much worse time than us."

"Oh, stop your questions," Meg ordered, "why do you want to know all that stuff anyway?"

"Go on with your knitting woman," Jeb chuckled, winking slyly at Dan and Nancy. "This conversation is far too intelligent for you to understand!"

Meg's knitting needles stopped clicking. Raising her head, her eyes narrowed and her face went beetroot red.

"Laddie, I reckon your way would be to shoot the poor man!"

"Well, it would sure cut out all the jawing!" Jeb laughed.

"He's pulling your leg, Aunt Meg," said Dan in a soothing tone. "Come on Mrs. Brown; let me take you to bed."

"A pleasure sire," Nancy replied tiredly. "I'm having trouble keeping my eyes open. Just give me a minute to say goodnight to my boyfriend."

Meg giggled as Jebediah, blushing, shuffled back in his chair.

"Control your wife, Dan!" he bleated as the redhead slid onto his knee and planted a sloppy kiss between his eyes. Gently pushing her away, he sighed in resignation. "God knows, I love you, girl," he whispered.

"Soppy!" she chuckled, going over to Meg and hanging over her shoulder to give her a hug.

The next morning Dan forecast sunshine after studying the elements —his sailor instincts noting the antics of the birds, although it was still dark. He had risen early as usual even though he was going into town with Nancy this morning. Walking by the orchard, he was suddenly alert as a rustle of leaves caught his attention and Sam revealed himself.

"Hungry Sam?" he called, but the old hermit disappeared back into the darkness so Dan went inside to tell Meg. He watched with interest as the Scot hurriedly found meat, cheese, and bread, wrapping it in an old newspaper and handing it to Jeb.

Minutes later, bundled up against the cold, Nancy slipped into the passenger seat of the truck, wound a blanket around her legs, and tucked her bag, containing several envelopes of money, safely in beside her.

"Looks like I've got a promotion!" Dan exclaimed, going to crank the truck before climbing into the driver's seat.

The mud of Ash Road, hardened by the cold, caused a bumpier ride than usual as they headed into town along the new gravel surface. Almost alone on the road, when they reached Maude Hunter's little corner store at Shelbourne and Cedar Hill Cross Road, in the low light, Nancy was surprised to see what appeared to be a light in the building.

"I've never seen Maude's store open so early," she commented.

"We'd better check it out," Dan mumbled, pulling up and stopping as Nan quickly opened her door. "There could be something amiss."

Nancy sniffed the air and looked around as she got out. "There's something burning!" she cried, racing for the door.

It was open and the little shop appeared empty, even though a lamp were burning. Not a soul was in sight as Dan hurried inside calling loudly. Panic clutched at the redhead's throat as she pointed to a wisp of smoke curling from under the back door. Dan cautiously tried to open it but it flew aside hitting him with a wall of hot, stifling smoke.

Then they saw the flames, leaping high into the air from a small out-building. Through the swirling smoke he saw a shadowy figure and realized it was Maude. He yelled at Nancy to close the door. Maude was flinging water onto the flames using a heavy metal bucket, but he quickly pulled her away from the fire and took the bucket from her.

"Let it burn," she called over the noise, "me candle dropped!"

"Is it your storehouse?" Nancy called.

"It's only the blasted chicken shed!" she replied fiercely.

"Take her inside, Nan," Dan ordered, refilling the bucket. "I'll stay here and make sure it doesn't spread."

By 8 o'clock the fire had almost burned itself out when John Sadlier, the new Gordon Head Store owner, arrived. Going into town for supplies, he said he smelt burning and followed his nose.

"I hope she didn't lose much," John muttered sympathetically.

"Only a chicken house," Dan chuckled, "sounds like she was searching for eggs with a candle! The chickens flew away."

"Well if she finds an egg now, it'll be well cooked!" laughed the Tyndall Avenue store owner.

Inside the store, Nancy and Maude were also laughing over the incident. In true pioneer spirit, Maude quickly recovered and was already planning a new home for her birds.

"Fire scares me," the redhead murmured as she and Dan resumed their drive to town. "I can still hear the crackle of the flames from the day Government Street burnt down."

"That was eight years ago in 1910, wasn't it? I was at sea on the Belfast and came home to see the mess."

"I was still at the orphanage but I worked at the Temperance Hotel."

"That burned down too, didn't it?" Dan asked, frowning.

"No, thank goodness. We were safe."

Traffic was light on Bay Street as they hurried past the small, well-kept farmlands of Fernwood. Crossing Quadra, Nan watched fascinated, as a milkman's horse pulling a cart walked slowly up the street, stopping to wait for the owner at predetermined places.

"Isn't that lovely," Nancy sighed, "so simple and innocent."

"What is?" Dan asked, looking around.

"Oh, just a milkman and his trained horse back there."

"That's yesterday's world, Nan. It's 1918, things are different now and soon those horses and carts will disappear as automobiles take over."

"I hope it doesn't happen too quickly," she murmured, continuing to look out the window but realizing Dan was right.

Chapter 17

Yellow smoke smelling of sulphur, swirled around the foundry on Government Street as they passed. Mixing with the foul odour from the gas works and the Store Street railway sheds, the air became totally distasteful to breathe. They covered their mouths and noses until they were past.

"I don't know how men work in that stink," she commented, grimacing disapprovingly.

"I wouldn't mind working *there* for a day or two," said Dan, pointing at the big iron gates of the Victoria Phoenix Brewery.

"You don't want to work there; you just want to get at all that beer!" she chortled.

Continuing up Government Street, Dan noticed a group of people milling about outside the fire station behind city hall. Then he realized there were an unusual number of men standing in groups on the surrounding street corners, too.

"What the devil's going on?" he muttered.

"I was about to say the same thing. No doubt Jeb or Waldo will solve the mystery for us," Nan replied as they reached the turn to the dock.

Dan parked the truck beside Jebediah's car and, leaving Nancy to find Kate in the office, made his way across the jetty to check on the *Stockholm*.

Around the corner he was surprised to find another group of men. Jeb, Waldo, Dumpy, Tom Ben, Jim Morrison, and several of Rithet's drivers were watching a growing crowd across the harbour in front of the legislative buildings. Vessels of all sizes were converging on the harbour. Partially blocking the view, a hospital ship, fumigated and now loaded with eager young men—conscription recruits fresh from training camp and, anticipating they would be saved from real war duty—enthusiastically waved to dockside relatives as they prepared to sail.

"Has anybody talked to Fred?" Dan called, jumping aboard the *Stockholm*.

"Barrett's listening for news," Waldo growled. "He says the war's over. News is trickling through that there's going to be a national announcement very soon now."

“How did all these people find out?” Dan asked. “We passed crowds just standing about up by city hall.”

“Damned if I know,” the haulier replied.

“Well someone’s spreading the news,” Tom Ben, a cigar salesman with E.A. Morris observed. “I’m going over there. Those folks need a good cigar and they’re obviously not coming into the shop this morning!”

Old Jim, the blacksmith, chuckled as the rotund cigar salesman hurried away. “Never misses a trick, don’t Little Tom, he’ll be selling cigars at his own funeral!”

Nancy had already left for her regular visit to her Burnside area families, when the official news finally came through. It was just after 11 o’clock when Fred Barrett burst out of his door at the harbour master’s office and began yelling with uncontrollable excitement across the docks.

“DANNY, THE WAR’S OVER! IT’S OVER, IT’S OVER!”

Loudspeakers at the legislature also suddenly burst into life, but over at the Brown and Wilson dock it was impossible to hear what they said. A cheer spontaneously rose from the legislature crowd, growing louder and louder as the news spread along Belleville into Government and the Empress Hotel.

“It’s finally over, thank God. I better go call Margaret,” Waldo gasped, snatching his pipe from his mouth as he hurried away.

Offices along Wharf Street emptied, as people rushed to join the cheering crowds already in the street. Victoria had abruptly sprung to life despite the health restrictions.

Suddenly feeling light-headed, Dan grabbed the *Stockholm*’s rail for support, sitting down heavily on the floor. His breath came quickly as he closed his eyes and memories of the sacrifice he and his men had made on the battlefields of France flashed through his mind. He felt a hand on his shoulder and looked up to see Jeb beside him. He knew the old detective understood as they both wiped tears from their eyes.

It was almost 2 o’clock when Nancy headed back to the city, still unaware of the news. She watched with amusement at the large number of people scattered along the streets waving flags and acting strangely. As she reached Government Street, further puzzling things were happening—streetcar drivers were incessantly ringing their bells and cars and trucks were hooting their horns. Above the noise, she heard the church bells peeling from several churches all over the inner city, each with their distinctive sounds.

"The war's over," she whispered, heaving a deep sigh as realization struck her. She began to cry as her own memories of those long days waiting for Dan's letters that didn't come and, then the news of his injuries, flooded her mind. Thinking also of her ladies waiting for long-lost husbands, she hoped this would bring them all home soon.

Wharf Street was almost impossible to negotiate with noisy revellers filling the street while the almost unbearable noise of steam engines and foghorns from harbour vessels added to the confusion.

Suddenly Dan and Jebediah were in front of her, clearing a path through the crowd. Showing great patience, the two men coaxed the revellers to part long enough for her to turn onto the boards of their dock.

Jumping out of the truck, she ran over to give both men a hug. "I assume this means the war is over!" she shouted. Seeing their happy reaction, she continued, "We'll never get out of here today!"

"I'm not leaving until this mob goes away anyway," Dan muttered, moving back up the dock toward Wharf Street. He stopped several men who were straying onto their property, pushing them back toward the road. "This could get very ugly," he called back at Jeb.

"The army's here, Dan!" Jack called, pointing back toward the road where Victoria policeman, Sergeant Walker, and six soldiers were labouring to make their way through the crowd toward them.

"Sgt. Brown!" called the city policeman. "These men are here to guard your property. I'll leave you to deploy them as you will."

"I don't see how we can get out of here," Dan confided to the policeman in a concerned tone. "There are too many people on the streets."

"Of course you can!" Walker snapped turning to leave. "Use the boat like Nancy did in 1916!"

Standing smartly in a straight line outside the door of the office, the young soldiers waited for Dan's orders. Kate came outside and went over to stand beside Jack and Nancy, while Jeb stood off to one side and lit his pipe. They all curiously watched Dan as his demeanor took on a new, unfamiliar appearance.

Squaring his shoulders, Dan faced the recruits.

"Stand easy men," he snapped with authority, "you're going to guard this dock with your lives, do you understand?"

"Yes sir," six voices chorused.

Nancy and Kate exchanged surprised expressions and tried to keep straight faces.

“Any questions before we deploy?” Dan inquired loudly.

“How much force are we to use, sir?” asked one young soldier of about 19 years.

“Whatever it takes … short of killing anyone!” he replied curtly.

“C-can I ask you a question, s-sir?” stammered a soldier who looked a lot younger than his years.

“Yes.”

“Are you the famous gunner our artillery officers talk about, sir?”

“I think not, lad. I was a soldier just like you.”

“Th-they say you could hit a man from a m-mile away,” the recruit persisted, awestruck at meeting his famous hero.

“Be glad it’s over, lad,” Dan hissed. “I fought in that hell. All I did was my best, like you will.”

“Yes sir!” the young man replied, standing up even straighter.

“Now, you four men take your posts up near Wharf Street keeping everyone off the access road. You two will guard the dock from anyone entering from the harbour side,” he instructed the others. “Take your positions and don’t let me down.”

In that few moments it took to deploy the recruits, Nancy and the others realized why Dan had been such a competent and respected soldier. His instant authority and control startled them at first, being a revealing switch from the usual easygoing man they all knew.

“It’s going to take us hours to get home, Jack,” Kate groaned, breaking the silence.

“No it’s not,” Dan replied with a ready grin. “We’ll drop you off on the rocks at Seaforth, by West Bay, Kate. Jack you know where I mean?”

“Sure,” Jack chuckled, “we’ll be home in no time from there, Kate.”

“Did anybody call Aunt Meg?” asked Nancy as she locked up.

“I did,” Jeb growled, “she said she already knew the war was over.”

“How?”

“I never asked,” he retorted as they boarded the *Stockholm*.

The young soldiers watched as the legendary Sgt. Brown eased the *Stockholm* away from the dock and into the congestion of the harbour. Progress was slow and demanding as bottle-waving sailors drunkenly danced on the decks of boats and nearby wharves, paying no attention to local liquor laws.

Cautiously working their way through the mass of vessels now packed into the harbour, the *Stockholm* crept toward the West Bay shore. They kept tightly to the rocks until Dan was able to put the Dumpfords safely ashore. Waving goodbye, Dan took them past the harbour entrance and away from the commotion.

As they moved along the southern coastline of Vancouver Island darkness was quickly falling and they made out several bonfires burning in Beacon Hill Park. The noise from hundreds of high-spirited revellers drifted out to them across the calm water.

Pushing on the throttle, Dan made good use of the last grey threads of daylight speeding around Gonzales Point past Oak Bay and the long stretch of green lawns marking the Victoria Golf Club. Farther along, he swung wide at Cormorant Point, cautiously avoiding the explosives factory, as darkness draped the last few miles of coastline leading to their little cove. They had barely touched the dock before Nan leapt onto the boards and raced up the cliff stairs. She reached the porch just as a surprised Meg opened the door.

"I didn't expect you to come home by boat, lassie," her aunt cried as the girl threw her arms around her.

"The war is over and the city has gone crazy, Aunt Meg!" the redhead gabbled excitedly. "Streets are blocked solid with people and traffic, even the harbour was full of every boat imaginable. Nothing is moving but we managed to get through it. It was the only way we could hope to get out."

"Have you eaten today?" Meg asked pointedly, seemingly unmoved by the news as she pulled Nancy into the warm kitchen.

"Not much, but it's so exciting; the war's finally over!"

"I thought the influenza regulations were still on," Meg commented.

"They are, but nobody's taking any notice of them. Sgt. Walker called in the army to help keep order. He sent six soldiers down to guard our dock."

"You mean they're rioting, like they did in 1914?"

"No silly, they're happy this time!"

A sharp cold draught suddenly blew through the house as Dan and Jeb came stomping in.

"Shut that blasted door, Danny!" Meg scolded. "We need wood for the fire before you take your coat off."

Isolated and oblivious to the celebrating crowds rampaging through the city, the residents of Cunningham Manor enjoyed the first evening of worldwide peace in the warm, cozy atmosphere of their Gordon Head living room. A phone call from Gus made them aware that the American city was also going wild, quickly arranging a victory parade.

The next day persistent warnings were posted all over Victoria, issued by Dr. Price, clearly stating that the influenza restrictions were still in force and must be strictly adhered to. Doctors' Tubble in Seattle and Underhill in Vancouver issued the same warning. The influenza epidemic was definitely waning but, nevertheless, was still dangerous and caution needed to be taken or it could flare up again, they said.

Through the following week Nancy heard many arguments and opinions from city businessmen—everyone wanted the city open for business again. Nancy accompanied Dan to Seattle on the 15th and Terry chatted freely about the local council meeting which had managed to lift the influenza restrictions. He laughed when he explained how the city health officers had been bullied into cooperating with big business, but also pointed out that many people were still taking precautions by wearing masks in public places.

Gus welcomed them with open arms, obviously relieved that Beth was now fully recovered and although positive that Jebediah's port wine had helped, they now realized her symptoms had not been the same as the deadly flu strain.

Bubbling with life, Beth received news of Nellie Cornish and James Moore, both hard at work arranging the grand re-opening concert at the theatre on the 30th of November and Bill, acting on the girls' behalf, was making arrangements to record the concert.

Nancy and Dan, overwhelmed by all the good news, made speed on their uneventful trip home, talking quietly of a time in the near future when Victoria would be back to normal.

"They're home," Meg murmured to Jebediah as they sat reading in front of the fireplace.

"Wait until they see this," the old detective replied grinning broadly. He folded the newspaper to show the headline story and handed it to Meg just as the door flew open.

"They've lifted the influenza restrictions in Seattle!" Nancy squealed.

"Look at that headline in today's *Colonist*," Jeb grinned. "I'll bet they're going to cancel the restrictions here, too."

"They're having an Armistice Ball at the Empress!" Dan said incredulously, reading the headline and staying to talk to Jeb as the women went to get dinner ready. "I'll bet Dr. Price is fighting to stop that from happening."

"When is it?" Nancy asked from the kitchen.

"The 28th," Dan called back.

"That's a Thursday, an unusual day to have a big dance." Nancy came into the living room and sat on the arm of Jeb's chair, peering over his shoulder at the newspaper. "They have Professor Louis and his orchestra booked," she added excitedly, pointing to the paper.

"Do you know him, Nan?" Meg asked from the doorway, cocking an inquisitive eyebrow at the girl.

Dan took the paper from Jeb and followed the women into the kitchen sitting down at the table and spreading it out in front of him.

"Danny, I thought you were hungry, lad, find another place for your dirty paper!" Meg clucked, shooing him away.

Dan grabbed up the paper, folding it quickly as Meg deposited a handful of cutlery onto the table. He grimaced a warning to Jeb who was standing well back, grinning as he watched the familiar scene.

"Yes, I know the professor slightly," Nan continued, as if nothing had happened, "he came to one of the Seattle concerts and James introduced us. Nellie knew him already from her music circles. He's the conductor of the Empress Hotel Orchestra."

Discussions over dinner ranged from the decreasing number of influenza victims to the excitement of victory rippling through the city with prospects of business returning to normal.

"There'll be a lot of heartache yet," Jebediah predicted, "when the army gets around to finally informing all the families about their missing boys."

"I hope Tom comes home soon," Nan whispered. "Eva's terribly lonely."

"He's in administration," Dan said thoughtfully, "they might post him to the occupational force."

"You mean he might have to stay in Europe?"

"That doesn't seem fair," Meg muttered, "he's been away since 1914. It's time they let him come home."

It was late when the lights went out at Cunningham Manor that night. Moving out of the dark safety of the tree line, Sam with his dog, Flash, shuffled noiselessly toward the house. His senses ever alert to the night sounds as he stopped and listened before cautiously moving on—the soft whimper of his terrier leading him to the parcel of food on the doorstep. Silently moving over to the cliff stairs, he began his nightly vigil, unaware that the old detective was watching from a dark, upstairs window.

As the country district of Gordon Head settled into sleep, an emergency meeting was going on a few miles away at Victoria City Hall. As the mayor and councillors argued with the provincial and city medical officers regarding the lifting of health restrictions, angry words erupted in the stately chamber room. They were all aware that Seattle and Vancouver had already lifted theirs, yet Dr. Price was adamant they should remain in place in Victoria. Throwing insults at the medical officers, some of the politicians accused them of being too cautious and strangling the city's businessess.

Observing the discussion, several members of the legislature including Premier John Oliver, listened with interest to Mayor Todd's futile attempts to keep order.

"Businesses are going bankrupt!" one member wailed. "They need our help."

It was after two in the morning when the frustrated mayor finally called for a vote. Dr. Price continued his fierce objections in a loud, booming voice and, when the mayor attempted to silence him, he stomped out of the meeting allowing the mayor to press on with his agenda. When the votes were counted, it was found that an overwhelming majority had voted in favour of revoking the influenza restrictions. Premier Oliver nodded his agreement and the welcome sound of the gavel concluded the eventful meeting.

Chapter 18

Dawn was minutes away as Dan eased the *Stockholm* out of the cove the next morning with both Jeb and Nan aboard as their vehicles were in town. By the time they arrived in Victoria, news of the council's decision had leaked onto the streets and many shops were already open. Although the public seemed rather happy that the restrictions had been lifted, there were those who were obviously apprehensive, avoiding close contact with each other, and, still others, who continued to wear their gauze face masks.

"Damned useless!" Waldo snapped when asked his opinion of the masks.

The city began to relax even in spite of newspaper stories telling of the increasing death toll attributed to the epidemic. Commenting that Victoria had fared much better than other cities, they also heaped praise on the diligence of the local medical officers. Basking in popularity and praise, Dr. Price again showed his bitterness to council by angrily refuting it was his decision and claiming caution was still important.

Kate, now well-rested, enthusiastically opened the *Wounded Soldier Restaurant*. She and her girls handed out free coffee and tea to patients, hospital staff, streetcar drivers, and delivery men, advertising they would be open for normal business the next day.

Driving carefully over the icy, frost-covered roads, Nancy felt a touch of excitement at the restaurant's re-opening and decided to go over and see if she was needed. *Things can finally get back to normal*, she told herself. Reality suddenly pushed the thought from her mind when a convoy of army trucks crossed in front of her at Cook Street and her thoughts turned to the homecoming soldiers they were now expecting. She momentarily wondered what injuries and mental wounds the Red Cross and other services would have to now contend with, then pushed the unhappy thought from her mind.

Steam was already rising from an open kitchen window as she parked the truck in the back lane. Greeted with a cheer from several early customers, Nancy went to talk to them briefly. By mid-morning Dr. Price arrived, sternly warning the redhead they were taking a risk.

"There could be a resurgence of the disease," he proclaimed loudly, making his views known to all in the room, "and it's people like you who would be the cause of it spreading!"

"Now you just hold on there, mister," a young man argued angrily. "This little watering hole is our only source of pleasure."

"I could order you back to the hospital!" the doctor growled.

"Try it!" the man invited ominously, wobbling unsteadily onto his crutches, showing he was missing one leg. As he faced the doctor, he snapped a threat of his own. "You do that, boyo, and I promise you'll need a bed in the hospital yourself!"

"Stop!" Nancy cried, rushing in between the combatants as another group came in the front door. "Why don't you both sit down? I want to talk to you."

Grateful for the intervention, the young man sat back down and grinned mischievously at the doctor, tapping the chair opposite him with his crutch in an unmistakable invitation.

"Come on Dr. Price, it won't hurt to get to know these men, they're all soldiers who are missing their families and eager for conversation," she coaxed diplomatically.

Muttering to himself, the doctor pompously went over to the empty chair and sat down, glaring at the new faces gathering around the table. Nancy straightened her apron, brushed an imaginary hair from her face, and went to stand at the end of the table.

"First," she suggested, "why don't you introduce yourselves?"

Dr. Price began, at first hesitantly, but ending in his well-known pompous style. "I'm Dr. Arthur Price, Chief Health Officer for the City of Victoria."

"Private Stanley Stone, Nova Scotia Artillery, sir," said the lad.

"You're a long way from home, private." The doctor's voice softened a little.

"I'm from Halifax, sir. It's pretty much like Victoria, but a lot bigger."

"You lost your leg?"

"Yes sir, I'm a cripple now but still one of the lucky ones."

"The lucky ones?" Dr. Price asked sounding surprised.

"Yes sir, I lived to tell about it!"

Wiping his brow, Arthur Price struggled to understand how this young man could accept his fate without bitterness—just grateful to be alive.

Biting her lip, Nancy reached out and touched the young soldier's arm. "They're all heroes, doctor, every last one of them," she whispered emotionally, sweeping her hand across the room which was now almost full of obviously wounded soldiers.

"Don't you believe her, sir," retorted another soldier, blushing. "She's the hero—our bit of home here in Victoria. She's the one who makes us all feel special. There ain't a man who's ever been here who could easily forget this red haired angel!"

A murmur of quiet approval ran through the restaurant. The doctor solemnly studied their faces, noting their bandages and injuries.

"It ain't medicine that gives these lads hope, doc," commented a streetcar conductor as he got up and headed for the door, his money bag jingling as he moved.

Dropping his eyes in not-often felt embarrassment, Dr. Price began to digest the situation and felt Nancy's hand on his shoulder.

"We know you're doing your best doctor, but consideration of others never cost a cent," she said softly.

Wincing, Dr. Price raised his head, offering his hand across the table to the young private from Halifax and smiling as it was quickly accepted.

"Private Stanley Stone," he said with gentle firmness, his eyes locking on those of the wounded soldier's. "Please accept my apology; I am proud to have met you." Excusing himself, the doctor got up and moved toward the door. Pausing before opening it, he glanced back at the redhead and nodded slightly.

As the door closed behind him, lively chatter erupted and Nancy busied herself collecting empty cups.

All day long, there were reports of armistice celebrations being arranged and hotels serving liquor behind closed doors, in violation of prohibition laws. Eva called in the late afternoon, looking tired as she provided the latest news of the epidemic, expressing her opinion that the worst was indeed over.

"Why don't you take a few days off?" Nancy suggested.

"Why don't you?" Eva returned with a raise of her eyebrows. "I know you've visited all our widows and May Coolridge told me what you did for Ted Lancaster. You talk about me needing a rest!"

"I didn't do anything, it was Jim Morrison's idea," Nan declared.

"Someday, Mrs. Brown," Eva sighed, "folks will learn about what you've done for them."

"Any news of Tom?" Nancy changed the subject.

"No, not for a long time," her friend replied, lowering her eyes.

"But you know where he is?"

"Yes, but he doesn't answer my letters anymore," she said, looking distraught now that the subject had been broached.

Thankfully, a call from the kitchen drew Nancy away, leaving Eva to wipe a tear and bravely gather her composure.

"Would you like a ride home, Eva?" Nancy called when she put the phone down.

"Yes please, if it's not inconvenient for you."

"No trouble at all. I'm going straight home and would enjoy the company."

Slipping her coat off, Eva donned an apron, found a tray, and began to clear the now empty tables as only a few stragglers remained. When she entered the kitchen with a full tray and began to put them in the sink, she giggled at Kate's reaction.

"What on earth are you doing, Eva?" Kate asked in astonishment.

"I'm paying for my ride home!"

"Is Jack coming for you, Kate?" Nancy called from the back of the restaurant.

"No, I'm catching the streetcar into town; I want to see if the fabric shop on Government has opened again, then I'm meeting him at the dock."

"You go then—maybe you'll catch them open, and remember it's Wednesday tomorrow. I'm off to Seattle with Dan."

A few minutes later, a streetcar rattled into the turnaround across the street. Kate grabbed her coat and dashed out into the cold evening air, shouting 'good night' as she ran. Nan locked the door behind her and helped Eva with the rest of the cleanup. In 15 minutes they were finished and went to get their coats.

"You and Kate must be so proud of this place, Nan," Eva murmured wrapping her woollen scarf around her neck and following Nancy outside.

"Yes, I suppose we are," Nancy replied, locking the door.

As she started the truck and proceeded toward the road, a builder's truck stopped at the end of the lane blocking her exit onto Richmond.

"Are you closing early?" the familiar voice of Jack Duggan boomed out of the darkness.

"Closing early, my foot!" she squealed, running over to the truck and giving him a hug. "What the heck are you doing here?"

"On my way home, honey, but I thought I would just catch you before you left."

"Why, is something wrong?"

"No, no, lass, the boys heard you were open again and I just wanted to say hello."

"Well hello, you big bear, how's Nellie?"

"Good now, she's had a cold and we were a bit worried with the flu scare and all, she's better now. Dan and your Aunt Meg are well, I hope."

"Of course they are. Uncle Jeb's elixir takes care of all of us!"

"His what?" the builder asked.

"Oh we'll tell you later. Now get outa here! Go home! Your Nellie's waiting dinner for you."

"How did you meet the Duggans, Nancy?" Eva asked as Jack pulled out of the way and they turned onto Richmond.

"They were friends of the Joyce brothers, the whalers who employed Dan. They were all Newfies."

"Dan's from Newfoundland?

"No silly, his bosses and Jack were."

Smiling in the darkness, Nancy left Eva to puzzle it out while she concentrated on her driving, crossing over to Shelbourne's new surface. She knew the Red Cross worker would have more questions and would ask them when ready.

"But how did you meet them, Nan?" Eva persisted finally.

"Dan and I signed the adoption agreement at their house; they were witnesses when we became a family," Nancy replied, knowing this would further confuse her, but she still enjoyed teasing her friend.

"Now I'm really confused!" Eve sighed.

"Danny and I met in the orphanage as children; he looked after me until he left to go find work. When I finally left that place years later, we found each other again and he decided we needed to be a family, so we adopted each other."

"I thought you'd lived with your Aunt Meg?"

"No, she worked for the Joyces and treated Dan like a son, so we adopted her, too!"

"You're pulling my leg, you mean she's not your real aunt?" Eva giggled.

"Not Dan's either! Now, let me really confuse you because we adopted Uncle Jeb as well. Look, look over there at the store," she cried, changing the subject. "Did you know Maude had a fire the other morning?"

Eva stared at the well-known corner store where a light in the window indicated it was still open for business. "The store looks all right; how do you know she had a fire?"

"Danny helped Maude put it out. We were driving past and saw the lights. It was so early in the morning we were concerned and then we saw the flames out back. We were shocked to find Maude throwing water onto a roaring fire in her chicken house. The poor woman said she dropped a candle!"

"Oh my gracious, she was lucky you came along."

"She had actually done quite well on her own but it was too much for her and could have gotten worse and spread to the store, I dare say."

"I have some news, too. I heard at city hall that the CN is going to stop running the railway to the Saanich Peninsula and also that the V&S is in financial trouble."

"It's the first I've heard of it," Nancy admitted.

Refusing to let Nancy drive her all the way home, Eva got her to stop on Ash Road and she shouted a cheery goodnight before she walked off into the darkness.

"I know," the redhead sighed to herself, knowing why Eva liked to walk. "It's thinking time. I had many nights worrying about Dan, too."

Continuing to think about the Todds as she drove the rest of the way home, Nancy wondered how she could help the tireless Red Cross worker, but no solution came to mind.

Meg opened the door for her when she came up the steps.

"Well, how did the restaurant opening go?" she asked, her eyes sparkling with curiosity.

"Wonderful! Kate's in her element again."

"Did all the staff turn up?" the Scot persisted.

"Yes, cook and Kate were both there when I arrived and Linda arrived a bit later; it was just like old times."

"Old times," Jeb snorted from behind his newspaper, "you've only been closed a few weeks!"

"Five weeks and two days to be exact and it feels like a year!" Nan retorted, looking around. "Where's Danny, he's home, isn't he?"

"Upstairs changing," Meg chuckled. "He fell off the dock!"

"What! I gather he's all right."

"Aye, just a wee bit damp is all!" laughed Meg.

“He could have picked a better time of year for a swim!” grunted Jeb, causing Nancy to giggle.

“Yes, I agree, Uncle Jeb!” came Dan’s voice from the stairway. “I’ll remember that next time,” he added, accepting a sympathetic hug from his wife.

“Eva dropped in at the restaurant and I gave her a ride home,” Nancy told them over dinner. “The poor soul is still waiting for news from Tom. He’s not answering her letters and yet she knows where he is. It’s all very puzzling and I’m worried for her. She also mentioned she heard some news about the problems the Sidney railways are having.”

“I heard about the V&S having money troubles last week,” Dan commented. “Walt Bohannan told me Victoria had withdrawn its subsidy and they would, no doubt, be going bankrupt.”

“You never told us that,” Jeb muttered.

“I didn’t quite understand it all and forgot about it. Walt said the CN was taking over some of the lines and would be doing all the freight for the lumber yard.”

“You mean Mr. Bohannan who owns the Sidney newspaper, don’t you?” Nancy asked. She watched Dan nod. “He should know, he writes all the news.”

“Aye and probably makes some of it up, too!” quipped Jeb.

“We had a visit from Dr. Price today, too,” Nancy murmured nonchalantly, getting their instant attention. “He got quite upset with us and one of the soldiers, too.”

“He wanted to shut you down again?” asked Meg.

“Sort of, but he got more than he bargained for.”

“He will get more than he bargained for,” Jeb threatened, “if he doesn’t leave you alone.”

“Restrictions are off,” Dan said firmly, “he can’t shut you down.”

“I know,” Nancy agreed, “but he’s worried we could have another outbreak now that people are mixing together again. He could be right—we still have to take every precaution.”

“Oh dear,” sighed Meg, “that must have been embarrassing for you.”

“No, not really, a young amputee from Nova Scotia took exception to what he was saying and we had the support of the other soldiers and a streetcar conductor. The boys were so glad to have us back. It was wonderful seeing their smiling faces.”

“A maritimer!” Dan laughed. “Those lads don’t take too kindly to being lectured.”

"No, he didn't, I thought he was going to hit the doctor with his crutches!"

"What regiment was he?"

"An artillery unit."

The blood drained from Dan's face as he whispered in a far-off tone, "Good lads, they were on the firing line with us before I got hurt."

"Hey," she slapped his hand, "come back to us, you're at home now."

"You haven't told her of the invitation yet," interrupted Jeb, turning to Meg.

"Gracious, I forgot!" the Scot replied. "They've invited you to sing at the Armistice Ball, Nancy.

"Have they? Who called?" Nancy asked.

"A man called Turner."

"Professor Louis Turner, remember he's the conductor of the Empress Orchestra and one of Nellie's musical friends. If he calls again Aunt Meg, ask him if that invitation includes Nellie."

"I will, but now it's bedtime and you need your rest. Take that man of yours with you, young lady, he's falling asleep in the chair!" Meg remarked.

On October 20th, rain gently beat on the windows as Nancy and Dan woke to the sound of Meg's voice calling them for breakfast. It was an earlier start for them as they had to go to Victoria first to load up before heading to Seattle. Over their meal, Jeb remembered to tell them what he had heard about planned celebrations for the city.

"Huge evenings of dancing at the Empress, YMCA and the Union Club are apparently being arranged," he told them.

"It seems like an awful waste of money," Nan complained. "I could think of a lot better way of spending that money."

"Let the toffs have their fun," Jeb growled, "then we can get back to normal."

"I suppose the government will take care of the wounded soldiers now," Meg murmured.

"We'll see," Nancy commented sarcastically, getting up and pushing her chair under the table, "they haven't done much of a job up to now!"

Fifteen minutes later, huddled together under a single umbrella on the clifftop, Jeb and Meg watched as the *Stockholm* slipped out of the cove and disappeared from view around Cormorant Point.

On board, a heated discussion was taking place continuing the subject they had discussed over breakfast. Dan, taking exception to one of

Nancy's comments, said that the army would come through and support its wounded men. Angrily, she reminded him of the help, or lack of it, she had been given on discovering he was wounded and recovering in a hospital. Only luck and a chance meeting had found him convalescing in Whitby, England.

"You watch," she argued, "they'll push you off with a medal and a handful of beads, like they did to the Indians."

"I never realized how bitter the war has left you, Nan," he replied with a frown, "you hate the army, don't you?"

"No, I hate the way they won't tell us women the truth; how they don't care if we spend months and years wondering what's happened to our men, or where they are. You're the ones who get wounded, but in the end it's us women and the families that get hurt."

"Well it's over now, thank God," Dan chuckled as they rounded the breakwater and scooted up the harbour.

"The war might be over, darling," she said, looking up at him and grinning, "but the fight for justice is only beginning!"

Jack was waiting on the jetty as the *Stockholm* swept up to the dock. Catching the line, he quickly secured the bow while Dan leapt over the stern rail with his rope, bouncing quickly back aboard to release the hatch cover and begin the loading.

Wandering aimlessly up the dock while the loading was in progress, Nan spotted Jebediah's black car coming along Wharf Street. Looking over to the corner of Fort, she spotted Waldo puffing on his pipe as he waited to cross the street to visit his friend.

Going into the office, she filled the still-warm kettle to make tea. Hearing the door open, she shuffled Jack's stained coffee pot over to make more room on the little stove.

"Off to Seattle," Waldo growled, more as a statement than a question. Not waiting for an answer, he added, "Pour me a drop of Jack's coffee."

When Jeb opened the door, the sound of laughter and cursing followed him inside.

"Now what's happened?" Waldo asked, his eyes brightening as he saw the sheepish look on Jeb's face. Deciding to go and take a look, he picked up his hot coffee mug, holding it gingerly as it warmed his hands.

Following Waldo, Nancy burst into laughter at the sight before them. Sitting on the wet dock in front of Jeb's car was Fred Barrett still cursing and yelling abuse at Jebediah who had evidentially almost run over him.

"Damnit Jeb," Waldo chuckled, to his friend standing in the doorway. "Can't you do nothin' right, you've hardly dented him!" Offering no help, the haulier downed his coffee, passed the cup over to Jeb and, muttering to himself, walked past the harbour master as he left.

"Danny, don't just stand there laughing, help him up!" Nancy ordered. "He'll feel better with a warm drink inside him."

Standing with his back to the pot-bellied stove, Fred was soon steaming as his pants dried and the hot coffee, helping him to now see the funny side of his misadventure, warmed his insides.

"What happened?" Nan asked.

"I was rushing to catch Dan before he left and that blasted dog that hangs around here tripped me up just as your Uncle Jeb's car came onto the boards. I thought he was going to run over me!"

"I tried!" retorted the old detective, stifling a chuckle.

"Stop it, Uncle Jeb," Nancy ordered, giggling. "Why did you get so cross, Fred, it was only a tumble."

"Oh, I don't know, guess I felt rather silly," Fred mumbled, dropping his eyes.

"First honest feeling you've ever had, lad!" Jeb retorted.

"Well," continued Nancy, "you've got to admit it was funny. I'll bet Uncle Jeb got a shock too, when you appeared out of nowhere in front of him."

"We have to get going, Nan," Dan interrupted, poking his head in the door.

"Oh, Dan, I almost forgot what I came for. Capt. Gray called," Fred announced, "said to tell you he would be waiting for you in Copley's Bay."

"Why?" asked Dan.

"How on earth do I know, I don't even know where Copley's Bay is. All he wanted was to make sure you were told."

Chapter 19

Avoiding a large freighter being escorted to the mouth of Victoria harbour by two small tugs, Dan smiled as the *Stockholm* made its way toward the open sea. He loved seeing the miles of open water stretching out before him, reminding him of the exciting and often dangerous whaling trips with the Joyce boys. Things had changed so much since those days. Whaling was finished and, with the war over, port traders were already experiencing an improvement in merchant shipping. With the oceans safe from the German U-boats a resurgence of ocean travel and commerce was expected. Already they were seeing more schooners and freighters lining up in the Royal Roads shipping lane awaiting their turn at the dock.

"It's good to see merchant vessels in the harbour again," he commented into the redhead's ear when she took the wheel.

Nodding, she concentrated her attention on the group of fishing boats ahead, seeing Algenon Pease's harbour patrol vessel, *Legal Limit*, among them.

"They're American," Dan muttered reaching for his binoculars, "swing wide and slow down, honey."

Doing as he said, Nan slowed to a crawl giving them a wide berth. She noticed the *Legal Limit* pulling away from the group and heading out to intercept them.

"Hold it," Dan called, lowering his binoculars. "Looks like Algy wants us."

Leaning over the rail as the harbour patrol vessel came alongside, Dan yelled, "HAVING TROUBLE?"

"NO, JUST FISHERMEN SWAPPING NEWS, THANKS FOR CHECKING," Algy replied.

Pushing off, Algenon watched with envy as the red-and-gold *Stockholm* wheeled about in a flurry of spray, then streaked off toward the US border.

With no further incidents to delay them, they headed down Puget Sound paying close attention to the numerous small craft running along the coast. Turning into Useless Bay, Dan's hand settled on her shoulder, warning of caution as their eyes fastened onto the familiar sight of the US Coast Guard cutter sitting just off Bay View Harbor.

Racing across the bay which had held the German freighters captive in 1916, Nancy pulled the *Stockholm* up alongside the coast guard vessel. Prewarned of their arrival, Capt. Gray met them at the rail and invited them aboard, his serious expression disturbing Nancy as she followed Dan across the deck.

"Something wrong, John?" she asked, as a member of the crew brought refreshments.

"I shouldn't be telling you this," he confided hesitantly, "but Admiral Johnson is waiting for you at the Jorgensen's."

"Then why are you telling us?" Dan asked suspiciously.

"So you're not taken by surprise; I just want you to be prepared."

"Oh come on, John," Dan replied, "you expect me to believe you called Victoria just to warn me that your boss is waiting for me at the Jorgensen's for some unknown reason. If you do, you're an idiot!" Pausing, he watched Gray's expression carefully. "You were going to tell us something more, but now you've got cold feet, haven't you, lad? What's the matter, do you think I'd tell them about this conversation?"

John Gray dropped his eyes in frustration. Dan Brown was the man he admired most on the West Coast, his experience as a whaler and his efforts in the war put the young captain in awe of this Canadian. Knowing the nature of Dan's coming altercation with Admiral Johnson, his intention had been to protect his friend.

"They've investigated your background, Dan, and are going to offer you a job."

"I have a job," he replied, not taking his eyes from the younger man's face.

"This one is something new. It's dangerous and I think you've seen enough of danger."

"We don't have to listen to him," Nancy offered.

"Well, thanks for the warning, captain," Dan saluted his friend and grinned. "Is that all you wanted us for?"

"No, actually it wasn't! My wife would like two tickets to Nancy's new show on the 30th."

"Go and buy your tickets, you cheeky devil!" Dan laughed.

Dan's spontaneous comment eased the tension and Nancy let out her breath. "I'll make sure you get those tickets, John, don't take any notice of him."

“We tried to buy tickets,” Gray added defensively, looking point blank at Dan, “but the show was already sold out.”

Dan looked over at Nancy and winked.

“I’m sure we’ll be able to find you some, don’t worry and thank your wife for her interest,” called Nancy as one of the men helped her clamber back aboard the *Stockholm.*

Capt. Gray waved them off, smiling as the pretty redhead took the controls and sent the red-and-gold craft surging toward Puget Sound.

“We should check on Zeke,” Dan directed, leaning over her shoulder as he pointed toward the entrance to the hidden cove across the waterway.

Automatically adjusting her direction, she glanced over at Dan who was scouring the hillside with his binoculars, checking for the old man’s beacon which would be difficult to see in daylight. Cautiously approaching the hidden entrance to Apple Cove, Nancy stopped the boat and pointed. There on a rock, just to their left, sat Ezekiel with his rifle laid across his knees.

“Easy Nan, don’t get too close,” Dan ordered in alarm as Nancy attempted to push the *Stockholm* closer. “There’s a rocky ledge just under the waterline in front of him.”

“How do you know that?” she asked.

“I can see how the water is moving.”

“Does he know the war’s over?” she asked, peering into the waves and marvelling at Dan’s knowledge of the water.

“Probably not,” Dan replied.

“Are you all right, Ezekiel?” she called.

Waving his rifle, the old man signalled he was fine. Rising, he leapt from rock-to-rock with the agility of a much younger man until he disappeared into the heavy tangle of undergrowth.

Turning the boat away, Nancy glanced back over her shoulder at the hidden lair of Ezekiel Plunket, wondering how he would fare through the winter months ahead—she had grown quite fond of the old recluse, despite his roughness.

A lone figure stood by the boathouse at the Jorgensen jetty, watching the launch speed toward him.

“They’re here,” he growled to the men waiting out of sight in the boathouse. “Gus wants a word with you two,” Terry rasped as the Canadians stepped onto the dock.

Hurrying up the garden path to the mansion, they saw Bill waiting in the open doorway, his wheelchair rocking with excitement as he waved to them.

"Hi Dan, Nancy, so good to see you again. It's all arranged, Nan!" he bubbled enthusiastically, pulling Nancy onto his knee.

"We know the concert has been arranged," she laughed, wriggling out of his grasp, "in fact, John Gray told us it's all sold out."

"Not the concert," Bill grinned, backing his wheelchair inside so they could get by, "they're going to record the show live. It's the first time its ever been tried under show conditions."

"How did you manage to talk them into that?" she asked.

"Dad bought the controlling interest in RCA and amalgamated it with Victor. I'm going to run the new company!"

"You don't know anything about recordings," Dan interrupted.

"I don't have to—the technicians do all that—but I do intend on learning it."

"Are you three going to stand out there in the hall all morning?" Bill's father called from the living room. "Come in here, and then we can all talk."

Nancy hurried into the living room, jerking to a stop when she saw the two visitors. General Greene stood up and opened his arms to the girl he had met for the first time when she sang for his men at Camp Lewis. Taking note that he was thinner than she remembered, no doubt from his bout of flu, she happily noted his hug was just as strong as it used to be.

Then, just as John Gray predicted, Admiral Johnson rose and strode toward her, smiling as he took her hand.

"Nice to see you again, Nancy," he declared warmly, looking past her as Dan pushed Bill's wheelchair into the room.

Excusing herself, Nancy moved across the room to Beth, kissing her gently on the cheek as they embraced.

"It always feels like I'm at home when I come here, Beth. How are you?"

"You are at home, dear," Beth assured her, "you and Dan are part of this family and, I'm feeling well, thank you."

"Why am I always last on your list, young lady," Gus grumbled, coming over to kiss her. "Don't you care about the old man anymore?"

"I always keep the best for last," she whispered affectionately into his ear as they hugged.

"Is Jorgensen her father?" Admiral Johnson whispered to the general.

"No more than I am!" the general muttered sharply.

"Why don't you take Nancy upstairs, my dear," Gus suggested. "Show her the dress Hattie Rhodes sent over for her."

"Are you trying to get rid of us?" Nancy asked pointedly.

"Yes, actually, these gentlemen would like a private word with Dan," laughed Gus.

Beth took Nancy gently by the arm, eager to have the redhead to herself, although knowing full well she would have liked to stay. Nancy glanced back at her husband and seeing his mischievous wink, allowed Beth to lead her from the room.

"Can you find something to do for a few minutes, Billy," Gus tried to dismiss his son who was not making any move to leave.

"No dad, I can't. I wouldn't leave Danny alone with you three! I want to know what the devil you are up to first."

"It's not your business son, now—please leave us."

"No," Bill stated defiantly, "he's my brother and he might need my advice."

"Let him stay," General Greene ordered as Bill rolled his wheelchair over beside Dan, "actually I'm rather surprised Nancy left so easily."

"Sgt. Brown, we have a proposition to put to you," the coast guard officer began, "this is not official yet, but you can take it from me, it will be."

"Before you go any further, sir, I'm not in the army anymore. I'm just plain Dan Brown."

"Yes I know, lad, we've checked your army record. You were invalided out with head wounds and, subsequently, made a full recovery," Admiral Johnson detailed. "You spent your youth as a whaler on the *Belfast*, owned by the Joyce brothers. Oh yes, we know all about you, son!"

"Get on with it, man," General Greene growled irritably. "We don't need a speech!"

"We would like to recommend to the governor, that you be selected as a secret agent for our government. Dan, we desperately need a man of your calibre, knowledge, and ability, out there in the straits," continued Admiral Johnson.

"To work for your government? Doing what?" asked Dan, looking from one to the other.

"Catching the dogs who are murdering our fishermen," General Greene interrupted. "Two more were killed last week."

"Rum runners?" Dan's instinctive comment brought a cold grin to the admiral's face.

"Yes, you and I know why, but how do we stop them, Mr. Brown?" he asked, chuckling as he waited for Dan's reaction.

"You think I can stop them, sir?"

"You're the best we can think of."

"Have you forgotten I'm a Canadian? They would hang me in Canada if they found out I was working for the US Government."

"Dan," General Greene interrupted, "I don't think you've got the picture yet, lad. Actually, we don't want you to work solely for us, we plan to negotiate with your government so you would work for both countries."

"They'll never go for that, sir. Premier Oliver is a farmer; he wouldn't spend a penny protecting fishermen, especially rum runners!" Dan replied emotionally.

"But would you consider it, if we could negotiate an agreement with your government?"

"Tell them no, Dan," Bill interrupted, growing quite red-faced as he listened to the conversation. "They're talking about dangerous stuff, pirates, and waterfront riffraff who don't think twice about murder."

"Let me get this straight," said Dan, leaning forward as deep thoughts caused a ridge of furrows to appear across his brow. "All you want from me is to say 'yes' I'll consider it, then you can go ahead and try to negotiate with the BC Government. Is that correct?"

"We want to be fairly sure you'll do it, yes," Admiral Johnson growled, "or what's the use of us going to all the trouble."

"Danny," Nancy's voice called from the hallway. "Look at this dress Beth got me!" She burst into the living room obviously excited with the beautiful formal gown draped across her body. "Isn't it wonderful, Dan?"

"It's beautiful, honey, you'll look like a queen," he responded warmly, glancing quickly over at the admiral who looked none-too-pleased at the interruption.

Coming up beside her, Beth slipped her arm around the redhead's waist and proudly announced, "Gentlemen, may I introduce you to the Queen of Seattle!"

"Very nice ladies, but could you give us a few more minutes of privacy," the admiral asked irritably. "This is a matter of national security."

"Stay Nan," Dan murmured, focusing his attention back to the admiral who had acquired a tinge of crimson on his ruddy cheeks as he realized too late the penalty for his rudeness.

"They want us to clear the straits of bandits, Nan," Dan grinned coldly. "Admiral Johnson here seems to think we could do it."

"I did not include your wife," the admiral denied angrily, "and I presumed our conversation was in confidence."

Smiling, Nancy handed the dress to Beth and she quickly passed it to the hovering butler who removed himself and closed the door. Spinning around to face them, Beth Jorgensen's flashing eyes gave them a quick warning.

"You forget your manners, sir! I will not be dismissed so flippantly in my own home. Nancy and I are waiting for your apology."

Holding back a smile, Gus lowered his eyes and made no attempt to intervene. Not many people had ever seen Beth really angry but he knew, when roused, his wife had the courage of a lion and the ability to use words like a sword.

Stumbling over his own words as he attempted to allay Beth's anger, Admiral Johnson made a half-hearted apology. "I'm sorry ma'am," he said, frowning, "this matter is extremely important; we are talking of national security."

"And, of course, good manners have no importance at all!" Beth insisted.

Beth's sarcasm took the admiral by surprise. Sighing in frustration, Richard Johnson lowered his eyes, unable to find the words that would appease the angry lady of the house. The squeaking of Bill's wheelchair broke the silence as he moved to allow Nancy to sit on the arm of Dan's chair and, having their attention, now took up the conversation.

"Don't you think Dan has faced enough danger, admiral?" he stated heatedly. "How much does a man have to give to satisfy you, you …?"

"Billy!" Beth quickly intervened.

"It's all right, mother," Bill murmured, "but don't you think this family has given enough, admiral?"

"Yes, I do, son," Admiral Johnson replied.

"Would someone please tell me what you're all talking about?" Nancy asked in frustration.

"It's my fault," General Greene admitted. "I talked the admiral and the governor into it."

"You talked them into what?" asked the redhead, still appearing confused.

"We need someone on the water who can take care of the lawless element that's plaguing the straits, somebody both our governments will trust with the responsibility," the general continued.

"And you think that's us?" Nancy looked aghast.

"I am sure Dan is that person," added the admiral. "He knows these waters like the back of his hand and he has marine experience as a whaler. Combined with his army record of exemplary courage and your own experience, nobody could question where your loyalties lie—either of you. Look at what you've done for your widows and orphans, Mrs. Brown."

"He's talking about catching pirates and murderers, Nan," Bill pointed out in a distressed voice. "Tell him no, it's too dangerous."

"Hold up for a minute, son," Gus interrupted. "This idea is just a pipe dream; they haven't even talked to the BC Government yet. This is just a tentative chat. Say yes, you'll think about it, Dan, and then wait and see what happens. You never know what they'll offer."

"This is not a business deal, Gus." The general looked disapprovingly at his old friend. "It's more of a patriotic gesture."

"We almost gave our lives on the last patriotic gesture, general!" Bill snapped. "Perhaps this time we can make a much better deal."

"Well, Sgt. Brown, do you have anymore to add?" General Greene asked, smiling through almost-closed eyelids.

"I have," Nancy murmured and then raising her voice continued, "we get unrestricted access to both sides of the border."

"Agreed," replied both men in unison.

"The full co-operation of the coast guard," she continued.

"Agreed," Admiral Johnson stated, with a sigh. "We'd be proud to serve with Sgt. Brown."

"And you pay all the expenses?" she went on.

"We'll do better than that, Nancy," General Greene chuckled. "We'll pay all the expenses and donate one thousand dollars to your orphans' fund every month!"

"I take it we can proceed with the plan now?" asked the admiral, forcing a smile.

"Yes sir," Nancy replied, smiling as she watched the two men closely. "You can begin your negotiations as soon as you make your first donation to the orphans!"

"That's blackmail!" snorted Admiral Johnson, looking over at Dan who beamed his approval of his wife's negotiations.

"It's worse than that, Richard," the general laughed, "we still have more Canadians to deal with! We have to persuade their government to share this scheme."

Happy to have Dan's agreement to cooperate, General Greene and the admiral quickly left the house and Beth ordered the butler to serve lunch. Sitting around the dining-room table, Bill obviously still had reservations about the plan and he began to voice them immediately.

"I still say it's too dangerous," he muttered.

"Oh quiet," Nancy giggled, "we get a thousand dollars a month for our charity and it could take years to get our government to cooperate!"

"That was a pretty slick move, my dear," Gus nodded approvingly.

"None of you noticed the other interesting side agreement, did you?" Dan asked, looking sideways at his wife and smirking.

"What do you mean?" asked Gus.

"They agreed to unrestricted access which means we can bring your booze over the border without fear of being stopped or searched."

"My word, you're right!" Bill exclaimed, banging the table with his hand as he began to laugh. "I'll bet that never crossed their great military minds."

"Now you know why I put Nancy in charge of the refit on the *Southern Bell*, back some years ago," said his father with a wink at the redhead. "I wish you lads were half as smart as she is!"

Nancy and Beth nearly choked on their food. They looked over at Dan and Bill who were pretending to look hurt over Gus' teasing, and they all burst into laughter.

As the meal progressed, they caught up on the local news of both countries and the Canadians learned that wild celebrations of the war's end were continuing in Seattle. However, sadly in the midst of all the rejoicing, a second wave of influenza was causing a panic in nearby Tacoma. Gus told how the army base at Camp Lewis had also suffered from a second bout with the epidemic, but thankfully the general was able to prevent a relapse.

"The old fool won't give in and rest," Gus sighed, "he thinks he's immortal."

"He's trying to arrange a concert for you at the camp in December," Beth announced. "He's contacting all the stars who performed with you in 1917 trying to persuade them to come back, hoping the influenza is gone by then so they will travel."

"Strange he never mentioned it today," Nancy mused.

"He obviously has other things on his mind," quipped Bill who went on to relate his experience of reorganizing the recording company. "It's new and exciting," he bubbled with enthusiasm, "seems like we have new innovations every day and I know a lot more about contracts now. Your friend, Mary Pickford, is already under contract with us, Nan, but of course you know she's also a Canadian, and Nellie Cornish is on the board of directors as an advisor."

"Good, I hope you pay her well!" Nan quipped.

Gus and Beth chuckled at the redhead's blunt reply. Always ready to stand up for her friends, they watched in amusement as Bill squirmed under his adopted sister's scrutiny.

"Of course I do! Ah hell, don't start on me now, sis," Bill whined. "How come you don't ask me about your own contract?"

"What should I ask; you're looking after it, aren't you?"

"You could ask how much money you'll be getting."

Dan glanced over at Gus and Beth, putting his finger to his lips and waiting for his wife's reply.

Nancy cocked an eyebrow.

"I know how much. It's for a good cause and I'd better be getting 60 percent of it."

"Where did you get that figure from?"

"You, when you said you were going to be my agent."

"B-but we have expenses to consider, Nan," he wailed.

"So we're starting our association with lies, are we?" Nancy purred.

"No, no, I didn't lie to you."

"Then keep your word and pay me 60 percent!" she insisted.

"Give it up, Billy boy," Gus laughed. "She's got you coming and going. You don't have a chance of beating her."

"Well I know one thing she can't argue with," Bill murmured, grinning as he looked across the table at her. "Nancy, my darling, I love you!"

The sun was just setting behind Whidby Island as the *Stockholm* slipped away in the pouring rain, leaving three waving figures huddled together at the boathouse door. It would be dark before they hit Canadian waters making for a slower and more dangerous trip as they kept watch for deadheads and other vessels without lights. Straining to peer through the windscreen, Nancy felt the closeness of Dan behind her as she picked out the coastal lights and got her bearing. Quickly checking Ezekiel's signal beacon on the hill, Dan swung his binoculars toward the sleepy little town of Woodway and then beyond to the myriad of twinkling lights on the Edmonds' waterfront.

"There seems to be a boat sneaking along the coastline without lights," Dan commented with a chuckle, pointing to show Nancy.

"Forget it, Mr. Brown, we're heading for home!" she replied, pressing the throttle forward in defiance.

"We should talk to Uncle Jeb about the general's offer, Nan. I'm sure he'll have some interesting thoughts on how to approach it. You know, I expected you to have more objections."

"I'd already had time to think about it. I knew what they wanted."

Feeling Dan's fingers tighten on her shoulder, she giggled.

"Beth told me while we were upstairs. She'd been there when Gus and the others were discussing it before we arrived."

"So, you were already prepared when you and Beth came back into the room—the dress was just a ploy. You sneaky girls!"

"Of course, we women stick together you know. Beth made sure I knew all about it—she also told me most of it was Gus' idea."

"I'd swear Bill wasn't aware of it though."

"You're right, he wasn't—they never told him."

"You sneaky devils," Dan muttered.

Conversation petered out until they were beyond Admiralty Inlet and the rain and lights of Keystone were behind them.

"Look at that boat leaving Victoria," Dan said suddenly as they crossed onto the Canadian side of the strait. "Douse the lights, let's see what he's up to."

"You just can't resist some excitement, can you?" Nancy teased, switching off the running lights, turning the *Stockholm* to face Victoria, and slowing almost to a standstill. Peering into the darkness, she could just make out the shape of a distant boat silhouetted against the Ogden Point light.

"They're running without lights," she ventured the obvious.

"Rum runners," Dan grunted, "we'd better warn them."

"You're going to try to stop them?"

"Either stop them or scare them. Put your lights back on and head straight at them."

"But why? We're not working for the coast guard yet."

"Because they're heading straight into trouble—the US cutter is waiting in Useless Bay. They'll never make it to Seattle. Come on, Nan, get moving. I want to catch them on the Canadian side of the line."

Reacting to Dan's urging, Nancy switched her lights on and sent the *Stockholm* surging forward, weaving back and forth until she caught the silhouette in a distant light then, holding the line, she screamed across the water to intercept the oncoming boat.

Veering away, the quarry now headed back toward the Vancouver Island coast, hoping to disappear into the darkness, but the *Stockholm* was hot on its stern. Dan's eyes pierced the darkness as he gave her directions.

Suddenly lights came on in the fleeing vessel, slowing to a stop as the *Stockholm* came cautiously alongside, illuminating two terrified young men with their hands in the air.

"David Stern what on earth are you doing out here?" Dan's voice cracked in the evening air.

"Danny!" the young fisherman whimpered in relief. "I thought you were the law."

"Pull in close, Nan," Dan ordered. "I know these two."

Sighing with relief, Nancy held close to the other boat as Dan yelled a torrent of abuse at the boys, ordering them back to Victoria and threatening to contact their fathers.

"Now we can go home," he told her, feeling pleased with himself as they watched the fishing boat set its running lights and head back for Victoria harbour.

"Who were they?" Nancy asked.

"I know David, he's Jim Stern's son. Jim's a fisherman—keeps his boat at the Hudson Bay dock."

"I think you scared him, you're not going to tell his father, are you?"

"No, but I hope we've scared him out of anymore thoughts of rum running—he's only a boy."

"Yes, a boy of the sea like you once were and a boy with initiative—sometimes a dangerous combination!" Nancy remarked solemnly in the darkness, unable to see her husband's wide grin.

Chapter 20

Jeb's pipe glowed in the dark as he stood high on the clifftop, braving the cold wind as he strained to catch the sound of the *Stockholm*'s engine. Hearing it, he sighed with relief. *They're sure late tonight*, he thought, then he moved quickly back inside to get warm and tell Meg of their arrival. He didn't want to alert them to how worried they both were.

It wasn't long after meeting the young redheaded waitress at the Occidental Hotel back in 1910 that his crusty exterior was broken and Nancy had won his heart. After all these years, by his reckoning, she belonged to him and he was allowed to worry about her. The war was over now and the dreaded influenza epidemic appeared beaten in their area, but his intuition could still sense danger in the air. Although nothing specific disturbed his mind in recent days, he promised himself to be ever wary.

"They're here?" Meg posed her question hopefully as Jeb slipped off his coat.

"Aye lass, they're coming, just came 'round the bend."

When Dan looked up at the house, the clifftop beacon light was there to guide them in and Cunningham Manor's lights glowed warm and inviting.

"You know, Nan," he mused as they docked, "I'm always so thankful when we get home."

"I know, I feel the same way. This is our little piece of heaven, Danny, our own special haven. You picked this spot well."

Fussing over dinner, Meg demanded all the news from south of the border, raising her eyebrows in concern when Nancy told her General Greene still looked thin from his illness. She smiled thoughtfully when Nan told her of Nellie Cornish's involvement with Bill Jorgensen and the new recording company.

Listening quietly, Jeb at last broke his silence. "Why was General Greene there to meet you?"

"He wanted to talk to me," Dan muttered.

"He wanted to talk to you? Who was with him?" the old detective asked suspiciously.

"Admiral Johnson, he's …."

"I know who he is," Jeb interrupted scornfully. "It's what he wanted that bothers me."

After Dan explained the details of their meeting, adding Nancy's subtle negotiations, he waited for Jeb's expected opinion.

"Why didn't you just say 'no'?" the old man growled.

"What's the matter, Uncle Jeb," Nancy teased, "are you too old for a little excitement?"

"I'm too damned old to be stupid!" he corrected her.

"Well, you won't be involved," Meg snorted, "and who knows if Premier Oliver will go along with the Americans."

"Oh be quiet woman," the detective snapped, getting to his feet and heading for the door. "They wouldn't have asked if they weren't sure Oliver would cooperate, the pigs have an ace up their sleeve. I know how they work!"

Once they cleaned up the dishes, the women joined Jeb and Dan in the living room sitting around the roaring log fire, and Meg put Nancy's record on the phonograph. Jebediah's attitude softened as his thoughts turned to the planning of a safe campaign against the Puget Sound marauders.

During the night, another storm lashed the cliffs at Gordon Head, leaving a mess of branches littering the lawn and driveway. As dawn neared, Meg hurried her charges through breakfast, then watched the taillights of their vehicles as they disappeared through the mist and up the drive. She laughed as Dan, dressed in his cumbersome oilskins, came to say goodbye.

"I'm off to Sidney to pick up a delivery that goes to one of the islands, Aunt Meg. I'll find out which one when I get there so it will probably take most of the day." He gave her a fond hug and opened the door.

"You be careful now, lad, this weather isn't fit for man or beast!" the Scot complained, quickly shutting the door behind him.

Following Jeb's big black car up the drive and splashing through the mud holes of Ash Road, Nan knew his mind was at work when he turned onto old Cedar Hill Road. Instead of following him, she took Shelbourne as far as Cedar Hill Cross Road. Reaching the lowland area, she groaned when she saw the flooding and cut over to Richmond.

Katherine was already serving her first customers—night staff from the hospital, a streetcar driver, his conductor and one lone soldier—when Nan arrived.

"You must have slept here, Kate?" she called, hanging up her coat and slipping on an apron.

"Almost, I was here at six. Jack had an early start to Jordan River."

"Was it stormy over your way last night? Boy, the wind was howling in Gordon Head. There were tree branches littering the roads everywhere this morning," Nancy informed her.

"No, it wasn't that bad in Esquimalt. I wouldn't have wanted to be out in it though," Kate replied.

The kitchen staff arrived soon after, shouting that the rain had stopped and, in no time, the *Wounded Soldier Restaurant* was a hive of activity. It was almost ten when Eva walked in and took a chair in the corner of the kitchen.

"How did you get into town?" Nancy asked taking a cup of tea to her friend and sitting down with her for a minute.

"I came in with John Sadlier, he was delivering vegetables to the hospital."

"That was handy."

"Sometimes I come in with Mr. Williamson, the mailman, or other neighbours. You're all so kind. I sure miss Dorothy since she went off to school."

"How is she doing with her studies at The Normal School?" Nancy asked.

"Oh, really well. She's almost finished her nine-month course and then she has to do two years experience to get her teacher's certificate. She's very excited about it all and I'm thrilled for her."

"Good for her," Nancy replied, excusing herself to look after some customers.

Finding a bit of time here and there between customers, Nancy was surprised that Eva didn't seem to be in any hurry to leave. She told Nan that her position as supervisor with the Red Cross had changed substantially and she was now helping returning soldiers find jobs and rehabilitate with their families—a difficult task in some cases. At the same time, she was also keeping an eye on Nancy's list of charity cases.

"I don't know how you manage it all, Eva," said Nancy, admiration in her voice. "I tried to do it when you were helping with the influenza victims but I didn't think I was very good at it although it sure gave me a sense of accomplishment to be trying."

"You did an amazing job, Nan," Eva assured her. "Dora Alcock thinks you're wonderful and what you did for Teddy Lancaster is little short of a miracle. I hardly recognized him when I saw him yesterday and, by the way missy, Teddy's one of their family now! They all love the arrangement."

"I'm so pleased but that wasn't me," Nancy retorted, blushing, "it was Jim Morrison who helped that boy."

"I suppose it wasn't you that gave Mrs. Wright some extra money when her son came home either."

"It was only five dollars."

"Well, when her son Jim learned you and your fund has been paying his mother's rent and giving her money for food, he cried, Nan. He could hardly believe anybody could be so kind and caring. Why don't you let me tell them where the money comes from?"

"No, please don't," Nancy implored her friend, a look of desperation on her face.

"All right, you know I won't just now," Eva sighed reluctantly, "but someday Victoria's going to find out. Now, I don't imagine you can guess why I'm here?"

"Let me see, you couldn't possibly need money, could you?"

"I'm afraid so," Eva giggled.

"Kate," Nancy called her partner over. "Can I borrow a hundred dollars from the cash box?"

"Of course you can, just put an IOU in the drawer."

Carefully putting away the money Nan gave her into her purse, Eva quickly left the restaurant and caught the streetcar to her next destination. Resourcefully, she had stumbled on a way to ride the city streetcars without paying—her friendly smile and a quick flash of her Red Cross identity tag worked wonders with sympathetic conductors. She only wished the streetcars went out to Gordon Head—it would save her a lot of walking.

Professor Louis Turner startled the redhead early that afternoon when she noticed him sitting quietly in a corner with a lady companion and went over to greet him.

"Hello Louis, I didn't notice you come in. Have you been served?" she asked hurriedly, going by with a tray of drinks.

"Hello Nan, yes thanks, your girl has taken our order," he replied. "This is a wonderful place you have here, so friendly and cozy."

Nancy went and delivered her order and, on returning to the kitchen, Louis called her over.

"You are coming to the Armistice Ball, aren't you, Nancy?" he asked.

"No, I don't think so, Louis. Dan and I would be lost among all those toffs!"

"But I was hoping I could persuade you to sing for us," continued the popular Victoria maestro, pretending to pout.

"Oh you'll manage without me I'm sure," she replied, moving quickly away to assist a wounded soldier, steadying his shaking hand as he raised a full cup of hot coffee to his lips.

A rush of customers caused the professor to slip from her mind until Kate quietly informed her he and his companion had left, but the maestro told her to wish Nancy the best of luck with her Seattle concert.

"I think he was quite disappointed you wouldn't sing at the ball," Kate murmured.

"I'm a working girl, not a socialite, Kate," the redhead replied flippantly. "I'd be just as happy to sing for our customers."

"Are you going to Seattle tomorrow?" Kate asked late in the day, as the two experienced waitresses flashed around the restaurant, doing the last cleanup.

"Yes ... Kate, I thought you were catching this streetcar?" said Nancy looking out the window. Seeing Kate run for her coat, she continued, "It's moving! It's leaving!"

Squealing, Kate ran out of the door Nancy was holding open. Racing across the street, she accepted the conductor's hand and scrambled aboard the slowly moving iron monster as the passengers shouted their encouragement. Laughing, at the restaurant doorway, Nancy waved.

Finishing her work half an hour later, she flicked out the lights, locked the door, and went to her truck. She gave it a crank and slipped into the driver's seat, adjusting her hat before slowly moving out to the road. Sitting for a moment, she looked over at the lighted hospital windows and noticed the shadowy figures through the curtains. Sighing, she briefly wondered if there were any new influenza cases, then drove out onto the dark, deserted street.

Resisting the temptation to go home via Lansdowne, she laughed at her thoughts and continued through the lightly falling rain to Cedar Hill Cross Road. She watched as two youngsters in a small boat played in the water which had collected in the lowland basin. Driving more quickly along the pothole-free road, she suddenly felt an urgency to get home.

Meg was busting with news when she walked into the house, unable to contain herself as Nancy hugged her.

"They're coming for the Armistice Ball, they're all coming!" she blurted out.

"Who's coming?" Nancy couldn't help but smile at her aunt's excitement. "Where's Danny?"

"Changing his clothes, he was soaked to the skin. Would you take that pie out of the oven for me, lass?"

Picking up the two potholders on the counter, Nan opened the oven door and sniffed the wonderful aroma of apple pie and cinnamon. Lifting it carefully out of the hot oven, she pushed the door shut with her knee and had almost set it down when Dan came up behind her.

"Stay right there, Nan," he laughed. "I'll get a spoon and eat it right out of your hands!"

"Get out of here," Meg chastised him, slapping his hand and chasing him out of the kitchen.

"You know, lassie," said Meg as they were getting ready to eat a bit later, "I never told you that Danny once ate one of my apple pies all by himself!"

"Maybe he was hungry," Jeb chuckled, winking at Dan.

"It had just come out of the oven," the Scot laughed, "and Ned and Tim were waiting for it to cool when that little devil ran off with it!"

Both Dan and Meg burst into uncontrollable laughter as they replayed the scene from years before.

"Ned chased him up Wharf Street," Meg gasped through her laughter.

"He never caught me though," Dan chuckled.

"Och, you ate the whole thing," Meg panted. "Ned would have drowned you if he could have caught you. You even slept in the shed that night because you daren't come home!"

When things quieted down, Dan wiped his eyes and rose, pulling Meg's chair out from the table with her on it. He surprised everyone by kneeling in front of her.

"And I thought you'd forgiven me!" he moaned, resting his head on her knee.

"Right lad," Jeb said solemnly. "I think we've got the message. Best not let you get near our pie in the future."

During dinner Meg finally got a chance to tell them her exciting news that Beth had phoned and the whole family, including the boys, were coming to Victoria for the dance and expected the four of them to be their guests.

"Gus has already booked their rooms at the Empress. They'll come back with you on the *Stockholm* next Wednesday and return on the 29th."

"Well, we better hope it doesn't rain," Dan laughed, "that's eight people and Bill's wheelchair—it'll be a squeeze in the cabin."

"Isn't it exciting," Meg purred, "fancy us rubbing shoulders with rich folk."

"Professor Turner called at the restaurant today," Nancy added quietly, "he wanted me to sing at the ball."

"You said no, didn't you, lass?" Jeb surmised knowing how she felt about the too-fancy occasion.

"I said no because I wouldn't even consider it if you three weren't invited."

"But it's such an honour to be asked, dear," retorted Meg, "maybe you'll change your mind."

"Aunt Meg, to be really honest, I get enough pleasure singing for the soldiers at the hospital and doing my Seattle concerts."

"But this is a special occasion, honey, and I think you should consider it," continued Meg. "I'd love to be there when you sing at the Empress."

"Yes, especially for all those toffs!" Jeb added.

By 9 o'clock, tiredness was overtaking Nancy as they sat relaxing in front of the fire. Eyes drooping, she snuggled closer to Dan on the chesterfield, oblivious to conversation as her thoughts projected ahead to the Seattle concert.

Before dawn the next morning, they headed for Victoria to pick up their Seattle shipment. A fleet of fishing vessels was just leaving the harbour as the *Stockholm* rounded the breakwater.

Dan grinned, pointing to a motor launch mixing closely with the fishing vessels. A well-known rum runner was chancing his luck in a run for the American coast.

"Looks like Johnny Schnarr is going to try his luck going to Port Angeles today," said Dan.

"He can't outrun the coast guard in that old tub," Nancy declared.

"The coast guard is down in Useless Bay and I'll bet he knows that. Johnny is a smart one and his *Rose Marie* is faster than you think."

Pulling smoothly into the Brown and Wilson dock they found Jack waiting. Nancy shut down the engine and leapt onto the boards, racing for the office.

"What's wrong with her?" Jack asked.

"My guess would be nature's calling," Dan growled and, looking around, continued, "did you order that liquor yet?"

"Waldo sent a truck for it, here he comes now."

Yelling orders at the truck driver, Waldo Skillings' voice carried down to the water as he directed the ungainly vehicle past the office and over toward the boat.

"I've done this before ya know!" the driver grumbled at the haulier as they began to unload.

"Aye, but you won't be doing it again if ya don't listen, lad!" Waldo threatened.

Staying on the dock and helping them load the *Stockholm*, Waldo mopped his brow with a rag as the last case disappeared into the hatch. Grinning to himself, he reached for his pipe.

"Time you two were outa here, come on get moving!" he ordered.

"Don't you start on me, Mr. Skillings," Nancy whispered mischievously, "or ...."

Backing away from the redhead until he bumped into the office wall, Waldo yelled at Dan. "Danny will you control this blasted woman of yours!"

"Nancy," Dan called authoritatively, "give the man a kiss and let's get going!"

Waldo looked up, pretending to be panic stricken and made a dash to escape, still gripping his pipe firmly in his teeth, he scampered away.

"I think you scared him that time, Nan!" Jack laughed.

Nancy waved, then jumped aboard and expertly took them out of the harbour carefully watching a couple of merchant ships being towed by harbour tugs. She slowed when they cleared Ogden Point, seeing a hospital ship coming toward them.

"Another load of heartache," she said sadly, looking up at Dan.

Dan held her shoulders and fondly kissed her cheek, knowing how badly the stark reality of war affected her. There was little conversation until he pointed out the coast guard cutter in Useless Bay.

"I told you they were here, didn't I?" he said. "Somehow Johnny Schnarr knew, too."

"How could he have known?" asked Nancy.

"Spies, someone is telling him where they are."

"Johnny is nobody's fool and he's a whiz with engines. Check Ezekiel, Dan, I don't want anything to happen to that old man."

"I will, you just keep your eyes on what you're doing."

There was no light in the tower on the hill as Dan's binoculars scrutinized Ezekiel's warning system. Lowering his attention, he caught sight of a wisp of smoke disappearing quickly as it left the tree tops. At the cove entrance, he followed the movement of a fishing boat sailing close to the coastline, but saw no suspicious activity from the crew and lowered his glasses again.

Down the coast, Terry stood waiting in the shelter of the Jorgensen boathouse. He was worrying, as was his habit when the Canadians were making a delivery. Now, more than ever, he knew the risks as new elements crept into the Seattle waterfront trade—Eastern gangsters were taking an active interest in the West Coast liquor trade—while talk in political circles were of national prohibition. Police Sgt. Roy Olmsted had already warned him they could soon be seeing open warfare among the rum runners.

Sharp hearing warned him the *Stockholm* was coming, but caution caused him to stay out of sight in the shadows until he saw the familiar launch streaking toward him.

"Gus said you were to go straight up to the house," he informed them curtly once the motor was silenced.

"Sourpuss!" the redhead commented sharply, making a face at him and grinning. She knew the gangster was more sensitive than he pretended and always concerned for their safety.

Ignoring her, Terry cracked orders at his men, urging them to put more effort into their task.

"I wonder what's biting his arse?" Dan mused on their way up to the house.

Hurrying to escape the bitter cold wind, they were grateful when the butler quickly opened the door.

"The family are upstairs waiting for you," Joseph told them, "you could try Master Bill's elevator if you like."

"An elevator!" Nancy giggled as the butler took their coats and scarves and they removed their boots.

As they did so, they looked around them for some new construction.

"Where do you keep this elevator, Joseph?" Dan asked.

"Right here on the stairs sir, let me show you."

Walking over to the stairs, the butler excitedly explained in great detail how the steel plate, big enough to carry Bill's wheelchair, folded down from the wall. He pointed to the drive chain, which carried the platform all the way to the next floor, neatly running up the side of the stairs.

"Stand on it, please," Joseph invited, lowering the platform.

Doing as he said, Nancy held tightly to Dan's arm as the butler turned a switch, giggling as the whole contraption suddenly began to lift.

"Ooh, that feels funny!" laughed the redhead as they moved upward.

"You like my latest toy?" Bill's voice boomed down from above them. "Now I can get up here without any help."

"I think it's wonderful," Nan admitted enthusiastically as they reached the top. "They should have these lifts on all stairs."

"They will someday, sis," Bill grinned, offering his hand. "Dad had the men at the shipyard build it."

Beth and Gus were having tea in their apartment when the others entered. Eager to talk of their intended trip to Victoria, Gus chuckled with enthusiasm questioning Dan on the city's shipping merchants and expressing his desire to make the acquaintance of local businessmen like Rithet, Dunsmuir and Wilson.

"I found you a new party dress, Nan," Beth whispered while the men were talking. "You'll love it. I can't wait to see it on you."

"Another one! Oh you shouldn't have, Beth. I have all those lovely dresses you and Hattie Rhodes have given me."

"Those dresses are for your Seattle shows; this one is for the Empress Ball, a socialite's extravaganza!" she exclaimed, exaggerating her words. "All the best families will be there, dear."

"And you expect me and Aunt Meg to fit in with that bunch?"

"No, I expect you to dazzle them and, by the way, James is also coming. He'll be escorting Nellie."

Bill joined their conversation, trying to explain to Nancy the new technology the recording company had developed for the Seattle concert.

"We'll be able to capture the ambiance of the whole theatre," he babbled.

"Yes, I'm sure it will," Nancy rolled her eyes.

"We've already tried it," Bill replied defensively. "Nellie played for a test record last week."

There was a light tap at the door and the maid entered.

"Lunch is ready to be served, ma'am."

Starting down the stairs, they moved out of the way as Bill negotiated his elevator, grinning impishly as he passed them.

Chapter 21

After lunch, Gus took Dan and Nancy outside and walked down to the dock. He told them of some new plans he had for the boat.

"I've ordered Sven Sorenson to design and install a canopy for the *Stockholm*, in case it rains for our trip to Victoria!" he chuckled. "He may be here now."

Terry's still here," the redhead exclaimed, seeing his car out on the road.

Inside the boathouse, the Swedish engineer was erecting the framework of a canopy on the *Stockholm.*

"Hello Dan, Nancy, nice to see you both again," Sven exclaimed, shaking hands with Dan.

"What have we here, Sven?" Dan asked, climbing aboard.

"It's quite a simple structure, easy to erect and remove as needed. The cover will be waterproof sailcloth affording a measure of protection from the weather."

"So what do you think, Dan?" Gus asked.

"It's a wind trap!" Dan replied, scowling. "I wouldn't want it on permanently; it could cause us quite a problem in a gale."

"You're right," the engineer agreed, "it's only for special occasions. You're an experienced sailor, Dan, you can make the decision whether you use it or not."

"Yes, that's right, lad," Gus agreed. "It's your boat, but it will give you more flexibility, especially when you have visitors aboard."

"I'm not trying to be ungrateful, sir. These are treacherous waters and the weather can change in an instant. The *Stockholm*'s a mighty fine boat, but it still pays to be cautious."

Terry poked his head in through the boathouse door.

"We have visitors!" he exclaimed, sounding worried.

"Who?" Gus asked quietly.

"Police!" Terry hissed.

Angry voices sounded outside as Terry blocked the pathway to the boathouse. Bill spun his wheelchair for the door, eager to lend his support but Dan bounded over the rail to charge after him.

"What the devil!" Gus growled as he followed the boys.

Nancy felt Beth grip her arm and then they heard Dan shouting.

"LET THEM THROUGH, TERRY, IT'S ADMIRAL JOHNSON!"

"What's all the security for Gus?" the admiral grumbled. "You boys stay out there," he shouted to the two city policemen accompanying him.

"Well move, Bill!" Admiral Johnson hissed at the wheelchair-bound man blocking his approach. "I need a word with Dan."

"Not until you identify that one." Bill pointed at the man in a suit and tie behind the admiral.

"Damnit, move!" Richard Johnson snapped irritably, reaching for the wheelchair.

"I wouldn't advise that, admiral!" Dan's voice was threatening as he stepped closer, his hands balled into fists.

Startled by the obvious threat, the admiral stepped back, uncertain how to proceed.

"Well, identify yourself, man, before I turn these two young hellions loose on you!" Gus added, moving toward the group.

"You know who I am, Bill," Richard Johnson said with a frown, "and this fellow is a government agent who will be working in Victoria. Now move and let us pass."

"His name?" Bill asked, somberly.

"Marley, Tom Marley, now are you satisfied?"

Glancing up as he felt Dan's hand settle reassuringly on his shoulder, Bill backed his wheelchair out of the way and allowed the men to pass.

"We're finished for now, Gus," said Sven, emerging from the boathouse and quickly disappearing up the path. "We'll have the cover ready for Wednesday."

"Well son," Tom Morley chuckled reaching out his hand to Dan, "it's a pleasure to meet you. I've heard so much about you and your wife in the last few days."

Frowning in deep thought, Dan felt the strong, warm handshake of the government man and sensed his honesty.

"We'll leave you now," Gus murmured. "I don't want Beth to get a chill. We'll be ready on Wednesday, so don't be late, son."

Hugging the Americans, Nancy said her goodbyes and watched them walk up the garden path to the house, waving again before they disappeared inside.

"We would like to talk to Dan and his wife in private," the admiral remarked, looking directly at Bill.

"He's family," the redhead said decisively, "he stays."

Nodding, Morley appeared to have no objection to Nancy's decision, stating, "First, I'd like to see this boat of yours."

Following Dan, Nancy, and the two men into the boathouse, Bill parked his wheelchair just inside the door where he could see and hear everything.

"Halleluiah, what a boat!" the government agent exclaimed excitedly. "I'll bet she's a speedster."

"Fastest boat in these waters," the admiral bragged, "nothing could catch them."

"And nothing could escape either," Tom murmured, glancing over at Dan. "You were a whaler, weren't you, Dan?"

"Yes sir."

"He's the gunner who shot a freighter—the one I told you about," continued the admiral.

"You shot a freighter by accident?" Tom chuckled.

"No sir, on purpose."

"Now why would you do that?"

"To get a line onboard and claim salvage."

"A wreck, harpooned in a storm, you're exaggerating aren't you, lad?"

"No he's not, mister, my dad owns that freighter and they kept the evidence—they chrome plated the hole in the bow!" Bill Jorgensen replied.

"I'm impressed," Tom Morley said thoughtfully. "You were also in the Canadian army?"

"Now that's enough, sir," Nancy exclaimed, wagging a finger at him. "State your business. It's time we were leaving."

Glancing up at the beautiful redhead standing on the deck above them, Morley could feel Nancy Brown's protective anger. He had been warned by Admiral Johnson and realized too late he had touched a sensitive nerve.

"Sorry ma'am," he muttered. "I just wanted to check my facts," Tom continued, unwisely offering a feeble excuse.

"She said 'that's enough'," Terry O'Reilly's voice hissed from the doorway with a menacing overtone, "and that means your business is finished, mister!"

"All right, no more questions," Tom agreed amicably. "I shall be working in Victoria, Dan. No one knows me there but we should keep in contact. I might have some useful information for you."

"I'm not working for you people yet!" Dan replied defensively.

"Well you know what Nancy said, Dan," Admiral Johnson added, "she told General Greene you would consider it as soon as he started paying into her orphans' fund."

"Yes, I remember."

"He's already made the first payment. Nellie Cornish has an envelope for you."

"The old devil!" Nancy laughed, as Dan threw the bowline on board and stood waiting for her to go start the engine. "He is serious, isn't he?"

"I'm afraid it's a very serious situation, Nancy, and we really need Canada's help," Morley added, watching as Nancy moved in behind the controls of the large launch. An amused expression spread across his face.

Nan started the engine and the boat began to move as Dan threw in the last line. Bill and Terry waved as Dan skillfully jumped aboard the moving boat and went inside to join Nancy. She opened the throttle and, with a roar of power, the *Stockholm* swept away from the boathouse.

"Surprised ya, didn't she?" Terry asked coldly, turning to Morley. "Don't underestimate that gal, she can handle that boat as well as Dan."

Checking the new canopy frame as Nancy headed for home, Dan marvelled at the Swedes' ingenuity—their work was always of the highest quality. Stepping into the cabin, he touched Nancy's cheek.

"Oow," she squealed, "you're freezing!"

Laughing, Dan teased her with his cold hands as they made their way up Puget Sound.

Back at the Jorgensen's, Bill was already making plans to assist them with the general's proposition. Watching the *Stockholm* disappear among the array of boats in the vicinity and, gladly seeing the last of the visitors, he casually began to solicit Terry's participation.

"You know most of Seattle's dockland scum, don't you, Terry?" he asked while watching his friend close the boathouse door.

Terry half-smiled, making no effort to deny or affirm Bill's statement. Unaware of the arrangements made with Dan, he wondered where the conversation was leading.

"There must be some talk around of who is responsible for the murders of those fishermen in the sound," Bill suggested.

"What the hell are you talking about, Billy?" Terry snorted as they went outside. "My men don't mix with those bums!"

"But you could put out some feelers, couldn't you?"

"Spit it out, kid. I ain't one for riddles; tell me straight what's biting at ya."

"Aw hell," Bill groaned, "all I'm trying to do is keep those two out of trouble!"

"Those two?" Terry asked solemnly. "Nancy and Dan?"

"Yes, I'm not much use to them without legs, but they're going to need some help in the near future."

Terry paced the dock, fiddling with his hat as he tried to make some sense of Bill's request—his immediate reaction was to go down to the Seattle docks and force someone to talk. Luckily, logic quickly tempered his thoughts. Knowing heavy-handed action would start a war with the criminal element there and no one would be safe, he settled on stealth.

"Right, you leave it with me," said Terry, turning back to Bill, "let me see what I can find out."

"I want to keep this between us two," Bill muttered.

"Fine by me, now let's get you back to the house."

Farther up the waterway, Dan and Nancy were enjoying their trip home in daylight and good weather for a change. At home Meg was outside standing on the clifftop listening and watching. Long before she could distinguish the red-and-white boat cutting through the high waves, she heard the welcome sound of its engine and turned back to the house to finish preparing dinner.

Nancy helped Dan tie up and then, carefully carrying her new dress, went up to the house. By the time Dan arrived, she and Meg were engrossed in woman talk with Nancy changing into the dress to show it off then filling Meg in on all the news.

Feeling neglected, Dan disappeared outside to cut some wood. Losing all sense of time, his mind strayed to thoughts of the American's proposition and the dangers it posed. He realized the daylight was fading when he heard a vehicle approach and put down his saw. Moving to the front of the house to see if it was Jeb, he grinned when he recognized the Parfitt Brothers' truck and saw Jack Duggan coming toward him.

"Are you folks going to the Armistice Ball at the Empress, lad?" Jack asked.

"Yes we are. Gus and the family are all coming up on Wednesday—we're going with them."

"You folks are all well? You didn't get touched by the flu, did you?"

"No, everybody's fine, Jack. Uncle Jeb came up with one of his homemade remedies; he's been dosing us with port wine."

"Port wine eh, sounds like a fine remedy to me!" chuckled the Irish builder.

"Come on in and I'll give you a bottle," Dan invited, knowing how much Jack enjoyed his liquor.

"Hello Jack," Nancy squealed, standing on a stool while Meg knelt at her feet, stitching the hem of her new dress. "What are you doing out here?"

"Nellie gave me orders to make sure you were going to the Armistice Ball and I was out this way, so thought I'd stop by."

"Get the man a cup of tea, Danny," Meg peered over her spectacles.

"I will, but he wants a taste of Uncle Jeb's port wine first; do you want a tea or coffee, Jack?" Dan asked.

"Tea, but get that bottle out, lad, I'm eager for a taste of it now that you've mentioned it!"

Dan brought the port wine and a glass over, pouring out a liberal amount before handing it to the builder. Holding it up to the light, Jack studied its colour. Nancy jumped down off the stool, helped Meg to her feet, and waited for Jack's reaction. Pleasure spread across the Irishman's face as he sniffed, sipped, then suddenly drained the glass.

Best medicine I ever tasted," he exclaimed, grinning broadly, "any chance of another wee sip, lad!"

"No, but I'll get you a bottle to take home and share with Nellie," Dan replied. "We think it's kept the flu away from us and Beth took it after getting sick and got better very quickly."

"That's good. I'm much obliged, son, now I'll take that tea." He waited until Dan brought the cup of tea to the table, then turned to look at the redhead. "That's a mighty fine dress, Nancy," he commented, "for the ball I presume?"

"Beth Jorgensen bought it for me," she replied, smiling as a car was heard out on the driveway. "I think Uncle Jeb's home, Aunt Meg."

"I know," Meg called from the kitchen, "are you staying for dinner, Jack?"

"No thanks, Meg. I just wanted to tell Nancy that I'm working in Fernwood, building new soldiers' houses."

"We're working on three houses in Walnut Street. They back onto a little farm at Denman where we get our sandwiches and milk."

Nancy looked puzzled and wondered where the conversation was leading when Jebediah came stomping into the room, hung his coat behind the door, and, went to stand by the stove, warming his hands.

"You're building in Fernwood, you said, Jack?" Nancy coaxed the builder to continue.

"Yes, yes, we met a young man there."

"Jack, what are you trying to tell me? I'm not a mind reader you know."

"We met Ted Lancaster, he works on that farm and he told us what you did for him."

"I introduced him to Jim Morrison and Jim did the rest making those fancy contraptions for his legs."

"The mayor and several councillors were with us that day. Ted told them you had arranged it all and he showed us what those metal legs looked like. Dr. Price said he was going to talk to Jim Morrison to see if they could help other amputees."

"That would be wonderful. They should talk to May Coolridge or Eva Todd at the Red Cross office. They will know other amputees."

"Dinner's ready," Meg announced. "If you're staying, Jack Duggan pull up a chair, if not, off you go home to Nellie, we're eating!"

"I'm going," the builder replied, not offended in the least with the Scot's bluntness. He stopped at the door with his hand on the doorknob. "Nancy, you did a wonderful thing for that lad. Thanks for the tea, Meg. See you all at the Empress."

"If they only knew what you've done for this city," Meg muttered, swinging her attention onto the old detective. "Jebediah are you listening to me?"

"Oh be quiet woman," Jeb growled, winking at Nancy. "I'd have to be deaf not to hear you!"

During dinner Jeb told them of some news he'd heard—city police were trying to find the source of liquor that had suddenly appeared in the hands of revellers, still celebrating the end of the war. They were having little success—it seemed. Waldo told him there were still a few cases of the flu around, although no one was paying any attention to the restrictions anymore, and the police weren't enforcing them. He laughed when he told of a harbour pilot who had rammed the dock at the rice factory on Store Street, after drinking a bottle of rum.

"Anybody hurt?" Dan asked.

"No lad, it did a fair bit of damage to the dock though, but none to the freighter."

"Good, do you know where the booze is coming from?"

"Yes, Jim Goodwin told me."

"Who's selling it?" asked Nancy.

"It seems a farmer in Saanich brings it in from Alberta and sells it out of his barn. A lot of work but he must be making good money."

"Drug stores sell it, too," Dan murmured, "but only with a doctor's prescription."

"It's stupid," Meg added, "almost anybody can get liquor if they want it. What's the use of having prohibition?"

"You're right lass," Jeb mused, "even the mayor thinks prohibition has outlived its usefulness. He says as soon as John Oliver finds a way to tax it, he'll call an end to it."

"That would have to come from the feds," Dan pointed out, "but they'd probably leave each province to make their own decision on how to implement it."

Nodding his agreement, Jeb changed the subject and told them of all the activity at the Empress as preparations were made for the ball. "They're stringing banners and flags across the front of the building and waterproof canopies are being erected at the entrances. A staff member told Waldo the ballroom will be decorated with flowers and streamers."

"Did you book me any deliveries for tomorrow?" Dan asked.

"Yes, you have two, to Salt Spring in the morning and a machine part to Cowichan Cannery. Jack's going out to the lumber camp at Renfrew."

Neither Dan nor Nancy mention the meeting with the admiral and Tom Morley, having agreed to keep it a secret until it became official.

A strong wind noisily rattled through the trees along the cliffs at Gordon Head and Dan announced he was going to go down to the dock to check the *Stockholm.* He slipped into his oilskins and went out into the darkness, taking one of the lit lamps with him. Forcing his way against the wind, he descended the cliff stairs into the shelter of the cove. Standing for a moment, he listened to the pounding waves and the creaking of the *Stockholm* straining at the lines. He added an extra tie line on the stern before making his way back to the house.

"Fred forecast a gale for tonight," Jeb growled as Dan came back into the house. "It's going to be rough tomorrow."

"It'll blow itself out before morning," Dan predicted. "It's coming from the south."

Chapter 22

The morning proved him right, the wind dropped, but logs littered the beach and rocks along the coastline, showing stark evidence of the storm's power. Jeb encountered a fallen tree on Cedar Hill Road and cursed when he had to find an alternative route, while Nancy sped along Richmond splashing through the mud holes.

"Wild night," Katherine called as the redhead burst into the restaurant. "Somebody's porch roof is hanging off up the street from us."

"Are the streetcars running?" Nancy asked.

"Yes, they are, and here come our first customers."

The door flew open and the night staff from the Jubilee noisily arrived calling for coffee even before putting two tables together.

"Hey girls!" one young man shouted to Kate and Nan. "Have you heard the latest rumour? The word is out there won't be anymore hospital ships coming to Victoria. Isn't that wonderful?"

There were whistles and cheers from the group, and then a streetcar driver told of a foundry building being blown into Douglas Street, stopping the traffic. It wasn't until after lunch that a truck driver told them the street was clear again.

All day long the restaurant buzzed with activity and the doctors and nurses talked excitedly of the upcoming ball at the Empress. This was the social event that was going to officially end the doldrums of war and everyone felt Victoria was ready to boom again.

Harry Maynard called in, whispering he had just talked to a politician who said the Empress would be serving liquor at the ball.

"And that my girl," he chuckled, "would be the thin end of the wedge. It would mean the government was thinking seriously about repealing the prohibition law."

Time passed quickly over the next few days and new rumours surfaced with amazing regularity—always finding their way to the restaurant. The two city newspapers vied with each other to report the latest celebrity to book into the Empress Hotel while, on the inside pages, they continued to update the list of local soldiers missing or dead. Nancy knew there were many, many wives and families still waiting for their special someone to come home.

Dan noticed his wife was still showing little enthusiasm for the upcoming ball and was noticeably more quiet and short-tempered than in the past week. He couldn't imagine why she might be feeling out of sorts so he decided to talk to her about it. The first opportunity arose as they left the harbour on Wednesday morning.

"We don't have to go to the ball if you don't want to, honey," he murmured in her ear.

She looked at him with a puzzled expression. "What makes you think I don't want to go to the ball, Danny?"

"You haven't been as excited as I thought you would be, even after getting your dress, your enthusiasm just hasn't been there."

"You certainly know me, don't you? You're right, I suppose, but Beth really wants us to go and I promised."

"But what's bothering you; why don't you want to go?" he insisted.

"This fancy ball has turned out to be a party for the rich folk and it should be for the returning soldiers and the ones in the Jubilee Hospital who almost gave their lives," she said adamantly, her voice rising. "Do you think anyone has thought to invite them?"

"We can soon rectify that, honey," Dan murmured with a mischievous sparkle in his eyes. "Maybe someone should do a little quiet arranging."

"Let's do it, Danny," she responded excitedly, her attitude taking on a complete change. "It would give the boys some recognition and show the toffs that while they're partying, the war is not over for these broken young men."

"Good, we'd better push on. We need to get home quickly. This only leaves us one day to arrange it all."

Pouring on the power, Nancy showed her skill with the *Stockholm*, flashing past other vessels as Dan watched the coastline and the water ahead through his binoculars.

"They're in a hurry," Terry warned his men when he heard them coming.

Racing up to the dock, Nancy spun the red-and-gold craft around with the ease of experience, sending it shooting backwards into the boathouse.

"You go get the folks," Dan ordered as the redhead leapt onto the dock. "Terry did Gus show you the new canopy? I need to get it on quickly."

Terry went over to a shelf in the boathouse and picked up a large parcel wrapped in brown paper.

“Is this what you’re looking for?” he asked, handing it to Dan. “Gus said to give it to you.” Seeing Dan’s grateful nod, he turned to watch his men and cracked out an order, urging them on to greater efforts as they unloaded the secret cargo. Returning to the boathouse after his men had gone, Terry called out to Dan. “Need some help with that cover now?”

“That would be appreciated,” Dan growled, “pull that corner over the frame would you, Terry.”

Slowly they worked the tight-fitting canopy cover into place and Dan lashed it firmly to the frame using the cords provided. He still had a few misgivings about the whole contraption, knowing it could present a hazard if the wind came up, but was firmly resolved to try it and it would make travel much more comfortable for their passengers.

Bill was the first to arrive with his overnight bag strapped to his wheelchair. The boys lifted him over the side, sitting him on a bench while they got his wheelchair aboard. Then Joseph arrived with two servants, each carrying several bags of luggage. Dan and Terry quickly got them stowed into the hold.

“We’re almost ready to leave,” Dan called to the others who were talking outside the doorway.

Fifteen minutes later, with Beth and Gus safely settled into the cabin seats, Bill’s wheelchair tied firmly in the stern under the canopy and Christopher standing at the rail, Dan cast off.

As Nancy sent the *Stockholm* speeding out into the Puget Sound, Terry realized how much he envied and admired the young Canadians and wouldn’t want any harm to come to them. That moment he vowed he would give Bill Jorgensen his full assistance to find the murdering thugs who plagued their waters.

“I can feel the difference in the handling, Dan,” Nancy murmured as they sped past Apple Cove.

“Let me see.” Slipping in behind the wheel, Dan felt the *Stockholm* pulling a little to the left.

“Is it a problem?” asked Gus.

“I don’t think so, it’s just the wind on the canopy, which is to be expected,” he explained. “It’s pushing the stern over—we’ll just cut our speed a little.”

With Dan in the captain’s seat and Gus keeping a watch, it gave Nancy a chance to stretch her legs. Putting on her heavy coat, she stepped out on deck with the boys.

"Nan, I heard the Navy held some German freighters somewhere along here during the war. Do you know where that was?" Chris asked, searching the coastline for clues.

"Useless Bay over there," she replied, pointing. "Would you like to use Dan's binoculars?"

"I would," Bill replied. "I'd really like to take a closer look at the coastline."

"There must be hundreds of tiny little coves all over this coast," Chris said thoughtfully as Nan moved toward the cabin. "I'll bet nearly every house on the water has a sheltered dock."

"Well, you're right, many have," she agreed, entering the cabin and quickly returning with the glasses. "Anyone could be lurking in one of those inlets, the Eggers tried it with me a couple of times."

"Were they the rum runners you fought it out with, Nan?" Bill's voice filled with excitement. "Dad told us the story of how you wiped them out one night, shot them up pretty bad!"

"I guess I did but they were asking for it. It took awhile for them to regroup after that, but the next time I had the coast guard for backup."

"Was that when Dan got hurt?" Chris asked.

"No, that was earlier. Do you mind if we don't talk about this," she pleaded, turning to look through the window at Dan. "It brings back so many horrible memories."

Changing the subject, Bill focused the binoculars on the coast.

"I'll bet you and Dan know every light on this coast."

"He does—that one is Keystone and the next one is the Ebey light."

"It must be exciting when it's pitch black out here," Bill continued, "a real test of your nerves and confidence."

"You want some excitement, Billy Jorgensen?" Nancy asked. "We'll give you some excitement in Victoria."

"Oh yah, what have you got in mind, little sister?"

"We're going to crash the Armistice Ball!"

"You can't crash it; Dad's already bought the tickets!"

"Dan and I are going to bring some wounded soldiers who are not invited and don't have tickets!"

"Now that would be a lark I could go for!" Chris proclaimed. "I hope you intend including Billy and me in your plans."

"Oh I'm sure you will be after I tell Dan."

"You mean you haven't told Danny yet?" Bill chortled. "I wonder how Mum and Dad will react."

"No silly, of course Dan knows but we won't tell your folks until it's all over—by then everyone will know!" Nancy laughed. "I'd better go back inside, but don't say a word to anybody it's just between the four of us."

Glancing over his shoulder as his wife stepped into the cabin, Dan noticed the twinkle in her eye and her eager happy chatter. *That's more like my Nancy. I wonder if she's up to something*? he thought.

An hour later they left the protected waters behind them and Vancouver Island came into view.

"My goodness, look at the size of those waves," Beth exclaimed staring wide-eyed through the window at the angry waters of Puget Sound.

"Hold onto Beth, Nan," Dan ordered, "this could get a little bumpy."

"Better check the boys, Gus," Beth gasped as the *Stockholm* plunged though wave after wave.

"They're fine," Dan interrupted, looking outside. "This will wake up their sense of adventure. Are we taking you into Victoria?"

"Yes, we'll book into the Empress and hire a car to come out to the house," Gus explained, going to look out on deck and seeing the exhilaration on his sons' faces.

It was almost 2 o'clock when they turned into the harbour and the Goodwin Tug hooted a welcome. Slowing to avoid a row of herring boats leaving Fisherman's Wharf caused a flood of questions from Beth.

"Where are they going, Dan?" she asked. "Are those the boats you used to work on?"

"No, no, Danny was a whaler, Beth—those are herring boats," Nancy explained. "I think I heard there's a herring run in Barkley Sound and that'll be where they're going."

"Where's Barkley Sound?" Beth asked.

"Way up the West Coast of the Island."

Jeb, Jack, and Waldo were working out on the dock, loading boxes onto the *Highliner*, as the *Stockholm* nudged the dock behind them. Jack ran over and caught Nancy's line.

"Well, I must say this has been the most exciting boat ride I've ever had!" Beth declared as the engine went silent.

"Looks like you're starting a ferry service, Nan!" Waldo growled. "My word, it's the whole Jorgensen family!"

"We're the CP line's opposition," Nancy retorted, jumping down onto the boards, "didn't you know?"

"Waldo, we could use one of your hacks to deliver these people to the Empress," Dan called as he extracted their bags from the hold.

"Will one be enough?" Waldo asked with a smirk, watching him.

"Waldo," scolded Beth, "we've only come for a couple of days!"

"I know all about it. You ladies like to take enough for a month when you travel light!" he retorted, chuckling, as he headed off toward Wharf Street.

"You going somewhere, Jack?" Dan asked his manager.

"We got an urgent order from the machine shop on Store Street to make a delivery to the Nootka Cannery. I won't get back tonight. Make sure you let Katherine know, will you Dan? She wasn't at the restaurant."

"We'll look after it, Jack," Nancy called back.

"He's going to be out all night?" Beth asked, as Nancy helped her onto the dock. "Poor man, he'll be awfully cold."

"No, he won't," Nancy giggled, "he'll stay overnight at Port Renfrew at the old whaling station and be back tomorrow."

By the time Dan, Jeb, and Chris emptied the hold of the luggage and piled it on the dock, Waldo was back with one of his station hacks.

"We won't get the wheelchair in the cab," Waldo muttered, looking distressed when he saw Bill.

"Don't need to, Waldo," Bill laughed at the haulier's confusion. "I'll drive myself over, that's why I have wheels!"

"And I'll walk with him," Chris declared.

"Walk!" his brother declared, "you'll have trouble keeping up!"

"You can go out to Gordon Head anytime you like," Nancy called after them as they got into the hack. "Aunt Meg's expecting you."

"Time you two ate now," Jeb growled after the Jorgensens had gone. "Meg made some extra sandwiches just in case you wanted them."

"I need to borrow your car today, Uncle Jeb," said Nancy, winking at Dan. "You can go home on the *Stockholm* with Dan."

"And if I don't want to go home on the *Stockholm*?" the old man grumbled as he brought the tea and sandwiches to the table.

"Then you'll have to sleep here, won't you!" the redhead said flippantly.

"You could come get me," he suggested.

"I have to go to the restaurant, the Willows army camp and maybe over to Esquimalt and I don't know when I'll be back."

"What are you going to the Willows for, Nan?" Dan asked.

"We're going to take some wounded soldiers to the Armistice Ball, remember?" she whispered.

"We are?"

"You and I talked about it on the way to Seattle this morning," she said, looking exasperated.

"I remember you said it should be the soldiers who ought to be at the ball, but you never said we were going to crash the party."

"Well now you know, so I'd better get some arranging done, fast!"

"She's right lad, and nobody knows better than you. They should be thanking all you lads that went over there," Jeb agreed. "I'll do what I can to help, lass, and be proud to do it."

"Mostly I need you not to tell anyone about it!" Nancy retorted.

"You little devil," Dan laughed, "that's what you told Billy and Chris on the boat, wasn't it?"

"Yes, and they want to help, too, but no one else knows."

"I knew by the look on your face when you came back into the cabin, that you were planning something."

Awhile later, heavy footsteps coming down the boards indicated Waldo was back again. Stepping into the office, he marched over to the cupboard, acquired a mug, and poured himself a steaming cup of tea.

"Now then, girl," he said roughly, "are you going to tell me?"

"Tell you what?" the redhead purred innocently.

"Don't play that innocent little-girl thing with me, lass. You forget I've been watching you for years. I know when there's something perturbing you!"

"I want to crash the Armistice Ball at the Empress with 30 soldiers from the hospital," Nancy stated abruptly.

"Hell, you'll have the place in an uproar!" Waldo exploded.

"Don't you think, Mr. Skillings, that they should have a part in any celebrations? After all, it was they who fought the war, they that died, and they who are now suffering. I say they should be there."

"You're right," the haulier's voice dropped almost to a whisper. "Tell me how I can help."

"You can provide the transport."

"I can't just go to the hospital and ask for 30 men!"

"You'll pick them up at the Wounded Soldier at seven-twenty."

"Right," Waldo nodded. "I won't be there but I'll make sure you have enough vehicles. I suppose some will be in wheelchairs?" Watching her nod, he continued, "How long will they be staying at the Empress?"

"About an hour."

"I'll have the boys wait and take them back to the hospital."

"Thanks, old friend," Nancy purred. "I appreciate the help."

Draining his mug, Waldo stood up and went over to Nancy.

"Come here!" he said roughly, taking her hand and pulling her to her feet. Uncharacteristically, he gave her a hug and whispered emotionally, "By my oath, you're a very special lady, Nancy Brown." Releasing her quickly and turning away, but not before she felt a wetness on her cheek, Waldo strode to the door and was gone.

"You can take the car," Jeb grinned, "and I reckon I can keep a secret for one day."

"Good," she replied, giving him a quick kiss on the cheek. "Right, I'm off to the restaurant; can I have your keys please, Uncle Jeb?"

Dan and Jeb sat thoughtfully listening to the car start and make its way up to Wharf Street, before either of them spoke.

"She's quite a gal," Jeb whispered, "did I ever tell you how we met?"

"No, I don't think you ever did, Uncle Jeb."

"It was at the Occidental Hotel when she was a waitress, just a slip of a girl about 16, I believe," he paused staring off into space and taking a puff on his pipe. "She was ready to fight a big bully to protect me and she was going to pay for my meal."

"Why would she do that? You stopped her, I presume?"

"Actually, Waldo intervened, he put the run on the bum, but it was obvious he was watching out for Nancy. I was undercover at the time—looking rather shabby and she thought I was destitute." He stopped to chuckle. "Quite a gal she was even at that age, no wonder you took a shine to her, lad!"

"Yeah there was something about her made me want to help her even when I was a twelve-year-old and she was only four. Hey, I just remembered," Dan exclaimed, changing the subject. "I brought a pair of Aunt Meg's shoes in to get repaired last week and forgot about them. I've time now to slip up to the cobblers."

"They're done, lad," Jeb snorted. "Meg mentioned them and I found them in the cupboard and took them up to Arthur Hibbs. They're in that bag over there; I just keep forgetting to take them home!"

Chapter 23

Nancy pulled into the lane behind the restaurant and realized Jeb's big car wasn't going to fit quite as nicely into the lane as her little truck. Finally, managing to get it parked, she told herself nothing was going to spoil her day and went inside.

"Hi Kate," she called cheerily, opening the door so quickly she almost knocked a full tray out of her partner's hand. "I'm back … oops, oh my gosh, I'm sorry!"

"I can see that, silly!" Katherine giggled, barely managing to keep the tray upright. "Jump into an apron and give us a hand, we've been full all day."

She glanced quickly around the restaurant and as she got into her apron she remembered to give Kate the message from Jack. As she went to work she soon noticed there were no civilians in the place. Every table was filled with soldiers and even two wheelchairs were parked in the aisle.

Now's the time, she thought to herself. "BOYS!" she shouted above the noisy chatter. "I have an announcement to make."

The noise subsided and everyone curiously turned to face her. Even Kate and the kitchen staff crowded into the kitchen doorway to listen.

"I need 30 volunteers," she called, then burst into laughter when every able hand in the room was raised. "Don't you think it would be better to wait until you know what I want you for?"

"Don't matter, Nan," one soldier shouted. "We're with you!"

A burst of laughter from the kitchen doorway, brought a blush to Nancy's cheeks. She hadn't expected this kind of reception.

"Listen boys," she giggled. "I want to take you all to the Armistice Ball at the Empress Hotel tomorrow."

The look of shock and anticipation on the boys' faces was instant.

"Tie and tails, Nancy?" a wheelchair-bound, young soldier called out boldly, amid an outburst of laughter.

"No, just as you are, but wearing your regimental caps."

"Can I go, too?" a blind soldier asked. "I used to be a musician in the Winnipeg Orchestra."

"Of course you can, you'll love the professor's music."

Kate touched Nancy's arm and whispered a warning. "Did you see that nurse who came up and stayed just outside the door, I think she's gone to tell someone at the hospital."

"Right lads, here's the plan," Nancy carried on, nodding at her partner's warning. "You'll all meet here at 7 o'clock; we'll feed you dinner, then take you to the dance for an hour."

Those who could, rose to their feet and cheered, the others joined in. As the cheering subsided, Nancy realized that the nurse had returned, accompanied by the uniformed matron.

"Miss Wilson!" the matron snapped coldly. "I think I need to have a few words with you, young lady."

Nancy's eyes twinkled with amusement and she whispered demurely, "Why of course, ma'am, I was expecting you."

"You were?" the black-uniformed woman replied abruptly, pursing her lips. "Can we go somewhere private?"

"This is as private as it gets in here, ma'am."

The matron nervously glanced around at the soldiers before beginning her angry lecture. "Miss Wilson, you must stop this nonsense immediately. I will not allow you to take these men anywhere."

Katherine nudged the cook excitedly when she saw her friend's hands tighten into a ball at her side. "Look out," she whispered. "Nancy's getting cross."

"I know you occasionally sing for the men and they all love to come over here," Matron stated firmly, "but taking them to a fancy ball at the Empress is simply ridiculous."

"Miss Simpson," the redhead purred, "my name is Mrs. Brown. We haven't been introduced so I'll forgive your first mistake! My husband is Sgt. Dan Brown who was badly injured while serving in Europe. So you see I have some knowledge of the suffering these soldiers have experienced."

"My apology for not knowing you were a married lady," Matron Simpson interrupted, "and I was not aware your husband was a soldier."

Whispers ran around the tables as the men relayed the conversation to their hard-of-hearing companions.

"You seem to be misinformed, Miss Simpson, for I *am* taking them to the ball, ma'am, and you have no say in the matter! These men can get a pass to be out until ten-thirty and I promise to have them back before you lock the doors."

"We don't lock the doors!" Matron snapped. She softened her tone before continuing, "If you're so adamant, I must insist you take six nurses along."

"Thank you, you're right, of course. I'll leave it with you to have them all here at seven-thirty tomorrow evening. Oh, and could you make sure the men have their regimental caps with them, if at all possible."

"Yes, I can do that," Matron Simpson replied meekly, wondering how the confrontation had suddenly turned against her and now had her agreeing to participate.

The nurse accompanying the matron also looked startled at the turn of events. Seizing the opportunity, she quickly asked her superior, "Ma'am, may I volunteer to go with them?"

Cheers erupted around the room, causing a blush to appear on the matron's cheeks. She nodded to the nurse and held out her hand to the redhead.

"It's been a pleasure to meet you, Mrs. Brown," she whispered.

Holding onto the woman's hand briefly, Nancy whispered back. "It's Nancy, and thank you."

Walking back to the hospital, the matron suddenly stopped and turned to look back at the *Wounded Soldier Restaurant*. She pulled her cloak tightly around her body to shield against the wind.

"You'd better go back to the restaurant, Nurse Robinson," she said. "We'll need the names and regiments of the men who are going to the Empress. My word, this is very exciting don't you think? Off you go now."

When Nurse Sarah Robinson returned to the restaurant, she was much happier than she had ever been after talking to matron. She had been employed at the Jubilee Hospital for more than seven years and had never seen such a pleasant change in the woman. Feared by everyone inside those grey walls, she fiercely ruled with a rod of iron—her decisions always unbending and harsh, and yet, after spending half an hour in the restaurant that day, she had emerged with a totally different outlook.

Strange, Sarah thought, *could it be she felt Nancy's determination to do a good deed, or perhaps the enthusiasm of the men*? Puzzling it over in her mind, she knew the nursing staff would welcome the knowledge that the matron's frosty personality did indeed have a softer and more sympathetic side.

With another call to make at the Willows army camp, Nancy took her leave at 5 o'clock and, with difficulty, extracted Jeb's car from the narrow lane and out into traffic. Driving down Cadboro Bay Road, she was soon at the army camp on the old agricultural fairgrounds.

Chuckling, she remembered the day Gus and Beth had brought her here to the horserace when she had first met them so many years ago. One of the sentries on duty stopped her and asked her reason for wanting to enter the camp.

"I want to borrow about 60 soldiers," she replied.

"You want what?" the sentry asked not being able to contain his grin.

Repeating her request, she watched a surprised expression now cross the sentry's face as another soldier came up to join them.

"Can you see the light in that office?" he asked, pointing to a building a short distance inside the gate. "Park your vehicle there and ask for Sgt. Morgan in the office."

Following his instructions, she drove through the gate, waving coyly at the sentries as she passed.

"Can I help you, miss?" a soldier at the front desk asked politely when she stepped through the door.

"Sgt. Morgan, please."

"Come this way, ma'am."

Following the young soldier down a dimly lit hallway, she waited while he tapped on a door, opened it, and announced her.

"Come in, my dear," an older sergeant with a patch over one eye invited her gently. "Tell me how can I be of assistance to you."

"I would like to borrow 60 soldiers for an hour or two tomorrow evening, sir," Nancy purred.

"Are you sure you only need 60?" he asked seriously.

"Yes sir," she replied, trying to keep a straight face. "I need them to form an Honour Guard from the street to the main entrance of the Empress Hotel."

Frowning, Sgt. Morgan sat back in his seat and let his one good eye roam over this young woman with the strange request. He could see the bright red hair under her woollen hat and the honest intensity of her twinkling eyes.

She's serious," he thought with an inward chuckle. "Why don't you tell me the whole story, my dear."

"Well sir, it's the Armistice Ball at the Empress," she began. "I'm half-owner of the *Wounded Soldier Restaurant*, across Richmond Road from the Jubilee Hospital, and I'm taking 30 of our wounded men to the dance. I thought they should have an Honour Guard."

"You're absolutely right, they should!" Sgt. Morgan agreed, touching his eyepatch. "Has the hospital agreed?"

"Well, sort of, I've discussed it with the matron and she's helping us."

"Then I'll make sure you get your Honour Guard and, by the way, we know about your restaurant—it's a mighty fine institution. You're doing a wonderful service for our wounded men." He paused for a moment before asking, "How the devil did you manage to get tickets for them?"

"Oh, we don't have tickets, sergeant, we're crashing the party!" she quipped, grinning broadly.

"Holy hell!" the sergeant yelped.

"I consider they should have included the men who fought the battles, the lads who paid the price with their bodies, and are still suffering—not just the rich folk!" Nancy explained fiercely.

Sgt. Morgan was stunned by Nancy's outburst. He himself was wounded in the first year of fighting, and now, missing one eye, was doomed to a desk job.

"Stay right there, ma'am," he instructed. "I'll get the captain over here to meet you, Mrs. …."

"Mrs. Nancy Brown."

Smiling, she watched him charge out of the office and listened to his footsteps pound away down the corridor. Glancing around the office, she rose to look at a group of pictures on the wall and gasped at the brass plate beneath them. They were artillery; she had come to Dan's old regiment without realizing it. Oblivious to the sounds around her, she stared in mesmerized fascination at the pictures of battlefield guns, unaware the sergeant, with his captain, had returned and were standing watching her from the doorway.

"That's a very famous gun, ma'am." The sergeant's voice startled her. "It's the one Sgt. Dan Brown used on the western front. He knocked out 20 enemy guns with 20 shots—he's a legend in this regiment."

"And what happened to him?" Nancy managed to gasp, still staring at the pictures as tears began to course down her face.

"He was badly wounded, ma'am," the sergeant rasped, "the regiment lost track of him. I'm not sure if he survived."

"Yes, he did," said the captain. "The British had him hospitalized for a long time but I understand he came home. What can we do for you, young lady? Please have a seat."

She wiped her tears away with her hand and, turning back to face the men, realized she was losing the feeling in her legs. Only the captain's quick assessment of her difficulty and his strong arms prevented her from falling as he eased her toward a chair.

"Are you all right, ma'am?" he asked kindly.

Nancy opened her purse and took out a handkerchief as her tears began again.

The men looked helplessly from the young woman to each other as she dabbed the hankie to her cheeks.

"Dan Brown is my husband," she whispered in a shaky voice. "Please forgive me; I have never seen these pictures and it brings back terrible memories."

"Oh my word! The captain sat down on the chair beside her and took her hands. "I-I'm so sorry for being such an insensitive pig, Mrs. Brown. I had no idea, Sgt. Morgan, give this lady anything she wants and I will sign the order papers."

"She wants a guard of honour, sir."

"Then give it to her and, for goodness sake make sure she gets home. Perhaps a cup of tea would be a good idea, I'll wait here while you get it, sergeant."

"Yes sir," muttered the sergeant, hurrying from the room.

Nancy shook her head and managed to thank the captain for his kindness. He asked about Dan and, by the time the sergeant returned with a cup of tea, she was gaining back her composure. She told the men that she had never expected to see a picture of Dan's gun or even stumble into contact with his old regiment. Fate often seemed to steer Nancy's footsteps and this was just one more obstacle she would have to overcome.

"Well, Mrs. Brown," said Tom Morgan after the captain left them, "you've got your guard of honour—just tell me when and where you want us."

"I want you to be at the Empress' main door on Belleville Street tomorrow night at eight-fifteen. We'll be there with the soldiers by eight-thirty."

"We'll be there, ma'am—the boys will be thrilled to see Dan again."

"Thank you, sergeant, I'm sure the feeling will be mutual."

It seemed a long drive home to Gordon Head that night as darkness fell quickly and she stopped when she reached Ash Road, seeing no one around. She knew that her face would still be a sight and pinched her cheeks to try to even out the redness. She could only hope no one would notice so she didn't have to explain it all.

"Where the heck have you been, lassie?" Meg admonished as she opened the door. "You had us all worried to death. The Jorgensens came for awhile but decided not to wait for you. The boys seemed to think you had some things to do which would make you late."

"Did you find what you wanted, Nan?" Dan asked, helping her with her coat and being surprised when she took it from him to hang up herself.

"I found more than I wanted," she replied softly, keeping her back to him as she fumbled with her purse. "Matron, at the Jubilee, is going to help and the army are delighted to be part of it," she continued, keeping her voice low so the others didn't hear.

"Part of what?" Meg asked, setting Nancy's dinner plate onto the table.

"Oh, it's just … just a little surprise," Nancy said secretively, sitting down at her place but not looking up.

Slowly folding his newspaper, Jeb leaned his elbows on the table and took a deep puff on his pipe. He listened to Nan's evasive answers and knew it was something about her surprise for the ball but his curiosity was aroused as he watched her eat. He noticed her reddened eyes and knew she'd been crying although she was trying to hide it. *What the hell's happened*, he wondered.

The mystery deepened as the old detective continued to observe her behaviour during the evening. Her need to be close to Dan and the looks she gave him were giving Jeb a clue and he resolved to find out what was wrong.

Chapter 24

Typical November weather blew across the island as dawn broke on the 28th, the day of the much-anticipated Armistice Ball. Nancy was humming a tune as she drove to the restaurant. This was the day she was going to shock the establishment—to register the complaints for all the wives, mothers, and wounded soldiers who had suffered for so long.

Lights were already on in the restaurant as she passed and drove around to the back. As she walked to the door, she heard laughter coming through the open kitchen window.

"What time did you get here?" Nancy called to her partner as she changed into her working clothes.

"Remember Jack's away, I slept here last night."

"You're crazy!"

"It saved the hassle of getting here this morning," Kate grinned mischievously as Nancy picked up a tray. "Now I know that chesterfield is not meant to be slept on!"

All morning, customers kept them informed with the progress of the celebrations. Banners and flags were being raised around the Empress, streetcars were decorated with signs showing names and insignia of local regiments, and Government Street was buzzing with rumours of dignitaries who were coming to attend the victory ball.

In the early afternoon, Nurse Robinson and matron appeared and finding the place quite full, took seats at a table with a group of soldiers.

"Would you like tea, ladies?" Nancy asked.

"Yes please," Matron replied then dropping her voice to a whisper asked, "and could we try a little of your lemon meringue pie?"

"You'll love it, ma'am," whispered one of the soldiers, whose eyes were bandaged, trying to keep his voice low. He raised a blush on the matron's cheeks when he added, "it's a damned sight better than hospital tucker."

"Shut up Aussie, that's the matron!" declared the soldier next to him, digging his elbow into his friend's side.

"You can bring the same for me, please Nancy," giggled Nurse Robinson.

Hearing the conversation, Nancy hurried back with the tray, setting the tea and food in front of the ladies.

"Now boys!" she called loudly, waiting for the noise in the room to cease. "Let me introduce the two ladies we have with us today. This is Matron Simpson and Nurse Robinson, so please behave yourselves."

Conversations among the men returned, now in hushed whispers, as the two women ate their pie. Glancing around the room, Matron's gaze settled on the soldier with the bandaged eyes.

"Are you really an Australian, young man?" she asked. "Did I detect an accent or is that just a nickname your mates gave you?"

"Yes ma'am, I'm from Fremantle, on the West Coast of Australia," he replied, exaggerating his accent.

"Your family live here?"

"No ma'am, my family are all in West Oz; Downunder we call it."

"Then how on earth did you land here in Victoria?"

"By cattle boat, like the rest of the lads."

"You mean hospital ship, but you have no family here."

"We have Nancy and Kate and this place is home for most of us lads, ma'am, so don't you worry about us. I might even stay now the war is over."

Over the next half hour, Matron Simpson saw a different side of a wounded soldier's life as she listened to the men tell stories of their homes and how Nancy and Katherine made their lives more bearable.

"You need the nurses here at seven-thirty, don't you Mrs. Brown?" matron asked as she prepared to leave.

"I told the men seven—they can come for dinner if they like, but everyone has to be here by seven-thirty."

"The boys will be here at seven-thirty and they'll be eating at the hospital; I'll supervise their tucker myself," said Matron. "This has been a most enlightening afternoon, you will see me again. Oh, and the pie was wonderful!" she said quietly, causing a few chuckles from the nearby men.

Things were just getting back to normal when Chris Jorgensen poked his head in the door and called, "Do you have room for four, sis?"

"Chris!" Nancy spluttered, hurrying over to the door and looking outside, "is the family with you?"

"Of course we are," Gus laughed, coming up behind Chris and pushing him inside. Holding the door open for Beth and Bill's wheelchair, he added, "We want the best seats in the house!"

"SHUT THE DOOR, MATE!" the Aussie shouted, causing Gus to step inside quickly and pull the door shut.

Hugging Beth, Nancy steered them to an empty table and shouted to Kate to bring tea while Chris and Bill made their way among the wounded soldiers, causing a few raised eyebrows when introducing themselves as Nancy's brothers.

"Those two sons of ours certainly make themselves at home," Beth whispered to Nan.

"There's a special bond between wounded soldiers, Beth," Nancy replied, "they've shared many of the same traumatic experiences as their brothers-in-arms."

"Someday, we might know what this war has cost our young men," Gus sighed, "but governments seem to easily forget."

"They won't easily forget these men," Nancy whispered sharply, "by tomorrow everyone will know who they are."

"How Nan?" Beth asked, looking puzzled. "There won't be any wounded soldiers at the ball tonight, will there?"

"You'll see," Nancy said secretively.

Jumping up to serve some new customers, Nancy excused herself and left Gus and Beth wondering about her comment. Gus felt a cold, uneasy feeling creep up his spine as concern, for the girl he loved like a daughter, mounted. *I hope she's not going to get herself into any trouble*, he thought.

"It's time you went home to change, Nan," Kate called from the kitchen door after the Jorgensons had left. "We need you back here by seven."

Suddenly the telephone rang and, balancing her tray of dishes in one hand, Nancy answered it.

"*Wounded Soldier Restaurant*," she announced into the mouth piece. A smile spread across her face as she listened. "Hang on a minute Jack, she's right here," she exclaimed. "Kate, it's Jack."

"Go home, Nan!" Kate repeated taking the receiver.

Slipping into her coat and waving goodbye to everyone, she went out to her car, knowing Dan was on his way home, too. Doubt began to creep into her thoughts. *Will the army and Sgt. Morgan keep their promise? What will we do if he doesn't? Oh well, it's too late to worry about it now.*

"Nancy's home," Meg informed Dan, glancing out of the kitchen window.

"She's going to be in a hurry if I know my Nan!" Dan retorted. "Aunt Meg, we're going back to the restaurant before we go to the ball."

"I'm not going with you two?"

"No honey, you're my date tonight," Jeb grinned, "that's if you'll give me the pleasure of your company!"

Hitting the door at a run, Nancy burst in the door. Putting her purse down, she wriggled out of her coat and hung it on the chair. "I don't want a lot to eat, Aunt Meg, I'll get dressed first," she announced, dashing up the stairs.

Grinning, Dan continued eating, carefully watching Meg who kept looking toward the stairs and scowling.

"Why do you have to go back to the restaurant tonight, Danny?" she asked. "I thought we were meeting the Jorgensens at the Empress at seven-thirty."

"You are meeting the Jorgensens," Dan assured her. "It's just that *we* may be a little late. You can save us some seats at your table. I'm going to go and change, too."

"Aunt Meg, Uncle Jeb come look at this!" he called excitedly from the hallway.

As they joined him, Nancy slowly descended the stairs dressed in the beautiful blue gown Beth had bought for her. Swinging her shoes in her hand, she was a picture of radiance as her curly red hair danced about her shoulders.

"What a picture," sighed Meg.

"You look beautiful, Nan!" Dan exclaimed, holding out his arms.

"Don't you dare touch me with those dirty hands, sailor boy!" she giggled.

"Stop, right there," Meg exclaimed, as her fingers explored the hem and waistband she had altered, assuring herself everything was as it should be before giving Nancy a hug. "I don't know what all this secretive stuff is, but I only hope you both know what you're doing."

"It will be fine, Aunt Meg, you'll see," Nancy assured her as Dan went up to get dressed. She sat down at the table, giggling as Meg spread a clean dish towel across the front of her dress.

Waiting for Dan as the time crept closer to six-thirty, Nancy fidgeted impatiently, then turned expectantly toward the doorway when she finally heard him coming down the stairs. Both she and Meg gasped when Sgt. Dan Brown stepped into the room, looking every inch a soldier in full dress uniform. Moving quickly into his arms, Nan whispered in his ear.

"You're almost as handsome as the sailor I married, Mr. Brown, shall we step out together tonight?"

Meg, clucking happily, and Jeb now looking resplendent in his new black suit and tie, exchanged kisses and hugs with the youngsters at the door. Gathering up her coat and tiny purse, Nancy took Dan's arm and they hurried out to the truck.

Dan drove quickly along Shelbourne, splashing through the water at Cedar Hill Cross Road and swinging left onto Lansdowne. They bounced over the streetcar rails and then turned right onto Richmond. Nearing the restaurant, they could see a row of cars and station hacks already lined up in front of the Wounded Soldier.

"I hope they've left us space to park," Dan grumbled.

"Go around the back."

Not a sound came from the restaurant as they climbed out of the truck. Nancy's heart skipped a beat. Was nobody there—had disaster already struck her plans?

Dan opened the door and deafening cheers drowned out her thoughts. Nancy blushed self-consciously as he pushed her through to the main room where they found Matron Simpson and six nurses surrounded by soldiers.

"I know we're early," matron quietly explained, "but we just couldn't control the men's excitement. They were so eager to get here. Oh and by the way, my first name is Eleanor—may I call you Nancy?"

"Thank you, Eleanor, I would really like that," she replied.

Nurse Robinson was watching Dan as he mixed easily with the men.

"Goodness, he's so handsome," she murmured, blushing as she spilled out her thoughts. "Is he your husband, Nancy?"

"Yes, he is."

"He's in the army," Nurse Robinson continued, "uniforms do so much for a man."

"No, he's not actually in the army anymore," Nancy replied. "He was invalided out after being badly wounded just over a year ago. Excuse me for a moment, ladies."

Making her way over to the kitchen, she found Kate watching them. "Tell them there's tea, coffee and cakes on the house for anyone who wants them," she urged, "we're not leaving here until seven-thirty."

"I think you should do it," her partner replied.

Shaking her head at Kate's reluctance, Nancy turned around and raised her arms. "Quiet please!" she called, pausing until the noise died down. "We have tea, coffee, and cakes for those who would like something before we leave. We're not leaving until seven-thirty and it's all on the house!"

A cheer rose and the men began to shuffle toward the counter. Eleanor made her way to the redhead's side, tugging gently on her arm to get her attention.

"Nancy," she whispered, "I have acquired three dozen bottles of beer; would it be all right if we gave them to the men?"

"Gosh yes! How did you manage that, where are they?"

"In crates outside your back door under a burlap sheet, and you don't want to know how I got them!"

"Hold it, lads!" Nancy called. "We have a surprise for you. Dan, can you come give us a hand?"

Pushing his way through the crowd, Dan quickly grasped the situation and, under Eleanor's direction, went outside and recovered the beer.

"RIGHT LADS, ARE YOU READY?" Nancy shouted above the noise.

"YES MA'AM!" they shouted back.

She waited for them to quieten down.

"Matron has found some beer and there's one bottle for each of you. Now how about three cheers for the matron!"

"HIP HIP HURRAY!" rang in one massive crescendo, reverberating out into the street.

"What's going on in there," one of the drivers asked.

"I don't know, lad," an older man laughed, "but I'm for joining them!" He began to move toward the door.

"Don't do it, Charlie," another driver advised. "Matron's in there, she'll have your liver cut out and fed to the cat!"

"Yeah, I wouldn't want to upset that old buzzard!" Charlie laughed, turning back.

"It's seven-twenty, Nan," Kate reminded the redhead, "maybe we should start getting the wheelchairs loaded, it'll take awhile to get everyone organized."

"I'll get Dan to deal with it," Nancy replied, waving to get his attention. "The drivers will know how they want the wheelchairs loaded." When he arrived, she explained what she needed and he quickly went outside to talk to the drivers.

“We’re ready for loading,” he announced. “There are six wheelchairs and 28 men to go, some of them on crutches.”

Standing back, he watched as the drivers went into a noisy discussion. Emphasizing their opinions with arm-and-hand gestures, they finally reached a consensus and went to their vehicles.

Twenty-five minutes later, under the matron’s watchful eye, the last vehicles were being loaded and Dan and Nancy felt safe leaving for the Empress. Nancy was nervous but hopeful that the last piece of the puzzle was ready for setting into place.

It was almost 8 o’clock, when Chris and Bill excused themselves from their father’s table on the perimeter of the ballroom floor. Well aware of Nancy’s schedule, they found the perfect observation point in the foyer and settled down to wait for the action to begin.

“Go have a look, Chris,” Bill urged his brother, “this is almost like waiting for a battle to begin!”

They’re coming!” his brother hissed urgently on his return. “I could see Nancy and Dan outside and there are two army trucks unloading soldiers. A hack has just pulled up and they’re unloading wheelchairs. She’s either in big trouble or she’s brought plenty of support!”

Suddenly, they heard the distant shouted orders of an officer and the sound of heavy boots hitting the pavement as many soldiers trotted into position. They went closer to take a look and watched the soldiers lining up on the steps and along the driveway.

Nancy’s own level of anticipation was growing by the second and hotel guests were already stopping to watch, thinking it was part of the celebrations. Two hotel security guards appeared and Dan went over to explain the situation. They quickly removed themselves, melting into the crowd.

“Jeepers look at that,” Bill hissed, as several more hacks and various other vehicles drew up to the sidewalk, depositing their human cargo of obviously wounded soldiers, all wearing regimental hats, despite their hospital or civilian attire.

Striding into the foyer, Carlo Calza, the hotel manager, glared at the slowly approaching procession of wheelchairs and wounded men. In the lead, was Dan in full military uniform, with Nancy on his arm. She looked stunning in her beautiful, ankle-length, blue, evening gown. It was a military parade extraordinaire and, so far, the crowd loved it.

Standing his ground, although astonished by what he saw, the manager made a quick decision. Holding out his hand in a gesture of welcome, he greeted the young couple with his warmest smile.

"Mr. Calza, I apologize for not giving you warning of this intrusion," she began, intentionally not introducing herself. "I'm afraid I'm responsible for this display and it was planned so quickly, I simply didn't consider letting you know."

"No need to apologize, but you'll need some chairs."

Thinking quickly, she replied, "Thank you, we'll need about 20 chairs for the hospital group."

Calza thanked her and, turning away, found several of his staff gawking at the soldiers.

"We need 20 chairs, find them!" he ordered. "Set them up wherever there is room, quickly now!" He turned back to ask Nancy her name but she had disappeared into the crowd.

Meanwhile, soldiers in the Honour Guard were peeling away from the line to help lift the men in wheelchairs up the short flight of stairs also assisting any of the others who required their help. It was all going remarkably smoothly. Once the row of soldiers was formed in an orderly fashion, Nancy and Dan led the way through the large foyer, now filled with curious people, and entered the ballroom.

Professor Turner's orchestra was playing but the maestro noticed the new arrivals and his baton arm drooped in amazement. Excited chatter became a deafening silence, as every eye in the room centered on the unusual procession of men entering the room led by the handsome young couple.

"What the devil is she doing?" Harry Maynard growled across the table to Jack Duggan and Waldo Skillings.

"Shut up and watch!" Waldo snapped back, obviously enjoying himself.

"It's Nancy and Dan with a group of wounded soldiers," Nellie Cornish whispered to James Moore and the Seattle theatre crowd she was sitting with. "Well I'll be …! We need some special music!" Jumping up, she hurried over to the orchestra and spoke to the conductor. "Louis, it's Nancy, she's brought some soldiers with her. Play something special for those boys."

"Join us, Nellie," he suggested and, as soon as the orchestra finished their number he followed her lead and they moved right into a popular marching song.

When the song finished, Nellie returned to her seat, nodding to the maestro. At the Jorgensen table, Meg and Beth stared in disbelief as guests moved toward the wounded soldiers, shaking hands and talking with them as Dan made introductions.

"I'll bet they're all in on it," Gus grinned, noticing his sons were still with Dan greeting the soldiers. "Jeb, this is an amazing tribute to your military. I wonder who thought of it?"

"Oh, I think it's a fair bet to say it's our Nancy. Look out she's heading for the orchestra," the old detective chuckled. "I don't think she's done with this lot yet." Jumping to his feet, Jeb moved quickly to the edge of the ballroom floor as a wandering security guard made an attempt to cut Nancy off.

"Where's Jebediah going?" Beth whispered.

"To protect his daughter," Meg sighed.

"He won't be needed," Gus laughed, "look at Bill speeding to her rescue!"

"You keep going, sis," the young American muttered, passing close beside her. "I'll take care of him!"

A murmur of apprehension ran though the guests when Bill aimed his wheelchair at the oncoming guard. Leaping wildly to one side, a ripple of laughter spread through the crowd. Acknowledging the audience with a wave, Bill spun his conveyance in a gesture of success, before charging again and chasing the guard off the floor.

"See," Gus glowed with pride, "she's got three real fighting men out there taking care of her."

Grinning and shaking his head, Jeb returned to his seat as the guests rose to give Bill a standing ovation, unsure that what they had seen was not part of the evening's entertainment.

Watching with fascinated interest from a side door, the hotel manager caught the attention of his assistant. "I like it, John, find out who these people are."

"I have a feeling we should know that young woman, sir. I mean the one with the red hair talking to Mr. Turner. She looks very familiar."

"Yes, I agree, matter of fact she spoke to me outside," he continued thoughtfully. "Did you notice the reaction of our guests to this interruption? I wasn't aware any of this was going to happen, were you?"

"No sir, but I would respectfully suggest that we don't interfere, everyone seems to be enjoying it."

The hotel manager nodded his agreement and moved back into the ballroom.

"What is this all about, Nan?" Nellie asked as Nancy walked past her.

"Steal their piano again, Nellie!" Nancy commanded with a broad smile. "I'm going to sing for these soldiers. Louis, may I borrow your microphone?" Meekly handing the redhead his microphone, she took it, and added, "Get ready to follow Nellie's lead."

Professor Turner turned to his orchestra, his mind in utter confusion. He had wanted Nancy to sing at the Armistice Ball, but had given up all hope when she had declined and no arrangements were forthcoming. Now, he had a sneaky suspicion that Carlo Calza might have sprung this surprise on him.

"Ladies and gentlemen!" Nancy's voice rang through the room with the help of the loudspeaker system. "That group of young men over there are only a few of our soldiers who were wounded fighting for Canada and world freedom in The Great War. They are our heroes, so let's give them a rousing welcome." Her last words were spoken so excitedly and loudly, the crowd came to their feet, instantly cheering and clapping with enthusiastic energy.

Outside, Sgt. Morgan and the Honour Guard heard the thunderous cheer and as the rest of the hotel became aware of what was happening in the ballroom, guests and staff crowded the foyer all eager to see what the commotion was about.

Holding up her hands for silence, Nancy continued, "I would like to introduce three young men who are very special to me. Danny," she called, "would you bring Bill and Chris out onto the floor where we can see you all."

Cheers rang out as Dan, blushing profusely, pushed Bill's wheelchair out onto the floor, followed by Christopher.

"Take a good look at these three handsome young men," Nancy purred. "The one in the wheelchair is William Jorgensen, an American, and to his right his brother, Christopher. These boys were wounded in Europe and are very special to me as they're my brothers!" Pausing briefly, she felt the poignant silence as the crowd waited for her to continue. "The soldier in uniform is my husband, Dan Brown, also wounded in Europe, and believe me folks, I've spent many lonely, worrisome nights wondering where he was! Thank you boys, you may go back to your seats," she laughingly dismissed them. "Now it's my turn to say, 'thank you', to all of you."

Glancing over at Nellie, sitting at the piano, she began to hum a few bars of the soldier's love song, *Lili Marlene*. Instantly Nellie picked up the tune and Nancy turned back to the audience and began to sing.

"I know who she is!" Manager Calza whispered to his assistant. "That's Nancy Wilson, they call her Seattle's sweetheart but she lives right here in Victoria. I heard her sing at the James Moore Theatre last year. I read she got married earlier this year."

Also hearing the music, Sgt. Tom Morgan decided it was time to go and speak with Dan about meeting the Honour Guard from his old regiment. As he made his way to the ballroom, he found his way blocked by a large crowd standing in the foyer. They were obviously listening to the music and trying to see inside the ballroom. He was totally unaware that the singer was the same woman who had been in his office the day before. His intentions forgotten, he now stood with the crowd totally enthralled by the woman's lovely voice and the songs she was singing.

Completing three songs, Nancy bowed graciously, then went over and pulled Nellie onto her feet so they could take a bow together with the orchestra. Waving to the audience who continued to roar and clap their appreciation, the women went back to their seats.

The loud cheering brought the sergeant back to the present and he began to push his way toward the ballroom door. From behind, others, eager to get a glimpse of the singer, pushed their way forward also.

"DAN, DAN BROWN," the sergeant shouted over the noise, seeing him not far away.

As Nancy arrived at Dan's side, she heard the sergeant's voice and looked around to see who was calling her husband.

"Dan, there's Sgt. Morgan who I met yesterday at the Willows camp. He wants to talk to you."

Dan turned in the direction she indicated and, hearing his name, waved above the crowd. They watched as the tall, uniformed soldier with the eye-patch pushed his way through the knot of people surrounding the wounded men and made his way toward them.

"Sgt. Brown," he said crisply, saluting the retired soldier. "I'm Sgt. Morgan from Willows Barracks. Would you and Mrs. Brown do us the honour of inspecting the Honour Guard, sir?"

"Yes, certainly sergeant," Dan replied. "We'll do it on the way out, then I can meet some of the men who shared the same hell I did. Would you please call the vehicles up for our men?" Waving his arm he indicated the wounded soldiers. "We're almost ready for leaving."

"Yes sir!" Sgt. Morgan snapped to attention, saluting Dan again and quickly departing.

Nurse Robinson heard Dan's statement and spread the word readying the men with smooth efficiency for the ride back to the hospital. Within ten minutes, with the Jorgensen brothers in the lead, they began to make their exit as cheers followed them through the foyer. Reaching the outside door, the Honour Guard was ready with rifles and bayonets forming a walkway.

Getting the men loaded into the lined-up vehicles took awhile, but nonetheless went smoothly, cheered on by the eager and noisy crowd which spilled out onto Belleville Street.

"Mission accomplished, Mr. Brown," Nancy chuckled, taking his arm as the last of her soldiers drove away and the crowd began to disperse.

"Not quite, Mrs. Brown," Dan replied, looking back at the two rows of soldiers standing patiently as civilians jostled around them. "We have an Honour Guard to inspect."

Chapter 25

Standing rigidly to attention, the soldiers of Dan's old regiment waited as their comrade, Nancy, and the Jorgensen boys, whom Dan had asked to join them, slowly walked up the line, spending a few seconds with each soldier and finding he knew very few of them. Afterwards, Bill and Chris left to join their parents in the ballroom and Dan turned back to the soldiers.

"There's one more thing, Sgt. Morgan," Dan commented, turning to face the soldiers, "have you told these men the Golden Rule of our regiment?"

"Oh, yes sir! Right, lads, tell Sgt. Brown our Golden Rule."

"NEVER VOLUNTEER FOR ANYTHING, SIR!" 60 voices chorused loudly.

Dan went over and shook Tom Morgan's hand and thanked the soldiers for taking part. Then, their commanding officer gave the order to move toward the army trucks waiting nearby. Minutes later, Dan and Nancy were left standing alone on the steps as only a few people remained outside in the cold. Nancy put her arm through Dan's and they looked out over the harbour that had played such a large part in their lives.

"You love this city, don't you, Nancy?" a voice said from behind them. "I know exactly how you feel. Let me introduce you to someone else who feels the same way."

"Mr. Wilson, it's so good to see you," Nancy bubbled, on recognizing the Government Street clothier.

"Congratulations on your wedding, Waldo told me all about it," added Mr. Wilson. "Did Danny ever find out how we tricked him?"

"Tricked me, sir?" Dan asked, looking puzzled.

"Ah well, no matter, lad," Wilson chuckled. "I want you to meet John Oliver, the premier of this fine province and the master of ceremonies for this evening's celebration."

"Hello Dan," said the premier extending his hand, "I seem to be inundated by people singing your praises. It would appear our paths are meant to cross again soon."

"Are they, sir?" Dan replied, pretending not to know what he was referring to as his mind flashed back to the meeting with General Greene and Admiral Johnson.

The premier continued, "And you, young lady," he said warmly, "have the most beautiful voice I have ever heard, but I must admit it's not the first time I've heard you sing. My wife and I were guests at one of your concerts in Seattle just before the influenza closed Seattle down. You've become quite famous on the other side of the border. I think …."

"John! John!" Carlo Calza, interrupted coming toward them, "they want you in the ballroom."

"Calm down, Carlo," Premier Oliver chuckled. "I want to introduce you to two of our finest citizens, Dan and Nancy Brown. They own the dockside delivery service on Wharf Street and Nancy runs the *Wounded Soldier Restaurant* opposite the Jubilee Hospital."

"That explains it!" replied the hotel manager as if he had just made a great discovery. "It was you who organized this visit from the soldiers at the hospital, wasn't it, Mrs. Brown?"

It was a wonderful idea," the premier continued, "and now you've given me one of my own … to hold an appreciation night specifically for our soldiers."

"That's nice," the redhead muttered sarcastically, "someone finally remembers the men who did the fighting!"

"Easy Nan," Dan whispered, slipping his arm around her shoulders. He looked down at her and winced when he saw the fire in her eyes knowing he was too late.

"And what, if anything, are you going to do for those men, Mr. Oliver?" Nancy hissed argumentativly.

"Right now I'm going to accompany you back to your table and meet your folks," the premier replied with a wide grin, "and sure hope you never go into politics! Mary Ellen warned me you were a fireball."

There were more surprises in store for the young couple when the premier moved ahead of them as they neared the Jorgensen's table. He calmly introduced himself and identified each person by name.

"Glad to meet you, Aunt Meg and Uncle Jeb," Premier Oliver chuckled. "Ah ha, you two must be Gus and Beth Jorgensen, and I know these two young men from Nancy's introduction tonight. Bill and Christopher, you boys fought with the Belgium Air Force. didn't you?"

As quickly as he arrived, the premier shook each person's hand, thanked them for coming and, turned to leave, but he suddenly turned around and taking a card from his breast pocket, offered it to Gus.

"My card, sir, if I can ever be of assistance, please call."

"That's two premiers I know now," Meg giggled, when he left. "Nancy, you once introduced me to Richard McBride at the Gorge Hotel."

"Yes, I remember, Aunt Meg. Sadly, he died in England."

"Oh dear," the Scot whispered.

"Now that's what I call a useful contact," said Gus with a grin. "You must have told him a lot about us, Nancy."

"No we didn't, we only just met him outside."

"Well, he knows an awful lot about us—too much," Jeb muttered suspiciously. "Somebody's been talking."

Unable to solve the mystery, Nancy decided to forget about it and enjoy the rest of their evening. She had so many people she wanted to talk to but men kept asking her to dance! Nellie finally saw her in the washroom later in the evening and handed her a thick envelope.

"What's this?" whispered Nancy. "Oh my gosh, I know what it is!" she giggled, trying to fold it but realizing it was too big to fit into her little purse. "Thanks Nellie, sorry we haven't had time to visit tonight."

"That's all right, this is your town and you know so many people."

"No actually, I don't, it's just because of the event. We'll see you Saturday anyway."

"Yes, we're returning tonight on a private boat, it's going to be a late night; perhaps I'll be able to sleep on the return trip!"

The girls hugged and returned to their tables in the ballroom. Nancy secretly gave Dan the envelope asking him to put it away safely. *Now we can really do some good*! she thought happily already planning how to spend the thousand dollars from the US government. There was more dancing but the time was getting close to midnight when Meg yawned and begged to be taken home.

"It's almost the end, Aunt Meg, let's stay for the last dance," Dan suggested, looking over at his wife. "I've a delivery to make tomorrow morning, so I think we'll be calling it a day, too."

"Don't go yet, Dan, I haven't had my dance with Nan!" Bill piped up, looking hurt. He was watching the dance floor and noticed it was almost empty.

"Okay Bill, what are you waiting for?" Nancy demanded, grabbing the handles of his wheelchair and pushing it out onto the dance floor.

Laughing, the two immediately went into their routine. Its effect on the remaining partygoers was electrifying as every eye in the ballroom turned to watch as the amputee and the beautiful redheaded singer moved about the floor, totally immersed in their moves.

Professor Turner's baton waved majestically but he turned to watch the unusual display out of the corner of his eye. As many of the onlookers began to clap, those who were leaving returned to stand and watch, some moving to the edge of the dance floor. At the end of the song, the ballroom erupted with applause and cheering as Nancy landed on Bill's knee, giving him a kiss.

Returning to their table, Nellie came over and spoke to her.

"Let's do one last song, Nan," she pleaded, looking quite excited. "They would love it if you sang *We'll Meet Again.*"

"Do it, Nan," Beth encouraged, overhearing and nodding her head in agreement. "It will round off a perfect evening."

"I'll warn Louis," said Nellie and not waiting for her friend's reply, she hurried off.

Nancy sat back in her chair and took a deep breath.

"Dan, I want to dance with you for the home waltz."

"Can't you do both, Nan?" suggested Beth.

"I'll find a way, be ready sweetheart," she exclaimed quickly taking a sip of her drink and leaving them.

Professor Turner was smiling as he looked around for Nancy, obviously eager to comply with Nellie's suggestion. Speaking into the microphone, he made the announcement introducing Nellie Cornish as 'an American musical director and talented pianist from Seattle' and Nancy as 'Victoria's own beautiful songbird.'

"Gentlemen, bring your ladies onto the dance floor for the last dance of the evening—a special treat with the lovely voice of Nancy Wilson Brown!"

Nellie's fingers bounced over the ivory keyboard playing the introduction as Carlo Calza listened from the doorway, his pulse quickening. After she had sung the main verse and chorus, she handed the microphone back to the maestro and hurried toward Dan. He saw her coming and moved to her side, causing laughter from those who realized what was happening. As they danced, to the crowd's utter delight, she continued singing.

It was obvious everyone had enjoyed the show for no one moved even as the last lingering note faded away. Then the ballroom erupted in loud appreciation and, slowly, everyone returned to their tables or headed off to get their coats. Swamped by well-wishers, it took half an hour to extract themselves and make their way outside.

"Never again," Jeb grumbled when they all finally made it outside. "We could have got squashed to death in there!"

"We'll see you two at home," Nancy laughed, calling after them as Jeb escorted Meg across Belleville Street to his car.

"How do you kids feel about coming back to the hotel for awhile?" asked Gus, coming toward Dan and Nancy as they stood by the truck.

Looking at his wife, he suddenly realized how tired she looked. "Nan are you all right, honey? Don't you think you've had a long enough day?" he asked, going around to her side of the vehicle.

"I think you're right, Danny," Nan replied softly, reaching out to steady herself. "All of a sudden I do seem to feel quite exhausted." Dan hurried around to her side of the truck and opened the door. "We'll visit tomorrow," she murmured, sinking into the seat.

Dan bent over and gave her a kiss. "It's all right honey, they'll understand." He closed the door and went to talk to Gus and Beth.

"Thanks for the offer, but it's time I took Nan home. It's been an exhausting week for her and we're so pleased everything worked out. Have you made any arrangements to come out to the house tomorrow?"

"Yes, I believe the girls were talking and Meg invited us for dinner. You go take Nancy home; she worked so hard to turn this evening into something extraordinary and succeeded. We'll visit tomorrow," Gus replied.

"I must admit I'm pretty tuckered out myself!" Beth added, hanging onto her husband's arm. "I guess we're not getting any younger for all this partying and excitement."

"Nonsense!" Dan replied, going to give her a hug and shake Gus' hand. "Have a good sleep."

City street lights were extinguished by the time they drove up Government Street and passed the foundry in the hollow below Bay Street. It was the only building that appeared to be in use having its usual glow, due to the fact their furnaces were never allowed to go out. Negotiating the roundabout at Gorge and Douglas, they headed up Hillside.

As they turned onto Cedar Hill Road, Nancy broke the silence. "Danny, I've got something to tell you. I've been trying to find the perfect time but there has been too much going on the last few days."

"Why so serious all of a sudden? Are you all right, honey?"

"I'm pregnant, Danny!" She was so excited to finally be able to tell him, she just blurted it out. "We're going to have a baby!"

Swerving, Dan slammed his foot on the brake skidding across the road as he whooped like a drunken sailor, finally bringing the truck to a shuddering stop.

"Are you sure?" he laughed, pulling her into his arms. "Oh Nan, that's the best news."

"I haven't told anyone," she said, "but the doctor says we will be parents about June 15th!"

"Gosh, maybe you shouldn't go to Seattle on Saturday," Dan whispered in concern.

"It's all right, sweetheart, I have to sing at the concert. Take us home, Danny, all three of us, we're getting cold!" she giggled, cuddling up to him.

Grabbing the blanket from the back seat, he tucked it around her, gave her another kiss, and put the truck in gear. "Do you think we should tell Aunt Meg when we get home?"

"No silly, not tonight, she'd never be able to get to sleep!"

"Hmm, you're probably right, we should surprise them all at dinner tomorrow." Taking her hand, he squeezed it gently. "He's ours Nan, he's all ours."

"And if it's a girl?"

"I hope she's just like her mother. I love you so much, honey!"

"I love you too, now drive, we'll take whatever we get and love it to pieces."

They talked for awhile but soon lapsed into silence as Dan concentrated on his driving and, Nancy relaxed, thinking of the changes a baby would bring to Cunningham Manor.

"Bring in a couple logs for the fireplace, Danny," Meg shouted as they came onto the porch, having arrived home before them. "The kettle is still warm, I'll make you a hot cup of tea, lass."

"Thanks, Aunt Meg but I'm going straight to bed and probably Dan will, too. He has a fairly early delivery. Where's Uncle Jeb, has he gone to bed already?" she asked.

"No, he was out in the kitchen getting some food together for Sam. We're going to have a quick cup of tea. It was a lovely evening, lass. I did so miss hearing you sing."

Nancy went over and took her aunt into her arms and hugged her.

"I'm so glad you had a nice evening, Aunt Meg. We did too; it really felt like we were accomplishing something good when so many bad things have been surrounding the city for so long."

The next morning, dawn revealed dark clouds hanging low over the pounding waves of the strait, hiding the San Juan Islands in a thick mist. Habit wakened them at their usual time and although yawning they ate breakfast together unable to stop talking about the Armistice Ball.

"Why don't you tell them now, Nan," Dan suddenly urged his wife.

"I thought we were going to wait until dinner," she whispered, but seeing him shrug his shoulders, she quietly continued, "You tell them if you want, it's yours as much as mine."

Frowning suspiciously, the Scot looked from Nancy to Dan. "Now what are you two up to?"

"How would you two like to be grandparents?" Dan asked, reaching for Nancy's hand under the table.

Meg's teacup rattled violently on its saucer causing her to let go of it as a look of utter shock came onto her face. "A baby … a baby?" she gasped, tears coming to her eyes. "Aye, that will be wonderful!"

"When is this going to happen?" the old detective asked nervously, catching his pipe as it slipped from his lips.

"June 15th, the doctor says," Nancy replied, getting up and going over to Meg and allowing her aunt to hug her happily. "It'll be an early summer baby."

Excited conversation bounced around the table as Meg began making enthusiastic plans. "I shall start knitting straight away," she chortled, "it will need booties, bonnets and tiny little suits. The next time you go to Salt Spring lad, I'll get you to bring me a selection of that extra soft wool from Jane Mouat's."

Awhile later, Dan went off to work and Nancy got ready to go into the restaurant.

"I'll be home early so I can help you with dinner and visit with the Jorgensens, Aunt Meg. We'll tell them our news over dinner, so don't let the cat out of the bag," she warned.

"I promise," Meg replied. "I can't wait to see their faces."

The restaurant was a busy place with everyone talking about the Armistice Ball especially when the soldiers who had gone to the Empress dropped in over the course of the day.

By the time Nancy arrived home again, she was very tired but found herself most eager to tell her other family the exciting news. When they all gathered around the dining-room table, it soon became an even more joyous occasion than the Jorgensens expected as Dan and Nancy shared their happy news. Beth was beside herself with joy, as Meg was, and the boys dealt with it all in their usual manner by teasing Dan relentlessly.

Early the next morning, they were loading the luggage into the boat for their trip to Seattle and Dan found himself patiently listening to a new stream of Jeb's advice.

"I assure you dad, I shall always look after her. That redhead has been my life for so long I'd be lost without her, so stop your worrying!"

It had not gone unnoticed by the former Pinkerton man that Dan had called him 'dad' and it pleased him greatly.

When they were ready, Meg and Nancy came down and they were soon on their way to Victoria to pick up the Jorgensens. It was another misty morning with fog out in the strait, typical for this time of year, but otherwise pleasant and they made good time. The family was already at the Brown and Wilson dock but Jack was there so they were inside out of the cold. With the men helping, they quickly manoeuvred Bill and the wheelchair over the side and strapped it firmly in place. Dan located the canopy and while he, Jack and Nancy set it up, the others loaded the luggage.

By nine-thirty, with everyone sitting in their respective places, Nancy got them underway. Visibility had improved slightly in the last hour but speed was impossible anyway due to the restrictions of the canopy. Only a few small vessels were seen as they headed across the strait and several times they heard the rasping sound of a foghorn warning of a freighter but they never got close enough to see it.

Smoking a cigar as he sat waiting on the Jorgensen dock, Terry O'Reilly pulled his overcoat tighter about him and strained to catch the sound of the *Stockholm*'s engine. Hearing the distinctive sound among the foghorns, he got to his feet and shouted to his men, appointing one of them to alert the servants as soon as the vessel arrived. They would first need to get the luggage out of the way before unloading the liquor. He paced the dock until the boat finally came out of the fog and headed for the boathouse.

"You're a marvel with a boat, Nan," Chris complimented her admiringly, as she drew into the boathouse.

"Thanks Chris, I love this boat," she replied, turning off the engine.

"Brrr, it's cold," Beth exclaimed, taking Dan's hand to step over the side of the boat. "Let's get up to the house and have a nice hot cup of tea."

As they went outside, the servants arrived, taking the bags from Terry's men and hurrying back up the path.

"Any news, Terry?" asked Nancy.

"Yeah, there's been talk of a hijacking up by Maxwelton on Wednesday. They must have been out there waiting when you passed on your way home."

"Lucky for them, they didn't try to stop us."

"Don't get cocky, girl—you tell Dan what I said and be careful."

On their way up to the house she told Dan of Terry's concern, and the hijacking near Maxwelton.

"They don't know what we know," he said coldly, slipping his arm around her. "We've got speed and enough armour to blow them out of the water, but from now on, we come straight down the middle, unless we're looking for them. The first rule of combat is to know where your enemy is. If they have to show themselves to get to us, we can beat them all."

Dan's confidence and cold calculation startled Nancy. This was the first time she had heard him use his military training in relation to the rum running and knew he was treating Terry's warning seriously.

When they reached the house, they found Gus and Beth waiting for them in the hallway. They helped them out of their coats and hurried them upstairs to the warmth of their apartment. Later, the boys joined them and Bill grabbed Nancy as she went by.

"Stop mauling her, you fool," Chris snapped, "she's delicate now."

Grinning sheepishly, Bill kissed her hand and called for a servant to bring champagne.

"You seem to be our only shot at having grandchildren, Nan," Gus confessed. "We're all absolutely delighted you know—you can come to Seattle to have the baby, if you like. I'll pay all the medical expenses."

"Thanks Gus, that's very kind of you but no," Nancy replied. "We want our children to be born Canadian where we live in the most beautiful place in the world at Cunningham Manor."

The champagne and glasses arrived, brought by a maid who set the tray down on a small table and scurried away. Chris poured and passed around the glasses then everyone except Nancy stood up as Bill called for a toast to 'our new baby.'

It was almost two in the afternoon when lunch was served and conversation centered on the evening's concert. Bill ate quickly and left for the theatre saying he needed to oversee the setting-up of equipment. To their knowledge, this would be the first recording of a live theatre performance and he wanted to be prepared so nothing went wrong.

"You should have a rest, dear," Beth whispered, "we all had such a late night at the dance and such excitement. I'm going to lay down myself. Nellie is coming for dinner, so you girls can rehearse before we eat."

"I think you're right," Nancy sighed, stretching out her arms. "I'll grab 40 winks before Nellie gets here."

"Me as well, lassie, I can barely keep my eyes open," Meg agreed. "I'll come tuck you in."

Left alone, the men retired to the parlour to smoke as they discussed local politics.

"We're heading toward a national ban on liquor," Gus growled, "and now the war is over, there's bound to be trouble with the economy as we try to find jobs for the returning soldiers."

"Victoria's going to suffer, too," Dan agreed, "the whaling has gone and wooden ships are a thing of the past."

"Coal and lumber," Jebediah added, "Victoria and Vancouver will survive on its natural resources."

"The lumber industry won't hire crippled soldiers," Dan pointed out.

"It might, if we expand into mills and processing the lumber," Jeb argued.

"Pulp and paper," Gus added. "I think British Columbia will become a paper producer. Remind me Chris, we must look into that idea."

For the next hour and a half, the men discussed and argued, exchanging ideas and thoughts on the peacetime economy of both sides of the border, until the butler interrupted announcing Nellie's arrival.

"I'll go wake Nancy," Dan responded, leaving the room.

"Hi Dan, isn't it wonderful to have a concert again?" Nellie said excitedly, meeting him in the hallway. "My sources tell me Seattle can't wait to hear Nancy sing again."

"Hi Nellie," he replied. "The men are in the parlour, I'm sure you know your way. Nan will be down shortly."

Opening the door to the smoky room, she glanced around at their faces and giggled. "Have you been talking politics again, you look like the canaries who ate the pigeon!"

"Go away and play with your piano," Chris ordered, winking at her, "this is man's talk."

"Brat!" she countered, hugging him with obvious affection. "I might just do that while I'm waiting for Nan."

"She was having a nap, Dan's gone to tell her you're here."

"I know, we met in the hallway. Don't let me interrupt you!" she said coyly, backing toward the door.

Running up the stairs, Dan crept quietly along the corridor past the Jorgensen's apartment and Meg's room. Hearing the familiar sound of Aunt Meg's snoring, she knew she was still asleep. Grinning, he went on to the large guest room he and Nan used. He stealthily opened the door and tiptoed in, hovering for a moment not really wanting to wake her, when he heard her speak.

"Come lay with me for a minute, Danny."

"You're awake," he muttered, leaning over and kissing her. "You must have ears like a cat."

"No, I could hear you calling to me."

"But I didn't call you, honey." Grabbing his arm she pulled him onto the bed beside her and folded her arms around him.

"I can't explain it, Dan," she whispered. Remember how you could hear me singing to you when you were in France?"

"Yes, and I heard you again when I was coming home on the boat. Others heard you, too."

"How do you explain that?"

"I'm not even going to try; it's too big a mystery for me, Nan. Nellie's here."

"Tell her I'll be down in a few minutes," she replied, sitting up as he left the room.

She freshened herself up, slipped her clothes back on and brushed her hair. When she opened the door, she heard the piano softly playing in the distance. As she skipped quietly down the stairs, she began to sing softly, breezing past the men so deep in conversation, they didn't notice her.

Smiling as her friend entered the room singing, Nellie's fingers flashed over the keys, not stopping until Nancy slid onto the stool.

"So are we doing anything different tonight?" asked the pianist. "If so, we'll have to warn the conductor."

"Well, we need to find a baby song for one thing," Nan replied, blushing slightly.

"A baby song?" Nellie asked looking over at her friend with a puzzled expression.

"I'm pregnant, Nellie," Nancy giggled, "and I want to tell the whole world how happy I am!"

"Oh my goodness, Nan, that's the best news!" Nellie gasped, hugging her again. "How are you feeling?"

"I just found out last week and told Dan after the ball. I'm fine, only a bit tired."

"I guess you'll have to watch those late nights now, Nan," Nellie chastised her.

"I know, but how was I to prevent it without telling everyone?"

"Well, we'll just have to make sure you don't stay out too late tonight. How does Dan feel about the baby?" asked Nellie.

"Dan's quite sure he's going to get a son and he's very excited!"

"He'll get what you give him—there isn't any way he can choose," Nellie laughed. "Hey, just wait a minute, you want a baby song. One of my students brought me a lovely little song last week. She said her mother used to sing it to her when she was a child. It might be just what you're looking for and it should still be in my case."

Searching through her briefcase, Nellie pulled out a tattered sheet of music and smoothed it out on her leg.

"Just let me run through it a couple of times, then we'll have a look at the words."

Closing her eyes, Nancy let the music permeate her brain. As Nellie played the gentle melody again, she hummed along.

"You've got it already," Nellie said, smiling, "now take a look at the words."

"Are you sure she won't mind me singing it?" asked Nancy.

"Joanna's not a singer, she's a talented young pianist and she asked me if I would help her write an arrangement so she could play it."

"But it has music, you're playing it!"

"Actually, the music on the sheet is very rough from her memory; I'm composing as I go!" laughed the pianist.

"Oh Nellie, how lucky I am to have such a talented friend. Let's go over it a few more times and see if it's good enough for tonight."

Fifteen minutes later, Beth and Meg joined the men now gathered in the living room. As the butler announced that dinner would be served in 15 minutes, they realized the girls were practicing in the music room across the hall.

"Quiet!" Meg hissed, cocking her head toward the sound. "Listen, she's singing something new."

"Look at mum!" Chris whispered to Dan. "She's mesmerized by the music."

"Ach laddie, it's noo the music, it's the way that lassie reaches out to your heart when she sings," Meg sighed.

"I think we've got it, we just have to do it tonight, Nan," Nellie said excitedly as the song ended. "It's perfect for what you want and Seattle will love it. The words are pretty easy—should we write them down for you?"

"I think that would be a good idea. Don't forget to tell Joanna and thank her for me."

"She will be thrilled when I tell her," Nellie assured her as she got some paper and a pencil out of her case.

Conversation over dinner was exuberant as their discussion centered on the concert, songs and babies. They were soon talking about lullabies and each of the old folks mentioned baby songs they remembered from their childhood. They all laughed when Gus tried to remember the words to one of the songs he and Beth sang to the boys when they were young.

"Better leave the singing to Nancy, Dad," Chris laughed, "that way we can all enjoy it!"

Blushing, Gus accepted the criticism, muttering, "I was only trying to remember the words."

"There's plenty of time to remember them," Nancy assured him. "You can sing it to the baby when it arrives, grandpa!"

"Oh, the poor child!" Chris said solemnly, breaking into a grin. "Well I guess Bill and I survived—your singing can't be all that bad, dad!"

"Meg thought you were practicing a new song, Nan? Were you? It was pretty, are you going to sing it tonight, dear?" asked Beth.

"You'll have to wait and see, mom!" Nancy replied coyly.

"My goodness, look at the time. We'd better get ready," Beth announced, looking at her watch. "We need to be there early. Bill said he might need you girls for a sound test."

Chapter 26

Supervising the technicians scrambling under the stage, testing and checking their installations, Bill found himself getting both nervous and excited about the evening show. Having arrived early to supervise the final preparations, he fully realized the minutes were quickly ticking away. This would be the first live recording in a Seattle theatre and he was determined to make it the perfect recording.

James Moore was also having a busy afternoon meeting a group of special guests at the docks before taking them to his favourite restaurant for an early dinner. These were influential businessmen from Victoria who had quietly approached James at the Armistice Ball requesting seats to the sell-out concert.

Apparently, rumours had been circulating for the last year or so, especially within the legislative halls of power—stories of a red haired singer from Victoria who sang for a Victoria Widows' and Orphans' Fund at the James Moore Theatre in Seattle. Doctors' Price and Underhill also talked in glowing terms of a Victoria resident named Nancy Wilson when giving their report of the influenza epidemic, and an army surgeon from Esquimalt told a lengthy story of a determined and lovely redheaded woman's efforts to take care of her injured brother, despite his injuries and loss of memory.

Intrigued by his information and wondering if these women were one and the same, Premier Oliver's office made some discreet inquiries and he attended one of her Seattle concerts. Then due to the influenza problem, Nancy had almost been forgotten until her name again began popping up in the most unlikely places and he was introduced to her at the Armistice Ball.

Today, using the concert as a cover to meet with Mayor Cotterill and Admiral Johnson over their mutual shipping problems, Premier Oliver alerted no one in his office of his intentions. The Americans had already hinted at a solution to the increasing number of murders pertaining apparently to the rum running situation. With little in the way of coast guard vessels, however, Oliver's government was reluctant to participate, even though British Columbia was becoming unwillingly involved. America's request for closer cooperation amused the premier and his cabinet, but after four years of war they felt they had more important things to deal with.

Back at the house, two Bentleys provided by James Moore, arrived at the Jorgensen mansion and they all headed off to the theatre. Watching the gaudy lights of the signs and billboards as the cars sped into the city, Nan realized how much she had missed the concerts. Crowds were already jamming the streets around the theatre as their car crept up to the sidewalk, forcing several policemen to hold the crowd back from the protected walkway, laid with red carpet.

Inside, James Moore escorted the Canadian dignitaries to an executive box where drinks were served and the men were able to converse privately.

"Our idea is to put an experienced sailor in the Puget Sound area—one who knows the coastline," Mayor Cotterill began.

Sipping their drinks, the Canadians offered no comment.

"We would like British Columbia to work with us," Admiral Johnson took up the conversation, "and there's a man in Victoria we would like you to consider. He knows these waters like the back of his hand. He's an ex-whaler and a wounded army sergeant who fought with distinction and courage."

"That's fine, admiral," John Oliver growled impatiently, "we know all that, but what do you expect from us?"

"We propose that Dan Brown become a secret agent working to find the men responsible for the hijackings and murders in the waterways between our two countries. He would be a person whom we both trusted and could travel the border freely," pausing for a moment he levelled his eyes on Premier Oliver. "Dan Brown has an impeccable record of courage and integrity, and he's known to both our governments."

Half an hour later, increasing noise in the theatre alerted the men that the audience had arrived and they were surprised to discover most of the seats already occupied. Glancing at his pocket watch, John Oliver frowned, realizing the show was about to begin and he needed to go join his wife immediately.

"Gentlemen," he stated, rising to his feet, "in principle I agree, but there is still much discussion necessary. Now I suggest we join the ladies and enjoy the show."

Lights began to dim and the orchestra settled into silence as James Moore walked onto centre stage, his snow-white tuxedo glowing against the darkness of the lush velvet curtains behind him. He raised his arms.

"Friends," he called, "are you ready for a special evening?"

The eruption of cheers created a deafening crescendo which carried out into the street where 'theatre full' signs were now displayed. The doors closed and only a lone attendant watched for latecomers with tickets as the staff hurried to their own prearranged observation posts.

Standing his ground, the curtains opened revealing Nancy and Nellie in almost matching peach-coloured silk dresses. They came forward and stood on each side of him waving as the crowd showed their approval.

"Welcome back everyone!" the redhead announced, as Nellie made her way over to the grand piano and James disappeared into the wings.

Appropriately, they opened with an old favourite, *We're Together Again* and, from the first notes, Nancy had their audience captive, thrilling them with her selection of songs.

In a back corner, Bill's wheelchair swayed slightly to the music, his technicians watching their instrument board and making adjustments as dials and metres bounced crazily.

"This is wonderful," his music director whispered to no one in particular, "we're making history! What a show!"

At intermission, amid thundering applause, the girls took their bows before hurrying off to the dressing room. Dan and Chris quickly joined them, carrying a jug of lemon water and offering to get tea or drinks.

"The lemon water is perfect. I'm going up to see Aunt Meg for a minute," Nancy announced, "are you coming, Nellie?"

"I'm going to find Bill. I need to find out how the taping is doing."

"Good idea, you can tell me later," Nancy exclaimed, leaving the room quickly with the boys.

Nellie left right after them and managed to coax a stagehand to show her where the recording people were working. She sneaked up behind Bill's wheelchair and covered his eyes with her hands.

"Who is it?" she croaked in a foreign accent.

"Come closer and I'll whisper your name," Bill chuckled.

Leaning over, she rested her head on his shoulder and he suddenly yelped. "By the smell of that perfume, it's Nellie!"

"You cheated," she laughed, as he swung his wheelchair and pulled her onto his knee, hugging her until she squealed, "let me go, I want to see what you're doing."

Over in the Moore box, Nancy found Meg and Beth, telling them she was going to sing the new song at the end of the concert. Jeb directed Dan's attention across the theatre to one of the private boxes.

"What is it?" Dan asked.

"It's George Cotterill and that coast guard admiral, but I noticed John Oliver there before the show started."

"And what's that supposed to mean, Mr. Detective?"

"Don't know, lad," the old man replied, "it just looks mighty suspicious after Admiral Johnson talked to you about working for them. My guess is it's an informal meeting and they're trying to work out an arrangement."

"Not to worry, dad," Dan grinned confidently, "we'll know soon enough, but if you're right, why isn't General Greene with them?"

"He's right, Jeb," Gus interrupted, joining them. "He's the military commander in this area and would surely be involved."

"T'ain't military, it's civil," Jeb snorted.

The recall bell sounded, alerting the audience that the second half of the show would begin in ten minutes.

"Time to go, Aunt Meg," Nan said hurriedly, kissing her on the cheek. "See you after the show."

Also hearing the bell, Nellie excused herself from Bill and the technicians, finding her way around some stored stage props arriving back at the dressing room as Nancy came hurriedly down the back stairs.

"Hey there, girl," she said sternly, "you need to slow down in your condition!"

"Aw, hush your lips, Mother Hubbard," the redhead laughed. "I'm so happy I have energy to spare!"

After fixing their hair, lipstick, and rouge, and taking a quick drink of lemon water, they received a warning tap at the door. "Five minutes to curtain time, ladies," and went to take their positions at the piano.

On the other side of the curtain, James strutted around the stage, staring over the footlights as he solicited more donations from his auspicious audience.

"What the devil is he talking about?" John Oliver growled to his American counterparts before they parted company.

"She's been doing this for years, man," George Cotterill snapped pompously. "Get your money out, it's for a good cause and in your own city for heaven's sake!"

James left the stage, the lights immediately dimmed, and the maestro entered to polite clapping as stragglers found their seats in the low light. The strains of a well-known song filled the theatre as the curtain rose and a spotlight picked out the girls at the piano. Mayor Cotterill turned to one of the other men in the box and began talking.

"Shut up, the both of you!" Admiral Johnson snapped rudely.

The force of the admiral's order brought instant silence to the executive box as Nellie began to play the first introduction, backed by the orchestra. Nancy's beautiful voice rose majestically above them.

"My God, that girl can sing," Richard Johnson murmured.

Nancy sang a selection of both old and newer songs for the next forty-five minutes until, finally holding up her hands, she walked to the edge of the stage. The audience waited expectantly.

"Friends," she began in a clear voice, as many of you know, I was married a week after our last concert in April and now I have a secret to share with you. I'm going to have a baby next year and my next song is dedicated to the little stranger who is coming into our lives."

A gasp ran through the audience and Nellie winked at Nancy before resting her fingers on the keys. Nancy's red hair sparkled under the moving spotlights as she began to sing the lovely little lullaby.

When she finished, she bowed low, trying desperately to contain her emotions as the audience roared their approval, rising in a body as she and Nellie left the stage. Once again, the redhead's heartfelt singing plucked at heartstrings and many dainty handkerchiefs fluttered as ladies dabbed at wet eyes. Time after time, the applause drew them back on stage, until finally they agreed to sing one of their famous duets, bringing the show to a close as *We'll Meet Again* rang through the theatre and the curtain finally came down for the last time.

Excitement buzzed about the backstage area as James came to hug the girls, gushing his enthusiastic appreciation and congratulations.

"Wow, you two just keep getting better and better," he said excitedly. "Hurry now, the cars are waiting to take you to the party."

"Sis," came Bill's voice and Nancy looked around to find him.

"Bill!" she called, finding him stuck behind the stage props. "What on earth are you doing in there?"

"Can you get me out of here?" he pleaded, grinning sheepishly.

Getting a couple of stagehands, they were soon able to free him. Teasing him mercilessly, he went along to their dressing room where they collected their coats.

"You were both stupendous, knockouts!" he babbled. "The boys are thrilled with the recording."

"Thank goodness," retorted Nellie, "after all this buildup I was hoping you wouldn't be disappointed, Bill."

Meanwhile, up in the executive box, angry words were again being exchanged between Mayor Cotterill and the B. C. Premier as conflicting ideas were expressed on the nature of Dan Brown's involvement in the coast guard's problems.

"I cannot allow a Canadian citizen to be put in such danger," Oliver growled, "and if we did, we would want a measure of control."

"Do you want the situation to go unchecked?" Admiral Johnson retaliated heatedly, getting frustrated with the lack of a decision.

"The hijacking and murders go on in Canadian waters, too," George Cotterill, snapped sarcastically.

"Of course we want it stopped, but this is quite out of the ordinary, and who would pay for such an operation?"

"We would," the Seattle mayor retorted, "now will you please make a decision, sir."

"He would report to us?" Oliver continued, further aggravating the mayor.

"You would be kept informed," Admiral Johnson frowned, "there will be times when we have to work together, irrespective of boundary lines."

"Then I will tentatively agree to you talking to Mr. Brown; we can arrange a meeting in Victoria in a few weeks, to formalize the arrangement."

"Thank you," sighed the admiral, and he and Mayor Cotterill both breathed sighs of relief. Having refused the mayor's invitation to the customary after-show party, the Canadian premier and his party said their goodbyes and left, much to the relief of the Americans.

Watching intently through Beth's opera glasses, from across the theatre, Jeb grinned. "They're having a hell of an argument over there!" he muttered as Dan and the Jorgensens waited for his report. "He has a reputation for being a tight-fisted old devil."

"Who's tight-fisted?" Gus asked. "Who are you talking about?"

"Our Premier Oliver."

"He was very nice when we met him at the Armistice Ball," commented Chris.

"I noticed," the old detective grinned, "he was trying to make an impression."

"You mean you think he's been investigating us," Chris hissed in annoyance.

"For sure lad, didn't you notice how he addressed everybody by name—even Meg and your mother—he knows all about us and all about you," Jeb replied.

"Do you think he knows about the booze run?" Dan asked.

"No, that proves he doesn't, or you'd be in jail and he wouldn't be talking to George Cotterill and Admiral Johnson."

"Are we staying here all night?" asked Meg, coming back to see what was keeping them.

"We're coming, Aunt Meg," Dan assured her, taking Jeb's arm and moving toward the door as she gave poor Jebediah a withering look of disapproval.

Forgetting the other men, Jeb ignored her but sprang into action leading the party outside and into the waiting cars. Behind them, Nancy and Nellie waved to some fans as their car slowly left the theatre.

Mobbed by a group of women when they arrived at the restaurant, Nancy answered many questions regarding her baby but was relieved when Dan and Chris came to her rescue.

There were speeches from James Moore and a long-winded oration from the mayor before things settled down and the meal was served. Excitement had dulled Nancy's appetite, toying with her food as she glanced around the room at the sea of happy faces. These were her friends, people who had supported her through the war years, always giving generously to her fund.

"Try to eat something, darling," Dan's voice brought her back to reality.

"I can't," she whispered, lowering her head as a tear splashed onto the tablecloth.

"What's the matter, Nan?" Dan asked in concern.

"It's silly, but I never dreamed we'd be so happy," she said, quickly dabbing at her eyes and looking around to see if anyone else had noticed.

Dan took her hand under the table and squeezed it. She squeezed his back and picked up her fork, playing with her food.

As the meal came to an end waiters buzzed about the room, clearing plates and moving tables to make room for a dancing area. Chris was seen going to speak to the bandmaster. After a short conversation, he stood behind the microphone and tapped it for attention.

"Friends," he called, waiting until it was quiet. "I think it would be fitting on this auspicious occasion, if Nellie Cornish joined the band for the first waltz and Nancy and Dan Brown led off the evening's dancing."

The clapping and cheering indicated the rest of the room agreed with him and Chris returned to his seat.

"What a great thought, son," Gus whispered. "I'm proud of you."

Nellie was halfway to the piano when she turned with a grin and called to Nancy.

"Well girl, hurry up and get that man of yours out here onto the floor!"

Blushing, Nancy pulled Dan to his feet and the music began as they reached the dance floor. Dan looked ill at ease at first but grinned and took his wife into his arms—impishly, Nellie had chosen a number close to her friend's heart, knowing Nan would never be able to resist singing to her husband. Smiling, Nellie shut her eyes briefly as Nancy's voice lifted in song.

Thrilled by the happy spectacle, ladies dragged their escorts out onto the dance floor, holding them close as they swayed to the music, until Nancy's voice faded away.

"We won't be able to dance like this much longer!" Nancy giggled. Watching Dan's puzzled expression she continued, "Well silly, I'm going to be a fat girl soon!"

Blushing fiery red, he took her hand and led her back to the table, where Meg noticed his embarrassment.

"Has she been teasing you, son?" she asked. "You pay her no mind, I'll deal with her later!"

As the evening wore on, Nancy and Dan made the rounds, moving from table to table personally thanking the guests for attending the concert. At James Moore's table they found Mayor Cotterill and his wife talking with John Gray and his mother.

"John never stops talking about you two," John's elderly mother spoke up boldly as they shook hands. "I'm so glad his poor wife was sick tonight and I had to fill in for her! I hear you're going to be working together!"

Nan smiled back at Mrs. Gray, puzzled at her comment and it was as if no one else heard the remark even as obvious, and innocent, as it had been. She now knew that Jeb was correct in his assumption that there had been a meeting, with her and Dan as the subjects, and they had indeed reached some sort of an agreement.

"Did you hear that?" she whispered to Dan as they moved away from the group.

"Yes, I did, Uncle Jeb was right again."

It was almost midnight when Bill Jorgensen arrived, hair dishevelled and looking tired as he manoeuvred his wheelchair through the tables.

"Sorry I'm late folks," he sighed, "we were working on the recording."

"Late, you almost missed it, Bill!" Gus snorted.

Ignoring his father's comment, Bill bubbled with enthusiasm, going into technical details no one understood of how they were trying to edit some of the background noise from the recording. Nellie appeared fascinated, listening to every word, as she took a comb from her bag and casually tidied Bill's hair.

"Take your partners for the last waltz, folks," the orchestra leader announced.

Responding instantly, couples crowded onto the dance floor. Holding hands under the table, Dan and Nancy watched Gus lead Beth out onto the floor. They also looked on as Jebediah nervously invited Meg to dance, awkwardly holding her as they stood and swayed to the music.

"Oh Dan," the redhead whispered, "they're so cute! We'd better go join them."

Afterwards, many lingered to say goodnight before they left the restaurant. As they climbed into the waiting car, Nan heard a Seattle clock chime two. "Victoria will have been asleep two hours by now," she chuckled, cuddling closer to Dan as the lights of downtown began to flash by.

Sleep came easily to the Browns that night, settling contentedly in the luxurious silken sheets of the Jorgensen's mansion. Oblivious to the world, Nancy slept until well into the morning. On awakening, she opened her eyes and glanced around the room, Dan had already gone down to breakfast. Stretching, she looked at the alarm clock and was shocked to see that it was already 10 o'clock. She went to the window and, staring out at the dark storm clouds racing across the sky, she groaned at the thought of a rough ride home for Meg who didn't like boats even in the best weather. While she was enjoying the luxury of the Swedish shower, she heard Dan calling to her at the door.

"Are you going to laze about all day, wife?" he asked.

"Oh go away, I'll be down soon. If I had one of these at home I wouldn't stay in here so long!"

Everyone else was at the table when Nan arrived in the breakfast room, teasing her for her late arrival and pointing to the newspapers littering the table.

“Look what they’re saying about you!” Nellie said excitedly, pushing one of the papers across the table to her friend.

“Let her eat first,” Meg insisted sharply. “She hardly touched her meal last night and now she’s eating for two!”

“I’m all right, Aunt Meg,” Nancy responded, picking up the paper as Meg put an empty plate down in front of her. Reading part of the item, she saw Meg glaring at her. “Why don’t you dish up a small serving for me, Aunt Meg, not too much though, please.”

Meg gratefully got up and began to fill her plate from the heated trays on the sideboard. Trying to eat, read, and follow the continual chatter, she asked where Bill was and Beth said he’d already gone to the recording studio.

“I’ve never seen Bill so obsessed by anything,” his mother added. “He’s totally engrossed by this new recording business.”

“It’s good for him,” said Nellie, springing to the elder son’s defence. “It requires a good head on your shoulders to develop the recording business but I think Bill is the right person for it. It’s already been proven that there’s a future for it here and across the country as well. Having no legs won’t affect his thinking and I’m so sure he’ll succeed. I’m thrilled to be a part of it and I look forward to further opportunities.”

“Well Nellie, I hope your enthusiasm is infectious!” Gus laughed.

“Where’s Dan and Chris,” Nancy asked looking around, “and did you get our money bag last night, Uncle Jeb?”

“Dan and Chris are down at the boathouse with O’Reilly—he brought the money bag and newspapers over this morning,” Jeb replied.

“Oh good,” she replied, looking out the window. “The weather looks pretty awful out there; I think we should be leaving fairly soon.”

“I think you’re right, lass. I’ll go see what they’re doing,” said Jeb, draining his coffee cup and going to get his coat. Leaving the house, he glanced up at the threatening storm clouds hanging low over the water. “It’s going to be a rough one today,” he mumbled as he walked, holding onto his hat and bending into the wind. “Nancy thinks we should be leaving,” he announced, joining the three men in the boathouse.

“Anytime you’re ready, we’re all gassed up and ready to go,” Dan replied. “Terry says there’s a new gang in Seattle, Jeb. They’re trying to muscle their way into the booze business.”

“Do you know who they are?” The old man’s eyes narrowed as he studied O’Reilly’s face and waited for his reply.

“Roy says they’re Italians from Chicago.”

"Mafia?"

"That's what the cops think."

"Get the girls, lad, and let's be on our way, this trip's been long enough already," the old detective growled, ignoring Terry and dismissing any further conversation.

Jeb's natural abrasive manner angered the young gangster who, muttering under his breath, watched Jeb and Dan leave the boathouse.

Chris chuckled at the confrontation, offering his own advice.

"You should know better than try to tell that old man things you're not sure of Terry."

"Aw to hell with him!" Terry snapped, storming off toward his car.

Rain was falling as the Canadians said their goodbyes at the back door. Seeing the servants returning to the house under umbrellas, Beth called them over and, now with protection from the rain, the guests moved quickly down to the boat.

"Do you have the envelope, Uncle Jeb?" she asked, noting that the temporary cover was missing.

"It's right in here, honey," he grunted, patting his chest before going to help Dan stow the bags in the hold.

Meg went ahead of Nan into the cabin, settled into her usual seat, and wrapped a blanket around her legs. Nan took the helm seat and Jeb joined them as Dan gave the order for Chris to throw him the last rope.

"OKAY NAN, LET'S GO!" Dan shouted and, waving to Christopher, the engine obliterated any further conversation.

Chapter 27

Bucking and rolling, the *Stockholm* crashed through the pounding waves before turning north for the Canadian border.

"Try to use that freighter for shelter," Dan shouted into her ear, pointing to the lumber carrier heading back to Victoria. "That's the *Alma*, a Victoria ship."

He was unaware that aboard the *Alma* was a group of special passengers—John Oliver, his deputy, a member of his cabinet and Mayor Albert Todd, of Victoria, and their wives—heading home to Victoria from the concert. They were relaxing and discussing the weekend's events in the small, yet comfortable, passenger area.

Sitting back in his chair and puffing lightly on his pipe, Premier Oliver closed his eyes and again mulled over the American proposal regarding the safety of the nearby waterways. Soon, the others began discussing the same issue and, still with his eyes closed, he listened with grim-faced intensity.

"Victoria needs the waterways free from hijackers and murderers," Albert Todd stressed. "Now the war is over we shall be eager to welcome tourists again."

"Dan Brown is an excellent choice for the job but I wonder how the Americans came to choose him," Oliver muttered, opening his eyes as a steward refilled his glass.

"It's Nancy, sir," the steward whispered cockily, overhearing his comment.

"You say it's Nancy?" repeated the premier becoming instantly more alert. "Would you care to explain, son."

"The coast guard took care of her when Dan was away at the war, sir," the young steward expounded eagerly. "She sang for the army at Camp Lewis, it was in all the newspapers."

"Thank you!" John Oliver flashed the boy an infrequent smile. "That was very helpful information young man." He waited until the steward left the area before saying anything further. "It's General Greene, he's put them up to this. I might have known he'd be the driving force behind it all."

Staying in the shelter of the freighter until they passed the Keystone light, Nancy opened the throttle and felt the surge of power as the freighter veered away and the *Stockholm* charged on alone toward the wild waters of the Strait of Georgia.

Once clear of the islands and safely in open water, Capt. Hardy, master of the *Alma,* paid a visit to his illustrious guests. Alerted by his steward, he was aware there had been talk of Dan Brown.

"My compliments, gentlemen," he said pleasantly. "I hope the weather has not caused you too much unpleasantness and, by the way, Dan Brown and the *Stockholm* are just off our port bow, heading home toward Gordon Head, I would guess."

Chairs emptied quickly as the group of men scrambled for window space, staring through the rain-splattered glass at the red-and-gold boat jostling through the waves.

"Will they make it?" Bert Todd gasped in alarm.

"Of course they will," Capt. Hardy chuckled. "Dan's an experienced sailor and that little redhead's been out in worse weather than this when Dan was away in France. They'll be fine."

"You know them?" Bert asked.

"Yes sir, I've known Danny since he was a lad on the Joyce brothers' whaler. He was the best darn gunner on the West Coast and a good sailor even then. Nancy was a waitress at the Occidental. They're married now," exclaimed the captain with obvious knowledge. He paused for a moment before concluding reverently, "God bless 'em, they're the nicest young couple I've ever known."

Fighting their way into the shelter of Cordova Bay, Nancy kept well away from the log-littered coastline, noting that the yellow smoke normally belching from the explosives factory chimneys had cleared in the wind.

"Home," she whispered to Dan over her shoulder as she pulled into the cove.

"Someone's been here," called Dan, as he climbed the wet stairs, his hands full of luggage but noting the telltale rock on the last step.

Nancy also noticed the rock, Sam's signal to warn them visitors had called while they were away. Looking around, although she saw no sign of him, she knew he would be waiting to show himself to Jeb.

Fires were tended to as soon as they arrived at the house and, after quickly making a sandwich and wrapping it in newspaper, Jeb stepped back outside into the rain. Standing for a moment to stare into the dark undergrowth of the trees, he grinned when he caught a slight movement near the workshop.

"Who's been here, Sam?" he called.

The ragged half-breed stepped out of the shadows and eagerly took the package being offered. Quickly unwrapping it, he bit hungrily into the sandwich.

"Lady horse," came the reply after swallowing the first mouthful.

"A lady horse," the old detective chuckled shaking his head. "You mean a lady on a horse."

Nodding, Sam turned and shuffled back off into the forest, satisfied he had honoured his pact with Jeb.

"Who was it, Uncle Jeb?" the redhead called when he came back inside the house.

"A lady horse!" he replied, hanging up his coat and going to sit in the living room in front of the fire Dan had started.

"A what?" she giggled, rattling the plates as she set the table.

"Eva must have been over here on her horse," he called.

"What did she want?" asked Nancy.

"How the hell do I know, Sam ain't much of a socialite. I'll bet she never saw him."

"Money!" Meg shouted from the kitchen. "What else would Eva be looking for? You should phone her after we've eaten, lass."

Wind and rain continued to batter the coast as darkness enveloped the Gordon Head residence and Nancy went to the phone to call Eva.

"Nancy," Eva squealed happily when she heard Nan's voice, "I've heard from Tom!" She rambled off the gist of her husband's letter then paused and Nancy realized she was crying. "He has to stay in Europe with the occupation forces so he won't be coming home for awhile yet," she continued, attempting to control her emotions.

Knowing she couldn't find any words to comfort her friend, Nancy whispered how sorry she was, but Eva began chattering again.

"I don't think he wants to come home," she added solemnly. "I think we're going to be another casualty of the war."

"Don't you dare think that," said Nancy raising her voice, "you've got to trust Tom and hang onto your hope."

"We'll see, but I'm trying to face reality, Nan," Eva whispered, barely able to get the words out. "I just had to tell you."

The phone clicked and Nancy stared at the receiver hardly able to comprehend the conversation which had just taken place. Eva was her friend and she felt so helpless. Meg watched her from the kitchen having heard her reassuring comment and knew something was wrong.

"Come in here and tell me what's happened, lass," the Scot coaxed.

Nan went back into the kitchen, sat down and put her head in her hands.

"She's my friend, Aunt Meg, and I feel so helpless. She doesn't think Tom wants to come home. She's thinking the worst," Nancy moaned.

"Aye, Eva needs your friendship more than ever now, lassie. That's all you can do. She might have a long wait before she knows what Tom is going to do," Meg offered sympathetically.

"I know, that's the worst part."

Nancy, pregnant and happy, found herself wishing her time away as she waited for her baby. Encouraging Eva to visit often, Nan found herself driving the young woman into town more often as the Red Cross worker tried to fill her days, but sadly no more word came from Tom.

December 1918 brought joyful celebrations of concerts and Christmas parties, singing at the Empress for the Appreciation Concert in aid of the soldiers, and a special concert for James Moore in Seattle. Still no word came, however, from the government of John Oliver regarding Dan's appointment.

They all went down to Seattle for several days over Christmas where the luxurious and festive atmosphere of the beautifully decorated Jorgensen Mansion made it a special time for everyone. With all the boys home, it was a happy occasion with much teasing now that Nancy's normally trim figure was giving obvious evidence of the coming event.

Prior to the busy days of mid-December, Dan insisted that Nan curb her activities, including her long hours at the restaurant, so Kate hired another girl to help them out. Some of the wounded soldiers had returned to their distant homes but there always seemed to be others to take their place. Locals were also discovering the friendly atmosphere of the restaurant and thankfully there was no shortage of business.

Winter turned quietly into spring as April blossoms filled the Shelbourne Valley with a sweet-scented aroma. Her last concert in Seattle, on the 26th of April, brought the house down with appreciative applause when Nancy, heavy with child, finally left the stage.

Still driving the blue truck, although she was finding it difficult to squeeze in behind the steering wheel, Nancy continued to visit Kate at the restaurant although taking little part in the management or the work.

Tom Davis called in at the restaurant one day when Nan was there, informing them he was retired from his job as fire chief and was a civilian again. He pointedly told Nancy he was now able to go fishing whenever he wanted, chuckling as he promised not to get drunk while doing so.

"Why would he promise you not to get drunk?" Katherine asked her when they met in the kitchen.

"Oh, before the war, he took a little boat trip that backfired," Nancy explained. "Dan and I were coming back from Seattle late one Friday night when we found Tom and several of his friends adrift in their small boat. We towed them into our cove to let them sleep it off and when they woke up in the morning Jeb played a trick on them and they thought they were in Mexico!"

"If they had wives, I bet they were fit to be tied!" Kate laughed.

"They had wives …."

Noisy laughter suddenly shattered the quiet atmosphere as a group of soldiers arrived with Eleanor Simpson, finding themselves a table and calling for service.

"Behave yourselves!" Matron snapped at her boys going to join Nancy at her table.

Since the Armistice Ball, Eleanor was a regular visitor at the restaurant, often accompanying soldiers on their jaunts to see Nancy and Kate during the day.

"How are you feeling, my dear," she inquired with real concern. "It won't be long now, will it?"

"About six weeks," Nancy replied, touching her bulging tummy and smiling. "It's getting quite active and kicks me all the time!"

"Oh that's normal," Eleanor replied, blushing violently. "Are you going to have it at St. Joseph's?"

"No, my children are going to be born at Cunningham Manor. Mrs. Dunnett, who lives not far away, is a midwife."

"Don't you think you should have professional help, dear?"

"Mrs. Dunnett has five children of her own and has been a midwife for a long time. I trust her to know what she's doing."

"I have some time off coming," Eleanor quietly offered, dropping her eyes, "if you like I could be there as well."

Reaching across the table, Nancy took the matron's hand. "Thank you, Eleanor, I really appreciate your offer. I'll talk to Dan and Mrs. Dunnett and let you know."

"Nancy," Tom Davis called across the restaurant, "did you know the V&S railway is making its last run Wednesday at midnight?"

"Last run?" she repeated. "You mean it won't be going out to Sidney anymore?"

"They've gone bankrupt," Tom explained. "It's a shame but there won't be anymore passenger trains to Sidney."

"That's right," Eleanor confirmed. "I read it in Saturday's newspaper, though I've never been on it. I imagine it will be a real hardship for people who live out there."

More soldiers arrived, followed by Harry Maynard who joined Nancy and Eleanor at their table. Nancy introduced Harry and Eleanor and he eagerly joined the discussion, informing the gathering that a jitney service was now running a regular service between Victoria, Brentwood, and Sidney. There was also a new small freight service run by two ex-railroad men.

"I think it will be the lumber mill that suffers the most," he predicted, "they're producing record-breaking amounts of cut lumber and now have no way to get it to market."

"The government should force the V&S to sell their line to the CN," Tom interjected, "they're more experienced at railway management."

"Government is going to have its hands full enough," said Nancy, "who's going to take care of all these soldiers, when or if they get better?"

A cheer rose from among the men who were listening and one of them called out, "You tell 'em, Nancy!"

Excusing himself, Harry Maynard grinned mischievously as he hugged the redhead and left.

"Good gracious," Eleanor moaned, "I've been here an hour. The hospital will think I'm lost!" Quickly kissing Nancy's cheek, she hurried away.

In the late afternoon two streetcar drivers got into a violent argument while taking their break in the restaurant, shouting abuse at each other as they argued about the upcoming Victoria municipal election for mayor. Fists raised, tension flashed between the two combatants until a soldier on crutches tried to intervene.

"Sit down and mind your own business!" one of the drivers shouted at the soldier, coming toward the injured man.

At the start, Kate quickly moved to a position behind Nancy's chair, fearing it would be her friend who would try to be peacemaker. Then the door opened and the uniformed figure of Oak Bay's Chief Constable John Syme stepped inside. Quickly assessing the situation, he bellowed authoritatively at the two streetcar drivers.

"STOP IT YOU FOOLS!"

Nancy sighed with relief as the two startled combatants stepped back, dropping some coins onto the table as they nervously stammered an apology, and left.

"Thank you," Nancy said gratefully, smiling at the policeman who she recognized but didn't know. "I think you were just in time."

"Glad to be of service, lass. Does this sort of thing happen often in here?"

"Goodness no, arguments don't often get that heated and I can usually deal with it myself," she replied.

"Not in your condition, you can't!" he exclaimed.

"I won't be in this condition for much longer," she retorted, blushing.

"That's not the answer," Syme replied, frowning down at her. "I think I'd better have a word with Victoria; they should be able to keep an eye on the restaurant for you."

Their conversation was disturbed as the group of soldiers rose to leave. Watching them make for the door Syme's eyes portrayed his sadness. Sighing, he shook his head, his eyes following the last man who, limping painfully, stopped at the door.

"Mister," said the soldier, turning to face the lawman, "we'll take care of our own girls!"

Not daring to comment, Syme turned back to Nan. "I have nothing but admiration for those lads. Many of them have nothing left but their courage." Following them, he left without another word.

"It's time you went home too, young lady," Kate hissed, clearing off a nearby table, "you've had enough excitement for one day."

On the way home Nan took time to stop and watch the cows and several new lambs at Dean's Farm. She noticed the fields of daffodils which formed a golden carpet of colour, broken only by trees on the fence line, and took a deep breath to see if she could smell the flowers. Gordon Head was home and the Shelbourne Valley was certainly the wonderland of all her dreams. *This will be a perfect place to raise a family*, she thought.

From the kitchen window, Meg watched the truck come down the drive and saw Nan stop to talk to Kent at the orchard. She sensed Nancy was enjoying her extra time for one of her favourite pastimes—

appreciating the wonders of nature. Meg was also surprised to find her puttering around in her little garden on a few occasions and talking of growing some of her own flowers in the spring. Nan had always enjoyed spring but was often too busy to really appreciate it. The orchard's apple trees were growing remarkably fast and some of the earlier varieties were already blooming presenting a delightful show of pink blossoms. Meg asked the orchard men if they could start a little vegetable garden out back and preparations were made for a spring planting.

May passed quickly for Nancy, but now barred by Dan from going to Seattle, she spent her time close to home under Meg's watchful eye. He did, however, permit a trip to Victoria for the May Day Parade on the 19th and a visit to the Maynard's that afternoon where the Skillings and Duggans gathered for their yearly picnic. Now too big to squeeze into the driver's seat of the truck, her contact with friends was mostly achieved on the telephone or when someone drove her.

As June arrived, time began to drag as Nancy counted the days until the 15th, hoping she wouldn't have to wait any longer. She was getting more uncomfortable as the days grew warmer and she was eager to see if she was going to have a boy or a girl, secretly wishing it was a girl.

Her birthday arrived on June 10th and Meg planned a quiet birthday dinner, but that afternoon Ruby Williamson at the Gordon Head telephone exchange shouted down the phone to Jenny Dunnett that she was needed urgently at Cunningham Manor.

Eleanor Simpson grabbed her medical bag and booked off at the hospital as soon as she received Kate's call that Nancy was in labour. Not having received a reply from Nancy regarding her offer of assistance she hadn't mentioned it again, but as the date drew closer, her concern grew. Eleanor decided to confide in Kate, who already having suffered the disappointment of a miscarriage, certainly didn't want her best friend to have any problems. So together they made the decision and Kate agreed to call her immediately upon hearing any news.

Dan, not wanting to be away in Seattle when Nancy was having the baby, hoped it would arrive before morning. However, that was not to be and her labour dragged on through the night keeping everyone awake and worried.

Next morning, Mrs. Dunnett informed him that she could not give him any advice regarding predicting the baby's arrival, so Dan decided to make his trip and return immediately. Meg would call the Jorgensens if there was any news.

Gus and Beth met him down at the boathouse telling him Meg had called just minutes before and there was still no baby.

"How exciting, Dan!" exclaimed Beth, giving him a hug as he waited impatiently for Terry's men to finish unloading.

"You look after that girl for us too, Danny," called Gus, as Dan climbed back aboard the *Stockholm*.

"Don't forget to call us with the news," shouted Beth, as Dan started the engine and waved.

He watched as Gus and Terry threw the ropes aboard and he moved off into the channel as quickly as he dared. Speeding up Puget Sound, Dan saw the US Coast Guard cutter laying off Keystone and wondered if Fred Barrett had received any word of Nan and would no doubt have contacted Capt. Gray. He would be laughing at his hurried trip home, being a father himself.

Worrying and wondering what was happening at home, he exerted every ounce of power from the *Stockholm*'s engine as it zipped across the open waters. Nearing Oak Bay, he winced when a sudden piercing pain struck him in the back causing him to ease off on the throttle. Gripping the helm wheel even more tightly, beads of sweat ran down his face as pain after pain tore at his back. With his head spinning, his knees began to sag and he sat down but, just as suddenly as it began, the pain went away. Wiping the sweat from his face with a handkerchief, he let out his breath and shook his head.

"I'll bet you've just had our baby, sweetheart," he whispered. "I'll be home soon."

As Dan suspected, at Cunningham Manor, Mrs. Dunnett and Eleanor Simpson had successfully delivered an exhausted Nancy of a baby boy who cried exuberantly exercising his lungs. Downstairs, Meg, hearing the welcome sound, flopped into the chair beside Jeb and began to weep.

"What's the matter, woman? I thought you females liked it when someone had a baby. You're supposed to be happy!" he grumbled.

"I am happy," she sniffled, "stop your griping. We're grandparents, Jeb! Isn't it wonderful?"

Jeb looked at her and shook his head; putting an arm over her shoulder, he silently gave her a hug.

Upstairs, Jenny Dunnett performed her midwife duties with confident certainty, unaware it was the matron of the Jubilee Hospital to whom she was giving instructions.

As Eleanor changed the bed, Nancy tried to sit up and watch Jenny who was bathing the baby, but she tiredly fell back on the pillows.

"Is he all right?" she asked, a worried note in her voice.

"He's perfect! He has ten fingers and ten toes and looks normal in every way," Eleanor declared, "and listen to those lungs. He's a healthy boy that is for sure."

"You can see for yourself in just a minute, Nan," the midwife exclaimed, dressing the baby in a tiny white flannelette nightgown and wrapping a soft white blanket around him.

She came over to the bed with her little bundle and lay him in Nancy's arms. Nancy gently pushed back the blanket to expose his face and kissed the little forehead. The baby wriggled and one of his hands came out and reached for her.

"Oh look at his tiny hand!" she whispered, then squealed softly as he wrapped his little fingers around hers.

"Are you ready for visitors, Nancy? We better let Meg and Jebediah come up or they're going to be dying of curiosity!" suggested the midwife.

"Oh yes, please call them," she agreed, not taking her eyes off her son.

Jenny went to the door and called. Within seconds the women heard footsteps on the stairs. Creeping expectantly into the bedroom, the old folks peered down at the tiny bundle in Nancy's arms. Meg gently stroked the tiny white hand still tightly clenched around his mother's finger and sighed.

"Honey, we're so proud of you," she exclaimed, kissing her forehead.

"Isn't *he* just adorable, Aunt Meg? What do you think, Uncle Jeb?" Nancy asked with glowing but tired eyes.

"It's a boy, is it lassie?" Meg asked, receiving a smile and a nod from the new mother.

"I think he was worth waiting for, girl!" Jeb exclaimed.

Nancy and Meg couldn't help but notice that the old detective had tears in his eyes as he tenderly touched the baby's face.

"Danny got his little lad!" said Meg, going to the window to look for the boat. "What are we going to call him?"

"We haven't chosen a name yet," Nan said sleepily, kissing her baby's forehead again and laying her head back on the pillow.

"We should let her rest now," Mrs. Dunnett suggested, putting the baby into his cradle beside the bed and ushering everyone out of the room. "I'm going to leave too, Nan, but I'll come back and see you in a few hours. If you are concerned about anything, just have Meg telephone me."

Nancy nodded and closed her eyes barely hearing them say goodbye.

As they went downstairs, Meg invited matron for a cup of tea which she gratefully accepted. Jenny joined them minutes later as Meg bustled about the kitchen pouring tea and putting out a plate of cookies.

Suddenly a thought occurred to Meg and she stopped, teapot poised in midair.

"Have you two been formally introduced yet?" she asked.

"Not really, we haven't had much time to think of introductions," matron admitted, winking at Meg, "but that can soon be rectified. I'm Eleanor Simpson, matron at the Jubilee Hospital and I understand you are Jenny Dunnett, a neighbour."

"Y-yes," Jenny stammered in surprise, causing her to choke a little on her cookie.

"You were wonderful, Mrs. Dunnett, may I call you Jenny?" asked Eleanor knowing the poor woman was embarrassed. "There's no doubt you've done many deliveries before and you certainly know what you're doing."

"No one told me you were coming," Jenny said shyly.

"They didn't know," matron replied, making up some of her story. "It was a spur of the moment decision. I happened to be in the restaurant when Katherine got the message that Nancy was in labour and I thought you might be able to use some help. It's been awhile since I worked in the delivery room but I love seeing the little ones come into the world."

Overcoming her embarrassment, Jenny found herself chatting with the matron about some of the deliveries she had attended. Jeb, feeling a little out of his depth and uncomfortable with the conversation, excused himself and went outside.

Going to the cliff stairs, he stared out to sea looking for the *Stockholm* but his attention was taken by an unusual noise coming from behind the orchard. Following the sounds to the edge of the forest, he chuckled at what he saw. There was Sam doing a dance in a clearing at the far end of the orchard. The orchard men were there also, watching curiously. Wearing a headdress of feathers, which they had seen years before when he blessed their new property and, waving his staff in the air, the old half-breed leapt and pranced in an ungainly dance, oblivious of his audience.

"What on earth is he up to now?" Jeb asked Kent Macleod.

"Says he's calling his ancestors to make the baby strong."

"How does he know about the baby?"

"We heard it bawling."

Jeb's head swung quickly toward the sea as his ears picked up the sound of the *Stockholm*'s distinctive engine.

"It's a boy," he called as he hurried away.

"Could you give Eleanor a ride back to the hospital, Jeb?" Meg shouted from the porch.

"Dan's coming in," he announced.

"Dan can manage without you!" the Scot retorted sharply. "Come on, she needs a ride and you can drop Jenny at home on the way."

Grumbling to himself, Jeb glanced out to sea and found the tiny boat in the distance, then changing his mind, he walked over to the car and gave it a crank. He didn't have to wait long until the two women arrived, thanking him profusely for his trouble. He held the car doors open until they were settled then climbed in. As he drove slowly up the drive, he looked back in his mirror to see if he could see the boat but it was hidden by the trees.

Coming in fast, Dan saw Jeb on the clifftop through his binoculars, but lost sight of him as he avoided some floating logs. When he looked again, Jeb was gone. He entered the cove and docked, pent-up excitement causing him to hurry. Tying the *Stockholm* carefully but quickly and grabbing the parcel Beth had given him, he bounded up the cliff stairs and ran across the lawn to the house.

"Hey hey, slow down, lad!" Meg laughed, "and not so much noise if you please. We have a young mother resting upstairs."

"Oh Meg," Dan exclaimed giving her a hug, "has she really done it?"

"Aye lad," she replied with a lump in her throat, "we have a wee new bairn upstairs." Hanging onto his shirt as he tried to turn, she warned, "Go up quietly now, she'll be sleeping."

Tripping on the stairs in his eagerness, his eyes awash with tears, Dan crept into the bedroom and stared down at the little bundle in the cradle.

"You got your wish, Danny," she whispered. "Isn't he a darling?"

"It's a boy?" he asked, watching her nod. "I knew Nan, I knew," he whispered, dropping on his knees by the side of the bed. "I felt your pain; it gave me a horrible backache!"

"Maybe you helped me. Mrs. Dunnett said I did very well although I began thinking it would never end."

Wrapping his arms around her, they wept together until a noise from their son took their attention and they giggled at the faces he was making.

"Go and eat, darling" she whispered, "your son is hungry, too."

The phone rang while he was eating and he answered it hearing Gus' voice.

"Are Nancy and the baby all right, Dan?" Gus asked in a concerned tone. "The coast guard told us you had a baby boy."

"The coast guard," Dan muttered, "how could they have known so fast?"

"Seems Fred Barrett contacted them and then John Gray called us."

"Good old Fred!" said Dan, thinking that his earlier hunch had been correct.

"Danny its wonderful news, congratulations!" a female voice interrupted as Beth got on the phone. "Tell Nancy we're all coming up on Friday. We can't wait to see him. Have you named him yet?"

"No, we haven't named him yet."

"Well, just give her our best wishes, son," Gus added.

"Thanks, I will," he murmured.

"Who was that?" asked Meg, putting his dinner on the table.

"It was Gus and Beth, they're coming up on Friday to see the baby."

"How did they know so quickly, we haven't called them yet," Meg mused, looking puzzled.

"I don't know but Fred passed on the word."

The mystery was later solved when calls kept coming in from friends and neighbours. It seemed Ruby Williamson was doing a sterling job informing Gordon Head that the Browns had a new baby. As Dan had already discovered, the news was spreading quickly along Victoria's waterfront and, throughout the city, after Fred Barrett told Waldo and Harry Maynard.

Jebediah took Jenny home and then dropped Eleanor off at the hospital. She thanked him profusely and rushed off to tell the staff and soldiers the news. Then he called in at the restaurant to tell Kate and the staff.

The lights of Cunningham Manor burned until 11 o'clock that night when Meg and Jeb went up to say goodnight to Nancy and the baby before they went to bed. Meg had made many trips up the stairs that day checking in on them to make sure everything was all right and giving Nancy some company. She was exhausted, although not admitting it. The days of worry were over; they had a new resident to consider and were already planning for his future.

On their way to bed, Jeb ushered Meg into Nan's room where Dan sat holding the baby. It was a lovely picture of a happy, new family.

"You have your own perfect family now," Meg murmured, thinking back to the day she had first met Nancy at the Joyce's whaling office.

Dan was out at sea that day but before he left, knowing how lonely Nancy was, he had suggested she go down to the dock and meet the older woman, who he said was also lonely. He had explained to Meg that he and Nancy had legally adopted each other as siblings so she could become his next of kin in case anything should happen to him. Meg quickly learned how much these two young people needed a family. Thus, she was very happy for them when Nancy came into an unexpected legacy and she and Dan decided to build a home in Gordon Head asking her to come and live with them. It all seemed so long ago.

"He won't be a sailor," she said sternly. "I've spent my whole life worrying over men who were at sea. He'll have a nice safe job in an office!"

"No chance," Jeb chuckled, "that lad's carrying the blood of adventure in his veins!"

"And I suppose you're going to be the grandfather who encourages him. Well, I'll be watching you, Mr. Judd!"

"I don't care what he wants to be, grandpa," Dan said softly, watching as Nancy changed his son's diaper. "He'll have more chance of a good life than me and Nan had—we'll make sure of that."

"Go to bed, lad," Meg urged, "you've still got work tomorrow."

"I know, Aunt Meg, I just have to put some things away downstairs," he replied.

"Honey, I think you should sleep in your old room tonight; we're going to be awake every few hours and you need your sleep," Nan suggested.

"I'd like to be here but I guess you're right. I'll come back and say goodnight before I turn in. I won't be long, Nan."

Fifteen minutes later, he opened the door and peeked into the dark bedroom. Listening for Nancy's breathing, instead he heard her whisper, "Danny, come hold me."

Chapter 28

Morning came too early for Dan, waking with a start when he heard Meg's voice and realized she was shaking his shoulder.

"How's Nancy?" he murmured. "I'd better go check on them."

"You leave them be. She's been asleep since three and I don't want either of them disturbed. Breakfast is ready."

Washing and shaving, then quickly dressing, he crept noiselessly along the passage unable to stop himself from taking a peek into their bedroom. Fast asleep, Nancy lay with her red hair spread across the pillow, one arm reaching out to the cradle with her hand touching the bars. He sighed and quietly closed the door.

"Did she wake up?" Meg asked, frowning as she put his breakfast in front of him.

"No, she's asleep, Aunt Meg."

"Have you given him a name yet?" she demanded.

"Not yet, we really haven't had much time to discuss it," he admitted between mouthfuls.

"You better discuss it soon, lad, we don't want to go on calling him baby forever and everyone will be asking."

"All right, as soon as I get home we'll talk about it," Dan assured her, gobbling down the last of his meal. "Now I have to get going, I've got a busy day ahead of me," he said, kissing her on the forehead.

As the men left, Meg lectured Jeb about starting his car quietly for a change, then wagging her finger as they went out the door, she called quietly after them, "I want you both home by five-thirty for dinner and no excuses!"

"Don't worry, lad," Jeb grinned, leading the way outside, "she'll calm down in a day or two. Right now she's acting just like a broody hen."

"I know!" Dan smiled back at him. "She's been like a mother to all of us and now she has a little one to worry about, what could be better!"

"You're going to Bellingham today, aren't you?"

"Yes, the Sidney sawmill needs a part in a big hurry, I'm going there now. You could order the liquor, Jeb. I'll load it before I come home."

Going their separate ways, Dan heard Jeb cranking up his engine and hoped it hadn't woken Nancy or the baby. *Baby*! he thought, going down the stairs. *We've actually got a baby that belongs to us*! Reaching the dock, he hurriedly untied the ropes and jumped aboard the *Stockholm.*

Battling strong tides, he cautiously cut through between the San Juan Islands taking the pass between Lopez, Orcas, and Blakely. He followed a freighter going between Cypress, Guemes, and Lummi, overcoming it and scooting on to Bellingham. Tying up at the city dock, he walked along the waterfront road to the machine parts warehouse.

"Hi Dan," shouted the clerk as the Canadian walked in, "did you see the coast guard as you came across?"

"No, why, are they snooping around?"

"We had a boat hijacked last night—two men were killed."

"Oh no, where?"

"They found them drifting just south of Cypress, in the top end of Rosario Strait. Your order is on that trolley, I'll send a lad out to help you."

Simon Welsh, the store clerk, was a little older than Dan and well known to most of the border shipping industry. Always pleasant, helpful, and a constant source of information, he was a man who always knew what was going on in his area.

"How'd you find out so quickly?" Dan asked as his interest peaked.

"John Gray told me, they were here just after dawn."

Mulling over the information, Dan followed the lad as he left the store dragging the heavy trolley down to the dock. Working together, they loaded the machine parts onto the *Stockholm*'s deck.

"How fast is this boat?" the lad inquired with interest.

"Oh she's quick, lad," Dan chuckled as he looped a rope around the parts and fastened them to hooks on the deck.

"Bet it's not as fast as that new one."

"What new one?"

"It's been in here a few times in the last month or so. It's real fast, I've seen it moving."

"Tell me about it," Dan coaxed.

"It's black and sits low in the water. She's a beauty—sleek as a fish!" he exclaimed, obviously thrilled he'd seen it.

"Any identifying markings?"

"No, but they have a peculiar jib, it's got a big hook on the end of it."

"Where's it come from?" Dan asked, his mind beginning to make wild assumptions.

"I don't know, but not too far away."

"How'd you know that?"

"I filled their coffee mugs last time and they were mighty grateful. They said they'd filled them at home and just finished them."

"Hell lad, they could have come from Victoria."

"No sir, those mugs were still warm."

Clever deduction boy, Dan thought. "Here's my mug, would you fill it for me, too?"

Scooting away the lad was back within minutes. Flipping him a quarter, Dan thanked him as he took the hot cup and started the engine. With the boy watching, he moved the *Stockholm* slowly away from the dock and out into the channel. Ten minutes later he took a sip, slowed, and threw half of the coffee over the side.

Farther yet, he thought, frowning at the hot coffee mug.

Ten minutes more and he slowed again, taking a mental note of his position with the surrounding islands and dumping the rest of the coffee overboard. He felt the heat still lingering in the empty mug.

"This is about right I reckon," he muttered glancing at the gap between Orcas and Blakely Islands.

Getting back to business, Dan sped through the American islands ever watchful of the coastline as his mind ran through all the known hiding places, emerging into Haro Strait and an almost calm sea. Opening the throttle, he let the *Stockholm*'s engines scream with power as he tore across the unrestricted open water into Sidney harbour, slowing well before reaching the dock and tucking the *Stockholm* neatly into an open space at the sawmill dock.

Moments later, three mill workers hurried along the dock to unload his cargo. Behind them came the familiar figures of the shipping foreman, Joe Mitchell, and Walt Bohannan, the Sidney newspaper owner.

"What's new Danny?" Bohannan asked, "where ya been for this lot?"

"Bellingham and, you might as well know, Nancy gave birth to our first child yesterday."

The men mumbled their congratulations and a note pad and pencil appeared like magic in Walter's hand. Joe cocked an amused eyebrow at Dan, leaving them to talk while he organized the unloading.

"Boy or girl?" Walt snapped.

"Boy."

"Time, lad?"

Pulling out his pocket watch, Dan replied, "Ten past one."

"Not that time, you idiot, the time the baby was born!"

"About three-thirty I reckon, it was about that time when I felt the pain."

"You felt the pain?" the newspaper man scowled over his spectacles. "Are you pulling my leg?"

"No."

"What is he called?"

"What?"

"What's his name!" snapped the exasperated newspaperman.

"We haven't named him yet."

"How much did he weigh?"

"I don't know. I don't think they've weighed him yet."

"What kind of news is that?" Bohannan hissed, storming away toward Beacon Avenue.

"What you done to old Walter, Danny?" Joe laughed.

"Nothing, all I did was tell him Nancy had a baby yesterday."

"Well, whatever it was, you sure set the old man's boiler abubbling."

Taking a wide course as he left Sidney harbour, Dan slowed to warily watch the barges bringing equipment to James Island from the Ten Mile Point explosives factory. A sense of relief had run through Gordon Head when it was announced they were moving the factory out near Sidney. Soon the air would be clean again and the clouds of yellow smoke would disappear.

Crossing wide of Cordova Bay, he focused his binoculars on the cove at Cunningham Manor and fought the urge to let the *Stockholm* head for home. He caught sight of Meg waving from the porch. *She sure knows the sound of this engine*, he mused.

It was a pleasant easy run into Victoria as a gentle breeze cooled the heat of the afternoon sun. Passing Finlayson Point, he saw children playing on the beach below the cliffs at Beacon Hill Park. He smiled to himself thinking what it was going to be like playing with his own son. As he rounded the Ogden Point breakwater, his thoughts turned to the news that the builders of the breakwater were suing the government for non-payment and, farther along, he watched as two freighters unloaded at Rithet's outer wharf. This added extra vehicle traffic to Dallas Road which had become much busier since war's end. *Victoria's starting to move again*, he mused, turning onto the Brown and Wilson dock.

Shouting from the harbour master's porch, Fred Barrett yelled his congratulations and Dan waved in acknowledgement. Jack was up at

Waldo's when they saw Dan arrive and hurried down the boardwalk to shake his hand.

"She almost did the double," Waldo laughed, "one day earlier and it would have been on her birthday!"

Dan mumbled under his breath and stormed off into the office.

Jebediah looked up from his newspaper with a hint of a smile playing around the corners of his mouth as he watched Dan pour himself a coffee and slump into a chair.

"You forgot her birthday, didn't ya?" he chuckled, pointing to a bouquet of flowers sitting in a glass of water on the counter. "Well lad, I saved your arse again."

"Thanks, Jeb," he said gratefully, picking up the flowers and wrapping them in some newspaper. "You're a life saver, I plain forgot."

"That bag goes home with us, too," Jeb informed him with a grin. "It's presents for the baby from the Wharf Street traders. I'll bring them and the flowers, I'll be home before you anyway. You'd better load that booze and get on your way. It's getting late and remember Meg's serving dinner at five-thirty and your son is waiting for you!"

Dumpy and Waldo had half the cases of liquor loaded by the time Dan came to help. Sweating profusely, Waldo groaned as he straightened his back, glad to let the younger men finish up.

"Are you bringing Kate over tonight, Jack?" Dan asked, loosening the mooring ropes and jumping aboard but not hearing Jack's answer. "I need to fill with gas; we're almost running on empty. SEE YOU AT HOME," he yelled to Jeb as he started the engine. He turned the *Stockholm* up the harbour and headed for the fuel pumps at Turpel's Point Hope Shipyard.

"I heard Nancy has a new boyfriend!" the pump man exclaimed.

Nodding, Dan chuckled at the ribbing, knowing these were his friends and it was their way of saying they cared.

Jeb was outside when he heard the *Stockholm* enter the cove. Going to his car, he picked up the roses and the bag of gifts and waited for Dan near the house where the women couldn't see him. When Dan came up the steps, Jeb silently waved him over.

"Thanks, Uncle Jeb," he said, going over and taking the flowers from him. "Did Jack say they were coming over tonight?"

"He didn't say."

Meg was visiting upstairs when she heard Dan arrive.

"You're daddy's home, little laddie," she whispered to the sleepy-eyed baby. Ten minutes later she picked up Nancy's supper dishes and turned to leave. "I imagine you'll be having company very soon so I'll be getting dinner dished up, lassie."

"Thanks Aunt Meg."

She was going down the stairs as Dan pushed the door open and entered quickly, roses in hand.

"Slow down!" she said softly as Dan closed the door. "Oh, you finally remembered did you, lad?" she chuckled, seeing the roses.

"No," he admitted, "Uncle Jeb did, I admit I clean forgot."

"Better go up and make amends lad, and don't forget to take those boots off so you don't wake him up."

Dan removed his boots and headed for the stairs as a sudden burst of excitement raced through his veins. Trying hard to be quiet, he clumsily opened the bedroom door and heard Nancy's voice.

"Come in, daddy, we've both been waiting all day for you," she whispered.

"I brought you some flowers for your birthday," he mumbled, laying the flowers on the dresser and dropping into a chair at the side of the bed. Taking her into his arms, he thought of all the dreams they had had for so many years, now culminating in a family and a child of their own. He held her tighter feeling her body heave with emotion as tears wet his shoulder and he knew she was thinking similar thoughts. The baby whimpered, breaking the spell, and they both turned to look at him.

"Look," she whispered, "he's smiling at you, Dan. He knows you're his daddy!"

"I'm going to bring my dinner up and eat with you both."

"No, you should eat downstairs, honey. I'm going to feed him now. Go and eat and then come back, Aunt Meg and Uncle Jeb need company, too."

Will you be able to come down soon?" Dan asked.

"Jenny says I'll be up and about tomorrow," she said smiling, obviously as happy as Dan with the idea.

Over dinner, Meg related the news of the visitors who had called or phoned during the day, extracting a promise from Dan that he stop at Apple Cove and tell Ezekiel. He agreed, then excused himself and went back upstairs. He found Nancy just putting the baby to bed.

"I'll be so glad when you can come back downstairs, we've missed you, honey. Say, have you given any thought to what we're going to call this son of ours? People are beginning to ask and Meg is giving me a rough time. I know we talked about it early on but we didn't come to any conclusion, did we?" he asked.

"No, we didn't, but I've been lying her thinking and I wondered what you thought about naming him after the Jorgensen boys."

"That's a splendid idea … Billy Christopher Brown sounds good."

"No silly," she laughed, "William Christopher Brown but I do like Billy for short."

"I think it's perfect," he replied giving her a kiss. Looking over at his son, he whispered, "Well, little Billy Brown, welcome to Cunningham Manor! You're going to have an amazing life!"

"Yes, being spoiled by all these grandparents!" Nancy giggled.

When Dan returned downstairs Meg cornered him immediately.

"Well, does that child have a name yet?" she demanded.

"Matter of fact, he does. He's William Christopher and we'll call him Billy," Dan said proudly.

"Aye, that's a fine name, Danny. The Jorgensens will be very pleased," Meg mused, with a faraway look in her eyes. "I once had a bonnie brother named Billy, he was a fine strapping lad."

Feeling the urge to question her, he caught a warning expression from Jeb and remembered that her three brothers were drowned in fishing accidents many years ago.

Going into the living room to sit with Jeb, Dan thought of his experiment with the hot coffee that morning. Raising the subject, Dan told him of the new murders in Rosario Strait and his conversation with Joe's lad.

"Smart boy," Jeb growled, "did you check it out?"

"Sort of, I did a rough experiment with my own coffee mug."

Jeb sucked on his pipe, scowling in thought as he waited for Dan to continue.

"I was halfway between Orcas and Blakely when the cup was still warm."

"Show me on the map."

Getting the map and rolling it out on the kitchen table, Dan pointed to the American islands.

"Get me a teacup, a ruler and a pencil, lad," Jeb ordered. Adjusting his spectacles, he studied the map until Dan returned. Carefully measuring the distance the *Stockholm* travelled from Bellingham, he placed three tiny marks on the map, connecting them in an arc with the rim of the tea cup and drawing a pencil line on the map.

They're somewhere inside that line," Jeb growled, "but that still gives them lots of places to hide."

"They'll need a ready source of gas."

"That should narrow it down a bit."

"Maybe they're not hiding at all. I wonder why John Gray's so interested in them."

"I should go with you tomorrow," Jeb hissed.

"No, we're not involved. I'll not be going after them," Dan replied.

"They might come after you!" Jeb suggested warily.

"I can run! Nothing can catch the *Stockholm*," Dan assured him.

"Yes I know, but you ain't the runnin' type, Danny, that's what worries me!"

Brilliant sunshine rose over the Cascade Mountains as the *Stockholm* pulled away from the Gordon Head dock on Friday morning. Nancy was standing at the upstairs window waving to her husband with Billy cradled in her arms. Checking the window with his binoculars, Dan yelped with pleasure when he saw them. Below the house on the clifftop, Jebediah stood like a statue, puffing on his pipe as he followed the *Stockholm*'s progress out of sight.

Now what's bothering him? Nan thought suspiciously. *He doesn't normally watch Dan leave.*

"Time you had some breakfast, young lady," Meg disturbed her thoughts, coming into the bedroom with her tray. "I presume you've fed his lordship?"

"I fed him twice in the night and once this morning, he's a voracious eater! Why was Uncle Jeb watching Dan off this morning? Is something wrong?"

"I don't think so, Nan, he was probably making sure Danny remembered to call at Apple Cove," her aunt replied, not wanting to worry her about the black boat.

"He's calling to see Ezekiel?"

"Yes lass, I thought we should let him know we have a little bairn in the house!"

"Thanks Aunt Meg."

A few minutes before nine, looking out of the kitchen window, Meg gasped when she saw Jenny Dunnett cycling toward the house, her bonnetted head bouncing up and down as she charged around and through the potholes.

"My gracious!" the Scot exclaimed rushing to the door, fearful their good-hearted neighbour would ride over the cliff.

Red-faced and grinning, Jenny's brakes squealed violently before she hopped off and propped it against the fence. Unhooking her bag from the handlebars, she ran to meet Meg on the porch.

"I didn't think I was ever going to stop the darned thing on Ash Hill!" she laughed. "The boys taught me to ride it last night. You should try it, Meg, it's a heck of a thrill."

"Ach noo, lassie," the Scot chuckled. "I could noo be so daring!"

"How's Nancy this morning?" asked the midwife with a sly smile. "Feeding one end and cleaning the other I presume!"

"Ach," she laughed, "she seems to be coping well, but then nature has a way of teaching mothers what's needed of them, don't you think?"

"Yes you're right, Meg, Nancy was meant to be somebody's mother. Look how she took care of Danny when he came home from the war and the stories I've heard of her visiting the war widows are legendary. Didn't I read quite a story in the newspaper when she took the wounded soldiers to the Armistice Ball?"

"I didn't need to read it Jenny, I was there!" Meg replied, sighing deeply. "She thinks of everything, that lassie, and is always concerned for others. She has made my life worth living again."

"Right, let's get Mrs. Brown out of bed then," the midwife chuckled.

"She's up already."

"Good, I'll just go check on her."

Meg clucked with envy as Jenny bounded up the stairs, then stood listening to their laughter before returning to the kitchen to clean up the breakfast dishes.

Satisfied that Nancy was recovering well, the midwife readily agreed it was time to allow the new mother to slowly return to some normalcy, although forbidding any heavy lifting or working at the restaurant for at least two months.

Knowing that finding something to wear was going to be a problem, Nancy had scoured her closet and drawers for some loose-fitting clothes. After talking with Jenny, she got dressed and with Jenny carrying Billy, they went downstairs.

Out on the water, Dan made good time on the unusually calm sea, keeping a close watch on other craft as he crossed the border. He was nearing Kingston when he spotted the coast guard cutter lurking close to the shoreline. It suddenly moved to intercept him. Swinging his bow toward them, he opened the throttle and felt the surge of power as the *Stockholm* leapt forward, tearing across the water straight at the cutter. Then he demonstrated his ability to stop applying his brakes and coming gently alongside.

"Capt. Gray requests you come aboard, sir," a crewman shouted over the side.

Tying the *Stockholm* alongside, Dan scrambled aboard and was quickly shown to the bridge.

"You've heard about the hijacking and the new murders, I suppose?" John Gray asked, motioning the Canadian to a chair at the chart table. "Any idea where to start looking?"

"Have you found the black speedboat yet?"

"You know about that too, do you?"

"Try a 20-minute radius of Bellingham," Dan suggested, grinning at John Gray's puzzled expression.

"Are you going to tell me why?"

"You wouldn't understand, captain, it's all because of a coffee and a kid!"

"You're right, I don't understand. I'm not even sure it's the black boat that's responsible." Worry appeared on the coast guard officer's face. Chasing a mystery boat who left no clues to its identity was proving an exercise in frustration. He needed help and Dan, with the *Stockholm*, was his preferred choice.

"Have you heard anything from my superiors, Dan?"

"Not a word from anyone, have you?"

"No," John replied bitterly, "they're all talk and no action."

"Well, if I run into the hijackers," Dan threatened, "you can be assured I won't be waiting for any official permission!"

A smile crossed John Gray's face as a memory flashed through his mind. "I'll never forget that day Nancy and Jeb fought the Egger brothers down at Apple Cove," he said, his eyes sparkling. "They were magnificent, but, of course, you know that because you were there."

"Yeah, but I didn't do anything!" Dan replied, remembering how helpless he had felt.

"She was a picture with her red hair streaming in the wind as she threw the *Stockholm* into the attack, and that old man standing in the stern with his Winchester ready. She shocked the hell out of us when she told us she was going to take out the boats to make it easier for us! And she did!"

"Don't count on that happening again," Dan growled, "she gave birth to our son on Wednesday afternoon."

"Sorry, I forgot to congratulate you, Dan, give Nancy my best wishes. I suppose you knew the Seattle newspaper already ran an announcement of the birth."

"No, I didn't know that," Dan laughed.

"They had an interview with Bill Jorgensen, right on the front page. That should sell a few more of Nancy's records!" John laughed.

"I guess that's a possibility," said Dan rising to his feet. "Well I'd better be off; I have orders to call at Apple Cove to see old Ezekiel."

"I was thinking of taking a look at Miller Bay," said Gray, "but now I think we'll mosey on over to Orcas and hope we get lucky."

Moving on, the *Stockholm* quickly made the trip over to Apple Cove. As Dan got out the whistles, he looked over at the overhanging branches at the entrance and saw the old man sitting on a rock cradling his rifle.

Cutting the engine, he eased the boat closer to the rocks using an oar to keep his distance while Ezekiel scrambled down from his perch and tumbled aboard.

"You knew I was coming?" said Dan.

"Saw ya talking to the law," the old hermit growled suspiciously, spitting his tobacco juice over the side. "I was filling the tower lamp."

Dan understood the old man's suspicions perfectly but didn't offer any explanation.

"Did ya bring me some jam?" he asked.

"Have you eaten all those bottles Meg sent already?" Dan teased as he used the oar to gently push his craft through the overhanging branches allowing the current to move him toward the rickety dock.

Dan watched, noticing the old man groan as he stepped onto the dock and limped away, going to sit on his log and rubbing his leg.

"What's the matter with your leg?" he called, picking up the case of Hamsterley Farm Jam and the two shirts Jeb had said to give him. He carried the packages onto the beach and put them down beside Ezekiel.

"He shot me!"

"Who shot ya?"

"That damned Pinkerton man!"

"Uncle Jeb shot ya?" Dan chuckled, realizing the old man was remembering long ago events.

"He did," Ezekiel blustered defiantly, "he tried to kill me."

"And why did he shoot you?"

"Oh it were a mix-up at a bank in Texas," Ezekiel grinned. "I were borrowing some money."

"More likely you were robbing that bank, old timer," Dan laughed, "and Jeb shot you in the leg to stop you getting away!"

"He shot me," Zeke repeated with a faraway look.

"Do you want me to bring some rubbing ointment next time?"

The question went unanswered as Dan watched the old man mumble incoherently to himself.

"Nancy had her baby," he announced, smiling as the old man began paying attention. "It's a boy and they're both doing well."

"Wow," Ezekiel whispered, jabbing a horny hand at his eye when a tear appeared on his weather-stained cheek. He muttered almost inaudibly, "She's a wonderful little gal. You take care of her, lad."

Climbing to his feet, the old man picked up the box of jam and went toward the cabin, leaving Dan alone on the beach. He was going to ask Ezekiel to watch for the mysterious black launch, but now he didn't feel like disturbing the old man's thoughts. His news of Nancy and the baby seemed to have a strange effect on the old hermit and he obviously wanted to be alone.

Still puzzling over Zeke's reaction, Dan carefully eased the *Stockholm* out of the hidden cove, checking the coastline before shooting out into open water.

Freighter traffic heading for Seattle was strung out all along Puget Sound causing smaller boats to keep their wits about them. Suddenly, he recognized a tug flying the Canadian flag, coming toward him. *What the devil is Jim Goodwin doing all the way down here*? he wondered, as the two Victoria boats came alongside one another.

"Hey Danny," Jim shouted, "you heading for Seattle?"

"No, I'm only going as far as Gus Jorgensen's."

"How's Nancy doing?"

"Fine, what are you doing down here?"

"I towed a launch into Marston's boatyard at Ellisport," the tug owner laughed, "fools hit the rocks off Cadboro Point."

"In daylight?" Dan frowned. "They must have been drunk."

"No lad, by all accounts it was at night, though it beats me what they were doing, and running so fast."

"Tell me about this launch, Jim, what colour was it?"

"Black as night, a powerful thing, long and sleek. It must have sat low in the water."

The hair on Dan's neck bristled. Had he traced the black launch by a quirk of fate and a chance meeting with his old friend?

"Who owns it?" he asked.

"Don't know, it was all arranged by an agent. They paid me well and in cash."

"Did you notice anything else about it?"

"Yes lad I did, now you come to mention it, they had a hook on the end of their jib."

Proffering no more questions and, not wanting to alert Jim to his interest, Dan changed the subject. "Have you heard anymore talk of late about that bridge?"

"There's been talk of that bridge from Johnson Street to Esquimalt Road for the last 20 years. They were talking about it when the railway bridge was built. Politicians like to talk but very rarely do anything," Jim ranted.

"I thought the city was going to do it."

"Same brew, different brand, lad!" Jim growled sarcastically.

Parting with a wave, Dan watched the Victoria tug chug away toward home, then he opened the throttle and turned southward.

Chapter 29

Pacing the Jorgensen dock, Terry suddenly stopped and shaded his eyes as he stared out over the water. Shouting orders to his men they watched the red-and-gold craft dart between two passing freighters before racing toward them.

"How long would it take you to get a couple of cases of beef, Terry?" asked Dan leaping onto the jetty.

"About 20 minutes," he replied without hesitation. "Do you want me to go get you some?"

"Yes, we have a meat packers' strike going on in BC, meat's getting very scarce."

They were almost finished loading the liquor onto Terry's truck when he returned in his car. He detailed one of his men to take the boxes of meat to the *Stockholm.*

Spending only a couple more minutes in conversation, Dan left the boathouse in brilliant sunshine eager to get home to Nancy and the baby. As he travelled he pondered the knowledge Jim Goodwin had given him on the whereabouts of the black launch. He became convinced that he must find the coast guard cutter and tell John Gray what he knew.

Luck was with him as he passed Keystone and came into the wide open waters of Juan De Fuca. Using his binoculars to sweep the coastline of Lopez and San Juan Islands, Dan spotted them. Firing an emergency flare to draw their attention, he headed toward them watching as almost instantaneously the coast guard vessel began to turn in his direction.

Capt. Gray hung over the rail as the two boats connected. "WHAT'S WRONG, DAN?" John shouted, his voice betraying his concern.

"I FOUND THE BLACK LAUNCH YOU'RE LOOKING FOR!" Dan yelled back grabbing the rail to stop them from drifting apart.

"COME ABOARD," the captain insisted, snapping orders at the crew to take care of the *Stockholm*, as he led the way into the wheelhouse.

Sitting down and accepting a cup of coffee, Dan quickly told of his chance meeting with the Victoria tugboat owner. Pointing to the chart on the wall, his finger found Marston's Ellisport Shipyard and he relayed the information he had gleaned in recent days.

"Why would they pay to have it towed all that way?" Gray asked.

"Maybe it's not the same boat," Dan replied, "could it be there are two of 'em?"

"If there are, this thing's more organized than we thought, but we'll know more in a couple of hours when I get to Ellisport. Thanks for the help, Dan."

Casting off, Dan watched the coast guard vessel pick up speed as it thundered away. As he made for home he could feel in his bones that something was wrong. *Could deliberately wrecking the speedboat in Canadian waters and gambling that the coast guard would find out and follow its trail, be an elaborate diversion? This would leave the area of the San Juan Islands unprotected.* The more Dan thought about the situation, the more he convinced himself he was right.

Speeding up, he crossed the open water and began to make a plan. *A call to Fred Barrett will reveal what ships are leaving Victoria. He'll also know their cargo and destination, and if anything looks suspicious. I'll need to be aware of any possible danger.* Charging across Haro Strait, he smiled as his binoculars focused on the Sidney Fish Plant barge loaded high with gleaming white shells being towed across to Bellingham.

It was almost five-thirty when the *Stockholm* slid into the cove and docked. Nancy was standing by the window watching him and wondered why he was so far to the east in Haro Strait. After Jeb's unusual actions of the morning, she had tried to put her suspicions from her mind but they now returned.

"Oh no you don't, young lady!" Meg said sharply, seeing Nancy put on a sweater and move toward the door. "You're not going out there. If I had my way you'd still be in bed!"

A whimper from the tiny bundle in the baby buggy near the bottom of the stairs snapped the redhead's attention from the window to her son. Moving quickly, she gave him a comforting whisper and adjusted the blankets around the tiny shoulders.

"Jeb's here," Dan called as he came through the door carrying a box of meat. "I brought some beef, Aunt Meg."

"Quietly, son," the Scot chastised, pointing to the buggy. "I know Jeb's here, I heard his car, and we need to order more ice tomorrow."

Still carrying the 25-pound box of meat, Dan went over to Nancy and peering over her shoulder at the baby, slipped his free hand around her waist.

"Look," she sighed, "he's watching us."

"Should you be up yet? I thought ladies stayed in bed for a week after having a baby?"

"How would you know?" she giggled.

Meg made sure the noise was kept to a minimum as they ate dinner with the baby nearby in its buggy. Nancy queried their day at work, inquiring from Jeb if he had heard from the Jorgensens who were expected the next day.

"They probably haven't arrived or we would have heard," Jeb murmured thoughtfully. "Don't worry, lass, they'll call when they get here."

"Anything interesting happen at the harbour today, Jeb?" Dan asked.

"Fred Barrett said Walter Findlay had been arrested."

"No!" Dan replied. "What's he been up to? He's a prohibition commissioner," he explained to the women.

"Making some easy money I guess," Jeb snorted, "like that schooner in the harbour that loaded hundreds of cases of liquor today."

"My goodness! Where are they heading?" Nancy asked.

"Waldo said Mexico, but I'll bet you they call into Seattle first. There's no market for high-priced liquor in Mexico!"

"Do you know when they're supposed to sail?" asked Dan, looking so thoughtful it caught Nancy's attention.

"All right, Mr. Brown!" she demanded. "Why are you so interested in this ship?"

"Oh, just interested in what's going on," he said, blushing as he realized he wasn't very convincing.

"Don't lie to me, Danny!" Nancy hissed across the table. "Please tell me the truth."

Meg and Jeb remained silent as they listened with growing interest. Nan was usually always able to squeeze the truth out of people, especially from Danny.

"John Gray's gone down Puget Sound looking for the black speedboat I suspect is doing the hijacking," Dan explained. "I sent him there, but on the way home I got to thinking about some of the little things that have been happening. Now I think it was merely a decoy to get the coast guard launch away from the area so they can hijack another boat!"

"Fred said they were sailing on the late tide," Jeb offered, "they could be using the dark to cover a delivery into Puget Sound."

"What vessel are you talking about?" Dan asked, his eyes not wavering from the former detective's face.

"It's the *Malahat.*"

"I know you want to do something about it, honey," the redhead said softly, "but what can you do?"

"I could call the Jorgensens to warn the coast guard."

"They're no doubt already here in town, they'll be here tomorrow," Jeb reminded them.

"I feel so helpless," Dan hissed.

"It could be dangerous trying to tackle them ourselves," Jeb began grinning broadly, "but we can make a mess of their planning if we give it a little thought!"

"Well I think it's a bunch of maybes," Meg snapped. "I think you both should leave it alone and forget it. It sounds too dangerous to me."

"We can't Aunt Meg," Nancy responded as the Scot moved away to check on the baby. "This is our backyard and we need it to be safe. Let's hear what Uncle Jeb has in mind."

Rubbing his chin, Jeb grinned at the girl he'd already shared many adventures with, and thoughtfully laid out his plan.

"You're looking at this thing from the wrong angle, lad," he began. "You want to stop a hijacking, then why don't we just scare the supply ship away. That would be the safe and easy route and, with what I am thinking, nobody would ever know it was us."

Dan glanced at Nancy and laughed. "You know, he's right, Nan, we could easily scare the *Malahat* away from Puget Sound."

"And how are you going to do that without getting too close?" she asked.

"By using exploding flares, they'll think they're being attacked and run!" Dan explained.

"How do we make exploding flares?" Jeb asked. "I ain't never heard of 'em."

"It's easy," Dan laughed. "Ned Joyce used to use them to keep the Indians away when we had to put into the coast."

"Well, how?"

"One stick of dynamite tied to the head of a flare and as soon as the flare strikes, it sets the dynamite off!" Dan explained, watching their faces.

Shaking her head at the simplicity of Dan's bomb, Nancy yawned and reached for his hand. "I want you to promise me you'll just chase the *Malahat* away and then come home to us, Danny," she begged.

Darkness was falling as the *Stockholm* slipped away from the dock and headed out into the rolling waves of the strait. A cold wind brushed the deck and tugged at Jebediah's coat as he adapted ten flares to Dan's specifications and readied the flare gun.

Staying well out in Haro Strait and steering by the warning beacon at the southern tip of San Juan Island, Dan sent the *Stockholm* cautiously moving toward the entrance to Admiralty Inlet. Seeing the light of the Point Wilson Lighthouse, he stopped just north of Port Townsend on the eastern shore, within sight of the Admiralty Head Lighthouse. From this vantage point, they had a good view of the strait and Victoria. Cutting the engine, Dan dropped anchor and looked over at the twinkling lights of their city, commenting how many more lights there were in recent years. Getting out his binoculars, he focussed them in the direction of Ogden Point and heard Jeb grumble in the dark.

"They'll be coming without lights."

"No, they'll have to have lights to leave the harbour," Dan replied, "I should be able to see them even from this distance."

Patiently watching across the dark waters as sounds of crashing waves echoed from the nearby Whidbey Island shoreline, Dan became aware of two moving lights near the harbour entrance.

"I think I see them," he announced, watching as the vessel turned southeastward. As it reached the outer limits of the harbour, the running lights went out and he could just make out a set of sails silhouetted against the darkness of the Gonzales hills. Putting down his binoculars, he quietly told Jeb what he had seen. He had guessed right, the *Malahat* was heading for Seattle.

Losing sight of the schooner, Dan knew he had to give them enough time to cross the strait but, with the wind blowing in their direction, it shouldn't take long. They were surprised when the faint sound of a motor was heard coming toward them and Dan turned his binoculars in its direction. Although running without lights as it entered Admiralty Inlet, Dan could still make out the name *Malahat* on its stern as it passed within 50 feet of them. Jeb quietly pulled up the anchor, allowing them to drift on the current.

"Ready Jeb?" Dan whispered and, hearing a grunted reply, hissed urgently, "Hang on!"

The *Stockholm*'s engine roared into life, leaping forward as Dan opened the throttle and moved after the *Malahat*.

Hearing the oncoming engine, a watchman on board lit a lantern, inadvertently giving their position away. Adjusting his direction, Dan hissed his next order.

"Right Jeb, let 'em go!"

In seconds, the sky was lit by a blinding flare, followed by a thunderous echoing crash, then another, and another. During the short bursts of light, they realized the mighty *Malahat* was doing exactly what they wanted it to do—it was turning away from the explosions appearing to head back the way it had come.

Jeb chuckled crazily to himself as he sent the last two flares screaming after the retreating rum runners. Grinning at the success of Jebediah's scheme, Dan turned for home still running without lights and well aware their fireworks display would attract many eyes from shore. Relying on instinct, he headed for Gordon Head, quite sure they had gone undetected.

Working late at the legislature, Premier John Oliver lit his pipe and wandered out into the gardens, pondering the problems which weighed heavily on his mind. Labour issues were getting completely out of hand and the liquor laws were driving him mad.

Suddenly, out in the strait, the first of Jeb's homemade bombs exploded with a distant roar and a flash of light. Flinching with surprise, and almost dropping his pipe, Oliver moved to where he could get a better view just in time to witness the second flash as it exploded into the dark skies, followed by several more.

"WHAT THE HELL'S GOING ON OUT THERE?" he yelled at a legislative guard as he rushed back inside.

Phones were already ringing all over the city as police and soldiers rushed to Dallas Road and the naval garrison at Esquimalt was alerted. Suddenly the city was wide awake and searching for an answer.

Meanwhile, at Cunningham Manor, unaware of the excitement they'd caused, Dan docked the *Stockholm* and he and Jeb wearily climbed the stairs, believing they had made the waters a bit safer, even if only temporarily.

* * *

The devastating disease which wreaked havoc on the world from 1918-1919 was referred to by the Allied side of World War I as *Spanish Flu*, so called because British doctors first identified it in that country. This is not to suggest that it started in Spain or, that it was peculiar to Spain, it was simply named such as an identifying mark.

The sickness first appeared in the USA on the 11th of March, 1918 at Camp Riley in Kansas and, before it was over, an estimated 28% of all Americans became infected.

By September 1918, Canada saw its first case of Spanish Flu in Quebec, brought home by returning soldiers. It quickly circulated among the general public and began its spread across the country. Vancouver, BC experienced its first admitted case of the flu in early October 1918. At that time, British Columbia health authorities learned from Washington State that the disease was already prevalent locally.

Strict measures were put into place as the epidemic attacked the West Coast and, in some areas, hundreds were stricken on a single day. Seattle banned all gatherings of more than seven people and schools and churches were closed. The wearing of gauze masks became mandatory and funeral gatherings were limited to 15 minutes.

Victoria followed these guidelines with the exception of making gauze masks mandatory—the city health officer leaving this decision to personal choice. A week before Christmas 1918, confirmed cases had mounted to 2,439. In 1919, a second wave of the flu caused more havoc on the West Coast.

A modern tally puts the number of worldwide casualties at 25-50 million people who perished from this viral infectious disease—a number greater than the deaths from Black Plague and AIDS. Of these numbers, 675,000 were American, 200,000 were British, and 50,000 were Canadian. In recent years, it was discovered that as many as 20 million may have died in India alone.

* * *

More Books by J. Robert Whittle

Lizzie Series

This popular multi-generational series begins in the year 1804 when Lizzie Short finds herself alone on the streets of London following her friends' arrest and deportation. Witnessing an accident, she discovers that going to the aid of a Napoleonic War veteran will become a life-changing event.

Set in the years when women were thought incapable of being in business, Lizzie begins the challenging life of a young entrepreneur. As teens, she and her friend, Quon Lee, aspire to use their business skills to help their friends and the needy. With sensitivity and humour, Whittle, once a child entrepreneur himself in Yorkshire, traces the youngsters' rise to fame from the age of nine to adulthood. They battle poverty, the establishment, jealous rivals and personal danger as they make dangerous plans for the war effort. *Lizzie: Lethal Innocence* became Whittle's first of three Canadian bestselling novels.

* * *

Released in 2007 and, winning rave reviews and their second Gold IPPY, don't miss Whittle's tale of a time travelling mortal angel in the Pacific Northwest.

Whispers Across Time

A first collaboration with his author/wife, Joyce Sandilands.

www.jrobertwhittle.com